THE CREATIVE FIRE

||| BOOK ONE *of* RUBY'S SONG |||

BRENDA COOPER

an imprint of **Prometheus Books**
Amherst, NY

Published 2012 by Pyr®, an imprint of Prometheus Books

Cover illustration © 2012 John Picacio
Cover design by Jacqueline Nasso Cooke

Inquiries should be addressed to

Pyr
59 John Glenn Drive
Amherst, New York 14228–2119
VOICE: 716–691–0133
FAX: 716–691–0137
WWW.PYRSF.COM

16 15 14 13 12   5 4 3 2 1

Library of Congress Cataloging-in-Publication Data

Cooper, Brenda, 1960–
    The Creative Fire / by Brenda Cooper.
        p. cm. — (Ruby's Song ; bk. 1)
    ISBN 978–1–61614–684–9 (pbk.)
    ISBN 978–1–61614–685–6 (ebook)
    1. Teenage girls—Fiction. 2. Revolutions—Fiction. 3. Social classes—Fiction.
4. Space ships—Fiction. I. Title.

PS3603.O5825C74 2012
813'.6—dc23

                                                                              2012023579

Printed in the United States of America

AUTHOR'S NOTE

This story was inspired by *Evita*, the musical about Eva Peron. It is not an account of a life exactly like Eva's, although as I prepared this novel I watched documentaries about her and read books about her and by her.

This is the story that grew inside of me after I was teased by Evita's legend. I am grateful, in advance, to all of the modern women who will forgive me for the way this story is told. I set the story far into the future, but I could not remove the patriarchy or the story would not have felt possible. But after all, the patriarchy remains in many places on Earth today.

To women everywhere who have fought for rights and freedoms.
Also to my mother: mothers are priceless.

PART ONE
YEARNING

ONE
A HOLE IN THE SKY

Four men in red uniforms surrounded three men wearing dirty gray work clothes. The reds muscled the less fortunate men down an orange hallway. Uneven light showed scars where bots and cargo carts had bumped the metal walls and two places where graffiti had been painted over.

Ruby pressed her back hard against the wall and waited for the group to pass her. She recognized all seven, even though they worked a different shift from hers. The looks on their faces were familiar: the reds stoic to boredom, their meanness hiding just under their bones, and the grays at once anxious and resigned.

She kept her silence as the knot of people passed. The closest red elbowed her in the stomach and stepped on her foot casually, as if she couldn't have been avoided. She knew his name. Vidal. He spoke without looking at her. "Waiting for your turn, Ruby? Keep being a little bitch and we'll get you as soon as you're old enough."

"Be nice, Vidal, and I won't have to talk truth."

The red didn't respond, but neither did he touch her a third time.

The youngest gray looked at her in desperation. She remembered his name. Hugh. They'd talked during the last Festival of Changes, and he'd been sweet and hadn't tried to kiss her. He was just a year older, but that made him an adult, which made it legal to lock him up without as much provocation as they'd need for her.

There were enough of them to take her, too. Ruby hesitated a moment, thinking through the odds.

She slid her journal free of her pocket and set it on record, glanced up to be sure they weren't looking back at her, and shoved the journal in the loose waistband of her gray uniform pants. The sharp edge rubbed painfully against her skin in one place, but she might need the recording. She'd just have to keep their attention on her face. Or her face and her breasts, she thought. Damned reds.

The group had gotten well past her before she took off after them. "Stop!" she shouted.

They didn't.

She dodged for an opening and passed around them as fast as she could, so they couldn't grab her. Their hands were busy restraining the grays, anyway.

Vidal almost managed to trip her, and she kept herself from stepping down hard on his foot—hurt any of the reds, and she *would* go with the other grays. She looked at the leader, a tall man with silver hair that she had no name for. "Hugh. The young one. What'd he do? I know him. He doesn't break your rules."

The man spoke to his fellow reds. "Don't listen to her. She's not here." He kept the group going. Ruby moved ahead of them, walking a little backward and a little sideways, careful not to slow them down while remaining impossible to ignore.

Hugh glanced at her and jerked his head sideways. Signaling for her to give up?

Ruby reached for her best sure-of-herself voice. "You gotta let him out by the morning anyway. They'll need him. He runs the trash compactor and his shift mate's been sick a week."

No response.

She sighed. "Let him go, or I'll report you."

Still no response. The reds had picked up their pace; they were getting too close to her.

She turned to face them, backing up as fast as she could.

They kept coming, Vidal's eyes so angry she'd be dead if they were weapons.

"I have the right to ask what he's being detained for."

Hugh spoke, his voice strained and shaky. "I didn't do a thing. I was just in the same galley with these two. I don't even know what they did."

The other grays were both older, people she'd seen but not talked to. Nothing she could do for them, for sure. Probably not for Hugh, but the fear in his eyes made her keep trying. "Let him go. He's never been in lockup. He doesn't deserve it now."

"Get out of our way," Vidal growled at her, tightening his grip on Hugh's arm.

Ruby ignored Vidal. He wasn't the power anyway. She looked directly at the older man. "I'll report you. Maybe it won't matter, but maybe it will. You don't need him."

Vidal's upper lip curled. "Are you sweet on him? Should I be jealous?"

The older gray winced and gave Vidal a harsh look.

Good. She had him. "He's just my friend," she said, dropping some of the anger in favor of sounding like she needed help. "Please don't hurt him."

"When you get old enough, we're taking you," Vidal hissed.

The older man looked genuinely irritated.

Ruby took another step back, keeping her eyes on the leader.

"What's that in your belly?" he asked.

She didn't answer. Lying could be bad. "Let him go, please." She fought the urge to touch her journal, kept her fists at her side. "Please."

He had stopped, so the others stopped. He looked at Hugh. "You don't know these two?"

Hugh swallowed. "Of course I know them. Know who they are. They work in the orchard. But I don't work there, and I don't know what they're in trouble for."

The other two grays were still silent, and one of them narrowed his eyes and bit his tongue. The other one said, "He's telling the truth."

"Shit," the leader said. "You could have told me that."

She'd won. It was the gray's fault now, or at least the reds could pretend that was so. It meant the other two would have it harder, but with someone to blame, the reds would let Hugh go. Surely they would.

The leader kept looking at her. When he spoke his voice was low. "I'll remember you."

She didn't say anything.

He did. "Hand me your journal."

Her mouth had become dry, and it was hard to even get the words out. "I need it back. I'm a student."

"I'll drop it at your parents."

He probably would. He'd actually been pretty straight with her, all things considered. Almost fair. "My mother's hab. Siri Martin. I have no father."

The man nodded and then spoke to Vidal. "Let him go."

Vidal slammed Hugh into the metal wall so hard that she heard Hugh's shoulder pop and the hard outflow of his breath on impact.

She stayed still until they left.

Hugh looked up at her, hugging himself and shaking. "Thanks."

She nodded. "Go. I know you have a girlfriend. Go to her."

"Can I thank you?"

"Stay out of sight for a few days." She smiled at him, trying to break the thick fear he was still wearing on his skin and in his eyes. "You're all right. They'll leave you for now." She didn't want him to stay. She wanted to be alone. "Go on."

He did, limping a little, but moving reasonably fast in the same direction he'd come from. Hopefully they *would* leave him alone. She didn't trust Vidal out of her sight, but the tall man might keep him in line. Reds needed some reason to lock up grays. Thin excuses were enough. But they needed something.

She let Hugh turn a corner before she took off, running. Her footsteps echoed in the long metal box of the corridor, the cadence of her anger matching her strides, hot and familiar.

She ran longer than she needed to, circling the whole pod twice before making a sharp right and emerging in an open space, trading the greasy orange of the ship's corridor for the pastels of the C-pod park. She barely slowed to swipe her wrist past the reader on the metal post marking the entrance.

On the far side of the gate, she stopped to catch her breath, drinking in the clean, airy smell of her favorite place. The open space rested in default mode. Thin white clouds slid across a pale blue roof. A soft breeze blew across blossoming orchard trees and sweetened the air. It was nearly shift change, and so everyone else was probably prepping or sleeping, not coming home late after a singing lesson.

Far off, a siren sounded. Ruby ignored it, muttering under her breath, "Damned sirens. Too many drills."

The siren stopped.

Her chest felt tight and her thighs hurt from running. Not running away from the reds. Never running away. Just running.

With luck she could be alone here for a few hours. She went to the control panel, forcing deep breaths.

Still no sign of anyone else. No noise.

The panel rose as she approached, stopping at the perfect height. It tilted toward her, as if requesting her touch. The oils of thousands of fingers had smeared the controls into a sea of red and blue and gray, but Ruby didn't hesitate. She tapped it into expert mode, playing it like she played her sound sheet, confident and familiar.

The surface flashed light back at her, conversing.

Ruby commanded the blue color of the roof to deepen and light to gather in the right-hand corner, flowing into a single yellow-white orb so bright she squinted. She sent a flock of virtual birds winging in random patterns across the fake sky. She strengthened and cooled the wind until the air flowing past her cheeks stung them red.

She shook her head, her arms, letting the scene in the corridor with the reds slide away from her. She needed to forget she was a grease monkey, a gray girl, someone who might end up in lockup. The park was the only place Ruby had the right to be where she could forget herself.

She left the controls and took the path, glancing up from time to time at the fake birds flocking above her. If she and Onor were right, and the other level of the ship was above her, then the birds winged below the floor of other habs the same way the cargo holds existed below her feet.

The path she walked circled and looped, sometimes recrossing the places it had been. A trick of the programming to fool her into thinking the space was bigger. The surface gave beneath her feet, absorbing the sound of her passage. Here and there, empty benches sat lonely in the pretend vastness of the park. It was big, bigger than any other open space in C-pod, and its connection to the fruit orchard and the vegetable garden made it seem even vaster. Display surfaces on the walls and the roof added depth, so it looked almost like she imagined a planet would, as if the sky were truly far above and the park went on forever.

She stopped at one of the benches beside a spindly tree. The trunk was only three inches wide, the top of the tallest branches just out of reach if she jumped. Probably a fruit tree that would get moved in next time the orchard lost one. The tree's roots were channeled into pots that hung below the surface, trimmed by some of the very bots she was learning to clean and test.

She touched the bark, running her finger across small knots and twists. The tree had real life in it. More real than the path or the sky or the birds. She plucked a leaf and crumpled it between her fingers, touching her tongue to the thin strip of bitter green blood that oozed from the severed stem.

Her throat choked up. She didn't let the tears come. If she were to start crying, her anger would leak away, and she liked her anger. It made her bigger.

The path bucked under her feet.

She drew in a breath, ready to scream. Instead, the floor slapped the air out of her, so she gasped and choked. She rolled. The tree was closer to her than the bench, so she reached for its trunk.

Light flashed bright and then dimmed. The displays that made the walls and floor and ceiling flickered and then faded to blank surface.

A crack opened across the floor, now a dead black, and the bench tilted but didn't fall.

Ruby pulled herself up, gripping the slender trunk so tight that the rough bark hurt her palms as her body lightened, the change in weight fast enough to unsettle her stomach and make her mouth taste bitter.

The ship kept tearing, metal pulling and screeching away from metal above her head. The roof opened almost directly above her, a slit longer than five or six people and as wide as one.

Ruby clutched the tree and looked up. The wind had picked up so much her shirt flapped against her belly and her hair stung her neck.

Through the crack, details competed for her attention. Stairs and corridors and handholds and flooring, all off kilter. Figures running away from the rent, grasping handholds and pulling themselves out of her vision. A light winked off. Another winked on, illuminating a humanoid robot that gripped the hand of a compact man in a blue uniform, keeping him from falling.

The sky of the new level was black, dead black. The roof above her and the roof above that, all black. The few lights above her were small points of white. She'd learned from drill instructions that power would be stripped from unnecessary things in an emergency, but her sky had never been black.

Broken pipes and wires protruded from the space between the levels.

A woman's scream came from far away.

The park jerked again.

The surface under her feet canted further, and she spared a glance for the bench just as it tilted almost straight up. A hole, like the one above her.

Gravity hadn't fallen quite low enough for her to float. Besides, all the drills said hold on, hold on, hold on. There were stories of people caught in gravity fluxes who floated up and then smashed down. Below, only the tall, cluttered service floor and beyond that, between her and the great rushing void of space, the cargo pods, and outside of those, the wall of the ship itself. If the outer shell of the *Fire* had been breached, she would already be dead.

She needed to stay calm in spite of the ever-cooler air rushing about and the thinness of her breath.

The hole in the floor of the park was immediate and close. It mattered now.

She redoubled her grip on the tree, whispering, "Please don't fall, please don't, please stay."

Another shudder opened the crack further. The bench dangled. The bolts that held it to the floor ripped away and it clattered below.

Ruby looked up. Where there had been birds, the man the robot had been reaching for fell through the rent in the roof. The ripped reflective surface of the roof flapped loose. The man caught it, swinging in slow motion, reaching impossibly toward the place he had come from. The metal man reached for him, then overreached. It tumbled slowly through the opening, its trajectory taking it right to the man, bumping him. Both fell slowly.

The pod jerked again.

The tree stayed in place. Ruby maintained her grip, holding her feet on the ground. The man and the robot fell, the two forms separating in the air.

Above them, the torn roof bled misshapen spheres of water and other fluids that refracted the emergency lights in shifting prisms behind the tumbling figures. The man tried to flap his arms like a bird, a reflexive silliness in the low gravity. He looked incredulous, his mouth open but not screaming as he fell through the air, now twenty feet above her. She hung on with one hand and reached toward him even though he was too far away to grab.

All lights switched off, except for three or four thin beams. The gravity generator activated and she was suddenly heavy.

The man thudded to the surface of the park with a grunt, a whoosh of breath escaping his lungs. He lay between her and the hole the bench had slipped through, the surface canted slightly toward the opening, like one of her shallow oil funnels. The robot fell feet first down the hole, reaching for an edge and missing. The expression on its face showed the placidity of all humanoid bots, and Ruby choked back a nervous giggle at the absurd vision.

Then her weight felt right. The gravgens balanced. She reached a hand out to the man. "Here," she called.

He twisted to look at her, his eyes wide. "I'm hurt."

"What? Can you reach me?"

The muffled ring of metal on metal told her the robot had collided with the floor far below.

The man slid sideways toward the hole, using one leg but not the other. "My foot."

"You have to," she said.

He crawled toward her, his face contorted with the effort.

She forced her hands free of the tree trunk and went to him, pulling him up.

His right leg buckled, taking him to his knees. "I can't. Walk."

"You must."

His muscles bunched across his neck and jaw. His brows drew in over startling blue eyes. Sweat shone on his forehead, but he stood, wobbly, one hand on her shoulder.

The floor shifted underfoot and he fell again. Ruby tugged on his arm with both her hands. "Come on. You can do this."

He shook his head.

"You'll die."

Another effort, and he was up. She took as much of his weight as she could, wishing for less gravity. His clothes felt slick and unfamiliar. She tested the ground in front of her as they went, unsure how stable anything might be. He grunted with each step, crying out once. "Keep going," she encouraged him. "We need something else to hang onto."

"It hurts."

"Less than death." Sweat stung her eyes as she supported him and led him to a different bench by a different tree, helping him sit. She grabbed onto the back of the bench with one arm and used her free hand to curl his hand around the top slat. "Hold on."

He did. At first that's all he did, grip and look around, his brows drawn together and his face white. The dim, strange light barely defined his features. A shock of red hair hung over bluer eyes than any she'd ever seen. He was older than her brothers. Maybe twenty-five? He wore a clean blue uniform with a darker blue belt. She blinked at the color; she'd never been so near a blue.

Clean. He looked and even smelled clean.

The ship shuddered and he gripped the bench so tightly his knuckles whitened. "What's happening?" he whispered.

Ruby shook her head. "I don't know. Maybe we hit something."

He winced. "If we hit something we'd be dead." He sounded entirely sure of himself.

"So what do you think?"

"Something broke."

Another sound of metal screeching and giving way came from below them.

Sirens started up, strident but far away. Probably from the living quarters. "Someone's alive," Ruby said.

"Is it always so cold in here?"

"No." She glanced at the hole in the floor. "The temp systems must have gone wonky."

"I can breathe okay."

"Me, too." The sirens stopped, the silence ominous if also a relief.

He seemed to focus on her for the first time. "Thanks for helping me."

"We all help each other. It's how we stay alive."

He hesitated, then asked, "You're a gray?"

Surely he could see her worn-out uniform. Really, who else lived down here except a few reds, and even in the awful light here he could tell she wasn't wearing red. "I'm Ruby."

It was the first time she'd seen him smile, and it made him look younger. "Glad to meet you. I'm Fox."

The light flickered up and then down. Nothing moved in the park, including them. It felt to her like *The Creative Fire* held its breath, unsure how to react to whatever had torn bits of its guts apart. She'd only ever seen a small part of the ship, but there had been pictures of *The Creative Fire* in school, so she knew it as a fat disk. She had been shown the layouts for the cargo bays and the places the grays inhabited: eight self-contained pods between the cargo ring and whatever hung above their heads. "Do you know if the whole ship's falling apart?"

He shrugged. "How would I? There wasn't any warning. The sirens went off just before the floor opened up under me. Thank god it wasn't during shift change. There'd have been more of us in the corridors." He rubbed at his ankle and grimaced.

Someone would come for them. Ix would know everything, Ix always did. Ix watched over everyone's safety. "At least the *Fire*'s not tearing herself up anymore."

"If we're lucky."

Ruby sat curled opposite him on the bench, the armrest digging into her back. It gave her a good view of his white face and the pain in his eyes. She pointed toward the roof. "Where did you come from?"

"J-pod."

That didn't tell her anything except that he wasn't from anyplace the grays lived, but she'd known that. Still, she hesitated, and finally chose not to admit she didn't know what he meant. "I've never been there."

He grimaced. "Of course you haven't. And I haven't been here. I never—" he shifted his position on the bench, grimacing—"thought grays would be so pretty. What do you do?"

She blushed, caught off guard. "I'm studying to maintain the repair bots. This is my last year."

He raised an eyebrow. "You don't look old enough."

She bristled. "I'm sixteen."

"It takes us longer." He looked lost in thought for a moment, chewing at his lower lip, then he smiled and said, "I guess we're slower." He looked around. "Someone will come, won't they?"

"They're probably worried about other things."

The idea seemed to surprise him. He sat back and closed his mouth tight, then nodded. Maybe he was right. Maybe the reds would worry about him and come rescue him. A blue might matter more than an apprentice robot-repair girl. "At least we can breathe. It could be worse."

He gave her a soft smile at that, like he approved of her positive statement or maybe needed it. "I might freeze to death."

"Ix'll get to us. It must have our body stats and know that you're injured and in the wrong place. So there's worse going on than us being cold and your ankle."

"I hope someone comes soon." He drew his arms in close to his chest.

He was a bit of a baby for a blue, she thought. His foot must be hurting badly.

Cold seeped into her lungs. With Fox's injury, he probably felt it even more than she did.

Someone should have come by now.

She didn't have her journal, so she couldn't use it to call out. Fox didn't have anything with him. At home, school, any of the work places, there would be first-aid gear. There would be a kit in the walls here, too, but she couldn't risk moving them away from the safety of the bench. There were no handholds on the floor of the park, and she didn't trust the gravgens. Not yet. If the gravgens switched off while she walked through an open space with no handholds, she could lose her grip on the floor.

Her shirt was a hand-me-down, big on her except across the chest and too long. She ripped a strip of material off the bottom and held it out to him.

"What?"

Whoever this Fox was, no one had apparently taught him basic first aid. She let go of the bench and knelt by his ankle, which was in front of him, his knee bent so his foot rested bottom-down on the middle of the seat. "I can give it some pressure, maybe stabilize it a little. If the gravgens go wonky again, grab me? I don't want to float away from you."

He nodded, finally offering a smile. "Be careful. It hurts like . . . a . . . like a lot."

She probably knew more curse words than Fox. Still, it felt sweet that he'd been careful not to use them around her. Even though his boot pulled off fairly easily, he grunted when she made her last tug. His ankle was twice the size of the other one, but the skin hadn't broken. He only cried out once while she wrapped it. When she finished, she said, "That should help. Not stop the pain, but maybe keep it from getting more swollen. We should get a cold pack for you."

"It's getting cold enough."

She laughed.

The lights went out, and she clutched his hand. She didn't think about it, she just did it. They were so alone, and everyone else could be dead.

If only she'd told someone where she was going.

The lights flickered again and came up lower than before. She let go of him, her cheeks hot.

"Here," he said, scooting along the bench and pulling her up beside him, his back against her shoulder. "There. I can keep you warm."

She wasn't ready to trust him, but she didn't mistrust him either. At least not like she did most men. Except for her shoulder being a rest for his back, she didn't touch him.

The act of breathing together in and out of the same dangerous dark made them almost like one being. She felt floaty, suspended between anxiety about the safety of the ship, and her family, and the strange excitement of being warmed by a blue.

TWO
THE WATER PLANT

The floor in the reclamation plant slanted under Onor's feet, forcing him to use the metal handrail to pull himself along the wall beside the water tanks. After the gravgen failures, his hands shook. He needed something to hold onto anyway, even though nothing worse than a banged knee had actually happened to him. Yet. The screams of stressed metal intake tubes above his head had softened to groans and mutterings. They were still louder than the strident but muffled sirens coming from a distant part of the ship.

Both made him want out of the corridor he was in quite badly.

Maintenance bots slid by on their own little strip of walkway, one of them clearly needing a lube job. From time to time, grey water sluiced through a pipe, burbling and rushing toward the hold where it would be trapped by plastine seals before it was allowed into the tanks. The corridor smelled of grease and damp and disinfectant.

The heavy metal door at the end of the corridor looked wrong. He searched around the edges where the door met the frame. Intact. But still wrong. The angle? There. The walkway he stood on had pulled slightly away from the wall in the corner, leaving an opening into blackness. Although the opening wasn't big enough for him to see through, he knew from his early training that a maintenance level ran beneath the water plant.

He held his breath and jumped lightly, testing.

The walkway creaked but held.

He reached carefully for the metal handgrip on the door and pulled. Nothing.

He braced his foot against the doorframe and pulled. It gave, but it didn't open. A second try produced a high, thin whine of resistance as the door scraped against its frame, but it opened far enough for him to slide though. On the other side of the door the sirens sounded louder and more eerie.

The corridor beyond looked empty. Entrances led to a small galley or to showers or offices. Everything looked right, in spite of the noise around him. Just abandoned.

He turned back to the door and focused on pulling it closed as tight as he could. It took three tries to get the seal tight enough to latch.

He turned, and almost jumped back against the door as Conroy stepped out of the galley and stared at him, seeming equally startled. The big man yelled to get over the background noise. "Onor! Where are you supposed to be?"

He pointed back at the door. "There's water leaking, a lot of it. From an intake toward the end of the row. A pipe—"

"Thank you." Conroy looked worried and distracted.

"We have to turn it off."

Conroy focused more closely on Onor, frowning. "Drill. Where the hell are you supposed to meet up during a drill?"

Onor blinked at him. "This isn't a drill. We have to stop the leak."

"Go!"

Conroy was his boss, but he was stubborn as hell and would probably stay and fix things himself. Except the damage was too devastating for all of them together to fix. "What happened?"

"Onor. For once in your life, do what I tell you to. Go now."

The look on Conroy's face didn't leave him any choice. Besides, Conroy was twice his size.

Onor went.

Ruby would know what had happened. Common. That was where Ix told people to go in drills.

Onor started heading toward common, jostled by people going every which way, surrounded by names being called, children snapped at, hushed voices full of worry.

The loudspeaker came on. Ix's voice, "All crew report to the transport station immediately."

As Onor turned along with the rest of the crowd, someone stepped on his foot. Tripping, he almost knocked an older woman down. The pain in his foot drove him to choose an empty corridor going the wrong way. He tested a door and ducked into one of the machine shops. He stuffed his pockets with energy gels and a full first-aid roll from the medikit. He glanced around the machine shop one last time to see if there were any other useful emergency items before he plunged back into the corridor to be swept along by nervous crowds.

Onor watched for Ruby, but the crowds were dense and confused, and he failed to spot her.

He'd never seen so much chaos. All one thousand two hundred and seventy-two inhabitants of C-pod appeared to all be trying to occupy a space meant for fifty or so at most. They clutched bags of food and bundled clothes and bedding, and they wore way too much jewelry. Many, like Onor, stood on tiptoe, looking for people they'd lost.

He spotted bruised cheeks, scraped arms, and one already purpling black eye. Here and there, a splint.

The crowd spilled through multiple corridors and into adjacent rooms. Loudspeakers periodically barked for order, which didn't emerge.

Being small let Onor slide and duck through the crowd, looking for the familiar bright splash of Ruby's red hair. Being small also made it harder to be sure he wasn't missing her. He finally found her little brother, Ean, and close by him, her mother. Ruby's mother had clearly once had her daughter's beauty, although in darker features, with intense black eyes and black hair barely touched with gray. She stood on tiptoe, trying to scan the crowded room. A boy almost as tall as she was clutched her arm, as if afraid he might lose her at any moment. Onor addressed her. "Suri? Have you seen Ruby?"

"No."

She didn't sound like she cared. He mumbled, "Thanks" and kept pushing forward until he reached the platform. The metal trains stood still, the doors that allowed people onto the boarding platform shut tight against the crowd. He asked people he knew. No one had seen Ruby. As he pushed out a different door than the one he'd come through, three reds in body armor were coming toward him. "Wrong way," the leader stated, but kept going without stopping Onor. The third red in line caught Onor by the arm and squeezed it hard enough to hurt. "The habs are closed." Onor noticed that the red wore half a uniform, a red shirt over blue pants that were a color he sometimes saw on men who talked to Conroy, but not to him.

Someone had called in extra help.

Damn it. Where was Ruby?

The reds—true and fake—continued down the hallway, clearing space with their voices. He spotted Conroy choosing people to help keep order in the lines. Onor turned around and followed the reds, going a longer way, cursing the time lost. If Conroy caught him and put him to work, he'd never find Ruby.

THREE

CONVERSATIONS IN THE DARK

The cold stillness of the park felt completely wrong. Ruby wanted to be moving, needed it. But the pain in Fox's ankle remained painted across his forehead in tiny, tight lines, and her belly remembered the loss of gravity. Every drill she could remember had taught her to stay put when the gravgens failed. Her teeth chattered with the cold, the only noise except for their breath and, sometimes, a far off screech of metal or the faintest hint of siren or loudspeaker.

She remembered something, or maybe it was just now sinking in. "You said we're almost home. What did you mean?"

"We're almost to Adiamo."

"Adiamo's a game."

"Locked down, so no one can change it. Did you ever wonder why? Besides, why do you think it's everywhere?"

"I don't play games much." She rolled the new meaning of the word around in her head. *Adiamo equals home.* She had seen the game, of course, had tried it a few times. It was where she'd learned about birds. "What do you mean by almost?"

He furrowed his brow at her, looking puzzled. "We've been slowing down since before you were born. We expect contact in a year or two. We're not close enough to see the details of the system yet, but it's changing how everybody acts."

"Not how *we* act." Why didn't she already know something so important? She shifted her weight around on the bench, swinging her feet in and out as a way to keep warm. "No one tells us anything. We're not too stupid to be told the ship's almost home."

He didn't say anything at all to that.

She spoke into the awkward moment of silence. "So what's Adiamo like? Is it much like the park?"

He laughed. "Black and dim?"

So he had a sense of humor. "Like the park usually is. Light. Happy."

"I don't know about the park."

"Does Adiamo have birds and trees and grass and sky?"

"Adiamo's the name of the star, but there are planets with birds and grass, I think. Like the parks."

"You don't sound sure."

"It's probably like the game."

All her life she'd known that the ship was going home, but never when it would get there. She'd assumed she'd die first. "So what happens when we get home?"

"I don't know. There's arguments about the value of the cargo and who owns what and all kinds of stupid nonsense going on."

She felt an extra chill, one that had nothing to do with the cold of the air around them. "Who decides?"

"Garth, I guess. The same people who decide everything else. But we don't even know what the choices are yet. First we need to get home."

Ruby didn't feel up to telling him she didn't know about Garth. She closed her eyes, felt the anger that had driven her here in the first place rising in her body, warming her a little. The world inside the *Fire* had been the same for so long that the idea it could be different simmered slow inside her bones. This was big. Bigger than the sky falling or Fox beside her. "Someone else is going to tell us what to do when we get home? Going to decide?"

"For me, too, I suppose."

"But you know about it." Her voice sounded bitter, even to her own ears. "You know we're going home. So you can talk about it. We can't even do that."

Fox narrowed his eyes at her, frowning. Ruby felt him reassessing, maybe withdrawing.

She settled, thinking hard about all she'd just learned.

Fox seemed content to be quiet as well. Their breath made faint white puffs in the gray air. The park sounded like silence. Spooky. There should be more noise.

"Tell me about your life," she said into the semidarkness.

He countered. "You first."

"I know about me. I want to know about you."

He laughed again. "I feel the same way, and I outrank you."

She wanted to say no, to make him go first, but he did outrank her. Damn him. "What do you want to know?" she asked.

"Start with your family."

Why did he ask that? "My big brother Macky works reclamation. My little brother Ean wants to do something in medical, but he doesn't know if he'll get picked yet. Mom works where I'm going, repairing maintenance bots. That's why I know the cargo holds have good air. We sometimes go to a special room that has parts."

"You don't seem to like your family."

Ruby bristled. "Sure I do. They're okay." Except Macky, who hated it that she was smarter than him. And her mom, who cared more about looks than brains, and who slept with men for favors and hinted that Ruby would have to do the same some day. Ruby swallowed, the familiar loss threatening to overwhelm her. Not here. "I like my brother Ean pretty well."

"Tell me about living down here."

"We work. When there's more to do than people to do it, we just keep working. Reds tell us what to do, mostly. Sometimes we're made bosses, but there's always a red calling the shots, even behind a gray boss." She glanced at his clothes. "We only see blues sometimes, and they usually come to talk to reds."

He didn't look surprised. "What do you do?"

"I fix robots." She held up her hands, so the grease in the creases of her fingers and the half moons of her nails showed.

He took her right hand and squinted at it and then let it go. She told him about the shifts and the crèches and the immersives. She didn't tell him about the black market stim, or the small gangs that gray adults broke up to save their own children, or about how some women made extra money. He probably knew all that, and he didn't need to know that she did. So she told him the surface of her life, which was bad enough.

He interrupted and asked her questions when she mentioned robots and parts breaking more easily, wanting to know the details.

She drew closer to him as she talked, his warmth welcome as the park cooled more. The cargo bays were always cooler than home, as if the cold of space crept into them. It had grown colder than that now, colder than she'd ever been. The chip in her wrist felt cold, and her earrings were like small ice picks in her lobes.

"What's best in your life?" he asked.

"Tell me about yours?"

He shook his head. "It's not important."

"I want to know about it," she whispered.

"Tell me what you love." His eyes looked bright and genuinely curious, and he smiled, as if that would soften the fact that he was telling her nothing.

"My best friends, Onor and Marcelle. And music. I love music. Singing and plays, choirs and instruments. All of it. I sing, too."

A funny look crossed his face, as if his curiosity had gone from the kind a teacher had to something deeper. "Sing for me?"

She swallowed. "It's cold."

"The breathing will warm you up."

Truth. One of the women in her pod was teaching her, a tall blond named Bari, with a rich voice. Bari listened to recordings she took from the library and sang along to them, and she taught Ruby to sing along to them, too. Singing was a secret hope, a dream almost as fragile as the hope of getting inward to the places the blues lived. Her cheeks tingled with nerves. "It's cold."

"And do you wear a coat when you sing?" His laugh came out soft and low, and it wasn't making fun of her at all. "Besides," he waved a hand, dark movement in a dark place, "I may not hear any other songs ever."

"They'll rescue us." She took a deep breath and sang the first thing that came to mind, something she knew was from the inner levels. The song, "Requiem for Grandmother," told a story of love between a child and grandmother; it ended with the child standing outside a hatch and singing the chorus for the grandmother, whose body had been sent free into space.

> *Grandma, will you watch for me?*
> *I'll be right here, growing old.*
> *Grandma, will you catch me*
> *The day I go out the door?*

She let herself feel it, the wistful lyrics drawing sadness into her core. It did warm her, although Ruby berated herself a bit for the choice. Fox was right; they might yet die.

As the last note trailed off, she waited for his reaction.

An extra bit of cold air blew in from above and rattled the broken pipes sticking out of the roof.

His next words didn't tell her what he thought at all. He just asked, "What else do you know?"

A few songs about how awful the reds and blues were. She picked a lullaby she'd heard came from the very beginning of *The Creative Fire*, one about watchful stars loose in the black of space. The song was so soft that it drew tears to her eyes. When she was really little she believed stars watched over them and that she would always be okay because the stars made it so.

Fox let the last note die out. She searched his face, and while he hadn't started crying, he looked soft. She'd affected him.

"Do you know 'The Black Hole and the Nebula'?" he asked.

Of course she did. "My throat's too dry to sing it. That's a Seren Gold song." Fox lived with blues. "Do you know Seren Gold?"

"I've met her."

She swallowed, wishing for water. "Tell me about her."

He sounded pleased. "She's older now, of course. I was only twelve when I first heard her, and I thought she had the best voice I'd ever heard. I used to lie in my room and turn off all the lights and listen to her before I went to sleep every night.

"I met her ten years later. She's very focused. That's what it takes, you know. Focus. She never stops practicing and working on new things."

"I've only heard three of her songs."

"I think there are four in your catalog."

The anger came back, a little, even after singing and even though she was hearing about Seren Gold. "So we don't get all the songs either."

"No one gets all the songs."

She breathed in and out with as much control as she could exert, not wanting to stay angry with him. Surely hours had passed, and surely Ix would send someone for them soon. Fox's head was turned far enough toward her that she could see his eyelashes, pale against the curve of his cheek. Everything about him felt different than the grays. He hadn't run out of hope or energy or lost his soul.

He knew real singers.

She swallowed. This was a chance, a gift. He hadn't said what he thought of her voice, but Bari had said that it was a great voice, and people did stop and listen to her practice.

"So take me home with you." She didn't expect the words until they were out of her mouth, but they sounded good and right. "Take me."

FOUR
THE JACKMAN

The crowd in the corridors stank of fear. Lines of people restless with waiting shifted and re-formed, inched closer to each other and drifted apart. Onor worked his way to the outer edge of the crowd, avoiding two more strings of reds converging on the transport station. The enforcers looked as scared as the grays they were herding.

He struggled the wrong way through people still streaming in, many clutching large sacks, extra clothes, or boots. He shuffled his feet to avoid tripping over discarded possessions, a sure sign of the total lack of discipline that had descended on the pod. They knew better; stuff became projectiles in a gravgen failure.

Thirst clawed at his throat, along with his fear. The energy gels were supposed to be consumed with water, but he didn't have any.

He stopped and sucked on a gel anyway, letting the corridors around him finish emptying. A red in full uniform came around a corner, brandishing a stunner. Onor quickly turned and knocked on the nearest door. The red stopped him, this one a rare woman in red. She had dark gray eyes that looked like a storm and didn't hold any trust in them. "What are you doing here?"

"They told me to look for stragglers."

"We can use the security cameras for that."

Onor dropped his eyes and did his best to sound earnest and biddable. "I'm just doing what I was told."

She pointed down the hall with her stunner. "Go on."

"I don't want to make the red who sent me mad. Besides, what if someone needs me?" Like Ruby. "Could be old, or sick."

He thought she wasn't going to buy it, but then she shook her head and said, "Be quick. I want to see you at the station before the last in line gets on the train. If you miss it, you might be stranded here when we power down the life support to do repairs. Do you understand?"

He nodded.

As if he hadn't nodded, she stared at him and said, slowly, "You'll die if you don't come back." Like he was stupid.

He nodded again and she left. He headed for The Jackman's door.

It opened just as he reached toward it, throwing him off balance. The Jackman stood in the doorway, so tall his head just missed the top. His long, white beard fell over his ample belly, and he had a wide grin on his face. "Onor! About time."

Before Onor could ask The Jackman anything, he found himself sitting down with a glass of water clutched in his hand, tilting the blessed sweet stuff into his mouth and feeling how it made him functional again. He drained the glass. "You're supposed to be at the transport center right now. Both of us are. They're herding folks to the other pods." He remembered the red's insistent voice. "They're gonna blow air on this one."

The Jackman raised a bushy eyebrow but didn't seem nearly as disturbed as he ought to be. They needed to be hurrying. "Do you know what happened?" Onor asked him.

"The ship's dying." The Jackman must have seen Onor's face, since he waved a hand. "Not today. But today it took a step closer, like when an old person breaks a hip. One of the metal struts that anchor the pod in place ripped, and that stressed some of the other parts, so the pod has been stretched like rubber. But they've already got bots working to stabilize the supports." A sly grin floated across The Jackman's face, and his eyes sparkled with a secret. "Worse for them, its torn holes between levels."

Onor leaned back in the hard metal chair, which had seen better years, just like The Jackman, but was still around anyway, also just like The Jackman. He and Ruby and Marcelle had been right. There were other levels. "How many? How many other levels?"

The Jackman didn't answer.

"I think there's three or four," Onor said.

"Not four. There's no room in the ship for four. I measured."

"I need to find somebody. Can you help?"

"Your girl."

Onor's cheeks got hot. "Ruby's not my girl."

"Would be if you could get her."

There wasn't anything to say to that. "I need to find her before they blow the air. Got views of the cameras?"

The Jackman had earned his name because he could access anything. But willing? That was always a harder one. The Jackman chewed on his lower lip for so long that Onor wanted to shake him. Finally he asked, "Where do you think she is?"

"I looked at the Transport Station. It's all chaos. Better look there again, I guess. She's probably not in common, since they moved everybody out of there. Maybe the park?"

The Jackman shook his head. "Park's falling apart. Better hope she's not there."

"It would be a faster place to look. Then we could eliminate it." The more he thought about Ruby being in the park, the more likely it seemed. "Please? 'Cause if she's there I have to warn her about the air getting spaced. It doesn't matter if she's at the Transport Station, except I don't want to be separated. But it won't kill her."

The Jackman held up a hand, laughing. "I'll help." The wall in front of him bloomed into a full-sized picture of the work habs. It showed at least ten reds walking down the corridors and looking in doorways, calling out. As they watched, the reds flushed a boy and girl, teenagers, from one of the bars by common. They emerged, red-faced, the girl straightening her blouse. Carolyne and Jay. And after they raced off, the reds laughed.

"Nosy reds," Onor said.

"Saved their lives."

The camera switched to darkness. "What's that? Is the camera broken?"

"No, that's the park." The Jackman grunted and pushed a button. The view changed to one high up, looking down in a wide angle. One area of the park was lighter than the rest. In the center of that, a hole gaped in the park floor. Something unidentifiable flapped in the camera's peripheral vision, completely out of focus.

Onor gasped. It looked like a giant knife had stabbed the park and ripped.

"Easy," The Jackman said, panning the camera. "There's your girl."

She and a red-haired man shared a bench. He took most of the available space, leaning against Ruby.

A blue.

The man's eyes appeared to be closed. His lips moved. The camera gave up no sound.

The Jackman let out a long, low whistle. "Maybe you wish I hadn't found her."

Onor flushed, but at least part of the heat blooming on his cheeks was anger. "It's not like that. That's no one we've ever seen. Can you zoom in?"

"Yes."

Onor peered at the image, Ruby and the stranger so quiet that it might have been a still frame except that the man's lips were moving, the cadence of his words showing in the whitened air around his mouth. "He's hurt—see his foot? He must have been in the park and got injured."

"Maybe."

"I gotta go."

The look The Jackman gave him was part compassionate, part hard. "She's not worth so much as you think, that one. She'll break your heart."

"I've got to warn her."

"Of course you do."

FIVE
THE DANGERS INSIDE

R uby shivered in the cold park as she watched Fox absorb her request. The very act of asking him to take her with him had opened all the possibilities in the world. She could eat well. She could sing. She could advocate for her people.

His jaw tightened.

She lifted her hand, touched his cheek, and let her hand fall again, holding her breath.

When he spoke, he didn't look at her. "It's dangerous where I live. You'd be eaten alive."

Heat flushed her cheeks. "It can't be more dangerous than this!"

"You don't understand."

"I learn fast. I haven't been killed here yet, or hurt. I haven't ended up in lockup yet. I'm first in my class." Damn it, she sounded desperate and young. She took a deep breath. "I'll do well there, I know I will. I'll have a better chance of singing—"

He cut her off, laughter licking at the edges of his face in spite of the way his lips were blue with the cold. "You don't understand."

"You think I'm not good enough. I am. I can do anything."

"Shhhhh . . . I know. You're good, but you don't understand. What's dangerous here and what's dangerous there are different. In my world, people aren't always nice to each other."

"Like they are here?" she shot back. "I didn't tell you the bad parts."

"Whatever they are, they're simpler than the risks I live with."

"I don't want to be a gray all my life." She plucked at his shirt. "I want nice clothes, and to sing, and to learn more things. I don't know who helps run the ship, but it's not robot jockeys." Her mind raced. "You could teach me. Help me."

He shook his head, still looking amused.

Her right hand rested on his shoulder and her left wrapped around him to rest on his chest. She felt hyperaware of every place her body contacted his. She clutched him closer, desperate for a way to convince him. His heart beat under her fingers.

The dangers and the breaking had made her stronger and faster and scared, but now all that fear had run out, leaving her too tired and cold to think as fast as usual. There had to be a way to convince him. If his ankle worked, they'd have gone a long time ago and found more people. Instead, it was just the two of them, nothing and no one else. That, and the cold, and the way the broken park looked surreal all around them made her feel like she was in a dream.

She had to think of something.

A low buzzing sound grew louder. She had taken it for background, but she was wrong.

Fox took her hand and squeezed it. "Thank you." A farewell.

She realized the sound was related to a cargo cart so quiet she'd not known what she was hearing. The cart sped just above the paths, the driver moving neither slow nor fast, inexorably growing nearer.

She glanced back at Fox. "You're welcome," she whispered, feeling him slip away already. "When will I see you again?"

"Maybe never."

"Take me with you," she repeated, hating the slightly desperate edge in her voice.

He didn't answer, but it felt like he wanted her to come, like something in his gaze told her yes.

She held her breath, drinking in the curve of his cheek, his dark eyelashes resting against pale skin, the specific blue of his eyes.

"Ruby!"

Her head snapped around at the familiar voice. Onor. At first she thought he might be on the cart, but he was on foot, racing toward her across the broken park. She winced. Trust Onor to show up when she didn't want him, or need him.

Fox's hand still rested in hers, warm in spite of the cold. He pulled it away, and she had to resist the urge to reach and take it back. He levered himself up, careful of her legs and of his ankle, squinting at the approaching vehicle.

The silver cart's surface was big and flat, meant for cargo. A driver stood at the back of the cart, balancing and holding on to a steering column in front of him, glancing around as if he expected to be attacked. He wore blue like Fox's, with a red cap stuck down on his head.

"Dayn," Fox called out, smiling, looking relieved. He waved him forward.

Onor had stopped a few feet away, watching the approaching cart and driver as well as Ruby and Fox. He looked far more uncertain than Ruby had ever seen him. He could wait. It was Fox she was losing.

She took Fox's elbow, helping to support him on his hurt foot. She walked with him toward the edge of the path. "How will I know you're okay?" she whispered, the approaching driver giving her words speed.

"I'll be fine."

Fox sounded distracted, as if he'd already left her.

Damn him.

She reached up and grabbed the back of his neck with her left hand, holding him still with her right hand on his waist, his weight off balance and leaning in because of his foot. "I will remember you," she said. He would leave and she wouldn't have another chance. "I need you to remember me. Find me."

He swallowed, his gaze filled with the desire she usually hated men for. But she needed it in Fox, needed him to want her. It was instinct, something that rose all the way from her belly and arced up her back and spine. Warm. Raw.

"Find me," she repeated.

Dayn had stopped, too, looking almost as confused as Onor.

"I'll remember you," Fox said.

He would. Ruby pulled him against her, hard, and kissed him. His lips resisted, cold and thin. She touched them with her tongue, opening them, touching his tongue, which pushed back at her. She gave herself into it, a lick inside him while she pressed him to her. She'd never done this, not so boldly, and it was as if a pillar of fire ran up her belly and her chest and skewered her heart.

Surely he felt it as well. He trembled.

Then his hands clamped down on her arms and he pushed a tiny bit. Reluctantly, she gave in, stepping away from him but taking one of his hands in hers "Do. Do remember me. Ruby."

He nodded, his voice thick. "Thanks for being here."

He meant it. If only she had more time, if only Onor hadn't come right now.

"Fox," Dayn said. "Leave off your flirting. We have to go. Now." Dayn gave Ruby a close gaze. She noted curiosity and surprise, like she wasn't what he expected to find. Or maybe it had been the kiss. She hadn't expected that, either. Now that it was done, she was surprised at herself. He spoke to both

Ruby and Onor. "You two better get, run if you can. You've got to evacuate. Get to the train."

"What?" Ruby asked.

"The train. Before they space the air."

"I know." Onor finally spoke, his face red. He looked hard at Ruby. "We have to go."

Dayn took Fox's weight, and Ruby let go of Fox completely, her skin suddenly cold. She went and stood by Onor. Neither of them said anything as Dayn helped Fox onto the cart and made sure he had a good grip on the low rail that ran along the side by the driver's stand.

The cart hissed back the way it had come, still low to the ground, as if its driver expected to lose grav at any time.

After Dayn and Fox had gone, Onor pulled her to him, his body and arm stiffer than she expected. "What was that?"

"Do we have a few minutes?"

"Maybe two."

She pointed up at the rent in the roof of the sky, at the torn fabric of the ceiling and the loose wires and broken pipes that dangled above them.

His mouth fell open.

"We were right. That's where they came from. Both of them, I'm sure. The hurt man—Fox—he fell from there. There's shiny robots, shinier than ours, and more, and there were more people, but they all got away to some-place safe. It's empty now, but it wasn't."

Onor licked his lips and stared up. "Did you have to kiss him?" His voice had a tiny bit of hurt in it, which tugged at her. But he was her friend, not her man, and so she ignored it. Besides, in truth, his anger had fled, his face showing only wonderment as he looked up. "Think we can get up there?" he asked.

"How?"

She looked around, but of course there was nothing. "Do you know what happened?"

"Maybe. The Jackman says the ship's getting old. They're making people line up and putting them on trains so they can fix this part."

"Can they fix it?"

"I don't know." He was still looking at the roof. An eerie quiet settled around them, with no sirens and no noise except the faint, slow flapping of the ripped material. "We should go," she whispered. "Besides, I'm cold."

He took a last look, and then he took her arm. "You're shivering. We should run."

They passed through the park's gates and pounded through the tunnel. It was a relief to be somewhere with lower ceilings and more holds on the wall. If the gravgens failed now, they'd be all right.

They raced through the corridors that led home. As they burst through the opening into the housing rows she lived on with her family, a red stepped in front of them.

He was thick-bodied, older than most reds, familiar. Ruby cursed under her breath and just managed not to run into Onor as he stopped.

"Ben." She gasped, nearly out of breath from running. "Hi." Ben had been scolding her and Onor for breaching safety rules since they were kids. If she let Ben tell her no she'd be lost. "I need something for Ma. She's sick, and she didn't bring anything with her. I've got to get clothes, too. My uniform. I'll just be a minute."

Ben narrowed his brows and started to shake his head.

Ruby's heart sank.

"We won't be long." A thin, dark-haired wraith of a girl emerged from behind Ben. "Come on, Ruby. Hurry." Marcelle looked up at Ben, her most winning smile pasted across her thin face.

The red stared down at her.

"I know. I'm supposed to be at the train," Marcelle pleaded. "But I was waiting here for Ruby. Let's go. We'll hurry. We know the dangers."

Ruby added, "We won't go anywhere else. You know our place is nearby."

Ben stepped aside. "Two minutes."

"Thank you." She reached toward him to touch his cheek, then decided he might trap her hand and keep her with him in spite of his step back.

Marcelle darted away, Onor right behind her. In moments, they'd crossed two corridors and turned down another, stopping at Ruby's door. Ruby held up her hand and the door opened for her. She stopped Marcelle and gave her a hug. "How'd you know where to find me?"

Marcelle grinned. "How do I ever know where to find you?" She pointed to Ruby's torn shirt. "You weren't going to let anyone herd you onto a train with nothing to wear."

Ruby laughed, almost giddy with exhaustion and excitement mixed up together in her body.

"And you'll want your journal."

The confrontation in the corridor seemed like days ago now. Ruby clenched her jaw, steeling herself in case the reds hadn't brought her journal back before the damage started. Thankfully, it lay on the table by the door. She grabbed it and then scooped jewelry from her one private drawer into a bag.

The floor nearly fell out from under her. Marcelle gasped as Ruby lost her footing and slammed into a wall of drawers.

Onor snapped, "Ready?"

Ruby shoved clothes into the bag and grabbed up a uniform shirt in case Ben asked her to show it. "Ready."

The sirens let out a short, high-pitched burst, and then another, and then they went off in an ululating cry so loud it drove them through the door. "Maybe we won't get your stuff," Marcelle told Onor.

"I know." His face was white and his eyes wide.

They headed into the corridors. Marcelle grabbed her own sack as they passed her door. It bulged even fuller than Ruby's.

They raced back the way they had come. Ben stepped aside for them like before, but this time he followed them. He'd been waiting. The care and concern his having waited implied touched Ruby. "Thank you," she whispered to him as she passed.

The old red made a hurry-up gesture, his serious dark eyes and the continuing screech of the sirens driving Ruby to pass Marcelle and Onor and lead them to the transport station.

The sign above the train proclaimed that it would be leaving in two minutes.

A woman from the crèche named Rebeck cried out, over and over, a soul-wounded sound. A pair of red women helped her toward the open doors, the taller of the two saying, "Surely he just got on the first train."

Cars filled and the station emptied.

As they stepped into the last car, Ruby smelled baby puke and urine when she was sure it should be all oily and clean. The car wasn't full. One family huddled close to each other near the back. Ben stood near the middle, where he could see everyone.

The train let off a loud squeal, warning that it would be leaving soon. Its dead-machine voice proclaimed, "Doors closing."

Ruby tugged on Onor's arm, guiding him into a seat. She strapped the bags she and Marcelle had brought into empty seats on either side of them.

The voice said "Doors—" and stopped.

The doors slid open and two people stumbled in. The young man's face was so bloody it took Ruby a moment to identify him. Hugh. Lya, his girlfriend, supported his right side, wincing as he leaned on her. Her face was flushed red with exertion and her reddish-blond hair wet with blood and sweat.

"What happened?" Ben asked.

Lya's voice sounded edgy. "Reds beat him up. We were . . . on our way here and they stopped us and beat him. His skull's split."

So they hadn't left him alone.

Hugh groaned.

Ben held a hand up to calm her, frowning. "Probably just his scalp. What reds?"

Lya spat her words at Ben. "It could have been murder. If they knocked him out we'd still be there. Missed the—."

Hugh said, "Let it be, Lya. You know Ben didn't do it. Let us by so I can sit down."

Ben nodded stiffly. "Strap in. I already used most of my medikit, but I'll look and see if there's any left on another car after we get going."

The train repeated its message about the doors closing.

Onor jerked his head toward their seats. "I've got fix-all and tape."

Ben raised an eyebrow at Onor. "Can you handle it?"

Onor nodded, his face white but his eyes determined.

The train's acceleration pushed Ruby back against the seats. Once it steadied, they unbuckled and began to work on Hugh.

He'd been beat bad.

Besides the gash on his head, one cheek was red and the other eye was going black. Ruby tore more material from the shirt she'd already mangled for Fox's foot. She handed strips to Onor and Marcelle, who pressed them against Hugh's head to stop the blood. After, Onor spread fix-all tape across Hugh's scalp. Lya clung to Hugh's hand, her knuckles white. Not a perfect job. Bits of dried blood stuck to Hugh's hair and stained his neck. Hugh whispered, "Thanks," his eyes slightly shocky and still full of pain.

"Keep him awake," Ben advised.

"I will." Lya squeezed Hugh's arm. A single bruise darkened the back of her hand and she winced from time to time when the train shook. So Lya'd gotten a little of whatever Hugh got.

Ruby sat back and closed her eyes, too tired to avoid the memory that Hugh's beating brought up for her any longer. It had been a year ago, but when she let herself think about it, it felt both more distant and more recent, like something so bad it couldn't have happened at all.

She remembered walking softly as she snuck down the corridor between habs. She hadn't wanted her mother to wake up and keep her home. If fifteen was old enough to be on shift after school, old enough to get in trouble, then it was old enough for her to solve her own troubles.

Or, more specifically, to help her friend Nona solve *her* problems. Nona was being stupid with dangerous people, and Ruby was going to stop her. It was bad enough Ruby was already scared her mom might be killed doing the same thing, and her mom was way smarter than Nona, had more edges and more toughness.

Nona had let it slip that she was meeting reds on the maintenance level. Stupid. Ruby had been there a few times, although never alone. She'd gone with senior repair techs to learn where the parts depots and the metal reclamation bins were.

No one had ever let her go to the maintenance levels alone.

The nearest entrance was in the corner outside the train station. The unmarked hatch in the floor swung up easily on well-oiled hinges. She climbed down a ladder, balancing the hatch over her head, letting it down slow enough that she barely heard it close.

The corridor here looked like the one above, except greasier and more banged up. Pipes and braces and way-finding signs hung overhead. The lights shone bright and stark, encouraging her to go about her business instead of standing still in their cold, square patterns.

Before she started off, she closed her eyes and took a deep breath. With any luck, she'd go straight to Nona, and she'd catch out the men who were using her. Reds were supposed to take care of you instead of hurt you. Reds were supposed to protect.

That's what they said in school.

It was a lie. Mostly. Sometimes it was a serious lie.

If Nona had told her the truth last night, protecting wasn't what they were doing to her at all. She'd come back with bruised forearms and a thick lip. She'd also come back with a flask of clear still and some pain cream her mom needed.

Everyone should be allowed to make *some* mistakes, but Nona had used up all the tolerance left for her, even though she was only a year older than Ruby. If she got caught skipping school or work again, she'd have to live down here the rest of her life.

Most lives down here didn't last very long.

Ruby frowned as she passed a door that had been permanently bolted shut. A toxic sign warned people away. Probably medical waste.

Ruby and Nona had sworn to graduate together and get on one of the good crews together, but it was only going to happen if Ruby made Nona act differently.

Her journal was folded into a sharp hard square and clipped to her belt. She opened it up and set it to be ready to take pictures.

It was nearly the end of second shift, and the corridors were so quiet Ruby heard her own breath and the laboring of the air scrubbers above her head.

A tall, lanky man with three half-height bots squeaking along behind him rounded a corner. Ruby hid in a side corridor and waited for them to go by.

She swallowed and kept going, passing the bottom part of the water reclamation plant, its doors all marked with the same familiar water-drop symbol that she saw on the maintenance doors of her own level and on some of the pipes above her head.

Nona had told her that the men met her just past the water plant, in some space that had once been a storeroom, and then offices, and was now a makeshift sleeping quarters.

Ruby planned to catch them and report them. Sex with underaged girls was against the rules, even if it happened all the time. All she needed was proof. Gripping her journal so hard that the edges dug into her palms, she turned sideways and sidled along the wall, trying even harder to be quiet. She wanted to see what was happening and get a picture of the men, but she didn't want them to catch her.

A squeak. A click. Laughter and then a harsh word, cutting it off. Footsteps around a corner from her, going away.

Heavy. Not Nona's boots. Whose?

Ruby shuffled as fast as she could go without making noise. Rounding the corner, she caught a glimpse of two red uniforms. She reacted before thinking, drawing back, hiding. When she got the courage to look around again, she cursed under her breath. These were probably the men she had meant to catch, and now they were gone.

Should she leave or go find Nona and confess that she'd been spying on her? Ruby sighed. Maybe she should wait a minute for Nona; but she was afraid that if she stayed down here she might lose all her courage. She took a deep breath, just the way Bari had taught her—the steadying breath to soothe her nerves before she sang in front of a crowd—letting it out slowly.

She walked as calmly as she could around the corner.

Only empty hallway, with doors on either side.

She whispered, "Nona?"

Silence.

She said it louder. "Nona. Are you here?"

Ruby took a few more steps, and her foot slid on something wet on the floor. She bent down and ran her finger through it, bringing it up to her nose.

Blood.

Her body went hot and shivery, her breath racing up and down the back of her throat and catching in her nose.

One of the doors hung a little open. Just a crack.

She stepped to it and pushed it the rest of the way open. It squeaked.

A dark room full of lumps and shapes. "Nona?" she whispered again, and this time she heard the faint scratch of fingernails on metal.

Her journal was still in her hand, so she told it to illuminate.

On the floor, Nona, on her side, her arms tied behind her back, naked from the waist down. Her shirt had been pulled up over her face. The hem was soaked and dark with blood.

The rectangle of light from Ruby's journal was too small to illuminate the whole room, so she flashed it around, making sure there was nothing else to see. There wasn't. A soft moan and a shudder told Ruby that Nona was still alive. She knelt beside her and touched her arm. Her skin felt cool.

"What did they do to you?" Ruby murmured as she untied Nona's hands and rolled her over.

"Oh, oh, oh." She heard herself gasping the word over and over as she spotted a dark metal shard of thin pipe or bar sticking out on Nona's side, blood welling out around it. "Ix!" she managed to scream out before she dropped her journal onto Nona's bare chest. She scrabbled around in the gloom, found the bottom of Nona's uniform, and folded it around the shard, applying pressure to try to stop the bleeding.

"Light. Ix. Light."

Damned machine. The cloth under her fingers was getting soggy. "Hang on, Nona."

Ix's voice, finally. "What's wrong, Ruby?"

"Nona's dying."

"Can you show me?"

"No. Send someone."

"I already have."

"Thank you. Light!"

Two of the four lights in the ceiling bloomed on. Ruby swallowed at her first real sight of Nona. She wanted a free hand to help cover her, but she didn't dare stop doing her best to staunch the blood. At least it wasn't gushing out over her fingers, but there was already so much on the floor. She'd never seen so much blood in her life, not even when Lou had cut off two fingers in the machine room. Ruby had been so close that his blood spattered her shirt.

Nona watched Ruby, her eyes intense in the white field of her pale face. She opened her mouth. "Thank you."

"Who did this?"

Nona shook her head, barely.

"You knew them. You met them here."

"Don't. Mess with It. Ruby." A long breath, thin, Nona wincing as she added, "Not safe. Don't be me. Stay safe."

"Shhh . . . stop talking. You'll be okay."

"No."

"Why?"

"Not. Good. Enough."

"What wasn't good enough?"

"Me."

"Of course you were. You're good. You're my friend. I need you."

Nona lifted a hand toward Ruby's face. She almost made it, but her hand fell away before their skin touched.

Ruby froze, her hands still over the wound, her voice shaking as she called Nona's name over and over.

Long after she'd lost all hope of helping Nona, and long before anyone came to help her, Ruby whispered, "I'll change this. I'll stop it. I'll do it for you." It became a mantra, and then almost a song, a shaky, scary little song that she sang over and over to the empty room while she waited.

"I'll change this. I'll stop it. I'll do it for you. I'll change this. I'll stop it. I'll do it for you. I'll change this. I'll stop it. I'll do it for you . . ."

The rhythm of the mantra matched the rhythm of the train, the rock and murmur of the cars, as they slid across tracks in the darkness between pods. Ruby whispered the words again into the near dark, feeling Onor's hand on her shoulder and hearing Lya whisper something into Hugh's ear. Ruby whispered, "I'll change this. I'll make them stop. Nona." Then she added, "Hugh."

SIX

KYLE

R uby jolted awake, blinking at bright light, surprised she'd passed so deeply into her daydreaming that she hadn't felt the train stop.

Ben stood in front of her, his arms crossed, using his best red voice. "Off."

Beside her, Marcelle had already gathered her things, and Onor looked anxious.

Ben gestured toward the door. Ruby clutched her bag to her chest. Where was her family? Why hadn't she asked Ben about them?

The B-pod transport station looked like theirs, except painted mostly blue instead of mostly orange. It smelled cleaner than the train, and far more sterile.

As soon as they stepped off, a red called them over, squinting at them as his journal queried their chips. After a moment, he identified them by name. Apparently satisfied, he launched into a few sentences that he seemed bored of repeating. "You will remain here until told to go anywhere else. Travel between pods is currently restricted. Resettlements are based on order of evacuation."

So she wouldn't see her family. She swallowed hard, listening for the red's next words.

"You will be expected to contribute to B-pod. Your ration allotments have already been switched in case you have immediate needs. Logistics will resettle you based on skills and family needs in the future."

"My aunt is here," Ruby said. "We can stay with her."

"If you have family who were settled to other places, logistics will try to resettle you based on skills and family needs in the future." The red repeated exactly.

She pursed her lips. "Maybe you didn't hear me. I'd like to find my aunt. Her name is Daria."

The red blinked at her as if she'd sent him into full stop. "Do you know where she lives?"

She hadn't seen her since she was ten. A long time ago. Maybe Daria wouldn't even remember her. "No."

"Then we'll try to help you find her . . . in the future."

Great. "In the future" meant don't bother me now. He looked at his journal. "Ruby and Marcelle, you've been placed with Kyle Gleason."

Ruby reached for Onor's hand and did her best to look lost. "Onor should stay with us. We're a family group." Their chips would tell the guard something different if he was paying attention. She held her breath, waiting, smiling.

The red's eyes had already been drawn to Hugh and Lya, who were coming off the train right behind them, Hugh's head bandaged and his clothes stained with dried blood.

A tall man came forward to take Ruby's bag. The man, who must have overheard, said, "I'll make room." He held a hand out toward them all. "I'm Kyle."

"Thank you," Ruby said.

Kyle's dark hair hung long over dark eyes, and his skin was the brown of used robot oil. She held her hand out to him. "I'm Ruby, and these are my close friends, Marcelle and Onor."

"One of you will need to sleep on the floor."

Ruby nodded. "We'll manage."

Marcelle said, "Onor will sleep on the floor," and then, a few seconds later, she squeaked.

Ruby didn't turn around to see what Onor had done to Marcelle. "Thank you. I hope we won't be here long."

"Might be a while."

It turned out that this part of the *Fire* had felt only small shudders, and no more. But they'd been told to expect refugees for weeks. They filled Kyle in on the barest details of their experience as they walked away from the transport station.

The corridors here were mostly blue as well, and a few of the walls had pictures of fish on them.

At home, the pictures had been of birds.

Kyle's place was like her family's hab—a small kitchen, a sink, a big shared-space room with a vid screen and a few chairs, a privy, and two small sleeping areas with two beds each. Shared walls with the neighbors on both sides. She asked for water, which tasted like the stars and a good song, and washed a bit of the scent of Hugh's blood from the back of her throat.

Kyle said, "I've got to go clean up a mess I left behind at work when all this started. I'll get that, and then I'll bring you dinner."

She hadn't been thinking about food until Kyle mentioned it, but now it was hard to think about anything else. She looked around. There were few personal touches. A picture of an older woman on one wall. On another, a painting of one of the planets the *Fire* had been to, a blue-water world with almost no land. It wasn't even the last one they'd been to, but somewhere in the middle, some place her grandfather's grandfather might have seen before he died. The picture stuck in her head though.

She dibbed the top bunk, and she and Marcelle stowed their stuff in drawers built into the walls.

Onor had no stuff, but he hopped up on the top bunk and sat beside Ruby, both of their legs dangling over. Marcelle, standing against the wall, opened her mouth like she was about to complain, but he produced three energy gels from his pocket. "This'll get us though."

Ruby thought she might kiss him. Except he'd like it too much. So she punched him in the arm and took the gel. After the sweet sticky stuff hit her stomach and got her brains working again, she remembered why the picture of the planet bothered her.

"I didn't tell you guys. We're almost home. Fox said we're going to be there soon, like in our lifetime. Maybe even in a year. The problems we're having—the stuff today—that's all from starting to slow down."

"Fox?" Marcelle asked.

Ruby dug the story out for them both, doing her best in spite of being tired. Because Onor had seen it, she couldn't hide that she'd kissed Fox. She didn't tell them how much she'd liked it, or how she'd asked Fox to take her with him.

When Kyle came with food, they swarmed him, eating silently and fast.

As he was clearing up, Kyle said, "There's a man who wants to see you. I told him tomorrow."

"Who?" Ruby asked. "We hardly know anyone here."

Kyle shook his head, and a thin smile showed one cracked tooth. "Owl Paulie."

"I don't know an Owl Paulie."

"Me neither."

"Or me."

Kyle smiled at the serial response. "We all know him here. He's kind of a legend to us—used to cause all kinds of trouble with the reds and get away with it. He said he owes you gratitude for wrapping up his grandson's head."

Hugh? "Okay, we'll meet him."

"That's what I told him. I'll take you on my way to work."

In spite of her exhaustion, sleep visited in slight waves, and she spent a lot of time thinking. She needed to know who would help her here and who wouldn't. Daria might not even remember her. Her family was far away, which was partly good, except that she'd like to know they were all right.

If only Fox had taken her with him. Then she'd be someplace strange, but it would be wonderful, too.

SEVEN

THE OLD MAN'S TALE

Onor woke from a dream where a rip in the roof led to the black of space. Lym, the home planet from the game Adiamo, swirled in the opening, a round, brown place riddled with seas and rivers, with mountains and birds and spaceships that flew for days or years instead of lifetimes. He hadn't even recalled its name until just now. *Lym*. Lym, with enough water for everyone, all the time. That's what he remembered the most about learning the game, the way his avatar could have all the water it wanted and never be thirsty.

That's it. He was thirsty.

And he smelled food.

The girls chattered to some man, all three of them laughing quietly. *Kyle.* He blinked and oriented himself to the direction of the voices. They must have gotten up and gone past him into the kitchen. Since he could hear all of them, it was safe to bolt for the privy.

Kyle fed them a better breakfast than Onor ever remembered tasting. It was the same base stuff as always, protein and vegetables, breakfruit and enhanced water, but Kyle had added a salty sharpness that lingered on Onor's tongue.

Ruby asked, "How'd you make that so good?"

"Magic," Kyle said and grinned.

"Nope." Marcelle teased him. "Magic's only in stories. What'cha got?"

Kyle pointed at dried flowers and plants hung upside down above the sink. "I have a friend who works in the gardens. He planted these for me."

Hidden resources. "That was the best breakfast I ever had," Onor told him.

Ruby asked, "Has there been any news? Will they tell us where our families went?"

Kyle grunted as he reached up to set two clean drinking bulbs into their holders. "Reds don't tell us much yet. I'm on day shift. I'll take you to see Owl Paulie on the way, if you like. I imagine C-pod was laid out the same, so you can find your way back."

They dodged more people in the corridors here than at home, probably from the relocation. Onor recognized a few, waving but not stopping. Hopefully the reclamation center and the gardens would hold up to so many new mouths.

They passed B-pod's common. It, too, was like theirs. Except it had pale blue walls painted with orange and red and yellow fish rather than pale orange walls decorated with gray and brown and black birds. Refugees wandered or sat on benches, looking lost and worried. He spotted old Ben standing against a wall, observing.

Ix's voice startled him, tumbling from all of the speakers at once. "All home personnel report for normal duty. Repeat. All home personnel, all pods, report for duty as usual. Anyone wounded in yesterday's accident is to report to medical by the end of this shift. All off-duty crew members are to report to common at 15:30."

Ruby looked sour. "They could at least tell us if the ship's still falling apart."

"I guess we get the day off," Onor said. "That's some information."

Ruby grinned at him, and Marcelle thumped him on the back, hard. Damn her. She could stop pushing him around any time.

Owl Paulie lived in the retirement warrens near medical: rows of small places with good access to doctors, extra handholds on the wall, and extra grime on the corridor floors and walls.

Owl Paulie's set of two rooms smelled like age—mostly dry but with a slight sour tang. Kitchen and living room had been crammed into the same space, with three locked drawers and one set of shelves that held pots and games strapped down. Ruby, Onor, and Marcelle pulled chairs out of the wall and sat close enough together to touch. The only padded chair was red, with handmade cushions. Although it wasn't big, it dwarfed its occupant.

Owl Paulie's limbs were knobby and thin as robot arms. His skull threatened to burst free of his skin, and big, laughing eyes hid behind folds of wrinkles. As soon as Kyle left them, the old man held his hand out to Ruby and said, "I've heard much about you."

Her cheeks reddened and she smiled faintly. She asked, "What do you know of us? From where?"

"Of you, Ruby." Owl Paulie shook a bit as he sat. His voice was so soft. Onor held his breath, leaning in close to the old man's dry, cracked lips. "Hugh's told me how you sing, and how you fight everything. He admires you very much. For both skills."

Ruby looked as surprised as Onor felt.

Owl Paulie took a tiny sip of water and kept going. "Hugh told me what he heard last night. That the sky gave way in your park and showed you the belly of *The Creative Fire*."

He went quiet again. Maybe he could only manage one sentence at a time before he had to rest.

Marcelle answered. "When C-pod started to stretch—that's what they said, it stretched—the roof tore. We knew there was another level, but we didn't know they were so attached," Marcelle looked up at the ceiling, "or for sure that it was above us and not beside us."

Marcelle hadn't even seen it. It wasn't her story to tell. But Onor kept his mouth shut.

Owl Paulie had gotten the strength to talk again. "My brother went there." Pause. "To other levels."

Wow.

Ruby leaned in, eyes wide. "How?"

Owl Paulie's breath sounded shallow and fast. "There's a test. They keep it from us, like everything." A break. "Can't have gray crap infect the ship. But you might get there that way."

Ruby's brows wrinkled deep. "A test? That easy?"

Owl Paulie said, "If we don't know what's possible, we don't reach for it."

Marcelle crossed her arms and leaned back. "How come *you* didn't take it?"

"I didn't believe him." A pause. "Ask Ix about Laws of Passage."

It sounded too easy. "Did you ever see your brother again?" Onor asked.

Owl Paulie nodded. "Once. He came back and told me he was okay. He was dressed in blue."

A stop while the old man's labored breathing ate any possibility of more words. When he could go on, he said, "He gave me a scrap of blue material and told me to tell someone one day."

"Did you?"

The old man winced. "Hugh didn't believe me." He looked at Ruby. "Do you?"

She was leaning forward, close to Owl Paulie's ear. She whispered, "I don't know what to believe anymore. After yesterday."

"Tell me your story . . ." Owl Paulie took a sip of water and coughed, almost choking. When he could breathe again he said, "What you saw. Tell me."

This time Marcelle was quiet and let Ruby talk. Onor listened closely when Ruby told the part about Fox. She wasn't telling him everything, or any of them everything. Even though her voice sounded higher and thinner as she blew past the parts she didn't want to talk about, she didn't miss a beat. She was good. If he hadn't known her story was true by being there, he still would have believed it. The way she told it, the danger felt imminent, and the hole in the floor sounded bigger than the one he'd seen.

When Ruby finished, Owl Paulie sat back in his chair and said, "Now I know why Hugh likes you. You have a gift for storytelling." Another pause. "Will you write a song about the sky falling?"

A smile played across Ruby's lips. Onor felt a sexual twist at the way she returned Owl Paulie's look, an adult look, almost but not quite predatory.

The inside speakers came on and repeated the earlier message, the recorded voice loud enough to buzz Onor's ears. After silence returned, Onor looked back at Owl Paulie, ready to ask him if he knew if his brother was still alive. The old man's head had tilted to one side. His eyes were closed. His breath was shallow and regular. In sleep, he looked even frailer than when he was awake.

Ruby glanced at Marcelle. "We're going to take that test. Right after we finish the last-years."

Marcelle grunted. "You think it's real?"

Ruby nodded.

Marcelle furrowed her brow. "Should we ask Ix?"

Onor couldn't help himself. "Maybe we should learn a little more. Ix is probably busy right now anyway."

Marcelle's reply came quick. "Ix is a computer. It can do anything it wants all at once."

"So? Maybe I want to learn more before we jump into this test. Maybe it's a myth."

Ruby glared at him, then softened and let out a long sigh, brushing fire-red strands of hair from her eyes. "Adiamo?"

"What about your aunt?" he asked.

"Tomorrow."

Good enough. He could already taste another day of Kyle's cooking.

Onor stood in the doorway and frowned. So many people filled the game bar; it looked like a festival night. Even the physical immersives along the walls were over half full. The multipurpose tables spread across the floor were full of students and players alike, some focused on group games, others chatting quietly or lost in solo trips. Surely the games were the same from pod to pod, but still the subtle differences in layout left him off center.

Marcelle and Ruby apparently didn't suffer the same imbalance, since they plunged into the room. Onor took a deep breath and followed.

The Adiamo players were young. Five kids around one console. Two standing nearly mute in front of the other one, using input boards.

The five played the advanced version of the game, glassed and wrapped, their every move creating change. Their only communication would be through the game interface, unavailable to watchers.

The two were younger, maybe five years old, and still fat fingered. They wouldn't be allowed to immerse yet. If they did, they'd probably pee their pants and scream at the scary parts.

His hands itched to try it again. He'd beat Adiamo as early as most people and hadn't played since he was eight years old. Now, he'd have a new eye for the game.

The new information made him fidget.

Onor yearned to see a planet. Always had, ever since The Jackman first told him that the park was designed to look like someplace where people didn't have to live inside a metal shell and do whatever the reds told them.

Ruby wandered the room, peering at various games. Onor and Marcelle stood behind the two boys with Adiamo input pads and watched them play. Since they were too young for immersion, it was easy to see what crops and animals and weapons and transportation they chose. Players did better against each other if they cooperated. But that was a late lesson, one of the ones you really understood just before you won the game. They only had to wait a half hour for the boys to starve each other out. When they were done, they walked off, chattering about what game to play next.

He and Ruby and Marcelle claimed the game chairs. They strapped in, goggled, gloved, and switched on communication.

The opening sequence played.

Adiamo spun up in front of them, tiny so that the whole system showed. A single brilliant sun, two gas giants. Cradled between, two inhabited planets. Game play took place on Lym, the planet with the most ground and the least water. Enough water for fish and birds and large mammals and humans, and air that didn't have to be scrubbed and rescrubbed inside a closed system.

On Lym, the breath of humans was no inconvenience at all.

The planet spun brown and busy in front of him, scattered with colonists and farms. Factories waited for players to gain control and grow them into cities and industrial bases, into centers of art and math, and—if you were winning—into active spaceports.

Onor paid so much attention to his own lakes and cities that he forgot strategy until he realized that he had less land than Marcelle and that three of his farms had lost crops because he forgot to check his water allocation for shrinkage.

Ruby was ahead of them both, but she had an instinct for the politics of games. She seldom played, but when she did, he no longer expected to beat her. He hadn't beaten her since they were eleven.

The game moved faster than he remembered. Ruby won twice before it was time to go to common. Even though they arrived fifteen minutes early, common was already almost full.

Hugh and Lya showed up right after them with Owl Paulie in a wheelchair, surrounded by a small crowd. Most everyone greeted the old man, who smiled at them and offered a bony hand to most. There had not been any one person that popular at home.

The promised time came and went.

An old woman on a seat near Onor began to cry. Three children raced through the few empty spaces, giggling. Their parents called them down with sharp tones and they obeyed for a few minutes before they went back to racing.

Marcelle tapped her toes. Ruby started walking the room, introducing herself.

Onor paced. He wasn't as outgoing as Ruby, didn't really understand why she wanted to meet everyone right away. They were stuck here. There was time. Besides, if he started shaking hands with people, they'd know his hands were sweating.

He felt nervous anytime he knew he was about to be told what to do. He hated it—hated people making him do things he didn't want to. But his parents had died fighting the reds. Ruby. Ruby was always a rebel, and he was a planet to her sun. He couldn't help himself, even though she scared him.

At least when the voice came it was human and not Ix, a man's voice that he hadn't ever heard. "Please take your seats."

There weren't enough seats for everyone.

More time passed, people slowly stilling until the group noise had been reduced to whispers and the quiet shuffling of bodies.

"Remain calm. C-pod may be uninhabitable for some time. The walls are too weak to provide safe life support and the gravgens remain unreliable. Students are to begin attending school immediately in the pod they now reside in."

A thin, willowy woman next to them chewed on her lip as she stood stiffly; her entire body looked like it was listening.

"Some people will be shifted in order to place elders and children back with their caregivers. This will take place after the Festival of Changes." The thin woman let out a long sigh and whispered, "So long?" as if she might break.

The voice repeated itself. "Approved moves will take place in two weeks at the Festival of Changes." There was a pause before it continued. "In the meantime, everyone is on ten percent reduced rations."

He'd expected that.

"No marriages will be allowed for a year. No pregnancies."

He looked around at the dismay on people's faces. If they knew they'd be home in a year, would they feel differently?

EIGHT

IX'S EXPLANATION

R uby tried to walk the park path fast enough to outdistance her nerves. Her belly tightened, the way she felt just before she sang for a crowd. She'd staged her conversation with Ix in the emptiest public place she knew.

Besides, public places meant cameras, and she wanted a record of the conversation.

The park was as empty as she expected it to be. Only one pair of reds, two serious men walking side by side deep in conversation. They might be a threat, but they hadn't noticed her so far. Reds at home knew her; in this new place she wasn't watched as much.

She walked a long time, keeping an eye on the reds, trying to look like she was there for exercise. Waiting for the others.

The last-years had been given two weeks of alternate work assignments in place of going to class. Ruby had been assigned grunt work in bot-repair. She recognized most of the pieces she was given to clean up as having come from C-pod. Onor and Lya worked on the C-pod reclamation. Air had been blown back into the pod after the initial repairs, but they had to wear pressure suits and face masks the whole time in case of failure. Marcelle helped with elementary classes in the crèche. Hugh chafed because medical kept him on rest.

Setting aside the idea of looking for her Aunt Daria, Ruby had returned to Owl Paulie four times in ten days, slowly pulling details out of him. The second time, Hugh had shown up to stand like a ghost in the background, his black eye and bruises goading her. He'd become a silent partner in Ruby's talks with his grandfather, bringing them water but adding neither comments nor questions.

This park was the same size and shape as her old one, but the controls refused to respond to her. The default breeze felt soft and warm. The flocks of birds and the fake flowers were more stylized and brighter, as if a different artist had worked on them. On the far edge, the orchard's branches hung heavy with bright yellow-gold and fully ripe breakfruit, half a season away from the orchard at home.

"Rruuuuuuby."

Marcelle, calling her. Loud as a three-year-old, as always. Ruby waited for her to catch up. "How did it go?"

Marcelle grinned. "The kids are damned cute. The extras put a stretch on lessons."

"Still got the five-year-olds?"

"Seven-year-old boys. It's a promotion."

"It's 'cause you know how to say no."

"Are you ready?" Marcelle asked.

"If Onor would hurry up."

"He's always here when you don't want him."

"And never here when I do." That wasn't really fair. "He's been my friend forever."

"He follows you around."

So do you. Ruby almost said it out loud. Nerves? That was probably what was getting to her stomach, too. The fluttering of her dreams. No, not dreams. Needs. "They'll be here soon."

"I heard about your story at work today. From one of the regular B-pod teachers. A little bit of a thing, shy as anything. She sidled up to me and almost whispered, wanting to know if I knew you."

"What'd you say?"

"I said yes. She wants to know if you're really going to get us a better life."

"Tell her I'll try, but I need help." She eyed the reds, still some distance away, and still not noticing her.

Marcelle grinned. "It has to be Hugh and Lya, or that old man. Spreading stories about you."

"Lies, too, from the sound of it."

Marcelle pointed. "Speak of the devil."

The ravages to Hugh's face had subsided to a red scar and the yellowed ghosts of bruises. He and Lya held hands. Onor walked on Lya's other side. All three looked tired and worn out, and Lya had a fresh red scratch across one cheek. Behind them, a couple of runners came up and then passed, moving easily right next to each other and talking in low tones. By the time the runners were out of earshot, the others all caught up.

Ruby wrinkled her nose at Onor, who stank of stale shipsuit and sweat.

Her pacing had taken them a bit away from the grouping of three benches she'd chosen for them to use, so she started back, the other four following her.

"I still think it would have been easier to use Kyle's place while he's at work," Onor said.

Ruby ignored him. The park and common were always recorded, and the recordings were kept for a long time, maybe forever.

She sat and gestured for the others to sit, making a circle on the fake grass. She took out her journal and balanced it on her knees, screen off private, mic open. Then she sat up straight and took a deep breath.

"Go on," Marcelle whispered.

Onor and Kyle and Lya watched her silently.

"Request to speak with Ix," she said, enunciating with care and maybe a bit too loud.

All journals were programmed to pass messages to Ix. The trick was getting real answers.

She got in three breaths before an answer came back. "Yes?"

Ix's voice. Or at least the computer voice that most often represented Ix. "Yes, Ruby Martin?"

She plunged right in. "I want to talk about rites of passage."

"Such as marriage or the birth of a child?"

"Passage inward. Passage between. I want to test to pass inward." Obtuse machine. Ix knew what she wanted, but it was as good at avoiding direct requests it didn't like as The Jackman was at avoiding orders from reds. "Ix, I demand to know about rites of passage."

"Laws," Hugh whispered.

Yes, that's what she'd said wrong. Ix was often literal when it wanted to be obstructive. Ruby felt sure Ix pursued its own goals within the rules that constrained it. Just like she did.

Ruby rephrased her request. "Laws of Passage. Tell me about the Laws of Passage."

"Laws of Passage apply to full adults."

She twitched. No fair!

Hugh spoke louder this time. "Ix, I am a full adult. So is Lya. The other three will be in months."

"The Laws of Passage are not currently in effect."

Hugh frowned. "Why not?"

"They aren't needed right now."

Ruby sighed. "So what makes them needed?"

Ix read from something. "The Laws of Passage may be invoked in times of need, when populations are at risk, and in war."

Hugh furrowed his brows. "Surely the accident on C-pod has unbalanced the population."

How? Ruby hadn't seen anything but a robot die. An inconvenience. There was another possibility. "Going home. Doesn't *The Creative Fire*—don't you—need more people who know more? To prepare to be at Adiamo?"

"The Laws of Passage cannot be opened from the gray areas."

Ruby wanted to scream. She settled for digging her nail into her palms. "But they're there to let us in. Why else have the laws at all?" Another thought came to her. "You need us. They need us. Without us, the *Fire* won't run for long."

Lya elbowed her and made a shushing shape with her lips. The reds were walking by them, looking *at* them this time. Ruby gave them her brightest smile and waved. They couldn't get them in trouble for talking to the ship's computer. It was allowed.

The reds kept going, not waving back, but not questioning them either.

Ix, who had also been quiet while the reds went by, asked, "Why do you care where you work?"

Sometimes Ix was as bad as her mother. "Look, you're a machine. You live and work everywhere. You don't get hungry or cold or feel bad when someone you love gets killed. You don't fear death and you don't need life like we do. We need to make a difference. We need to matter."

"Every crew member on the ship matters."

"Not equally," she shot back. "We deserve our share of whatever good happens when we get home."

"And bad?" the machine queried.

"And bad." Of course. She repeated it. "Good and bad. We want our share."

"There are no Laws of Passage to govern movement into the gray levels. Blues may visit you anytime they want."

"Fox? Fox can come here?"

Onor gave her a sharp look.

"Fox has no reason to be on the gray levels."

Ruby's whole body felt tight, like an instrument string. Ix was being even more obtuse than usual. She must be on to something important. "How do we study for the test? Whether the laws open up or not? If we just want to be ready?"

"First, you have to finish your last-year studies and do well. You have to be a full adult. The logistics section must authorize the potential for movement. And you must pass a test."

Now they were getting somewhere. "What kind of test?" Ruby asked.

"All of the things that you learn in your ten years of study matter. They will all be tested. So will your knowledge of the planets and people of Adiamo and the history of *The Creative Fire*, and the power hierarchy of the ship."

Onor whispered in Hugh's ear, and Hugh spoke. "We don't have access to that data. All we know about power is what happens here, in gray."

"The information has been classified."

Crap. Ruby broke in again. "What are the reds planning for us when we get to Adiamo?"

"That information is classified."

If Ix were sitting beside her instead of being air and sound and everywhere, she'd launch herself at it and wrestle it to the ground. She spoke loudly. "Ix. Consider me on record." Keywords to make the conversation publicly available. "I want to test into the inner levels. I am going to do exceedingly well on my last-year exams. So will my friends, and everyone else who wants to join me."

She closed her eyes and centered on her breath so she finished strong. "We want to know how to learn about the ship's structure and history. If you won't help us, we'll figure out how to help ourselves."

Ix said, "I cannot help you."

Nothing about it acted like a human. She could force it with more questions, but instead she turned her journal off. Damned machine.

NINE
THE FESTIVAL OF CHANGES

Common had been transformed to a feast of light and scent. Children's pictures and digital artists' work covered the walls. People perched on benches and low walls, scrolling through the new stories and songs that had been released to journals for the festival. Gold and green cloths covered tables. Flowers had been grown and picked, fruit ripened, and the fermented leftovers from the previous harvest canted into large clear bowls. Tables ringed the edges, laden with food and drink all along one side, clothing and jewelry on another.

A small crowd formed around Kyle's table as he arrived, reaching for cookies while Kyle laughed and held his platter out of reach.

Onor, Marcelle, and Ruby each cradled heavy decanters close to them. Onor's smelled sweet, Marcelle's tangy and salty, and Ruby's was filled with musky spices so good she inhaled repeatedly.

Ruby felt happy enough to hand the still over to Kyle. She'd have a cup later, when it was time, but for now she preferred a clear head.

Kyle took a handful of cookies and distributed them in bite-sized pieces.

Ruby heard her full name called and turned to find a woman who could only be her Aunt Daria. She had aged more than Ruby's mom; her hair had gone the color of her uniform and been cut short and a bit ragged. Her eyes were dark green, almost unnaturally green. The shape of her face was so close to Suri's that Ruby almost cried out at the sudden realization that she did, after all, miss her mother.

Daria smiled thoughtfully. "You do look like her."

"Not as much as you do."

Daria looked serious. "Suri asked me to look after you until she gets here."

"Mom's coming here?"

"There was more room for people to go from D to B than anything else. Besides, I'm here, too."

She was going to lose her freedom.

"I've room for you."

Ruby nodded, stiff with resistance.

"We can get your stuff after the festival."

"I'm settled now. I was going to look for you."

"Today," Marcelle added unhelpfully.

Daria didn't look convinced.

If only Ruby'd asked someone—anyone—before Daria found her. Now she didn't have any proof that she hadn't just been hiding. "Look, I'll visit you. But I can stay where I am." She pointed at Kyle. "We're staying with him, me and my friends."

Kyle turned toward them as Ruby pointed. He nearly dropped his tray of cookies as he leaned over and caught Daria in a great big hug. "Have you met Ruby?" he asked her.

"She's my niece."

He stepped back and eyed them as they stood side by side, then lifted an eyebrow. "Could be."

Daria told Ruby, "I cleaned out some space for you until your mom gets here. There's an abandoned hab on my row, and you can help me stake it out for Suri. She's afraid you're living with that boyfriend of yours."

"Onor's a *friend*."

In front of her, Onor tensed visibly.

No help for that. Ruby put a hand on his shoulder and turned him toward Daria. "Onor, this is my Aunt Daria. Daria, my *friend*, Onor." She grinned at Marcelle. "And my other *friend*, Marcelle."

Daria didn't even have the grace to look embarrassed. "I told your mom I'd get you today, and recorded the move with the reds on my way in. It's approved. I've got custody until Suri gets here."

Ruby didn't respond, afraid that anything she said would show her anger.

Daria noticed anyway. "Look, I have to go meet some people. I'll see you at the end of the evening, at the front gate, if I don't see you before."

"How about tomorrow morning? My friends can help me bring my stuff."

Daria glanced at Onor again. "Tonight." She kept her gaze on Ruby until Ruby nodded, and then she softened her voice and said, "It will be good to see you."

Ruby forced a smile. "Sure."

Daria nodded and took Kyle away to chat with him. Ruby let out a long trembling breath. She'd liked feeling like an adult.

Music spilled out of speakers and mingled with the background chatter. Ruby turned to Onor and Marcelle. "Let's go find Owl Paulie."

Hugh had found a place to pull Owl Paulie's wheelchair up to a little table so that well-wishers could stop to visit. Surrounded by healthy people, the old man looked even more insubstantial than usual, his face whiter, his eyes bluer, his shoulder more hunched inward and shrunken. Ruby stayed with him while the others wandered back for more of Kyle's cookies.

Owl Paulie took her hand in his thin one and leaned in near her. "I hear you're making no progress with Ix." He took a sip of water, then another, drinking like a bird and swallowing in little bits. "The ways between here and the other parts of the ship weren't always closed." A pause while two children came up to hug him and ran away, their faces sticky with something pink. "My grandmother told me it wasn't always that way, but she never explained."

Ruby'd felt that for a long time, like the world was too unfair to be right. "So do I give up on the test and look elsewhere?"

His headshake was the barest of movements. "You need to know those things anyway. Find the information."

She pursed her lips, still stinging from being found by Aunt Daria. "It shouldn't be so hard. It's not fair. This is our history, right?"

"We do remember. A little. That's why I'm talking to you."

She sighed. "So many people aren't even curious."

"Keep digging. You'll find it."

As if she could stop. She was going to figure this out and make things better, or die trying.

Owl Paulie's hand went limp in hers, and when she looked, she saw that he had leaned back in his chair and fallen fast asleep, as if an off-switch had been pressed. She set his hand down carefully and pulled the thin blanket across his chest. He was a sweet old man. Maybe she should have started spending some time with old people a long time ago. Maybe they were more important than she'd thought.

A few hours later, it was time to feast and drink the glasses of still. She and Marcelle and Onor had made their way back to Kyle. He was out of cookies, but he held a glass in each hand. She was going to miss seeing him every day, not to mention the best food of her life. "I've got to get ready to go to Daria's."

He raised an eyebrow and said, "That's good news, I presume. She's most excellent."

"Maybe."

Kyle took one sip out of each glass. "You must not know her. Daria's a good person. Creative."

Ruby smiled. "You've been great."

"You'll come back and see us for breakfast sometimes?"

"Wouldn't miss it."

He filled her glass extra full of the spicy still, winking. "In celebration."

She took a long, slow slip. She'd been allowed still since she turned fourteen, but like everyone, just at festivals. There were cheats, of course, but the penalty was lockup, so they were very, very careful cheats. She never drank much of it; it tasted funny.

She had been half expecting Ix or the reds to make ship-wide announcements. Instead, the music grew louder. Musicians showed up on the vid screens, laughing and playing and singing, their faces bigger than Ruby was tall.

She tapped her feet to the rhythm. This was what she wanted for herself. To be there, singing for everybody to hear.

She and Marcelle and Onor danced a bit sloppily to the band Fire Dream, an E-pod band that got play across all of gray for festivals, and the singer Heaven Andrews, one of the musicians she was sure really lived inside. Even though Ruby's voice felt rusty from lack of practice, she sang along with Heaven on the choruses.

Almost everyone else did, too. A whole pod and more singing, the sound not exactly harmony, but with its own magic.

When she stopped for breath after belting out the lyrics to three songs as loud as Heaven's voice in the speakers, maybe louder, Kyle handed her a glass.

Expecting water, she drank deeply, and then coughed and sputtered.

Strong still. Clear like water, but with a bite.

She grinned up at him and he grinned back.

Good Kyle. He not only made better cookies, he made better still.

She took a long and much slower sip.

She sang the next song even louder, feeling the still in her blood. The singer in the speakers, Kiya Kiya Too, had a tinny voice that Ruby wanted to drown out.

Three little girls who had been singing and holding hands stopped and watched her, their eyes big and their mouths open but silent. Their mothers stopped, then two women next to them, then the tenor behind her, whose voice she had been using as a harmony. Seeing so many people watch her shocked her into missing a beat, but Kyle put a hand on her shoulder, steadying. She smiled thanks, then plucked his hand off and sang louder.

Before she finished the song, everyone else in common had stopped singing or even talking. They were looking at her, making her cheeks flush red. She gave a little bow.

Kyle handed her a glass of actual water and a damp cloth to wipe her sweating forehead. The room spun a bit before settling down, most of the faces still watching her.

When the next song started, she didn't sing. Kyle leaned down and whispered in her ear. "You sound like good food tastes, like herbs and flowers and gardens. Thank you."

She grinned at him. "And you make things that taste good." He looked almost handsome in the shifting festival lights, and she forced herself to look away. He was not as handsome as Fox, and he was way too old for her.

Onor and Marcelle materialized as if from thin air and sat beside her, Onor babbling something about how everyone was watching her, and Marcelle looking worried.

By the time the festival was over, she decided that Ix, or the reds, or whoever, had been right to leave the day just a celebration, a marking of time. Nothing would really change because of it, nothing ever did. Except maybe, this time, a little bit would change for her.

A lot of people had stopped to listen to her sing. She would remember the bright, happy looks on their faces.

TEN

RECLAMATION

As the train approached C, Onor slid his helmet closed and drew in a deep breath that smelled of sweaty body and the clammy metallic scent of a suit that needed cleaning bad. They were supposed to get the day off tomorrow, and if they did, he was going to spend time scrubbing it down. Cleaning everything. Frankly, his nose was so irritated that he'd almost prefer going suitless, even in the reportedly unstable life support of the damaged pod.

Lya sat next to him, looking lost in thought, her long blond hair tangled and twisted down her back. In truth, it wasn't just their suits that needed cleaning. They hadn't had a day off since the festival two weeks ago. She nudged him gently. "Do you believe Ruby?"

"About what?"

"That we can test into a new life? That someday we won't get beat up just for existing?"

"I saw the other levels. They exist." When Ruby talked about them, they sounded fabulous.

"What if we die trying?" Lya bit her lip. "Hugh could've died when they beat him up. We might not have made it to the train. He was so heavy I was sure we'd have to stop. If I'd been hurt, too, or even twisted an ankle, he would have died. Maybe we would both be dead."

Onor put his arm across her shoulders. "This kind of talk makes me think of my parents. They died fighting for what Ruby believes. If I stopped, I'd feel like I was letting them down."

"I guess I want to live more than I want to win."

"I want to do both," he said, trying to sound as sure of himself as he could. "Look, we're almost there. Try and have a little fun today. Find something good." He swung his helmet up and strapped it on.

She dropped her faceplate down, his last sight of her mouth a grimace at her own smell. Or at knowing they were in for another long, hard day. Lya almost never looked happy, except when she was with Hugh.

When Onor climbed off the train, he split from Lya, going to his own detail of five people. There were a hundred total, but they'd been grouped in fives and sent all around the pod with different jobs. Lya spent her days cleaning out habs and bagging stuff to be sent to families.

Onor had been assigned back to the reclamation plant on B, under Conroy, who trained in from F-pod. Just like the old days, except not at all. During the first few chaotic days after the pod-wreck, as people now referred to the failure of the joining bolts and joists that kept the interior of the ship together, they had been surveying damage: cataloging angles that were wrong, blowing pipes for leaks, checking valves, and testing the cleanliness of the liquids at every inflow point. They hadn't found anything totally gobbed up, just stressed metal and a few joins between pipe and tank pulled apart by force.

Everything appeared fixable or replaceable.

In spite of that, the blues had ordered the system closed up and the water partly redistributed. The first few days, there hadn't been enough containers. More had been made and sent in. Water was heavy. Water sustained, grew food, and served as ballast and shield.

While his team and the plant's bots moved water, other people moved cargo around, some of it nonsensical on the surface except that it followed Ix's particular math of balance and weight. It felt all wrong to Onor. Too fast. Since he first started school, it had been burned into his head to do things slow and right, not to rush and take risks.

He'd asked Conroy about it. The big man had said, "Ix seems to know what it's doing," but Onor had a sinking feeling from Conroy's slitted eyes and slight hesitation in answering that Conroy didn't really think so. He just wasn't going to tell Onor anything.

This morning, Conroy looked like he wanted to kick something. Onor couldn't see Conroy's face well through the helmet, so Onor read the older man's mood in the stiffness in his limbs. And his voice, of course. "We're dismantling today. Begin with the offices, remove anything that could be useful."

Conroy called Onor's name.

"Yes?" he answered.

"Start with my old office. The bots will have already wheeled in some boxes for you. Rex can take the crew room beside you. The rest of us will head into the tanks and get the extra parts."

Great. He'd rather be working in among the big tanks. Instead, Conroy treated him like a green baby and stuck him with Rex the Lazy. Onor knew not to argue. His old boss sounded as foul and edgy as Onor himself felt. Maybe Conroy didn't want to be stuck in this new life either. In fact, maybe it was worse for Conroy—he'd been important as shift boss. Now what would he be?

Rex the Lazy was already ahead of him down the hallway, so Onor caught up and then passed him. There were two crew rooms: the office that Conroy had shared with the other shift bosses and a communal room for anybody assigned office work. The rest of the space included a small galley, showers, and a restroom.

Boxes sat in the middle of each room, placed just inconveniently enough to need stepping around. Dumb robots.

Onor checked that Rex had started working and then stood in the doorway to Conroy's office. He'd been in the room before, but never alone. It looked bigger and emptier without Conroy's bulk filling the center of it.

Piled boxes surrounded sparse furniture. Just a desk and three chairs, and walls full of monitors that used to show activity throughout the plant. All dark now, the power off. He sighed—a half a day's work, at least. Maybe more. He unscrewed lamps from the walls and took apart chairs, packing away the pieces in boxes that were the wrong size. After two hours he stank even more, and sweat dribbled down his back.

When he needed a break, he found Rex slumped in one of the chairs in the crew room, only one box filled in the time it'd taken Onor to finish two. Onor started toward him to make sure he was okay. Rex looked up and waved him away.

Well, whatever. Rex was senior, and bigger. Onor went back and started to carefully remove monitor screens from the walls.

He dropped a heavy screen on his right foot and pain shot up his leg. When he cursed, his helmet fogged over and he tripped and almost fell.

He ripped his helmet open and breathed in the greasy air of the plant, a smell far better than his own stink. He set the helmet close enough to reach.

His foot hurt. At least the monitor hadn't broken; his boot had taken the brunt of the drop. The suit hadn't been breached, either. The foot had a hard surface, top and bottom.

He ran his hand across the edges of the monitor, making sure there weren't any cracks.

His finger encountered a sharp ridge.

He picked up the monitor and angled it so he could see the ridge. It was dark, like the frame, but a slightly different dark. He tried to pluck it out with his bulky gloves but it was well and truly wedged.

He glanced at the door, listened. Then he compounded his safety sins by pulling his right glove off. He slid his index finger under the slender dark object.

A data stick?

He closed on it with his thumb and pulled.

It barely moved.

He tried again. On the third try, it slid loose into his palm. It looked like a data stick. If so, it had been well hidden. But what better place to hide something than in a monitoring room where the watchers sat, not being watched?

Footsteps sounded in the hall outside. More than one set.

Conroy poked his head inside the room, frowning behind the clear bubble of his helmet's face shield. His voice snarled across the comm. "Onor!"

Onor slid his glove on, hiding the slender stick in the middle finger between the first and second knuckles.

"I'll report you."

No, he wouldn't. Onor buckled his helmet and spoke to Conroy through the microphone. "I dropped this on my foot and had to check out my suit to be sure it's not torn. I needed my finger free to tell."

"Someday you're going to push me too far."

"Yes, sir."

Conroy didn't bother to answer. Onor's job was nearly done and Rex was only halfway through his task. But as if he needed to make a point, Conroy insisted on helping Onor finish while the other two helped Rex. "How'd you get done so fast?" Onor asked.

"Didn't. We filled the boxes. The bots didn't come when I called for replacements, so I figured we'd come help you and maybe then they'd be done."

The stick slid around in Onor's glove, almost stabbing him.

Whatever was on it had better be good.

ELEVEN

LILA RED THE RELEASER

R uby tried to sound nonchalant as she told Daria, "I plan to go to Kyle's for dinner." Ruby had just brought Daria tea, and now she stood beside her, watching Daria's hands as she polished a silver scrap-art pendant.

Daria looked up and gazed at Ruby, silent.

Ruby stood still, looking back as placidly as she could even though it seemed like Daria was trying to see inside of her.

Daria's lips thinned into something that wasn't quite a smile. "Have fun."

Maybe Daria was sick of babysitting, or maybe she just wanted to compose herself for Suri's imminent arrival. Her reasons didn't matter to Ruby. She knelt down and gave her aunt a brief hug. "I'll be back in a few hours."

Daria nodded, her attention already returned to her jewelry.

Ruby had the odd sense that Daria knew she was planning an assault on the status quo and that her aunt was maybe even a bit proud of it. But Daria never talked about what Ruby did away from her, even though she insisted Ruby be in early every night.

As she wandered down the hall, Ruby cataloged successes and failures to go over after dinner, when she and her friends would get down to real planning. She and Marcelle had talked some of the other students into believing in the test, or at least into working with them to study the other levels. Not as many as they'd hoped for, but maybe a quarter of the people in their class in this pod. Ix appeared to be offering occasional help in the form of stories or poems that would show up on her journal all by themselves. They gave her vague clues, but nothing concrete.

She didn't feel ready at all, and the end of the school year wasn't that far off.

When Onor greeted her, he seemed full of a great secret. Inside the room, Marcelle and Hugh and Lya and The Jackman had all gathered into the tight quarters of Kyle's living room, oriented toward the vid screen.

She had only expected Marcelle and Onor. "What's this?" she asked, perching on the edge of Marcelle's chair.

"Something I found," Onor said. "Something about an old story you told me once."

Really? She settled back.

The recording opened up with a woman's round face looking serious and filling the screen, her green eyes flecked with gold and her hair so red it looked more drawn than real. The camera backed up, showing the woman standing. She had an air of authority that was only partly because of her red uniform. A red woman with red hair. Ruby's lips parted and a name fell from them. "Lila Red the Releaser."

She'd never seen Lila on video. She'd seen a sketch, once, on a teacher's wall. A few days later, she'd found a photo of Lila's face on her journal, but she had never been able to find it again.

On screen, Lila moved with confidence, stepping back, taking Ruby along as if she walked beside the woman. Other people crowded Lila from time to time, offering handshakes and hugs or just reaching out a hand to trail fingers along her uniform. Lila gave them back gracious nods and small touches, but she didn't slow at all. She was in one of the parks, although neither of the ones Ruby knew. She spoke at the camera, "This is our last night of gathering. This is the last time I'll talk to you this way, for tomorrow we're going to change the way things are. And I hope you're going to help."

Lila walked away from the camera, heading for a bench that had been draped with white so that when she stood on it dressed in red, with black boots and green eyes and hair as red as Ruby's, she stood out from the landscape like a feral flower.

The sounds of a crowd settled away; the hundreds of people who had come to hear Lila had gone largely quiet, with only an occasional whisper disturbing the pregnant moment.

Lila stood and spoke. "We have almost a third of the ship so far, from every level. Mostly from here, from gray, from where the real work happens, from you. You are the magic that will matter as we shine light on change."

She waited, and the crowd reacted, hooting and calling and clapping.

Lila Red the Releaser continued. "There are too many of us for the traditionals to move against us anymore. I have been in lockup and I am free, and you have been in lockup, all of you, all of us together. Tomorrow we will be free.

"Tell your friends and your family, tell anyone who is not yet with us. Tell them that *we will win* and *we will become free*. We will lock up the leaders and make new ones who represent us all, including grays."

In the pause after her words a murmuring started and slowly grew louder.

Just as Ruby felt the need to urge Lila to stand taller and raise her arms, she did, and a great rush of applause filled the video speakers.

Lila lowered her arms and the sound subsided.

"When we finish this, we will feast, and then we will work together as equals, side by side with all our brethren. We will take off our colors. Blue shirts will work the reclamation plants and greens the crèche, and side by side we will all carry water and bring food and design new games and read star charts. Women will not be raped anymore. Young men will not die for fighting or for feeling their oats or back talking another young man in a different color shirt.

"We will all be free together!"

Lila extended her arms toward the crowd, palms up.

The crowd repeated, "We will all be free together."

"We will all be free together," she called to them.

They replied again, louder, "We will all be free together."

And then Lila lifted her hands and called for the crowd to say it again and they did, the sound from the vid filling the room.

Ruby felt complete awe. So brave, so strong. And shame, because she wanted to be that brave but wasn't.

The Jackman said, "That was her last speech."

The words were hammers, taking the breath from Ruby. The woman on the screen had been so alive. Marcelle gave Ruby a white-faced look, and Onor looked sick to his stomach.

Ruby stared at The Jackman. "Tell me about her."

The Jackman took another cookie and a water bulb. "I used to think she was a legend, something made up by someone who wanted hope. It's not just Lila—she may not have even been the leader. She was just the one everybody knew, the face of the Freers. That's the name of the revolution. The Freers. The formal story is that Lila Red betrayed her own, a whole level, and then the captain himself killed her. That's all part of the legend around why no one's lived in A-pod for a very long time."

"The captain?" Onor asked.

"The man who tells Ix what to do."

"Who is that now?" Ruby asked. "Who tells Ix anything?"

"Garth. Garth Galesman, but he's a lousy captain even though he wears the uniform." The Jackman stretched and looked uncomfortable.

"He's the one who killed Lila?"

"No. He couldn't be. It was too long ago."

"Tell me about Garth anyway?" Ruby asked.

"No. And we don't want to make Lila's mistakes either."

They were all silent until it felt awkward. Ruby mused, "Lila was a hero. I want what she wanted."

The Jackman's face grew hard and full of warning. "She failed. And she was one of them. A red. She had more chance than you do."

Ruby imagined people fighting through the corridors of the pods, inside the habs where people lived, shooting weapons across common. She could hear the yelling and the fighting, smell the blood and the fear. "How would anyone win a battle in a ship? There aren't enough people for all that death."

The Jackman stood up and shouldered his pack. "After she died, the levels were shut completely, like now. That's why you've never talked to a blue."

"I have."

"That doesn't count. It wasn't his fault he fell on you."

She managed not to lunge at The Jackman only because he was four times her size and she knew he was trying to bait her. Instead, she stared him down as he plucked the data stick out of the player and put it carefully in a box that he folded into his pack.

After he left, Ruby whispered. "He knows things he's not telling us."

TWELVE
SURI

Ruby's hand dipped and wove through the air, in and out of piles of bright beads. Her needle trailed a long, thin line of glass and metal across her thigh. Most of the beads were blue, but here and there silver caught the light and gave the strand extra life.

"So, Miss Sullen, are you ready for Suri?" Daria asked

"I didn't ask Mom to come here." She hadn't expected to wake up excited about seeing her mom, since she'd kind of dreaded it, too. Oddly, being happy about seeing Suri was winning by a long shot at the moment. But she didn't want to look happy, not in front of her aunt. She didn't expect to stay happy, after all. Suri was . . . Suri.

She kept her face as emotionless as she could, testing the strand's strength by pulling it through her fingers. "I hope she's in a good mood."

"She must have missed you a lot."

"Maybe she misses telling me what to do."

"Maybe she just misses you."

"She thinks about herself and about safety."

"Maybe she's more than you think."

Ruby sighed. She liked Daria better, but the women were alike. Willing to be led and bullied and happy to trade small favors for safety. With Suri it was sex. With Daria, it was jewelry and maybe more. No way to know.

Daria got her power somehow. The room they were sitting in was almost as big as Owl Paulie's whole hab. The walls were all shelves, with container after container of beads and tools, string and wire. Spare bot parts and broken bits of bot parts and odd little metal shapes she'd never seen filled wire-topped baskets on the lower shelves. A nest of tangled twine and metal filaments scrounged from a hundred previous uses tried to escape from one of them, as if the raw material of Daria's workshop wanted to make itself into art.

Three mismatched homemade chairs fit in the middle of all this, surrounded by end tables and footstools, leaving almost no actual floor space. She and Daria each balanced large soft-bottomed lap tables on their knees. The tables had cloth tops that beads and oddments could be spilled out onto without rolling into the corners, and soft, slight bumpers to keep escapees from rolling off.

Daria held up the complex beaded wedding shawl she was making and squinted at it. "I missed a red one three rows back."

"You told me to make at least one thing wrong in every piece."

"That's to know it's handmade." Daria frowned, "I'm up to four. That's not handmade, that's sloppy."

"It's a big piece."

"And it's due soon."

Ruby got up and pawed through the shelves for more silver beads. "They're still not letting anyone get married."

"This'll be needed the day the reds change their minds. There will be a shipful of weddings then."

"You're exaggerating." Ruby sighed as she sat back down. "I told you, we're almost home. Maybe they won't allow new families until we are."

Daria set the delicate lace of beads carefully across her lap and leaned back in her chair. "You might not have understood Fox."

Ruby picked through the silver beads for a medium-sized one. "I never told you his name."

Her aunt's voice was shaded with a slight bitterness, or maybe sadness. "You think I don't know all the stories they tell about you?"

"What do they say?"

"You're going to break the gates open and go inward. You're starting a revolution. You're in love with a man named Fox and he's coming for you." Daria's voice rose higher with each phrase, although her beads stayed in her lap, her hands still on top of them. "You figured out how to make the great test available again, even though no one ever heard about the great test before you got here. You're going to help us all become blues."

Ruby shook her head.

Daria leaned in toward her. "You're going to set us free. That's what they say."

"Are you accusing me, or wishing it was true?" Ruby found the bead she wanted and quickly popped three blue ones onto the needle behind it. She wasn't allowed to wear blue clothes, but at least she could wear blue jewelry.

"You need to be careful." Daria pursed her lips. "People are making you out like something you're not. If you disappoint them, they'll be mad at you."

"How am I supposed to create a revolution when you almost never let me go out?"

Her aunt laughed. "I let you go out last night. Are you unhappy?"

"I like making jewelry." And she did. Way back when she was eleven and they started her on the bot repair lines for training a few hours a day, she'd learned to sit and clean parts with both of her hands but only some of her brain. That left the rest free to be curious. It had become a blessing, which the pleasant monotony of beading also gave her. Even better, her hands suffered less than they had from degreasing parts. Of course, spending evenings in this close, cluttered place with Daria and the sparkly mounds of color was at best a pleasant jail. She wanted to be out with Marcelle and Onor.

She dragged her thoughts away from herself. Suri thought about herself all the time, and she wasn't going to be like Suri. "Daria? What do you know about what happened to us in the past. To the grays? Not to your parents, not to their parents, but further back?"

Daria picked up her beadwork and plunged her needle into a pile of pale yellow beads. "People get in trouble when they talk about history."

"How come all the old people are afraid?"

"Maybe you need fear to live a long life on this ship."

"What do you mean?"

Daria's voice had fallen to a whisper. "The accidents down here . . . you think they're all really accidents?"

Ruby flinched, dropping a bead. She saw Nona's dying look again. "No." She searched for another bead, accidentally poking the long, thin needle into the index finger of her other hand and biting her lip.

Daria's voice went soft, almost to a whisper. "Anything they don't like, you keep quiet."

"Who do you mean when you say *they*?"

"Ix and the reds."

"Ix is a machine."

"Ix is the one who sees everything, hears everything."

Ruby looked around the walls for emphasis. "Not in our habs. It's not allowed."

"Taping inside our habs isn't allowed as evidence against us, but that doesn't mean it doesn't happen."

Suri had always told her they could say anything they wanted in the hab. But come to think of it, The Jackman was always careful.

Daria hadn't answered her question about history. And she couldn't search the library without leaving a record.

The Jackman. She and Onor had talked about that, but he'd said that if the reds were watching anyone, it was The Jackman. She swallowed the knot of fear the idea drove into her sternum and picked up another bead, waiting for Suri.

She finished the necklace and started another.

The door let her little brother Ean in first. It slammed open, and she smelled him before she saw him; he always smelled of the medical creams he worked with, almost like robot grease but sweeter. Freckles flashed across his face, and his nose turned up like her father's must have. Macky looked like Suri, Ean was supposed to look like their dad, and she was in the middle. He grinned at her. "Hi, Sis. Mom'll be along in a minute. She sent me ahead to make sure you didn't escape to another pod before she gets here. She blames you, you know."

But his voice made it a joke, and Ruby let the string of blue and silver pool on the table beside her so she could fold Ean in her arms. "I missed you." She hadn't actually thought of him much, but now that she was happy to see him she knew she *had* missed him. "I really did. What have you been doing?"

"Taking care of Mom, you dope. Someone had to."

Her cheeks flared hot, but she didn't say anything about the cut in his comment. "Where is she?"

"Dragging luggage."

Ruby eyed the puddle of beads, but Daria was up hugging Ean next, exaggerating about him being knee high last she saw him. He rolled his eyes and mouthed the word "help" over Daria's shoulder.

"Daria, watch the beads." She grabbed Ean's hand and dragged him out the door.

Ean narrowed his eyes and grinned widely. "What? Are the beads going to run away?"

She stifled a giggle and whispered, "It will take her a minute to think that through."

He gave her a knowing look and picked up his pace until they rounded the corner and almost ran into two reds on patrol.

The reds glared at them. One of them put up his hand in a slow-down gesture.

She nodded at the red, slowing, and whispered, "Why didn't Macky come?"

"He's important now. Got an inspection job he doesn't want to lose." They turned a corner. "And a girl."

Ruby grunted, trying to hide her relief.

When they came face to face with Suri, she was pulling a wheeled cart laden with packed boxes and bags, everything taped and neatly labeled. A light sheen of sweat brightened her brow as she stopped, frowned, and then dropped everything and raced forward. "Ruby, you're okay."

Even though she'd just been dragging the cart, Suri's primary scent remained the soft perfume of juice-flowers, and for a moment Ruby felt small in her mother's arms, drawing comfort.

Suri pushed her away, still holding her, looking into her eyes.

"I'm okay, Mom."

"I've heard so much. I'm worried."

From Daria? Ruby shook her head. "I'm just me. In school. Same stuff."

Suri handed Ean the long tongue of the wheeled cart and waved him down the corridor. After the cart passed them, Suri grabbed Ruby's hand and directed their pace to match Ean's, staying behind him and out of his earshot. "Daria told me about Fix, or Fox, or whatever his name is, and Greg brought home a rumor that you're in trouble with the reds here, and I want you to tell me *everything*."

Ruby decided she hadn't missed Suri after all. If she really couldn't test inward, then maybe some other pod needed an apprentice robot-repair girl.

THIRTEEN

THE OWL'S TALK

A week later, Ruby looked up from her seat in common to see Hugh wheeling Owl Paulie to a nearby table. The old man looked determined, as if some secret store of energy drove him. Hugh had attended study sessions, but he'd never brought his grandfather. Ruby eyed them from time to time as she finished walking Salli and Jinn through a math problem. Owl Paulie watched her, contemplative. He seemed to draw strength the longer he sat there, as if he were drinking in the young people's energy.

A few students came up to greet him, and others waved.

They'd been meeting here for over a week. It had been Marcelle's idea to start a study group so they could get to know the other students and maybe get more people excited about testing into other levels. They'd done it by example and rumor and invitation. First, it had been Salli and Jinn, who never left each other's sides. Two days later, another group—three boys and a girl. And then they brought friends. There were two new students today. One was a pale girl, Nia, who had looked scared when Ruby stopped and introduced herself.

Right now, common held almost half of the last-years in the pod.

Ruby leaned over and whispered to Marcelle. "I half expect the reds to come bouncing in to break us up. An illegal gathering."

Onor glanced over at her, grinning. "Studying together is encouraged. We're not protesting. We're studying."

Marcelle moved from table to table, supporting, asking questions, and greeting today's crop of new people.

Onor went back to his journal. Ruby peeked. He was lost in a diagram of interactions between the water reclamation systems, the fruit and vegetable gardens, and the oxygen/CO_2 balance.

Ruby fingered the blue beads around her neck, small and hard against her skin.

"Cookies!"

The moment Kyle said it, Ruby smelled them. Kyle balanced two platters of his cookies, one on either arm, a great big smile on his face.

Ruby leapt up and stopped him in his tracks with a hug. She planted a kiss on his cheek, drawing a flush of red to his face, then took one platter from him. She pointed, sending Kyle to one end of common to start handing out cookies. She began at the other end. As she went, she asked questions that were likely to be on the tests.

"How many people can each pod feed?"

"How are metals separated for reuse?"

"What is the minimum amount of exercise required each day?"

She saved Onor and Owl Paulie and Hugh for last, and as Hugh took his cookie, he whispered in her ear, his breath ticklish, "Can you get everyone to be quiet? He wants to talk."

She smiled at the old man and took his thin, shaky hand. "What do you want to say?"

He looked . . . intense. Alive. "I need to give them fire."

"They have fire. But I trust you."

Owl Paulie squeezed her hand, his grip strong. She bent over and straightened his shirt. "Did you and Kyle plan the cookie break and talk together?"

Owl Paulie ignored her question.

She sat on top of a table and started humming, warming up her voice, thinking about Lila Red controlling a group with sheer determination. Salli and Jinn and the students at the next table over—four boys—stopped talking to listen, and for a moment she thought she might not have to work to get the room to quiet. But then conversations started back, so she began a song, letting her voice rise until it filled common. She sang just the first few stanzas, enough for most of the room to start singing with her. Then she trailed off, waited. She was still on the table, and all of the faces were looking at her.

"I'm glad you're here. Glad you're like me and you don't want to be gray forever." She touched her looped strand of blue and silver beads. "Glad you want to have the choice to wear uniforms that are this color, too. Glad you want to help me convince the reds and blues that we can all wear each other's colors, that naked, we're all the same."

She hadn't thought about saying that, it had just come out, the way a homemade song did. It sounded a little stupid, simple. Soft. But it was out. Best keep going. She pointed to Owl Paulie, waited for the room to quiet down. "You all know Owl Paulie. He has something he wants to say."

They came in closer with no protest, and she used the time to count them. Thirty-one, plus Kyle and Owl Paulie. They scooted together on benches, some of the girls squirming on boys' laps to make room for more.

Kyle stood outside the circle.

Owl Paulie watched the students settle, his large blue-on-pale-brown eyes suggestive of his name, his hands shaking a bit in his lap. Ruby stood beside him, Onor and Marcelle by her, Hugh on his other side. For a moment Ruby wondered if he was really going to say anything at all, then his chest rose and his nostrils flared. "I came to you because I'm old enough to remember things others don't want you to know."

As he stopped for breath, the students glanced at each other, a mix of excitement and confusion.

"We were not born inside this ship. Each of *us*, yes, but not humans."

Salli and Jinn scooted closer to each other. "We are going to where we were born. And when we left, we were not limited to the gray levels or the gray life."

Nia looked nervous, so Ruby offered her an encouraging smile in the time it took for Owl Paulie to get more breath.

"You have important things to do. If you don't do them, you and your children and their children will enter our old home the way we are now— grays. People with no rights and no claim on the value in our holds."

Ruby blinked. She hadn't thought through the implication of bringing *things* home. That was why they'd gone, of course. That, and to learn about other suns. She'd been in the holds outside of C, knew there were rocks and liquids and locked boxes and testaments of explorers, that there were sculptures that looked twisted beyond anything on the ship and dead animals that had been frozen. More. And even with all that, there remained a lot of empty cargo space.

Owl Paulie continued, raising his voice a little. "We were not always slaves."

Silence, except for the old man's in breath.

"I know because my family kept a written history. I used to read it over and over, because it had death and courage and freedom in it, and courage and freedom were both rare by the time I was old enough to read the history."

He paused, and the room stayed quiet, waiting.

"It's gone now, taken by a red." He paused. "There was a time when anyone could go anywhere on the ship."

A beat of silence. No one seemed to need to fill it.

"You're scared of the reds and the blues. They know how to do that to you. They know how to make you think they're stronger than they are."

More pause. He must be here today for this, to give this speech. He must have practiced it. Worried over it. She expected the reds to come before he finished, and she imagined standing in front of him, protecting him from them.

"But these reds and blues are afraid of you."

The students closest to her looked amazed, like the idea had turned something in their heads, like it had in hers the first time she'd heard it. Like suddenly she knew a secret that she should have always known.

"There are more of you than of them. You must be brave and strong and smart, and fight for the rights that are yours. You must tell other people."

Ruby, Marcelle, and Onor all glanced at each other, a small flash of fear showing in Marcelle's gaze before it was replaced by her usual cool control. Ruby took her friend's hand, squeezed. She could feel the fast beat of Marcelle's blood, and how it matched hers.

Owl Paulie continued. "You must fight like my brother before me. Like Lila Red before him. A name most of you know."

Hugh must have told him about the recording. That was why Owl Paulie chose this place. The same reason she'd used the park to ask Ix about Laws of Passage. *He wanted this moment recorded. He wanted it in Ix's public records so it could be seen by other grays. That is how he can say this and be safe.*

"Because we are close to Adiamo, to home, we need to be sure that our voices will be heard again."

A shorter pause. Ruby glanced around. Everyone watched her and Hugh and Owl Paulie. Kyle, too, standing still in the back.

"They were heard before."

A tall, dark-haired boy with thick arms cast a cocky glance at Ruby, Onor, and Marcelle, and then looked back at Owl Paulie and cleared his throat. "How do we do that, old man? My father's father was here like us. But his father was spaced for insubordination. I want walls around me and air inside the walls."

Ruby wanted to tell the dark-haired boy that he couldn't afford to be afraid, but he'd asked Owl Paulie, not her.

There was a pause while Owl Paulie drew in more air, wheezed, and breathed again. "Use your intelligence. Maybe this is not the time to fight." Pause. "Fighting made us what we are today, controlled. We lost. You need to know."

Then he pushed himself up so that he was standing, leaning on the table. A whisper would be enough to topple him. But the room stayed silent. "We are separate from the others because we became angry with them and they called it a mutiny even though it wasn't that. We have earned a better place in this ship with generations of hard work. And we must claim it."

The room felt full of such strong emotion that it seemed to weigh down the air. Fear and excitement, disbelief and anticipation.

"They need us to keep *The Creative Fire* alive." This time he didn't pause, and his voice rose as if he were in the middle of his life instead of near the end. "You must be strong. You must create change. Only you can do it. Most of the rest of us are too old. Follow Ruby." He started to fade. "Learn." Another pause, the room still, waiting. "Be free."

He sat back down, landing hard, and bowed his head.

Conversation started, low and whispered, and then grew bolder. Ruby let the moment hold, watching and listening. It felt . . . dangerous. Was this what Lila Red had felt before she went and helped start the fight that made A-pod a closed coffin forever?

She swallowed, realizing her breath had become shaky. She should send the students home so they wouldn't get caught out by reds. Surely there would be a reaction.

She put a hand on Owl Paulie's shoulder to thank him.

The light pressure of her touch bent him forward oddly, his body simply folding away from her. "Hugh!" she called. "Help!"

As Hugh pushed the old man up gently, Owl Paulie's head lolled back. His eyes had clearly gone—in that briefest of moments—to a place they couldn't see.

"Do CPR!" Marcelle screeched at Onor, then reached toward Owl Paulie herself.

But Hugh gathered his grandfather up in his arms, lifting him easily, and sat down on a bench with the old man's body draped across him, outside of Marcelle's reach. He looked at Marcelle and shook his head. "He asked me to let him die. Over and over."

"When?" Marcelle demanded.

"For years. But he stopped when Ruby came." Hugh gave Ruby a probing look. "Until yesterday. He knew." Tears brightened Hugh's eyes. "He asked again yesterday. He knew."

Ruby pushed to Hugh's side. She sat near the old man's head, feeling empty and confused. Bereft. She closed Owl Paulie's eyes. She managed to do it without flinching or stopping, even though her stomach knotted.

A crowd gathered around, the students standing and staring down at them with their mouths open, a press that stole the air from her lungs.

Hugh let out a strangled little cry and bowed his head.

Marcelle cleared her throat and started repeating, "Step away, step away."

As if jerked from a daydream, Onor began to do the same thing, following Marcelle, so the two of them walked side by side and repeated the same words. "Move along. Go home. Get your things."

Kyle helped.

Common cleared quickly, the quiet falling as heavy as the silence of Owl Paulie's stilled heart.

Ruby hooked her arm through Hugh's and helped him take the weight of his grandfather's body while they waited for the reclamation crew to collect him. She felt shocked and stilled and inspired all at once by what he said and because he had died after he said it, like an exclamation point at the end. The whole idea, the speech and timing, awed her.

Death usually happened in medical, or in accidents. It was almost never witnessed by a crowd.

Had he planned this?

FOURTEEN
THE OWL'S SONG

"I don't want you to go," Suri said for the fourth time, pacing around the small room, which had been transformed from Ruby's private place into Suri's domain. Daria was there, too, so it felt quite small and crowded.

"I don't care." Ruby counted out five strands of blue beads from the neat rows of finished jewelry in front of her. "Owl Paulie was my friend, and his family—my friends—asked me to do this."

"You didn't even know the old man before the sky fell," Daria noted.

"You did," Ruby replied. "Why aren't you going to common at least?"

"I am going to common."

"Good."

"And Suri's going with me," Daria added.

"I am?"

"Yes." Daria's face hardened around her tightly pursed mouth.

"I didn't know him," Suri said, staring in a mirror and plucking out gray hairs.

Ruby let out a long breath as she looped multiple strands of blue beads around her neck. She glanced at her mom, and at Ean, who stood silently near Suri like a shadow. "I'm singing, and you can hear me if you go to common. You haven't listened to me in a long time." Without Macky around there was no one big enough to tackle her, so she opened the door and went through it.

She met Hugh and Lya outside of the living habs. They looked solemn in their best gray uniforms. They all embraced. "Thank you," Hugh said.

"I loved him," Ruby replied simply, her throat thick. They walked side by side by side and silent, around medical and down a long industrial corridor with plain, dirty walls. Near the end there was a single door. On the other side, a blue would be waiting beside Owl Paulie's body.

The door opened as they approached. Hugh flinched. Instead of a blue, a red uniform. Ruby tensed and then felt relief. Ben. She squeezed Hugh's arm, offering reassurance. "Hi, Ben, what brings you here?" She glanced down at Owl Paulie's body. "Did you know him?"

Ben shook his head. "Not well. But Ix assigned a red, so I picked it up."

He didn't actually say he did it for her. If this weren't being broadcast she might have kissed his cheek, although she still wanted to know why there was a red here at all. There was always a blue to keep the form of the ceremony and say the last words. It was the ritual, the way of the ship, and expected.

There was, in fact, a blue. He stood beside the hatch on the far wall, so still he might have been a statue, except for his breathing. He was small and square-jawed, with dark skin and light hair, his uniform clean and pressed perfect, with shiny shoes and creases in his pants. Ruby stared hard at the blue to see if he would look at her, but Ben tugged her arm and refocused her.

She'd never been part of a funeral before. From the few times she'd sat in common and watched, she expected the room to be cleaner. The walls had been banged up over the years by maintenance bots gone feral or clumsy, a few of the gouges deep enough to collect grease and dust.

The five of them—Hugh, Lya, Ruby, Ben, and the unnamed silent blue— stood in a square room that was about ten meters on each side, big enough to make them feel small.

Owl Paulie's remains lay bundled at their feet, the old man's face left exposed so he'd be able to see the stars. His cheeks, which had been thin in life, had disappeared entirely into the bones of his face as if his skeleton wanted to free itself from his drained and desiccated body.

He seemed too small and weak to have been the force that set her in motion. Only in this moment did it sink in that she truly wouldn't see him again. Ever.

At home, arguing with Daria and her mom, singing for him had seemed like a natural thing, maybe an inevitable thing, but now that she stood here, Ruby felt scared and out of place. She had been thinking of this song as for her, but that wasn't right. She had to make it about him completely.

She bowed her head and stripped the strands of beads from her neck. She put one strand back on and separated the others out across her palm, dangling down and glimmering in the light. She walked along, handing one each to Hugh and Lya. She had to help Hugh put his on, and when she was done, he nodded and licked his lips, glanced down, and whispered, "Thanks."

Lya took hers with grave silence.

Ruby eyed the body below her. She'd planned to send him off with a strand of beads as a farewell gift, but the way he was wrapped, there was no way to fasten the beads on him well enough to be sure they'd stay.

She glanced at Ben.

He gazed back at her, his face emotionally flat. Looking red.

She stood on tiptoe and draped a strand over his shoulders.

He reached up and clutched them, his knuckles white.

She held her breath, waiting for him to rip them over his head or pull hard enough to break them.

His fist clenched tighter, the veins on the back of his aged hands turning to ridges. He didn't have to look at Ruby for her to feel the struggle going on inside him.

The blue remained still, but his eyes tracked the small, tense moment. He was younger than Ben by half, even if he was much older than Ruby, and he seemed to feel bound to stay quiet and play his role as observer and time-keeper.

Ben dropped his hand, and Ruby turned to Hugh and nodded.

The blue smiled coolly and asked Hugh, "Ready?"

Hugh nodded and gazed at the far wall, where the stationary cameras had to be hidden. Lya leaned in to him and spoke loudly enough for Ruby to hear. "They're watching."

As if her words had evoked change, a section of the wall bloomed into a vid screen, displaying the expectant faces of the crowd in common. There were so many faces; it looked nearly like a festival, except that they were looking toward the cameras, which were above their heads. Ruby spotted Onor and Marcelle next to Salli and Jinn, her mom and Daria in the back, and Ean beside one of his friends.

Hugh cleared his throat. "This man who lies at my feet gave me hope all my life. He told me that we should learn and strive. He told me I'd need to be everything I could be. He told me to be strong and smart . . ." He paused. "He told me to love and be loved." Hugh hugged Lya and Ruby close to him. "He told me to find people to admire."

The faces below stayed rapt.

"Owl Paulie told me to be ready whenever *The Creative Fire* needed me. He told me that all my life, and last night, he told me that time is now."

He stopped for a moment. Ben and the blue stepped forward.

Hugh waved them back.

Lya whispered to them both, "Be strong."

Hugh continued. "Yesterday afternoon, he also told many of you that the time is now. While I was wheeling him over, he told me that he is proud of this generation of young men and women."

Ruby was pretty sure she saw the people in her year group, and even the one below it, straightening up a bit. A girl clutched at her neck, her hand holding a blue cord. There were blue headscarves, too, and blue earrings. They were adorned in all the ways grays were allowed to wear color. Most of it was blue and a little red. The rest was the traditional black of mourning. The colors made Ruby proud and a bit awed.

Then Hugh added, "He told me we will *all* have to be strong."

A tear started down Hugh's face, then another.

The blue's body had tightened, his still face as stiff as the metal walls behind him.

Lya stepped in front of Hugh and said, "Ruby will sing now. Please listen."

Ruby's stomach twisted. She whispered in Hugh's ear, "That was good, you sounded like him."

Hugh gave her a shaky smile.

Lya pushed Ruby forward.

She stood staring down at the crowd. If anything, they'd grown even quieter. She glanced at Hugh and Lya, who didn't know exactly what she planned to do. She took in a deep breath, then another. "Many of you will remember the song, 'Requiem for Grandmother.' This is for Hugh's grandfather."

She had requested an instrumental version of it, so she stood quietly while the first few bars started. She smiled when she noticed some of the audience start to nod their heads as she began the last verse first.

Beloved Grandfather who kept me
Safe and taught me how to be
Part of Creative Fire's *journey*
Wait for me in the cold of space
For I too will pass in my day
And I'll need your lovely face
To see me on my way

She went right into the chorus:

> *Grandpa, will you watch for me?*
> *I'll be right here, growing old.*
> *Grandpa, will you catch me*
> *The day I go out the door?*

They had joined in, following along, a few getting confused and singing grandma instead of grandpa. "Now, just listen this time through." She started in on the verse she'd been up modifying in more ways than changing the gender.

> *Beloved Grandfather who kept me*
> *Safe and taught me how to be*
> *A person yearning to be free*
> *I'll don the mantle you left behind*
> *I'll hold you deep inside my soul*
> *I'll keep our histories in my mind*
> *And use them to reach our goal*

She didn't dare look behind her at Ben or the blue. "One more time."

She sang the same two verses (and the chorus) two more times through, using her hands and her body language to urge the crowd to sing. Behind her, Hugh and Lya sang, Hugh's voice soft and breaking a bit and Lya's loud and a tiny bit off key for all her enthusiasm.

Neither Ben nor the blue sang.

The last time through, Ruby closed her eyes and really let go on the last verse. As she sang, she felt like she meant the words, like Owl Paulie's spirit was in her, beside her, helping her sing to everyone who'd come to see him off.

When she finished, Ruby opened her eyes. Hugh and Lya looked shocked and a bit in awe.

Even on the screen, the faces of the people watching and listening down in common weren't streaked with tears, even though her own cheeks were wet. Instead, she saw . . . anticipation. Or maybe it was excitement. Only on a few faces, fear.

The blue startled her by moving. He opened the hatch in the far wall, slowly and exactly, every movement scripted and practiced.

Ben stepped back and gestured to Hugh, who bent down to grasp the stretcher on one side and with help from the blue, he lifted Owl Paulie's shrouded body and held it up to the chute it would slide into. The light caught the strand of blue beads on Hugh's chest, so they sparkled a bit as he moved. The two men slid the old man's feet in and then his legs, and then his torso, the body slightly tilted. This way, *The Creative Fire* herself took some of Owl Paulie's weight.

The blue spoke the closing words, his voice stilted and tinged with anger. "We of *The Creative Fire* thank you for being one of us. We counted the years with you as years of grace, and we will miss you among us. May the Universe hold you in her arms."

There was no sincerity in the words, just ceremony. He was doing what he'd been told. Ruby wasn't used to thinking of blues as people who did what they were told, but she was sure she was right.

They tipped the old man's body up a bit further and let it slide down into the chute and then shut and latched the hatch over it. Hugh moaned and Lya pulled him to her. The blue turned and stood formally, looking at the camera.

The video screen went dark.

As slowly and deliberately as he had dogged the hatch, the blue reached toward Ben and grabbed the string of beads Ruby had placed around his neck. The blue yanked, hard, and the beads spilled off their broken thread like a thin waterfall. They rolled and scattered across the floor, finding crevasses. Her first random thought was that she'd used almost all of Daria's blue beads, and her next was that they'd never free this room entirely of blue beads.

The blue's face looked serene, until she saw the fear in his eyes.

Fear. Real and dangerous, and far scarier than anger. Owl Paulie had warned them of this, but it had been a concept and not a truth to Ruby.

She gazed back as levelly as she could, but only for a moment. She didn't say anything; there was nothing a gray could say to a blue who had done nothing directly to her. She didn't dare look at Ben in case she'd gotten him in trouble.

She did resolve to make him a new necklace.

FIFTEEN
SYMBOL'S BIRTH

Ruby shook as she, Lya, and Hugh walked back from Owl Paulie's funeral. Lya clutched Hugh's hand tightly to her. She looked ovar at Ruby with her eyes narrowed. "Why're you shaking? You sing all the time. You're always brave."

"I never . . . never sang words I wrote before. Besides, the reds won't like what I had to say."

"So why'd you do it?" Lya's voice sounded slightly edged.

Ruby let a few steps pass, listening to the echoes in the narrow corridor. They were alone here, but she kept expecting a blue or a red to come out of a door or an intersecting corridor and stop them. "Are you unhappy I did?"

Lya shook her head, but she didn't look at Ruby.

Hugh spoke for the first time since they'd left the funeral. "He would have loved that song. Thank you."

Ruby flinched at footsteps in the corridor until she saw it was Marcelle and Onor, who had come to meet them. Tears fell down Marcelle's cheeks as she embraced Ruby and murmured, "I'm so proud of you. That was beautiful."

The exclamations continued back in common. Even Ruby's mother gave her a brief nod of recognition and clung to her for a few minutes, walking close, as if she wanted to be seen with her daughter. Ruby brushed Suri away by introducing her to Salli and Jinn's parents and suggesting to them that Suri might like friends in her new pod.

A few people ignored her. Some pointedly. Others came up and thanked her or just watched her curiously. The mood was hushed, and a bit wary, yet with an undercurrent of excitement she hoped had come from her song and from Hugh's words. Also from Owl Paulie's last speech, which she overhead three conversations about.

Whatever the varied reasons, there were enough eyes on her to make her back itch. Twice reds came in and left again, and both times they made sure to meet her eyes. A message.

In spite of that, maybe because of it, she talked to as many people as she could. She collected stories about Owl Paulie, shared some of her own, and nodded acceptance when people complimented her performance.

After about an hour, just as the wake was beginning to break apart, a hand grabbed her roughly on the bicep from behind, and she spun to look up into Ben's eyes. "That wasn't smart." His voice was harsher than she was used to from him.

She hissed a question at him. "Did you get in trouble?"

He shook his head. "No. But you will. You've been headed that way since I met you."

She swallowed. "Thank you for being there."

He licked his lips and leaned down and whispered loudly to her, his breath a bit rank from stim. "Be careful."

"I can't," she replied.

"You've gone past the kinds of trouble I can protect you from." He was still keeping his voice low. "You're not the only one believes life should be different. But more like it how it is. And you're getting pretty enough for a rape."

At the look she gave him, he said, "Not from me."

"I know."

"Some of the boys talk about it," he said. "Be careful." He pushed her away from him almost roughly.

Now she was shaking more than she had while singing the song. That had been fear and pride all at once, an edge that she liked. Ben manhandling her scared her. She left the room and hurried to Daria's hab and the quiet of the jewelry room.

She collapsed into the softest chair, suddenly grateful to be away from the stares of people. She'd wanted the attention, she knew that. But so many of the people had seemed to want something from her, more than ever before.

She ran her fingers through colored beads. Surely people had wanted things from Lila Red, too, and that was how she became famous enough to matter.

Ruby wanted to give the grays hope. That's what the beads and the test and everything was about, finding more . . . what? More freedom, more choice. For all of them.

Lila Red had been . . . well, a red. That was the secret. But she, Ruby, had Ben on her side. He'd been protecting her tonight, both by being there at the funeral and by warning her afterward. Except he was no hero. He was old.

But so was Owl Paulie.

Why was this so hard to think about?

The blue at the funeral had been afraid.

She felt afraid. A little. In this moment, anyway.

She stood up and paced as best she could in the tiny room. Most of the jars that had held blue beads were empty now, although there were more left than she had remembered. Enough for at least five more necklaces. She selected a jar of them. She started humming as she took down a container of red beads, setting it beside the blue. Then a gray, and as an afterthought, a small jar of black beads.

While she strung beads, her fingers moved in ways that had become practiced and smooth, like song itself. She hummed quietly and tried to think good thoughts about what the beads could change. Eventually she came to a place where she was thinking about nothing at all, and happiness seeped in between her fingers.

SIXTEEN
PREPARATION

Onor woke with the sheets tangled around his knees. On the bunk below him, Marcelle snored softly. He hadn't expected girls to snore, especially not any as petite as Marcelle. But she did. He was almost used to it after three months.

There was something he meant to remember, a bit of a dream bubbling up like a stray thought. He reached for his journal, flicked it on so he could see, and started writing. Reds lived on all the levels. If there were three levels, then they were gray and blue and something else. There must be at least one more level, no matter what The Jackman said, one more set of people with power that he never saw.

He'd woken up in the middle of the night possessed by the certainty that the blues did what someone told them. The blue in the funeral had ripped off the necklace Ruby gave Ben. But he'd done it after the video was off. He hadn't wanted to be seen. Since he hadn't known Owl Paulie (Hugh had sworn he'd never seen him before), it wasn't respect for the old man. But it was respect for someone.

Ix?

But the machine was run by men; it didn't run them.

So there were layers of blues, or there was something else.

Marcelle snorted below him and rolled over.

That was another thing to figure out. Ix. Ix saw everything, kept everything running. Ix obeyed rules and laws. In fact, it was very careful to stay inside all the bounds they knew about for it. One of his teachers had called Ix too stupid to think for itself, although Onor didn't believe the teacher was right.

Ix enforced rules—or at least it helped the reds enforce them. But that was like Conroy keeping the reclamation plant going or Ruby cleaning up crusty old bots. It was what Ix did, not what Ix was.

Marcelle's voice drifted up. "Do you ever stop thinking?"

"What?"

"I can hear you thinking from here. You're thinking about the test again."

"And you're not?"

Onor heard wrestling-with-clothes noises. He watched the ceiling until the sound stopped and Marcelle's feet scuffed on the floor. She stood up and leaned against the wall, her dark curly hair a soft tangle around her face. "I'll get stim."

"Don't spill it." He waited for the door to click shut behind her before he pushed his own covers away and pulled on his rumpled clothes.

How the hell did he end up sleeping with Marcelle instead of Ruby? Not exactly sleeping with her, but he wanted to hear Ruby breathing at night. Surely Ruby didn't snore.

Marcelle padded back in. He took a steaming cup of stim from her, liking the way it warmed his hands and smelled of mint. "Thanks."

"Are you sure The Jackman's going to be up this time of day?"

"He asked me to come. We need him if we're ever going to figure this out."

Marcelle blew on her stim to cool it. "What were you thinking so hard about?"

"Power."

She was silent for so long that they almost finished their stim before she glanced at him thoughtfully. "So you mean who has the power to tell us what to do?"

"The blues."

She held out her cup to him. "Your turn."

Onor took both cups and put them neatly in the sink in Kyle's neat kitchen. Then he slid his shoes on, grabbed his journal, and met Marcelle by the door. She wore a pale dress with darker gray straps and a gray belt, and she'd pulled a comb through her hair to make it lay in dark waves and rings across her shoulders. He swallowed back a compliment. It was Marcelle, after all.

Five minutes later, they knocked on The Jackman's door. It slid open a crack, and Onor whispered, "It's me and Marcelle."

The door opened wide enough to let them in, and after they entered, it closed quietly behind them. A faint light from The Jackman's sterile kitchen illuminated a bulky profile on the couch. Onor swallowed and wished the door hadn't closed.

"Onor," Conroy said unnecessarily.

"Good to see you." Onor blinked, trying to parse Conroy's presence. "Did you move here?"

"No."

He came for this talk? Onor let out a worried sigh. "Is Ruby here yet?"

"No," The Jackman answered. "We want to talk to you two first."

Great.

Conroy laughed. "You could move over to F with me. I tried to find you the day of the disaster."

"He wanted to be with his girlfriend." The Jackman laughed, a good-natured tease that still stung.

If only Ruby *were* his girlfriend.

Conroy stood up, his physical bulk intimidating. Onor stepped around him, flustered, instinctively trying for a little distance from his former boss. "I'm not working for you today."

"I can fix that." Conroy sounded matter-of-fact about it. Not bragging.

"Maybe. Maybe that'd be good again someday. I'm studying now. So why are you here this morning?"

Marcelle stuck her hand out and smiled up at Conroy. "Pleased to meet you. I'm Marcelle. The Jackman told us you're one of us."

Conroy's face twitched like he was swallowing a laugh. He glanced at The Jackman before saying, "I don't know who *us* is. I came to talk about you and Ruby. You're making enemies. Dangerous enemies." He looked at Onor. "I don't want to see you dead."

Marcelle answered, sounding for all the world like Ruby. "So we just lay down and do nothing? I don't want to stay here all my life, getting told what to do."

"What's so bad? You'll finish growing up and you'll fall in love and you'll have kids and you'll have a job and you'll have food."

Onor tried to keep up. That was exactly what Marcelle had always wanted, and Conroy had always grumbled at the reds. It was like the world was upside down, especially when Marcelle spoke with complete certainty. "I don't want my kids to be slaves. And if we're really going home, I want to help decide how things are. Where are we going to go when we get there? Are people waiting for us?"

The Jackman spoke from the dark shadows of the kitchen. "I told you they were naïve."

Marcelle flinched but stood her ground and looked from man to man.

"So enlighten us," Onor snapped at The Jackman, not liking that he was picking on Marcelle. "Owl Paulie said they were scared of us."

"I know. The vid went viral; we've all seen the clip of the Owl's last speech."

Conroy didn't live in this pod. Onor let that sink in a bit. "Everywhere. All the pods?"

The Jackman again. "And the 'The Owl's Song.' Ruby's famous." He narrowed his eyes at Onor, looking disappointed. "You all are, a bit. You might have succeeded before, when it was mostly quiet. We were watching you, and we thought just the three of you, and maybe Hugh and Lya, were going to take this on."

"We didn't do that," Marcelle said. "Distribute the video."

Conroy laughed. "No, you didn't."

"Who did?"

"There's a better question. Who didn't stop it from going viral?"

Onor drew in a deep, slow breath. "Someone out to help us?"

"Or not. Maybe to get you all in trouble. We don't know for sure."

"It's gotta be Ix," Marcelle said.

The Jackman shrugged.

Conroy spoke next. "You might have convinced Ix to let you in. Heck, you might have provided entertainment, been a curiosity. The blues might have decided letting you succeed quietly was better than the noise you'd make if you failed. But so many? They'll never let it happen. The test is lost."

"So they *are* scared of us," Onor mused.

The Jackman came out from the kitchen with glasses of water. "Sit down. We need to talk this out. *Before* Ruby gets here."

Marcelle flounced past Conroy, giving him a sharp glare as she went. She settled onto the frayed, dirty couch. "I want to know who *they* is. Is *they* all the blues on the world, or some of them, or is *they* Ix?"

Conroy gave her such a hard stare that she leaned back away from him, pressing her spine to the back of the couch.

Impressive, given that Marcelle never listened much to anyone, and here she was reacting to a stern look.

Conroy said, "*Them* is about who's in charge. Really in charge. Not about

the color of uniforms, which is just an easy way to tell you who you're supposed to think has power. And who you have to listen to. If you don't listen to
a red, they make you do extra work, or they lock you up for a day, or they get
you in trouble at school. Maybe, if they're told to, they do worse. But the reds
aren't power. Not usually. Others tell the reds what to tell you."

Marcelle said, "We were talking about that this morning. About power."

Onor, still standing, bounced on his feet. "It doesn't seem to be the blues
all the time either. Sometimes it's the blues in power, sometimes it's the reds."

Conroy looked the tiniest bit proud of him. "Good. That's what you have
to understand. Influence. Power. The ability to tell other people what to do.
Something you don't have any of. Zero."

Ouch.

Marcelle gaped at Conroy for the space of a breath, but she was obviously
thinking fast; she got the perfect question out before Onor thought of it. "Are
there grays with power?"

The Jackman and Conroy didn't say a thing.

"Ruby thinks she's one," Onor whispered.

The Jackman nodded. "That idea might kill her. She's wrong."

"What if Fox saves her?" Marcelle asked.

The Jackman laughed out loud, no gentleness in this laugh. Just a slight
derision.

Onor liked that. Damn Fox for existing anyway, and for becoming so big
in Ruby's imagination. Stupid romantic girls. He'd been beside her the day
the sky fell, and his memory of Ruby pushing herself on Fox was different
from how she remembered it. She remembered Fox responding, and Onor
hadn't seen that. "It won't happen," Onor said.

Marcelle looked at him like he'd betrayed Ruby. "How do you know?"

"She's gotta be a kid to him."

Marcelle scowled. "You know shit about men."

The Jackman cleared his throat. "The power on this ship isn't scared of
you, or Ruby, or for that matter even of me. Not by ourselves. We're not
much bother at all. Except in a large group. That's what they're scared of.
Losing us all." He let a moment's silence pass, the look on his face discour-
aging Onor and Marcelle from speaking. When he judged that his previous
words had sunk in, he nodded. "There's a history there, a time before when

things changed on this ship. I haven't quite figured it out, but I someday I'll understand. We all need to. So we don't make whatever mistake those poor buggers made."

For a moment, Onor felt all the generations on the ship, all the people who had lived and died in her, as if he rode with them all. He couldn't say if it was good or bad luck to be part of the generation that would bring *The Creative Fire* home.

The Jackman's next words dragged his focus back into the room. "I told you Ruby would get you in trouble. And she has. If you're not careful, if you don't make her stop," he glanced at Marcelle, "if you don't stop yourselves, you'll end up dead. They'll kill Ruby at least, but maybe all of you."

The Jackman meant his words.

Onor paced, angry. He couldn't stand up to the men, and he didn't have any idea what to say, much less what to think. There wasn't much room, so he paced, three steps one way, three the other, almost dizzying himself.

Marcelle stuck her lower lip out. "Tell me who *they* is."

Conroy's words came out sharp with frustration. "Figure it out, little girl."

Marcelle's eyes widened. For once she didn't have a snappy reply.

A knock on the door broke the awkward silence. The Jackman opened it, letting Ruby in. Her red hair had been caught back in a blue scarf, and at least seven strands of blue beads hung over her gray uniform shirt. Her cheeks were slightly flushed, her eyes bright.

Ruby looked surprised at the silence that met her. Then The Jackman smiled in greeting and said, "Come in," and Conroy introduced himself, even though they'd met before. At least they'd each talked about the other. Maybe they hadn't actually met.

Ruby settled into a chair opposite Onor, and he sat beside Marcelle. Conroy leaned against the wall on one side of Ruby, and The Jackman took the other side.

Ruby didn't seem to notice the tension. "So," she started in. "I was thinking that we should maybe show the students the vid Onor found. With Lila Red. But I'm not sure how to do that and not get caught. We can't just send it to everyone's journals. Ix'll strip it, and we'll probably lose it altogether." She looked at The Jackman, at Conroy, at Onor.

None of them said anything.

"We should at least show it to *some* others. Then they'll believe. I don't think most people think Lila Red's even real, and now we know." She forged ahead, talking fast. "Lila's story was history, and we should all know it. But they never taught it in school—" She broke off, as if the silence had finally sunk in. "So what's wrong?

Conroy spoke. "Rumor is you're drawing too much attention. I heard there's three crack peacers assigned to stop you."

Ruby looked up at him, blinked, and then reset her features into stubborn lines. "So I guess I need to stay in public. The last-years test is only a week away. I can manage that."

Marcelle nodded, but she looked uncertain.

Onor held his tongue, proud as hell of Ruby even though his stomach twisted at the idea that people might be trying to hurt her, might be trying to find her right now. He glanced at his old boss. "Where'd you hear that?"

Conroy just grunted. "From a friend that heard I might be looking after you."

Onor felt puzzled. "Me?"

"Yeah." He turned to Ruby. "I don't much want you hurt either, but Onor here was handy in the rec plant. I'd like him around to help me in the future."

Onor protested, "But I care about her!"

"Shhh . . . ," The Jackman said. He stepped closer to Onor and whispered in his ear. "Think, Onor. Don't waste yourself the way your parents did."

Onor clenched his jaw. They were gone. Ruby was still here, still beside him. He went and stood beside her, focusing on the brilliant highlighted reds in her hair and the way her lips pursed tight with determination. She practically quivered with focus.

He wanted to put a hand around her waist, but he didn't.

As The Jackman stood there watching them, he grew a little softer in the face and pulled on his beard. "Look, we don't know what happens if you do succeed." He was looking at Ruby, but Onor knew The Jackman's words were really for him. "Think about history. Think about the video we saw, Lila Red and her people right before they died. Whatever power they crossed, whatever waits inside the ship, was enough to kill adults who understood it. Lila Red had access to more of the ship than we do, wasn't gray, never was gray. She understood more than us by far, and chose to risk her life." He stopped for a long breath, but before Ruby could protest he said, "Take some time. If you haven't already got yourself in trouble past a beating, you have years. Spend them learning instead of fighting like a robot in a cage. No matter what you think, you're still a child."

"For a week."

The Jackman shook his head slowly, as if he were talking to a three-year-old. "Well, I wouldn't be brave enough to do what you're doing. I'm not brave, I'm old. Brave people die."

"Fine," Ruby said. "I'll die if I have to."

Conroy sounded extremely patient as he said, "We're trying to help you."

"So help me figure out how to play that vid Onor found. I want to show it to my friends."

Conroy look at Onor. "Is she always this stubborn?"

He didn't want to answer, but the idea of Ruby gone from his life was so oppressing that he blurted out words he didn't mean to say. "Maybe we don't have to be in such a hurry. Maybe we should just take our last-years and then wait awhile to challenge Ix. We can't be that close to Adiamo yet. We have time."

He'd seen betrayed, furious looks on her face before, but never directed at him. He couldn't think of anything to say until after she and Marcelle had both fled. And by then all he could do was whisper to the empty space where they had been. "Sorry."

SEVENTEEN

CHALLENGES

Ruby moved fast, leaving the hab warren with The Jackman behind, heading through the manufacturing shops and toward the crèche. Not because she was thinking about anything, but just because she had to keep moving. Onor's belief in her lived as part of her bones, part of her heart. It was a truth. Damn Onor.

Marcelle's footsteps followed her. Not catching up, but keeping up. At least she had the common sense not to say anything. There was nothing to say, no way to stop now. The test was too close, and she'd never get the momentum to do this again. If she stopped, she'd doom herself, forever, to be someone who once wanted something.

It made her think about Nona, who should be studying with her right now. It made her teeth tight in her face and her jaw quiver, and it made her walk faster.

Onor hadn't meant to betray her. He was just scared. He didn't mean it, and she wasn't going to start doubting him. She wasn't.

She trailed through corridors that would fill up with workers at shift change but were mostly empty now.

The people she did pass looked tired.

It was still early morning. Two crèche apprentices came toward her, walking two toddlers. The children wore gray harnesses, but the leashes dangled free in the handler's hands. They looked more vigilant than Ruby remembered her handlers being, but then there hadn't been any accident as bad as the sky falling when she was little. She'd been one to run away, and sometimes she actually got away.

Neither of these attendants looked likely to lose a child.

Marcelle had apprenticed in the crèche at home. She used to come back in the evenings full of stories about babies. There might not be any more babies. The new rule limiting marriages and childbearing fit with Fox's assertion that they were close. Why allow babies if they were almost home? It wasn't like they needed more crew, and babes in arms could be a liability in a strange place. Besides, the ship was already on light rations from the sky-falling day. Except she would allow them if it was up to her. At least a few.

Ruby sped up again as she hit the walkway behind the tall square of the crèche building, with its well-lit, bright corridors. She cursed as she bumped into a trash bot, scraping her shin.

The carrying arms of the short, sturdy bot held the rather pungent output from one or more of the smaller children, making running into it even more lovely.

If it didn't have any little kids to watch during the day, the bot would need to be reprogrammed and tested for a different job. She'd probably be the one stuck cleaning baby shit out of it for years. And she was going to have a whopper of a bruise on her shin.

Marcelle caught up to her, breathing hard. "If you don't start paying attention, you'll run into something worse than that. Shake it off. Onor's just scared. He's a boy."

Ruby fumed. Marcelle didn't usually stand up for Onor.

Marcelle took her arm. "You're supposed to stay in crowds. Let's go get breakfast. We've got time."

Ruby pulled away and then stopped. "Thanks. Thanks for following me. We shouldn't eat, though. We should be studying. We should be figuring how to play that damned video. We should not be scared." It felt like a mantra, calming her. "Ok, we go eat. But what did they tell you?"

Marcelle shook her head. "Nothing. Just called us stupid little girls and said we probably shouldn't be getting so many people involved. They just think they're special."

The community kitchen fed the old, and the hurt, and served as penance for ten to twelve year olds who got in trouble at school. Ruby'd been in similar kitchens dishwashing more than once.

She'd never seen them empty; it would be a safe place.

Was she really going to have to think this way? Were there really people after her?

If so, that's what she should have been thinking about first, not Onor.

"Who does it hurt if we get out of gray?" Ruby mused.

"There's our share of the cargo." Marcelle paused and raked her fingers through her hair. "If that's how it works."

"There's more to it than that. I just don't understand."

"Power needs someone to boss around."

Ruby laughed.

"Besides, what do people want to protect now? We're on our way home. They want us to be good grays and do the work to keep the ship moving. Especially since it's damaged."

"I'm tired of being good."

"Shhhhh," Marcelle said. "Me too. Maybe we should just slow down a little bit."

"You too?"

"No. Not like Onor. I believe in what you're doing."

So did Onor. Ruby's voice came out sharp as she said, "I can't afford to be afraid. I can't look afraid. If I look afraid, nobody will follow me, and nobody but me will pass the test."

"We won't if you're dead, either."

Did she have to fight with Marcelle, too? "If you don't take risks, nothing good happens. You just die after being boring." Ruby swallowed. Lila Red had died. "You can't change important things without taking risks."

"Lila Red died."

"Were you reading my brain?"

Marcelle didn't answer.

The smell of baking bread and stim wafted around the corner. Ruby softened her voice. "Let's take it to go. Get over to common. There'll be students there by now."

Marcelle looked doubtful. "It's pretty early."

The community kitchen was warmer than the corridor and smelled sweet and stale all at once. A few old people sat at one of the ten tables. They looked up as Ruby and Marcelle came in and waved at them.

Before Owl Paulie, old people had never even talked to her.

As they got in line, Ruby felt someone watching her. She glanced over her shoulder. Two reds headed her way. They hadn't been following her and Marcelle through the corridor, so they must have been in here already, maybe leaning against the wall.

Ruby forced a slow breath.

They weren't waiting for her. She hadn't known herself that she would be coming here until moments ago.

She and Marcelle both went along the same side of the buffet line,
Marcelle's eyes big, her head tilted a bit toward the approaching reds as if
Ruby hadn't seen them.

Ruby shrugged.

Then the reds stood opposite them, ladling gloppy, off-white morning
cereal and then fresh, sweet fruit into bowls. They were young, maybe just five
or six years older than Ruby and Marcelle, a man and a woman. The woman
had brown skin, black eyes, and white hair, a sort of shock look that most reds
didn't choose. Her partner was plain and dull, all browns except for hazel eyes,
walking behind her and watching Ruby and Marcelle nervously.

Marcelle's hands shook so hard that her spoon rattled against her plate.
Her face had gone white.

Ruby reminded herself that reds should make her mad and not scared.
Reds got hungry, too.

The woman smiled. "Ruby? And Marcelle?"

Ruby stiffened. "Yes."

The red woman brought her hand to her chest and lifted a strand of beads
from out of her uniform top.

Ruby drew in a surprised breath.

Blue and gray and red beads. Ruby didn't recognize the beads; she hadn't
made that strand. Daria hadn't either.

Some warning in the woman's eyes kept Ruby from letting the grin she
felt break out on her face. The red's hand disappeared, and the beads slid back
to rest under her shirt. She said, "I'm Chitt. In case you ever need me."

The man with her looked more scared than disapproving, and Ruby was
sure he wore no colored beads.

Maybe there were people after her, but she had them on her side, too.
"Pleased to meet you, Chitt."

She was rewarded with a look that no longer carried warning, although
Chitt's next words, while soft and conversational, were "Don't go anywhere
alone."

EIGHTEEN

THE TEST

Test day. Onor felt light-stomached and dizzy.

He and Marcelle walked side by side, their footsteps loud on the floor. Everything seemed amplified—sound, the greasy smell of the corridor, the way Marcelle's voice grated on his spine. He felt all the parts of him—fingers and toes and the backs of his knees.

Marcelle's face looked as if someone had washed the color out of it. "How do we know we studied the right part? Not for the last-years, but—"

Onor put out a hand to interrupt her. "Slow down and relax. It won't help you to be worried."

"But what if we fail?"

"Let it go. Relax."

"What if they make us fail?"

He snapped the word out this time. "Relax!"

Marcelle sneered. "Thank you."

He got blessed silence the rest of the way.

The exam was given in the biggest classroom, which consisted of three rows of chairs, four walls made of video screens, and two doors. They had to swipe their wrists through a scanner to get in. Here and there, teachers lurked at the edges of the room, looking serious. There were three reds—one in front of the room and two behind. None of them was Ben, or even familiar.

One red with good communications gear, a stunner, and Ix for backup should be able to manage a group of students.

One of the reds in back wore the three-color beads—red, gray, and blue. Visibly, too. Onor had become used to glimpsing hidden strands poking up along a neckline, but this deepened his worry.

A rising murmur behind them gave away Ruby's presence. She'd spent the last few days with her student following, which was why he and Marcelle had decided to walk over without her.

Ruby didn't sit next to them, but landed between two of her new friends.

Onor felt her absence. Ruby seemed to think her new followers would stick with her no matter what, that it was her they liked and not the idea of her. She was wrong. He took a deep breath while the scrapes and sighs and hushed chatter in the room faded to silence. Finally, each student had a seat, their journals, and nothing else.

The room smelled of sweat and adrenaline and nerves.

The red with the front position stepped forward and cleared her throat. She stood no taller than Marcelle. Her gray hair had been pulled back in a long ponytail that made her face look severe. "You may begin."

The light scratch of pens on journal screens and the shifting of feet made a small background hum to an otherwise oppressive silence. Onor focused down.

Basic math should have been harder, and he felt disappointed when he knew the answers were all correct even before the timer on the system pulled the pages away from his journal and presented the next part of the test. But then, he used math in his job, or he had. At the reclamation plant.

He hadn't actually had a job for the last few months, except for shutting their old pod down. When they finished, he'd been told to study. Most of the students had the last few weeks off. Maybe there were too many people for the *Fire* now that there was one less place to do work in.

The communication section came a little harder for him, but he finished on time. During the stretch break between test sections he squeezed his way to Ruby. "How are you doing?"

"Okay so far." She looked around at the other students who had oriented around her—almost half the room. Her next answer was clearly for them. "I think we're all doing okay so far. We all studied. We'll win."

Which meant she was nervous, or she wouldn't sound worried about it. Or more likely, she felt like he did. A combination of sour stomach and excitement, the knowledge that soon they'd know if the risks they'd been taking were going to pay off or hurt them. "It'll be okay," he assured her. She rewarded him with a grateful look and a nod.

In that moment, she seemed so strong and beautiful that he almost sicked up his breakfast. It was as if she had become too good to be true, and nothing too good to be true survived on *The Creative Fire*. Beauty was always ground down, aged, worked to death, or just disappeared.

Two more sections.

The next section covered safety measures. First aid. Gravgen failure drills. Oxy failure drills. Outbreak procedures. No problem.

Last, descriptions of every job in the pod and how they all interacted. Nothing, of course, about any other level. He licked his lips and told his racing heart to slow down and let him focus. Failures got three more months to pass, and a second failed test earned jobs as cleaners and sweepers and lockup guards, which meant a short life in barracks on the maintenance levels of gray.

He got halfway through rechecking before the pages disappeared on him. Glances full of either triumph or doubt or worry went back and forth between students. Marcelle looked confident. He felt confident. He glanced back at Ruby, but she was looking around at everyone else and didn't meet his eyes.

Were they all adults now?

Chairs scraped. People breathed a little loudly and someone coughed. It smelled like fear and exhaustion and excitement, or maybe Onor simply smelled himself.

Marcelle doodled on her journal, a picture of *The Creative Fire* hurtling through space toward a stylized sun.

Whispered conversations started.

The passage of time crawled through Onor's nerves.

Ix usually evaluated tests instantly.

The same severe female red that started them off stood in front of the class, waiting as students stopped stretching, or doodling, or in one case, sleeping.

The woman looked directly at Ruby, then at Marcelle, and then at Onor. Her dark eyes looked as steely and inflexible as a humanoid robot's eyes.

Then she looked at everyone else, one at a time. Enjoying the tension in the moment. She looked like one of the reds who would beat you in a dark corridor just for being there.

She cleared her throat. "Sorry for the delay."

Chairs scraped on the floor. The woman stood still, waiting for total quiet. "Ix had to double check the tests and the tapes from the actual exam. The results from this exam were hard for us to believe."

She looked at Ruby again.

Ruby gazed back at her, face implacable, strands of blue beads spilling down the gray front of her shirt, another strand wrapped around her wrist. Flamboyant and beautiful and defiant, even without saying a word.

No one made any noise at all.

"Everyone passed." Another beat of silence, the students all seeming to exhale at once and then inhale, and then the red said, "This class passed with the best test scores that Ix has *ever* seen."

NINETEEN

UNEXPECTED RESULTS

A split second after the freakishly severe red announced that they'd passed, the class erupted in hoots and congratulatory calls, in hand slapping and grins. Ruby sat still in the middle of the happy chaos, letting the idea of accomplishment fill her but not carry her away. They had achieved the little goal, the goal she knew was available.

She looked behind her at the tall red standing against the wall, openly displaying his mixed-color beaded necklace. He was middle-aged, serious-faced, as much like a typical red as you could get. He caught her watching him and gave her a warm smile. She smiled back, offering a thumbs-up sign. He didn't return the sign, but the smile remained on his face.

She tapped her foot, waiting for the room to quiet down. She'd waited this long, so long, but the next few minutes were surely going to feel like forever. She'd told everyone she could to stay, to be there when she challenged Ix.

It wasn't like this test, where they knew what to study for. But look how well they'd done so far.

Ruby watched the students spend some of their joy at passing. Of course, back home, if everything were still the way it had been, they would have all had jobs to start in three days. Some did, but not everyone. Onor, for example, had known what he would do at home. But not here.

She finished looking over the whole circle of the room. Something felt wrong.

Ruby swung around again and counted. Two more reds had come in after the announcement, during the excitement. She started toward Onor, careful not to run. She slapped his back as if giving congratulations—well, really giving congratulations—it was due. What mattered was the whisper of her breath against his ear as she hissed, "Look behind you. Casually."

He squeezed her hand. He'd heard her. He'd get it; he was good at worrying.

She went toward Marcelle, pushing past Salli and Jinn, who stopped her and grinned, silly, like girls at their first dance. Then they really looked at her, Salli wrinkling her brow. She looked about to ask a question, and for a split second Ruby hesitated, didn't know what to say, then she smiled and went on to Marcelle.

She glanced toward the door. Two more reds.

None of the reds in the room was Ben or Chitt.

The severe woman still stood in front of the group, watching Ruby. In fact, Ruby hadn't caught her looking at anyone else since she'd announced the good scores.

Ruby's skin itched. The oblivious chatter of the other students seemed louder and more cacophonous. For a second she thought someone might have slid her banned drugs, but surely it was just nerves, and too much stim, and not enough sleep.

And too many reds.

The room felt over-full with tension, even though the sounds were almost all still congratulations and even whooping. She reached Marcelle, who turned around and engulfed her in a relieved, excited bear hug, squeezing so tight that Ruby's chest muscles hurt.

Ruby pushed free, caught Marcelle's eye, tried to give her a brief warning.

Marcelle saw the look and stopped, confused.

Fair enough. Ruby didn't know herself what she was warning Marcelle and Onor about. Extra reds might or might not mean anything.

Maybe they'd come to offer congratulations.

Right.

It was time to take control, not give up.

"Stay near me," she told Marcelle, who nodded.

She looked for a place where she could be seen by the whole room. Close behind her, a table had been bolted to a long, doorless wall as well as the floor.

Well, okay. She needed an audience, anyway. This was partly Owl Paulie's plan, and he had left her before she could make it happen. Still, she felt him near her, as if some part of him was encouraging her to be brave.

Ruby swallowed hard and climbed up on the tabletop. It felt a little wobbly, but it held her.

She turned around to look the room over again quickly. Seven reds now, two leaning on each of the other three walls, and the woman in front, all of them quiet but very, very aware. The man who had smiled at her earlier guarded the door on her left.

Many of the students stood in a knot in the middle, mostly happy, talking, their voices still filling the room.

The severe red woman watched Ruby, her eyes rounded now. But something kept her from speaking.

They were waiting for something. Or someone.

Ruby caught Marcelle's eyes. She mouthed a single word. *Record.*

Marcelle fingered her journal, so apparently she got the message.

Ruby stood as straight as she could and whistled.

The chatter lowered; some looked at her.

She whistled again.

The room quieted. Two of the reds moved forward, but then they stopped as if jerked silent. Ix talking to them?

"Ix?" Ruby queried. Not right. She said it again, more demanding. "Ix! Speak to me."

It would have to. Ship's rules would make it.

She swallowed.

Damn. She tapped her toes, struggling to stay in control.

The room waited, everyone in it eerily still and quiet except for the shifting of stances and the drift of friends toward each other.

Ix's voice, choosing to sound like a machine. "Yes, Ruby Martin."

"I am a full adult now."

"Yes, Ruby Martin, you are."

Good. She needed to establish that. In her peripheral vision, two reds looked at each other uneasily, as if sure they should be doing something. She raised her voice. "We spoke in the park weeks ago. I'm sure you remember the conversation."

Ix didn't answer.

The students looked anticipatory, or in some cases confused. Not everyone had been drawn into the orbit of her talks and plans and songs and beads and dreams.

Two that she barely knew slipped out a door. No one stopped them.

She had made a statement. Ix didn't have to answer a statement. "Do you remember that we talked in the park?"

"Yes."

"We talked about the Laws of Passage, which were designed to allow people from one level of the ship to move to another. From gray inward."

The door opposite her opened, admitting a thin, bony man dressed in blue. She had seen him twice before. He had power. She'd heard him speaking sharply to Conroy once, and once with the head of the school. Even though he wasn't a big man, he felt like authority. He walked about ten steps toward Ruby, stopping almost in the middle of the room, as if he stood with his toes on a line that crossed the center, claiming the middle ground.

Maybe a table against a wall hadn't been a good choice.

"Ix?" Loudly, again, her throat constricting so she had to force the syllable past her fear. "Ix!"

The man spoke. "I will answer, Ruby Martin." He stepped so his legs were slightly apart and clasped his hands behind his back. She noticed his eyes as he looked directly at her, dark like grease and wide for his face. When he spoke, his voice was mild and cold. "Your understanding is correct. The Laws of Passage existed. They were created in the past, in a time when *The Creative Fire* was a different ship and the crew also different."

She didn't understand. Should she hope?

Everyone stood quiet, waiting.

"They were part of our beginning, but many things changed in the time we flew between stars." He almost sounded like he was reciting a lesson for the room, like he was a patient teacher and the subject was dry and factual, like math. "But laws are made by people, and for people. They change with time as we learn. One thing we learned about living in this ship is that it is easier to stay in one place and be part of that community than to yearn for things you cannot have."

"Easier for who?" she blurted out.

He broke his gaze from Ruby and spoke to the others. "You just did well. You received excellent scores, finished a tough education. You have excellent lives here. The gray levels are critical to the success of this ship we *all* call home." He paused, watchful, and then finished his speech, "These laws are for you; they protect you."

Ruby wanted to spit at his condescending feet.

Everyone watched him, the focus of the room shifted to blue.

She had never spoken directly to a blue except for Fox. She hadn't even had a conversation with the one at Owl Paulie's funeral. He'd said his words the way he was supposed to, told them when to do what, and ripped her beads off of Ben's neck, but they hadn't talked.

What should she say? She cleared her throat and rocked side to side on the table, catching attention. She started talking to the room and not to the blue. "We did well. We studied hard. We learned the things we need to know to go beyond where we were born." She nodded at the blue, trying to play his game. "To be useful to you in other places." That was it. Keep up the we, make this about more than her. It was anyway, she'd made sure it was. Almost half the room watched her now. "This is a fine group of adults." She spoke that word again. "Adults. We are down one pod in the gray levels, and there are too many people to easily support. Rations have been cut."

No reaction. But he knew all of this.

"You need to use us well. You need more hands to help us get ready to arrive home. We will get there in our lifetime."

The blue clamped his mouth shut, as if holding back words.

Surprise and doubt bloomed on faces. She hadn't told everyone they were almost home. Only a few. She'd stopped after those few didn't seem to believe her. She spoke as loud as she could. "We want to take the test. It won't hurt you to let us show you what we can be," she paused, "What we are!"

The blue blinked at her, not flustered, but at least looking like it cost him to stay calm. "No."

The man was a wall. She had expected Ix to be her adversary today, not a blue. The damned machine could be manipulated. Anger stiffened her back and thighs; she crossed her arms in front of her then dropped them again. "Ix! I demand to talk to you. If the Laws of Passage have changed, it happened since we talked." God, could they do that? Deny her this simply? Overturn an old tradition just to keep her from getting free? Ix had to answer direct, factual questions. "Ix. Tell me when the last change was made to the Laws of Passage."

The machine voice again. "Three hours and two minutes ago."

While they were already here, taking the test. Her instinct was to scream, but she forced herself to pause.

The red man wearing the multi-strand of beads stepped forward and spoke the words she held in her body. "That's not fair."

The blue didn't bother to look at him. He just gestured to the red to step back while he kept his gaze on Ruby.

The red didn't move. Not toward the man, not away. "That's not fair to these people. They studied hard, and we *could* use extra hands. She's right. Even if you make them peacers."

Some of the control slid from the blue's face. She expected anger, and it was there, but under the thinnest layer of anger, Ruby saw fear.

The Jackman had told her this. That they were afraid. So had Owl Paulie. Now she saw it.

The blue's mouth moved, although he didn't say anything she could hear. Six more reds walked quickly into the room. Two stood beside the one who had spoken back, taking one arm each. Her captured protector threw her a single glance, almost entreaty, as if she could do anything for him.

She smiled.

He saw she was watching him and smiled back, a brief expression replaced almost immediately by bewilderment. And then he and the other two reds left the room, arm in arm. He didn't struggle or fight it. He just went, head down.

After the door closed behind him and his escorts, she bit her lip, breathed. Onor and Marcelle had both made their way to her, and they stood by her side, although not up on the table. Three or four others had done the same. Almost half had drifted to the edges of the room. Others stood as if frozen in place. Salli and Jinn were in the center of this group. She should have known what to say to them.

Jinn turned away.

"No!" She breathed again, trying to breathe through her feet and up her spine, to get bigger. She spoke as loudly as she could without screaming. "We demand to test. We demand to be more free." She spoke to her peers. "They do need us. They haven't told you about Adiamo, about how close we are. They didn't tell us we would live to see our home. There must be more they haven't told any of us."

Jinn had turned back to her, challenge on her face.

"Our history. They haven't told us why they keep us separate. Why they changed the rules."

The blue man glared at her, anger the only emotion in his eyes this time.

"Well, I'll tell you. They changed the rules because *they are afraid of us.* Not of one of us at a time, not of me, but of all of us. Of all of us! There are more grays than all other crew on this ship put together." The whole room stared. She had to pour it on. "Remember Owl Paulie! It *is* our time to make a difference. If we don't do it now, we'll get home with nothing. But if we work together, we can change the rules."

Two reds shouldered their way to her, standing between her and everyone else, even between her and Onor and Marcelle. Onor looked stricken, almost ill. Worried. Marcelle simply looked like contained anger, switching her gaze fast between Ruby and Onor and the reds and the one blue who still dominated the room.

The blue spoke. "We can use you in other places. We have evaluated this entire graduating class and determined what jobs you should go to. We will read those off to you now, so that those of you going to other pods can prepare to leave tomorrow."

To leave? She held her tongue. Thoughts raced.

The woman cleared her throat. "Jinn Martel, you are assigned to D-pod to work on train scheduling." Jinn and Salli, who were never apart, somehow stood even closer together, bodies touching from shoulder to shin. From the stricken look on both faces, they had expected something else. Salli glanced at Ruby and her red escort. Her eyes narrowed and what looked like a curse passed silently across her face.

The next assignment sent a young man to work in food preparation in E-pod. He, too, looked surprised, and he, too, glanced angrily at Ruby, then turned away from her. He had brought her beads one morning, something from a broken set of his grandmother's, old and blue and yellow. She had pulled the blue ones out and closed his hands over the rest, and he had looked shy with her. His anger cut.

Each assignment felt like a small shock through the room, a moment of stiffening, of new fear, of a bit of anger.

By the time Salli was assigned half a ship away from Jinn, so much stony silence had fallen in the room that Ruby heard Salli's tortured intake of breath.

She would rather have been beaten.

She steeled herself. They were the last three. Marcelle, trained to work in the crèche, ended up in the water reclamation plant on E, in a place Onor would have been happy. But Marcelle hated being dirty and wet, and she hated being alone. Whoever had done this had sat there after they turned in good tests and chosen their worst nightmares. And they'd known them well enough to cause real pain.

Onor backed up toward her. The red at Ruby's right, under her, since Ruby was still on the table, blocked Onor with a hand, keeping him from coming close enough to touch Ruby. Onor's face turned up to her, shock the most visible thing, his first reaction to anything unfair.

"Onor Hall, you will report to D-pod for janitorial duty."

None of the students had drawn anything so bad. This would be below, where Nona was murdered. Below, where they put people who failed or grew too old for their jobs but not too old to work.

"Ruby Martin, you will report to cargo bay inspection here."

She nodded, nursing her fury. For now, she was well and truly beaten. Her eyes stung with hot tears and her fingers had curled into tight fists, the nails digging into her palms. And under that, fear.

In the silence that fell across the room after her assignment, fear of it sank in.

They were keeping her here to be a target for the families who had just lost children to the other pods. Besides, three people had died already this year in the cargo pods: one had suffocated, one had fallen in the grav failure the day the sky fell, and one had died of a heart attack. Maybe they wanted her to die.

The blue had left at some moment she hadn't seen, but the room was still ringed in reds, too many for resistance of any kind to matter.

Ix had gone silent.

There was nothing sane she could do except jump down as if she was just fine, as if it was all fine, as if her feet didn't hurt from the sting of the floor and as if the worst hour of her life hadn't just passed.

TWENTY

A RECORDING

O utside in the corridor, Onor drew a deep breath, struggling to get the stale taste of fear from the showdown between Ruby and the blue out of his mouth. Marcelle grabbed his arm, jerking him behind her. He stumbled before catching his feet.

"I take it we're going somewhere?"

She cast him a don't-ask glance and kept moving, eventually letting go of his arm, as if she no longer cared if he followed.

Maybe she didn't.

So he followed.

They'd been outmaneuvered. Ruby could get killed. He felt as if someone had picked him up and thrown him against a wall and broken him.

He was supposed to leave tomorrow.

He followed Marcelle all the way back to Kyle's and stumbled in after her. When the door closed behind them, she threw her stuff against the wall. She slammed her naked fist into the same wall, leaving a small dent in the thin metal. She cursed under her breath.

Marcelle the cheerful, upbeat, and polite.

He supposed he should be mad, too. Instead he felt dizzy and weak. At least Kyle was at work and they didn't have to tell him about the debacle.

He flopped onto the couch so hard it jarred his back. They would all three be in different pods. He wouldn't be able to protect Ruby at all.

What if he never saw her again?

He looked up to find Marcelle standing over him, her hands on her hips. "Snap out of it. We have things to do." She started clipping them off on her fingers. Index finger. "We need to make a list of who got sent where so we can set up a way to communicate." Middle finger. "We need to pack for ourselves." Fourth finger. "We need to tell Kyle thank-you and ask him to help us look after Ruby." Her voice sounded so controlled she might not have been slamming into things a moment before. Little finger. "We need to make a list of all the reds who were wearing beads." She grabbed her thumb.

"We need to see Ruby," Onor said.

A masculine voice answered him. "She'll be watched."

The door to Kyle's room, always closed when he wasn't home, slid open. Marcelle yelped and Onor tensed.

"You need to see me." The Jackman slid through the door.

"You broke in!" Marcelle managed to squeak out.

The Jackman shook his head and put his fingers to his mouth in an exaggerated gesture. "No. Kyle is one of us. How do you think you three all ended up here together?"

Marcelle crossed her arms over her chest. "There you go with all the *us and them* stuff again. Secrets."

"Some of those kids will be telling everything they know just to keep their old hopes alive. Anything anybody but you two knows, our enemies will know."

Onor objected, "I wouldn't rat you out. They'd kill you. They're not killing us." He swallowed. "Except Ruby! You have to help me. I need you to keep her safe!"

The Jackman headed to the kitchen and started heating enough stim for three glasses. "Good to see you understand the stakes." He looked as serious as Onor had ever seen him, which was saying quite a lot. "Did you tell any of those students there are adult grays just as dissatisfied? Did you mention my name, or Conroy's?"

"We're adults!" Marcelle protested.

The Jackman ignored her, keeping his eyes on Onor.

"No," Onor said.

"Did Ruby?"

He shook his head, biting his lips. "Not . . . no."

The Jackman turned to Marcelle. "You? Anybody? Or Ruby?"

Her eyes had grown wider, as if she'd finally stopped and thought about what he was saying. "No. Sorry. I . . . no one."

"Ruby?"'

"No one that I know of. Maybe her family."

He didn't look entirely satisfied. "See that you don't ever talk about people who help you. From this night forward. Either of you."

"Of course not!" Marcelle slid onto one of the kitchen stools. "You never tell us enough to tell anybody anyway."

The Jackman raised an eyebrow. "What happened today? Wasn't it exactly what I told you would happen?"

Onor took a deep breath to force his racing mind to slow down. The stim was beginning to warm, scenting the room.

Marcelle, still standing, went right up to The Jackman and stared at him, her face so close to his they must have been able to smell each other's breath. "They knew. So how do we know *you're* not telling on *us*?"

Onor sighed and took her shoulder, pulling her back. "Ruby didn't keep any secrets from anybody. She told people she was rebelling every chance she got. The Jackman and Conroy did warn us there'd be trouble."

The Jackman nodded at Marcelle. "That was a good list you started. We should do that. But first, did you get any of that recorded?"

"Oh!" Marcelle raced for her journal, abandoned the moment she'd come in. She scooped it up from the floor and plopped down on the couch, pushing buttons and frowning. "Maybe I . . ." She pushed something else, sliding her finger across the screen. "There it is!"

"Send it to me," The Jackman said.

Marcelle glared at him. "What are you going to do with it?"

The big man glared back.

Onor watched the crossed legs and arms and the tense jaws until he couldn't stand it anymore, then ran his hand through the air between the two of them. "Give it to him. If we can't trust The Jackman, then we might as well give up now."

Marcelle grunted. "I'm sending it to him and Ruby."

The Jackman almost spoke, but stopped himself.

Marcelle pushed a few buttons and looked up. "There. You should have it."

"You gotta help Ruby," Onor said. "You know they're going to have an accident."

It was apparently The Jackman's turn to grunt. "I'll do what I can. But remember what I told you last time you asked."

He remembered. "She might be past saving. . . . But maybe she's so well known now that it'll be easier to save her. It could work that way, you know."

The Jackman looked a little like he pitied Onor, and Onor squirmed and looked away, feeling defensive and a bit stupid all at once. "It could," he muttered. "People will notice if she disappears or gets hurt."

"Yeah, like some mom who's never going to see her kid again," Marcelle said. "That's who'll notice her."

The front door opened and Kyle came in.

"You're home early," Marcelle said.

Kyle went to the kitchen and started pouring the stim out, apportioning it so it would fit in five glasses instead of three. He handed one to Onor, one to The Jackman, one to Marcelle, and took one himself. He held up his glass as if toasting, "To the most blatant move against us in years."

Onor drank, wishing Kyle had got home in time to make the stim as well as pour it. Kyle could make the bitter drink taste almost good. He pointed to the fifth glass, sitting all alone on the counter. "Who's that for? Ruby?"

"No."

Onor recalled The Jackman's words and didn't get mad at Kyle for not exactly answering. "Thank you for taking us in. I appreciate it. And for keeping us."

Kyle blushed. How the heck was a man this soft part of an underground movement?

The door from the corridor pushed open and Daria rushed in, her hair a mess and her unusual green eyes glaring at The Jackman.

Onor stepped back. Daria didn't like him at all, had made Ruby stay away from him whenever she could. But he might as well have not been in the room. All of Daria's attention was on The Jackman.

"You told me she'd be safe!" Daria stood near The Jackman's chest, even closer than Marcelle had been earlier. "You told me you'd make sure they didn't hurt her or kill her or anything."

The Jackman wore a clearly amused look on his face, and Onor noticed a softness pass across his features as he folded Daria in his arms and whispered in her ear, loud enough that Onor could hear him say, "I'm not done yet."

Onor blinked, feeling stupid. This he would not have guessed.

Was every last gray part of a conspiracy?

Marcelle looked as sideways as he felt, her mouth open as she watched tiny Daria return The Jackman's hug, nearly disappearing in the big man's arms.

Onor went over and stood by Marcelle. He whispered, softly, right into her ear so no one else could hear. Not that anyone else was paying attention. "Have we been blind, or have we been manipulated?"

"I don't know," Marcelle whispered back.

TWENTY-ONE

THE CLOSED DOOR

Ruby dreamed herself cold and alone in a cargo bay. Her dreaming self tugged on a bolt that wouldn't let go. She braced in the low gravity to gain leverage with angle and torque, using her whole body as a tool, twisting. Just as the bolt snapped loose, the gravgens stuttered. She jerked downward, then floated untethered in an empty metal cylinder, knowing that at any second weight would return and force her to fall up, or down, or sideways. The dreaming jolt of gravity woke her, shuddering and moaning, sweat pouring down her face.

She used her fingers to brush her hair, then glanced down at her clothes. Still dirty from the day before, but clean enough to wear in public. She needed food. The floor dragged at her feet, her limbs thick and full of the dreams. She crept out the door, careful not to wake Suri or Ean, clutching her journal.

She needed stim. Thankfully the common kitchen was open this early. No one greeted her or said her name or even told her hello. They all ignored her, staying busy, keeping their backs to her.

Fine.

She didn't want to talk to anyone anyway. Her footsteps were loud in the warm kitchen, the bitter stim burn in the air offset only slightly with fruit so sweet it smelled near rot.

She bypassed food and took her cup to common, where she sat down on one of the benches against a wall. She slumped and tried to sip herself awake.

She had been undone. So fast. So easy. Except she'd thought she had the others, that they believed. That they'd rebel with her. At least some of them. But when it came down to it, they'd all been passive and scared. Her too. She'd run out of ways to fight.

For a while.

After all, what if she had fought? She'd have been stunned and sent to lockup. She ran her fingers across the slick bench, swallowing. She wasn't going to cry. That wasn't what she did. She dug her fingernails into her palm and savored the pain, biting her lip for more until she had control.

She opened her journal and sent Marcelle a note, asked her to meet her in common. For the first time ever she wondered if Marcelle would really want to see her.

Surely Marcelle would come. She had always come.

They could make a new plan.

A pair of footsteps passed by in the corridor. Students, a year or two behind her. One of them spotted her and pointed, whispering to the other, and then the pair glared at her as they walked on.

Ruby tensed, considering whether to stand up and chase them or just ignore them. Before she decided, they were gone. She sat back down with a sigh and curled her hands around the half-empty cup of stim, wishing she'd brought two. She felt powerless to move, as if the events of the day before had taken everything from her.

She needed to do better, to recover, to think.

There was an answer. If there was no way to change it all back, surely there was a way to change *some* things.

A pale orange blink showed new messages for her. Her mother, via voice, her tone not particularly worried, as if maybe she was talking to her mirror or a total stranger, except for a tiny extra high note at the end: "Why did you go and ruin everything? We just moved here, and no one will respect us now. What are me and Daria and Ean going to do?"

Ruby cut the message off, glared at her journal, and hissed, "There's a bigger picture here than you or me."

The note from her mom energized her more than the stim.

There was another message. From Marcelle.

A brief text: *Here. This came out pretty well.* The recording. Ruby thumbed it on and bent her head, listening. She heard herself challenge Ix, the blue and her talking, words barely discernible over background noise, the rubbing of soft things together—probably Marcelle's clothes—and footsteps from time to time as people walked by. Not completely clear, but at least she could make out most of the words.

Ruby brushed a stray bit of hair from her cheek and stared at the journal. Why had Marcelle been able to send her the recording? Ix knew about everything on anyone's journals; she'd gotten in trouble for writing down things she shouldn't before. So that meant . . . Ix had this recording, too? Ix approved of this recording? Ix hadn't gotten around to erasing it yet?

More importantly, what could she do with it?

She lifted her head and looked for Marcelle or Onor again. No one was in sight, no one even walking by. Surely they'd be here soon. They would make a plan together.

Two other videos had gone viral. "The Owl's Song." The Owl's last speech. She still didn't know why. It hadn't been her or Marcelle or Onor who set them free to run through the ship like a good rumor. Both of those had been real video though, and this was just sound, and not crisp, either.

"Ix?" Her voice sounded lonely in the big room. "Ix?"

Common, like the school, had speakers. She almost jumped when the walls addressed her. Not the computer voice this time; one of Ix's more human voices. "Yes, Ruby Martin?"

"Did you record the . . . the . . . What was the name of the blue in our test yesterday? The runt with all the control?"

"Ellis Knight."

She dropped her voice. "Did you record Ellis Knight and me talking, and the reds assigning the students the way they did?"

"I always record potential confrontations."

She grimaced. "And they are played for who?"

"Anyone who asks. Everything I record is free for anyone to listen to, unless it is specifically blocked by the peacekeepers or people in higher authority."

Good. Until she thought it through and realized it was another nonanswer. "No one has blocked this?"

"Ellis Knight blocked it."

She sighed and leaned back against the cool white wall. "If I send you a copy of a different recording, would you keep it safe so that I can request it again later?"

"The recording you have on your journal?"

"Yes."

"I will keep it for you."

She twisted the blue beads of her bracelet around and around, thinking. "As something personal? Not something Ellis can block?"

"And not something you can share."

Well, it was something. "You don't know if there are other copies?"

No answer.

"Ix?"

More silence.

She tapped her foot. Ix must have helped Ellis yesterday. Maybe mixing everyone up had been Ix's plan. Yet this morning, the damned machine sounded downright conversational. But if it didn't have any emotions, it wouldn't care how fair things were or weren't. Would it? She brightened. "The red? The one wearing the multi beads? He recorded it?"

"He was out of the room at the end."

"Is he okay?"

"Yes."

"Did anything bad happen to him?"

"Not yet."

Why couldn't the stupid AI just give her what she wanted? She forced herself to calm down and think the next question out. "Did Ellis Knight record the conversation?"

"No."

"You're infuriating."

"You called me."

"If you were physical I'd thump you for being so difficult!" Her hands were claws on the side of the bench. She forced the fingers to relax. "Did anyone else access your recording before Ellis blocked it?"

"Yes."

She forced herself to take a deep breath. "Can you tell me who?"

A masculine voice came from the opening between common and the corridor. "I did. And I shared it with my friends. And they shared it with their friends."

She twisted around, catching a flash of blue and then a shock of red hair.

Fox!

Her breath caught in her chest, and she put a hand up to smooth her hair.

"And I'm sorry if you're frustrated. I told Ix to keep you talking so that I could get here."

She felt her mouth open, as if she had things to say, even though she didn't have a single idea in her head at that moment. Except maybe that she should have dressed better.

Fox walked normally, with no limp. He stopped a few feet away from her, his red hair slightly long, hanging almost to his shoulders, his blue eyes warm, happy to see her—not severe like Ellis Knight's had been yesterday. Fox looked more confident than the man who had sat scared and injured on the bench beside her the day the sky fell.

He smelled like cleanliness and hope, like the world she wanted, like the long moments under the broken roof when suspicions had become truths.

He held a hand out to her. She wondered if this was a fevered dream from her lack of sleep.

His hand felt solid and real.

She leaned into him, drawn into his arms, which he closed around her, folding her inside of him, his palms a warmth on her cold back. He held tight. Her head fit into his shoulder and she pushed it there, putting her weight into him, feeling him brace and absorb her. She didn't dare a kiss yet, but wanted one, confused at the way her heart beat and her belly felt raw and fiery. She should be mad instead of weak. She should be worried, maybe even afraid, or angry.

But right now she felt safe.

Fox pushed her gently away and stepped back from her, looking down at her face. He kept his hands on her arms, a current of . . . something, passing between them. "You're as pretty as I remembered. I came as soon as I could this morning."

"Why not mornings ago? Why now?" Why after everything has fallen apart?

He spoke so softly she could barely hear him, and while he talked his hand ran along the curve of her cheek, distracting her. "I wanted to forget that I'd met you. But your song—"The Owl's Song"—played up there. On the regular vid, over and over until people started singing it in the halls. Because we talked, I knew what you were singing. Most of the others started out believing you sang about hope, but I knew it for defiance."

Something in her stuttered, a moment of mistrust. He was a blue, he was one of the ones who had just destroyed her dreams.

But he was Fox, and she had saved him.

And he had kissed her. Once. She turned her face up to him, hoping now for a kiss. He bent close, but only to whisper in her ear. "We need to go before Ellis or anyone else stops me."

"Go where?"

He whispered one more word. "Home."

She swallowed and stepped back. He would take her? Really?

"I couldn't bear to watch yesterday, the test and you being so brave and getting nowhere. But we were. A lot of us were watching, in a bar, on a . . . never mind. Ix helped. And I couldn't sleep, so I came here. We can talk later."

Her nerves screamed at her. If she went, it would be irrevocable. It might kill her, might get her locked up, might do anything. It was like stepping into blackness through a black door and hoping for light.

But she was already dead here.

This was what she had wanted, what she never, ever thought she'd get. She knew for sure now that she'd never actually expected to leave.

Onor and Marcelle.

She hissed, "I need to tell people I'll be safe. People need to know."

"It will make you less safe," he said, his voice laced with urgency, his hand on her back, propelling her toward the corridor. "We can find a way later. You're going to be a hit, you've already got a following. We can get a message through." He smiled. "We'll write a song for them later."

She didn't quite understand his words, but she understood the pressure of his arm and the urgency in his voice.

He walked fast, his boots softer than hers. They passed Jinn's parents, who glared at her. The woman, a tall blond with a scar on her nose and greasy hair caught back in a ponytail, smiled at Fox and said, "Thank you." The circles under her eyes hinted that she might have been crying, and her mate pulled her close to him and nodded at Fox as well, ignoring Ruby entirely.

Fox smiled back at them but didn't slow at all. He pulled Ruby harder down the corridor, making sure she didn't interact with the couple.

It took her a breath or two to realize he was playing the part of powerful blue taking the troublemaker in hand. For a moment she wanted to pull away from him and protest her innocence, tell Jinn's mom that she had done what she did *for* Jinn, for all of them, even for her. But the woman had looked tired and worn out, like she hadn't slept. Like life had nearly finished with her.

If she didn't go with Fox now, and if she didn't have any accidents, she would look like that woman all too soon, and keep her head down and hide.

She had her head down when they rounded a corner, and she spotted the bottom half of a red uniform. Fox sped up. Ruby glanced at the man. Ben. "Wait!" she called.

Fox tightened his grip on her arm, stopping just at the edge of pain. A warning.

Ruby read the set of Ben's face, saw worry there instead of mistrust.

He hadn't given up on her. Ben's eyes narrowed as he looked at Fox.

"It's okay, Ben," Ruby said. "Tell Onor and Marcelle I'm okay. Tell them to . . . tell them to keep going. To be safe."

Ben opened his mouth as if to respond, and in that moment, Ruby realized she might never see him again, or see any grays again, whatever happened. She threw her arms around the old red and squeezed tight. The hard nub of his stunner dug into her hip, and even as old as he was, he felt solid and safe and comforting. She didn't let go until he patted her back awkwardly.

"It's okay," he said, as if he understood the situation. "Do what you need to do."

"Keep them safe if you can. Marcelle and Onor, and my mom, and Ean and Daria and Hugh and . . . even Macky."

Ben hissed at Fox, "Keep her safe, or I'll find you myself."

Fox took a step back, then laughed. "It'll be okay, old man. Go on."

He almost sounded disrespectful to Ben. "He's my friend," she told Fox.

"I know who he is. I saw him in the 'Owl's Song' vid. Let's *go*."

Ruby followed, her stomach now twisted with hope and fear all together. She had to go. She would lose herself if she didn't follow. But she felt pulled apart, one arm into the future and one arm into the past.

After they left Ben, there were two more turns. Fox took her behind the school, in a corridor she'd never really noticed, a place scratched by the uneven wheels of bots and dented by carts. They came to a metal door with no handle, something she might have mistaken for a repair to the wall or a hatch to a storage closet.

Fox waved his wrist in front of it and it opened.

He went in and she followed him.

On the other side, light illuminated a long corridor that sloped up, lined with a metal handhold along one side and no-grav handles on the ceiling. It was cleaner than the place they had just left, unpainted and uncolored, a bit stark.

A fitting place to pass between lives.

The door closed behind them, a sharp metal on metal click that sounded like change and felt like it severed her from herself, made her lighter, and stole the ground from her feet.

Fox turned to her and took her in his arms. "Thank you for trusting me."

"I dreamed you would come."

"I did."

As they walked up the sloped wall, side by side, Fox near the handrail, what she heard wasn't their footsteps, but the metallic sound the door made closing behind them.

PART TWO

LEARNING

TWENTY-TWO
BECOMING BLUE

After the door closed on the gray world she'd grown up in, Ruby stayed close behind Fox, holding a hand out to touch him from time to time, to assure herself that this was no fevered dream. His closeness made her breath shallow and fast. She felt almost overwhelmed, as if an impossible thing had happened, as if Fox being here made the cruel events of the day before impossible, too. He felt like safety and the unknown all at once, warm and scary.

They hurried, breath and steps echoing in the corridor. Just when Ruby wondered if they'd walked all the way through the next level to the heart of the ship, Fox whispered, "Sorry. This is an old passage we found, and we thought it would be a better way to sneak you in."

"Sneak? Ix must know I'm coming."

"It's people that worry me. I want to get you into a better uniform."

She snapped out, "Clothes won't turn me blue," before she thought about it. Then she added, a beat late, "Maybe that'll help."

"Trust me."

She'd already made *that* decision.

A bot stood beside an airlock door, opening and closing the thick slab of metal so silently she didn't even hear the whisper of contact as the bot's metal hand grasped the metal door. The door squeaked as it moved. Ten steps up a rigid tunnel, holding the handrails this time, staring at the dented, graffitied walls that were inches in front of her nose. The tunnel swayed slightly. It looked thicker than the distance she'd seen between levels above the park, so they must be near the intersection of pods. If only she had a better picture of the details of the ship in her head.

She followed Fox through yet another lock monitored by another polite and complacent robot. She expected the second door to open into the blue level. Instead, it was another corridor with no interesting features except handholds and seams here and there, bland and clean. A few—far too few—deep nicks in the metal itself. No part of the *Fire* could possibly be newer than any other, but her senses told her she had come to a newer place.

A hundred more uphill-into-gravity steps later, Fox said, "Here. Be quiet."

A door she would never have seen opened, sucking light and the murmurs of conversation from the other side. She couldn't make out words, but the voices seemed hushed and curious.

Ruby pulled on Fox's shirtsleeve. When he turned back to face her she took a deep breath, looked at him as hard as she could, and searched for any sign that he might betray her. Seeing none, she reached up and touched his face, then nodded. They passed through the door, Fox in front, Ruby sliding around him to see a crowd of unfamiliar eyes filled with curiosity and welcome.

She didn't recognize a single face. Oh, one. Dayn, who'd driven the scooter and seen her kiss Fox under the broken sky. They were all near Fox's age or a bit older or younger, with neat hair and unscarred features. Clean. Here and there, a red.

Sweat stuck strands of hair to her forehead. She had not set out to leave home forever; her clothes were thin and stained.

The people were silent, curious. Their faces suggested they'd expected someone different. More downtrodden, or less?

A friendly voice, a little over-loud. "Hello, Ruby."

A woman she couldn't quite see. "Welcome."

"We knew Fox'd get you."

"Thank you for coming."

"Hello."

"Welcome."

And to Fox: "Was there any trouble?"

The warmth of the conversation fascinated her, making her stand a bit straighter, smile, hold out her hand. This was her first impression, her first chance, and she had to ace it, no matter that she stank and her hair was two-days-unwashed greasy. She smiled as hard as she could, stood straight, spoke charming words through tired lips. Fox stood beside her. He kept one hand on her back, steadying her.

She struggled to gather in the new names and remember them. Harold: a tall blond man with a wide smile. Lanie: a wisp of a blond-haired and fair-skinned woman who stuck close to Fox. Bo: a pale man with pale blue eyes and a slight limp. Harold was serious; Lanie had a warm smile that spread across her cheeks like a light turning on; Bo's hand felt clammy with sweat, and his handshake was a bit soft.

A tall woman with dark skin and dark hair and very light green eyes passed a thin stack of clothes above the small crowd. Fox stood on tiptoe and reached. "Thanks, Ani." He grabbed the clothes from above the head of a brunette woman and passed them to Ruby. "Take these."

A blue uniform, new and smelling of something sweet, soft against the exposed skin of her arm.

He pressed her forward and then pointed her into a privy. "I'll guard," he told her. "Hurry."

The dark woman, Ani, walked in right behind Ruby, carrying a bag over her shoulder. "Glad you're here, girl," she said, crowding in, filling more than half the small space. The bathroom looked like the ones at home except a tad brighter. Desperately thirsty, Ruby ran water into her cupped hands and sipped.

"Your singing is so pretty it makes me want to cry."

"Thank you." Ruby tried to hide her surprise as she grabbed a thin towel from a neat stack near the sink and scrubbed at her face. "What have you heard?"

"Just 'The Owl's Song,' so far. But that's why we wanted Fox to get you. We want more. We were all rooting for you. We couldn't bear the idea of you being a cargo-bay girl, not when you can sing like that."

Ruby wiped the sink and threw the dirty towel into the recycler, wondering if Ani knew the real risks of the cargo-bay job. "Why would you guys even notice someone like me?"

"Fox has been showing you to us. Making us listen." Ani looked down for a second. Her skin was so dark it was hard to tell if she blushed, but Ruby thought so. "We wanted you to pass the test."

Ruby looked away, sure her face would give away her confusion.

Ani laughed and pushed Ruby toward a privy stall. "Change into those and give me your old ones. Hurry."

The blue uniform slid easily onto her body, perfect except for the legs, which were a tiny bit short. She saved the necklace Daria had made her, the tri-color beads worked into clever lace that Ruby would never have had the patience to re-create. She also saved the blue beads she'd worn around her wrist. She found a pocket to fold them into. It felt good to keep a tiny secret.

Ani took her old clothes, muttering at Ruby. "We'll disappear these permanently."

Okay by her. Not that Ani seemed to need a reaction from Ruby. She dropped Ruby's old, gray clothes into the bag, tied the top tight, and tossed the clothes—bag and all—through a small, square hatch in the wall. A dull thud declared that they'd fallen into something below. A hairbrush appeared in Ani's hand, and she helped herself to Ruby's hair, pulling snarls out and muttering about showers.

When the brush disappeared again, Ruby wiped her face with her hand and stood up to stare at herself in the mirror, off-balance from the change. In blue, clean, with her hair brushed back, she looked older and smarter. More capable. She even felt different from her old self. "Thanks."

"Fox has extra uniforms for you. Let's go."

For an irrational moment, she expected to walk out and find Fox gone and Ellis waiting for her, but Fox stood very close to the door and came immediately to her side. "You look great."

"Now what?"

"We pretend we know what we're doing. I don't think you've been noticed yet. Follow me."

Ruby kept close to Fox, just behind, and he put his hand in hers, pulling her along. The danger they must be in made her feel tingly and hyperaware.

Fox stayed in the lead.

He pulled her into a big room full of tables and chairs and couches. People filled half of the seating, some in uniform, some not. Music played in the background, a song she didn't recognize but wanted to tap her foot to.

The sharp scent of fresh stim rose from a gleaming metal dispenser on a table. Bread and bunches of yellow orbfruit scattered across half-picked-over plates. Fox leaned down to Lanie, grinning at her, and pecked her cheek. "Find us a table? I'll bring you some stim."

He helped himself to two cups, handing one to Ruby. "I had breakfast, but if you want something, take it."

This place looked neater than the common kitchen back home.

Fox's entourage settled around Lanie at a table near the wall, Fox and Ruby next to each other and facing the door. The table held twelve. Ruby would be willing to swear she'd met more than that, and for sure Ani was missing.

Tasting the fruit reminded her she'd skipped breakfast. "What happens next?"

He swallowed. "We make our case."

"To who?"

"Ellis, I suppose. And the peacers."

He didn't sound particularly worried. Rather, he sounded like he was looking forward to something. "I want us in a public place when we get found."

Like her confronting Ix in the class yesterday. "That strategy only kind of worked for me."

He grinned. "It worked great. You're here."

"It didn't work so great for anybody else. The goal is to get all of the grays free."

"Impossible."

Ruby looked away from him, stung.

She glanced around the table. She knew the names of about half of them now. Three were reds. At home, she would never have sat down to eat by reds.

Two humans worked in the kitchen, supervising a set of five or six shiny silver bots that cleaned up tables, carried out trays of fresh food, and refilled the stim. At home there would have been a bot or two most of the time, but just for the jobs that people weren't strong enough or flexible enough to do. She had never seen some of these designs, and the mechanicals she worked on were all in worse repair. These didn't squeak in the wrong places or have parts of the wrong color welded on where something had broken a decade or a lifetime ago.

Their shiny surfaces reflected her in blue as they passed.

Other tables filled and emptied around them.

Dayn finally spoke Ruby's thoughts. "Maybe they're not willing to see her here."

Fox grunted. "Of course they aren't. That's the game. See who runs out of patience first."

"They can afford to wait us out," Dayn whispered.

Fox laughed. "I'm running a spot on the public channels promising Ruby will come to us and sing like the magic between the stars."

Dayn gave Ruby an assessing look, and Ruby stared back at him. She didn't understand what Fox had said other than that she would sing, but she could do that. She could sing. Whatever Fox was planning for her, she'd live up to it.

Dayn turned his attention back to Fox. "Sure you haven't gone too far this time?"

"They're all so busy fighting no one's going to know what to do with me. The *Fire*'s in loose hands right now." Fox got up and refilled his stim, leaving the conversation unfinished. When he sat back down he held the full cup without drinking from it, as if it gave him an excuse to hold the entire table of people there. Eventually, he leaned down to Ruby and spoke softly. "Ellis is not so strong as he likes to pretend, and he knows it. He's not well liked. He's only around because the ship's current leaders don't have spine enough to remove him."

There was a lot to ask Fox about in that sentence, and Ruby liked the taste of knowledge. She repeated the sentence in her head, setting it so that she'd remember it, choosing to wait until she was alone with him. In this brightly lit place with the crowded table, she didn't feel the same intimate pull that had threatened to overtake her in the corridors, but she was still aware of every move he made, every person he watched, of the cadence of his breath.

They waited a long time.

The door opened. The red woman from the class and two red-uniformed men she'd never seen before came through the door together and headed right for their table. Ellis trailed behind.

Ruby took a breath.

Fox whispered, "Let me talk."

She bit her lip and nodded, her hands shaking.

Fox smiled at the woman. "Hello, Sylva."

Sylva didn't even acknowledge him. Focused on Ruby, she snapped out, "You do not have permission to be here."

Ruby bit harder on her lip, drowning her need to answer for herself in pain.

Sylva's jaw was set as tight as the commitment in her eyes, as if sheer determination could make the world obey her.

In contrast, Fox sat relaxed, his voice and body language all implying there was no real problem at all. "I am allowed to bring talent from anywhere in the ship. I've chosen Ruby for her voice."

The taller of the two men blinked. "She has no . . ." he paused. "No training or experience."

"She has talent."

Ruby swallowed and kept biting her tongue. People seated at nearby tables watched them curiously. The confrontation touched the attention of everyone in the room except the bots, who ignored it entirely.

Fox addressed Sylva. "You can't stop me." He gestured around the table. "There is no rule. We looked. I verified with Ix. I saw you change the Laws of Passage. That governs her ability to ask to come here of her own accord. But no law controls my ability to ask Ruby to come. I have asked, and she has accepted."

"This is a bad idea," Ellis scraped out through clenched teeth. He didn't look as powerful here as he had down on the gray levels, although Ruby couldn't really put a finger on why. "You know the histories," Ellis said. "You know what a critical juncture the *Fire* is at now."

Dayn stood up and Ellis looked even smaller. "Look," Dayn said, "you can't change the rules now, not since she's here. Not without executive authority, and they're all worrying about who's on top when we get home. Are you going to tell them what a threat she is?" He pointed at Ruby. "She's not very big." He cocked his head. "Or very old."

Sylva gave Ruby a hard look, one that suggested she had made an enemy for life simply because she existed. "Why is she in dress blues?"

Fox looked up at Sylva and smiled. "Because she's working for me." He paused. "Go ahead and take her back if you want. But she'll have new things to say to the others down there, and you've already got a nest of discontent in your hands. Don't make her into a legend like Lila the Red."

Sylva's cheeks reddened. She stood, stock silent and glaring. Ruby wondered if there was nothing she *could* say. Sylva's expression screamed that she wanted to rip Ruby out of her chair, but for some reason she wasn't doing it.

Fox spoke. "Trust me. I'm helping you out." He looked at Ellis, his face relaxing, his voice as casual as his slouch in the chair. "*This* is a better way to make her disappear than the one you were contemplating."

Ellis pursed his lips.

Sylva narrowed her eyes and spoke to Ruby. "You should not be here. I will see to it that Fox pays for this, and if you misstep at all, you will pay for it, too." With that, she spun around, and the four of them left.

In Ruby's old world, if the reds wanted something they would simply take it. She let out a breath and then another, almost panting with relief.

Dayn sat back down.

Ruby was safe for now, and that was all she had ever been. "Thank you," she said, nodding at the door the foursome had gone back out of. "Tell me about her, and about the reds."

"Peacers," Fox said reflexively. A correction. Not an entirely respectful one either. "Sylva thinks it's her job to find everything hidden and wrong on this ship. She spends all day with her goons watching recordings and looking for mutineers."

"Mutineers?"

He lowered his voice, added drama bordering on comedy. "They tell us tales of the evil grays and how you tried to take over *The Creative Fire* the year we lost A-pod. They tell us how you're dirty and need to be kept segregated and worked hard so you'll be too busy to pick a fight. Oh, and entertained. That's been part of my job." He spread his hands wide, his eyes light with humor and relief. "The ship would fall apart without you, and we would starve or choke on our own poisons, but it will truly be the end of the world if you and I talk." He grinned at her. "That's why you scare them so."

He was making light of the whole thing, even though she was the one who might die for being here. "But why did you come to get me?"

"To prove them wrong."

And not because he remembered her and liked her and found her brave. Slightly stung, she said, "Surely for more than that."

"Of course." He squeezed her hand. "Later." He looked around the table. "Thank you."

The entire table full of people, except for Fox and Dayn, got up, swooped up their plates, set them in the sinks with a soft clatter, and left.

Fox held his hand out to Ruby. "May I show you around?"

TWENTY-THREE

VOICES

R uby stood between Fox and Dayn just inside a door on the narrow end of a long, narrow room. Along one wall, a row of swivel chairs had been fastened to the floor under a shelf. Attached to the wall were various levers and screens and headphones, punctuated here and there with tiny blinking gold or pale white lights that danced to sounds Ruby couldn't hear.

It looked quite fantastic and entirely new.

Data blinked across the other wall, lists and pictures and numbers making dark, moving columns on the light surface. "My studio," Fox said.

She didn't understand. "That's a workbench?"

"For recording. It's what I do. I manage the production of songs from here. It is . . . what I have to offer."

"Like I repair robots? You make sound?"

"Yes."

"For the whole ship?"

He laughed. "Of course. But I'm not the only one."

"All this exists just for songs? Just to entertain?"

"Of course not. This is one of two sound studios where we create and edit lessons, the formal histories of the ship, news, messages from command, and the stories you play for the children in the crèche. But I work with the singers."

"Heaven Andrews? Do you work with Heaven Andrews?"

Fox looked like he was about to choke on her question. "Heaven Andrews has been dead for two generations."

Oh. "Do you sing?"

He laughed. "Badly, and not in public. I produce." He glanced at her, the look heavy with conspiracy she didn't understand. "I needed a new voice, and I chose you. Our story will remain that simple."

"So you do think I sing well?"

"I can make you sound perfect."

Not quite the answer she wanted. She turned to Dayn. "What do you do?"

"Usually?" He grinned at Fox and gave a little bow. "Usually I help organize the output of the great producer here and prepare it for the ears of his waiting fans all over the ship." He shrugged, an exaggerated gesture. "Today, I am playing bodyguard so he is not caught unawares and does not lose the gray girl he has brought up to our land to sing to us of the travails of her people."

She savored the humor in his voice and the vague teasing look in his eyes. Both Fox and Dayn were very male, older than Onor or Hugh or her usual friends. Being close to them disturbed her belly and made her feel a tad bit giggly. Her reaction to Fox was the strongest, but her body wanted to speak to both of them or either of them, even tired and confused.

Or maybe she just wanted to be held and reassured. She couldn't tell, still barely sure this wasn't a dream.

She stepped out from between them to explore the room, running her hand along the cool surface and trying to puzzle out the meanings of the various controls. Surely this was a machine, and not entirely different from a robot. She could learn to do what Fox did. "Show me. How do you use this to record a voice?"

He came close enough to her to slide his arms around her from behind. She leaned back against him and Dayn cleared his throat.

She straightened, taking a step away from Fox.

"It's okay," he whispered, his voice warm against her neck. He brushed her hair back with his fingers and settled a thin wire across the top of her head. Then he cupped her ears with something warm.

She wanted a mirror, but there wasn't one.

He brought a thin thread down her jaw on both sides. His fingertips brushed her cheeks as he made tiny adjustments in the bend.

When he stepped away, she felt the absence of his warmth at her back.

He stopped a few chairs down from her, settling himself in and staring at the lights and keys above him on the wall. "Will you sing 'The Owl's Song' for me?"

"That's all I've ever sung for you. That and the song I made it from. I know more than that."

"Later. Sing me that one now."

She nodded, the wires along her jaw a nuisance. She twisted her face up, trying to loosen them.

"Relax. Be natural."

She blinked, the audacity of being here washing over her, making her almost swoon. What if she did this badly? What if the wires or the ear cup fell off? What if her voice wouldn't work in this cold, metal place?

"Breathe," he said. "Everyone worries. But you don't need to. Breathe."

The cups around her ears came alive, startling her, thrumming with the first few notes of "The Owl's Song," familiar and yet different, the instruments laying one atop the other, blending, clear and concise and exact.

She almost missed the in beat for her voice.

With the music in her ears, her voice sounded muffled and too soft, so she added to it, pulling strength up through her belly and closing her eyes, pretending she stood in the park.

After she completed the first verse she trembled with effort.

Fox touched the small of her back. "That's enough. This isn't a session. I just wanted to show you."

She reached up to peel the cups from her ears, but he whispered, "Leave them. Sit down. Listen."

He went back to his seat.

She sat, unsure what he wanted next.

He bent down, his hands moving gracefully over the surface in front of him. Then he nodded at her.

The music started.

She watched him. She took a breath as the in note approached but he put a hand up. She closed her mouth and listened to her own voice pouring through the cups in her ears.

She sounded . . . perfect.

"How did you do that?"

"Practice," he said. "Here, listen to the recording from when you first sang it." He made a series of gestures, then nodded, and she heard herself back at Owl Paulie's actual funeral.

The recording was clearer than she remembered ever hearing it. "That sounds great!"

He looked a bit proud. "I fixed it up a little. I've been playing it for them since the day you sang it."

Goose bumps rose along her arms.

Fox continued. "But that's not nearly as good as what you just did."

She blushed and listened.

He was right. The words she had just sung, tired and stripped down and raw, sounded great. He'd pulled her soul out of her voice, and sharpened it as well.

"That's amazing. Can you teach me how to do that?"

"Then I wouldn't have a job, would I?"

She frowned, not sure whether to take him seriously.

He came over, took the cups, and clipped them back onto the wall, holding out his hand to her. "Let's go get you clean, and maybe a rest would be good."

It would. She felt bone tired and a bit queasy. Her feet seemed heavy as she followed Fox and Dayn followed her, winding in a new direction that led to more crowded halls and rooms full of people working at desks, with interface sets on their hands and eyes. Everything looked and smelled different; she felt dizzy with the newness of it all.

Fox's hab turned out to be about the size of Kyle's back home. She had expected it to be bigger, more lavish, but the hab itself looked like it had been cut from the same plans as the ones on the gray levels. The walls were largely bare, the furniture simple. Fox dug out a towel and pointed toward the shower. "Go get cleaned up. There should be shampoo and soap."

As soon as he said it, she knew how much she wanted to be clean.

The privy room was as spare as the rest of the place, and the shower water turned off after the same amount of time as on gray. But she found a brush and toothbrush. A complete set of new clothes, blue and soft and clean, had been set out for her. She dressed and once again stared at herself in the mirror. The blue went well with her red hair. But no uniform could cover her puffy face and sleepy eyes.

She hesitated before she came out. Now what? Fox was a man and she was an adult woman now. She knew what that meant, but she felt shaky and unready.

She straightened her back and told her blood to cool. She stopped in the doorway to the living room, cocking her head to one side and preparing a smile for Fox.

Dayn sprawled across one side of the couch.

Fox was nowhere to be seen.

"Where did he go?" she blurted, before thinking, angry at how small and thin her voice sounded. "Fox?"

Dayn grinned at her. "He told me to watch you, said I should invite you to get settled. He's had three days worth of clothes brought in, and set you up with a sound system he downloaded his work into. He thought maybe you should sleep. He'll be back later."

Dayn looked like he was having entirely too much fun telling her what Fox had done and why he wasn't here. She bit her lip to stop herself from telling him what she thought of his tone of voice.

But damn, she wanted Fox.

She kept her voice controlled. "Did he say when he'd be back?"

"I expect he'll be back before morning."

She walked into the room and looked around more closely. A couch. A table. An entertainment rig. A rug. "He lives simply, doesn't he?"

Dayn laughed. "Want to play a game?"

Surely the entertainment rig here was up to it, but she didn't want to play with Dayn. "I'll just wait for him."

"Suit yourself."

She pursed her lips. "Where do you live?"

"Next door to you. That way I can keep an eye on you."

"But . . ." She let the word trail off, dripping from her tongue. What had she thought? That Fox had come down to rescue her because she was a little bit in love with him? That he would never leave her side?

Dayn raised an eyebrow. "You're a pretty bit to babysit, Ruby. Don't get me wrong, and I don't really mind the duty. You're spunky. But don't take it for granted. You'll have to earn your place just like the rest of us, and you won't always be Fox's new girl on the block."

Even with no meanness in the tone, his words felt like a slap.

"I think maybe I should sleep."

"I can show you where the bedroom is."

She glared at him. "I can find it. Go ahead and guard me, but do it from out here."

He raised his hands, pretending innocence she didn't think he felt.

She stalked into the bedroom.

An empty shelf and set of drawers and a big bed, big enough for three people, just like her mom slept on. The room was pale blue, the coverlet pale blue, the sheets brown. A door led to a small, private privy.

Maybe she shouldn't have been so mad at Dayn. It wasn't his fault Fox had other things to do. It wasn't hers either for that matter. Maybe it was just the way the world was here. He must be important.

She lay down on the bed and smelled the sheets, hoping for a stray scent of Fox in the pillows. But it all smelled clean and fresh and of nobody.

She wished for Marcelle. She tried to send her a message, but her journal errored out. It errored on Onor and her mom and everyone else she knew. As she tried to sleep, her mind's eye drew Sylva's face glowering down at her. Though she drifted through an uneasy rest, sleep hid from her. It made her bones heavy and stole the feeling from her feet, but refused to settle over her brain and soothe. Her tired mind supplied her with thoughts about people she already missed. Onor and Marcelle and Ben and The Jackman and Daria and Hugh and Lya and Owl Paulie and even her mom.

"I'll figure this all out," she whispered to the silent faces. "I will set you free."

TWENTY-FOUR
GRAY WITHOUT RUBY

Onor and Marcelle watched Ben's slightly slumped back as he shuffled away along his appointed rounds. Onor held on to Ben's last words, which carried more hope than the old red's body language. He'd said, "We couldn't have kept her alive here." He'd meant it, too, his voice full of the certainty of someone who knows more than he's telling. Maybe Fox could do what neither Onor nor Marcelle nor The Jackman nor Conroy nor all of them together could do: keep people with power from killing Ruby.

How would they ever know? If she went up there and died, if it was a trap, they might never be certain what happened. News that trickled to journals and vid screens on this level never said anything about anywhere else on the *Fire*.

While Ben told them about seeing Ruby in the corridor an hour ago, Marcelle slid ever closer to Onor. Her thigh warmed his and her left foot rested against his, toes touching him. It felt odd to be so close, and Onor slid away a few inches.

"I don't bite," she said.

"I can't believe she went with Fox."

"Without us."

Marcelle looked like she needed his arm around her, but he couldn't make himself do that, not with Marcelle. But still, she looked so lost. He nudged her softly. "It'll be okay. We have to pack."

"And then I won't see you ever again either."

"You don't even like me," he said.

"Maybe not." She gave a soft smile, stood up, and held her hand out for his. He let her have it, but stood up on his own.

"I hate her for setting us up and then leaving." Marcelle let go of his hand but stayed close. "Except I can't hate her. But aren't you angry, too?"

"No." He didn't elaborate, since Marcelle seldom understood subtle emotions like sadness that made your heart want to fall into the bowl of your hips and lay still. He would miss Marcelle later, but now he missed Ruby so much that there wasn't room to miss anyone else yet, or even to show his pain.

Kyle waited for them in the kitchen. Somehow the story had gotten to him before they came home, but then bad news beat the speed of light regularly. Kyle had the common sense to remain quiet and not look directly at either of them until he'd put plates of food and cups of his special steaming hot stim in front of them. The smell made Onor curl his hands around the cup.

Something else he'd eventually miss. He wondered idly if he would miss Kyle more, or Marcelle, or maybe The Jackman, but there was no feeling attached to the question at all.

For years he had had a goal, and Ruby beside and in front of him.

Kyle pointed at the fruit cut into tiny, sweet-smelling stars and placed on top of flat crackers spread with nut butter. "That's for you. A going away. You might need the strength."

Onor took one. "Thanks for . . . everything."

"It'll be okay," Kyle said. "It will. Everything seems worse when you're young."

Right. "I don't need anyone to tell me things are as bad as they'll ever be. I already know that."

Marcelle poked him in the ribs. "Maybe they won't make us stay away long; like a punishment."

"This isn't detention," Onor snapped. "It's jail."

"No," Kyle said. "Lockup on D is far worse."

Onor shivered at the first-hand knowledge he heard in Kyle's words.

"Making people hate them is stupid." Marcelle sipped her stim and made a sour face at the cup. "They'll figure that out." She took a cracker and ate, looking more thoughtful than usual.

Kyle spoke into the small silence. "Everything is changing, with us getting near home. Nothing can go back to how it was ever again." He slapped Onor on the back lightly. "Eat."

And then go become a glorified janitor. Or, more likely, a not-very-glorified janitor. They didn't need humans to clean. They had robots for that. So it was pure punishment. He ate, slowly, the food good in his mouth even though he didn't want it to be.

Kyle went with them to the transportation station, Marcelle's bags over his shoulder. People jammed the corridors, watching them, clearly curious about the exile; they stood in small groups, looking afraid or angry or empty. Marcelle walked close to Onor, her jaw clenched tight and her head up, her eyes glistening but tearless. Reds walked the halls in twos, their voices forceful as they broke up crowds and commanded people to keep moving.

Two reds stood at the entrance to the transportation station checking people in. They stepped in front of Kyle. "You can't go any further."

A flash of anger crossed Kyle's face as he handed Marcelle her bag. He paused to look closely at each of them, as if memorizing their faces, his lips a thin line and his jaw tight. "Good luck."

The look in Kyle's eyes made Onor wonder why he'd ever characterized him as mild-mannered.

The train swayed, screaming too fast along its rails. Marcelle's stop was first, and Onor squeezed her hand as they arrived. "Stop being so sad," he whispered to her. "You're stronger when you're angry."

She nodded, but she slumped against him a little, burrowing her head into his shoulder.

He held her closer than he ever had and then pushed her up and away. "You have to."

Before she left, she stood in the doorway and looked back.

The door opened onto D-pod. Salli, on the same train, glared at him with near-hatred in her eyes. He mouthed a single word. "Sorry."

"Are you?" she whispered back.

"Of course." He pointed at their surroundings. "For me, too."

"Then fix it."

He didn't answer, not sure what to say.

He'd received detailed instructions from Ix via his journal this morning. He carried them out to the letter, reporting for duty at the D facilities crew lounge before he even checked into his assigned hab. He had to pass the reclamation plant on the way, and he tried not to look at the door. He should be going in there for hazing right now, worried but only a little, getting clapped on the back. Of course, he should be reporting for duty in a reclamation plant in a pod that no longer lived, but the doors were marked the same, with symbols for water and transformation.

The big-machinery parts of the pods, where water and waste reclamation happened, were largely multilevel. The facilities lounge turned out to be a metal cave in the far back of the pod, under the sludge-processing part of the water plant. He half expected to smell the rotting stench of the waste-reducing bacteria at work, but apparently the gases produced there didn't travel down. Instead, it smelled like grease and stale stim and the citrus and bark smell of a clean corridor, so strong his stomach felt like it had been slammed. As he'd suspected, the large windowless room had been designed more for robots than for people.

Four semihumanoid bots stood loose limbed against one wall, their four feet grouped in twos for the moment, so they looked even more like people than they did when they were working. Straps held them to the wall by waist and torso. They didn't turn their heads to look at him or anything as he entered; their true eyes were sensors that circled them all over. Above the top row of sensors, they had painted-on eyes and metal faces sculpted to look human, but neither male nor female.

When he was little, he used to ask his mother where all the robots went at night. The memory brought a small, bitter taste to his throat.

There were about twenty other bots, sporting various appendages, most of them standing at the right height to bang his knees. Grease stains and the shiny scar lines of repair welds gave them individuality.

Hopefully he wouldn't look as bad as the bots after he'd been here for a little while.

None of the other exiled students had joined him in this particular misery. The benches along the one wall that wasn't full of bots held three hard-looking women, an old man, and a man with a bruised cheek and scars on his arms who couldn't have been more than a few years older than Onor. None of them looked like they used their shower rations.

Probably not. Probably they sold them for still.

He didn't feel like talking to any of them, man or machine, so he didn't. No one tried to talk to him either, although furtive glances passed between the others, often starting with a quick look in his direction.

A middle-aged and middle-weighted woman walked around the room unstrapping the bots from their cradles. As she loosed them by type, the machines lined up and went out the door together in small groups. In two cases, humans were sent with them, but most chores were apparently fine for the bots all by themselves.

A tall, thin man with a long ponytail of gray hair down his back called the other humans up one by one, speaking in hushed tones. Nothing passed between him and them except words, but Onor noticed they had their journals in small packs on their backs or bellies.

The last person called up before Onor was one of the women, a block on legs, with short, graying hair and a slight limp. As soon as she came up, the man nodded at Onor and waved him up beside her. "Penny here will take care of you today. She'll show you where the supplies are and how to deal with various messes."

Maybe he'd get lucky and the manual labor would drive Ruby's face out of his imagination.

Penny looked at him and smiled, but her dark eyes looked wary and her smile shed no light on her face. She smelled like sweat and dirt.

The man kept talking. "I'm Jimmy, and you work for me. You can leave your stuff here and get it at the end of shift, and I'll show you how to find your bunk. We take care of our own here."

Since his smile didn't touch his face either, Onor didn't feel very comforted. Or very happy about leaving his stuff. He tried to smile but couldn't. "Thank you."

Onor followed Penny through the door.

She led him down a corridor, boots echoing on the smooth metal floor. Bright overhead lights illuminated enough wrinkles around Penny's mouth that he revised her age upward. He should talk to her, but he didn't know what to say.

D-pod was similar to every other pod, but the underpaths they walked were mostly strange to Onor, who lost his bearings after fifteen minutes of walking alongside the surly Penny. The dark corridors were anything but clean. They dodged bots from time to time, and once Penny kicked a broken wheel assembly into a corner beside a few other bits of metal.

"Shouldn't you report that?" he asked. No trash was supposed to lay loose on the ship.

"Won't hurt anybody that matters down here. Besides, the reclaimers will eventually find it."

He and Penny both wore gray, but he felt like the world had bifurcated; in his old life he had been a rich and privileged slave and now he had been handed down to something darker.

At one point Penny was ahead of him by quite a bit, and she turned around and snapped, "Why are you dragging, boy? Think you're too good to be one of us?"

He shook his head at her. "Didn't sleep much last night."

"The slower you work here, the worse work you get." She sounded nervous, almost afraid. But he hadn't given her anything to be scared about.

"Hey! I'm a hard worker."

"Then keep up." She rounded a corner.

Onor followed her.

A fist took him in the gut and the weight of a heavy body forced him back. A foot hooked around the back of his ankle and a hand slammed him hard, forcing him to the floor.

He put his arms up over his face.

Someone kicked the back of his hands.

He held them in place anyway, afraid to be kicked in the nose or the mouth.

Another kick in his side and he curled around his belly, a ball of Onor on the floor.

A work-boot toe slammed into his thigh.

His breakfast threatened to leave him.

He split his fingers wide enough to look through them.

Three. Three attackers. All men, he thought.

No sign of Penny.

How was he supposed to take on three?

They were grays.

He'd expected reds, but then he hadn't seen any reds down here at all.

A man kicked his side so hard he let out an involuntary screech. He bit down on his lower lip, drawing blood, keeping back sound.

Nothing else happened immediately.

"Sit up," a voice growled at him.

He slid his hands a little down from his face to get a better look at his attackers. Definitely three, and behind them, leaning against a wall and looking away from him, Penny.

Onor loosed his hands, used them to push up into a seated position and scoot back against the wall.

The man closest to him had a distinctive scar that split his lip. He said, "This is so you know we can hurt you and so we know you can take it."

Onor's breath was fast and reedy from fright and pain. "You haze people to death down here?"

A laugh. "You could call this hazing."

"Who are you?"

The man shook his head. "We're like you. Right now, you're part of the reason we're being watched so closely." He cleared his throat, looking down at Onor. His face was thin, his eyes dark and full of confidence.

Onor would remember his face.

"This is a warning," the man said. "You drew a lot of attention back in B-pod, and you're to stop that now. Or we'll make sure you're never more than a cleaner. Got it?"

Onor bit his lip, looking up.

"Got it?"

"I heard your warning."

The man turned and passed between the other two men, and they turned as well, the three of them disappearing around the corner.

Penny came to his side and held out a hand.

He glared at her. "You were part of that."

She shrugged. "Not my decision. No way for me to stop it."

He swallowed and contemplated her answer. "You led me here."

"I didn't hit you." She was still offering her hand to help him up.

He took it. "Thank you."

"They beat me for longer the first time," she said.

"The first time? Do they beat people up regularly?"

A thin-lipped smile crossed her square face. "Only the ones worth bothering about."

"Now what?"

"Now we keep going. Got work to do."

TWENTY-FIVE
THE FOX'S DINNER

A knock on the door dragged Ruby awake from a dream as dark as the middle of the cargo bay, unformed, lonely as only a strange place can be. It took a few moments to register that she lay on Fox's soft bed, napping, waiting for him.

The knock came again.

Hope and an entirely different kind of fear goaded her to sit up and call out, "Right there!"

In the privy, she ran her fingers through her hair and brushed her teeth. Thankfully, she'd graduated from looking exhausted to merely looking tired.

Fox's slender form stood just outside her door. Almost as good, the hallway was filled with the subtle scent of cooking so savory it might have wafted up from Kyle's kitchen. Fox smiled at her. "Hungry?"

She stepped toward him. "You cooked?"

He raised an eyebrow. "Dayn and Ani."

She swallowed, her disappointment nearly as deep as her hunger. The only time she'd had alone with Fox so far had been the long walk up the hidden corridor. The food drew her out behind him, and the four of them sat at the kitchen table.

"Sleep well?" Ani asked.

Ruby nodded, looking the table over curiously. Kyle had served her similar food, a water soup with root vegetables and the curry tang of protein powder, yellow orbfruit, orange and red breakfruit, and flat bread with seeds baked into it. "Do you have gardens and orchards here, too?" she asked.

"You grow our food," Dayn said.

Fox looked disapproving. "He means the outer pods grow the food for the whole ship, except for a few herb gardens and some greenhouses over in the university. We have no parks as big as yours and no trees. Your parks serve us all."

So the separation of the levels had a cost for the people inward? But what had Ix said? "You can go there. Ix told me you could."

Fox nodded. "It's not Ix's rules that keep us out. The machine only cares about keeping the ship safe. But it listens to Garth and the other idiots that run this place."

"Doesn't Ix tell people what to do?"

"Us? Yes. But not the captain." He looked thoughtful. "I wish I'd seen the park working. I learned a lot the day you saved me."

"It's my favorite place. I go there when I need to be alone."

"Is it as big as they say?" Ani asked.

Ruby didn't know how to answer, but Fox said, "Bigger than I thought."

"It's very beautiful," Ruby said. "Almost always partly empty."

Dayn's voice had a small warning in it. "You can't go back, you know."

She'd never see a park again? "Don't you mean that if I go home, I'm stuck there?"

Fox answered. "I had to promise you wouldn't go back. And other things. I promised you wouldn't run loose here," he swallowed, looking apprehensive, "and that you wouldn't contact anyone you've left behind, and that we would watch over you."

She set her spoon down and sat back. "You've promised a lot for me."

"Ani will teach you. And you'll have to work. That part's the same everywhere. You'll start tomorrow with me, and we'll spend a week or so recording. At night, you'll stay here at first, then you'll go out with Dayn and me and we'll introduce you to people and teach you how to get along here."

"What access rights does she have?" Ani asked.

"None for now," Fox answered. "Basic com of course. Give me a few days and I can probably broker something." He looked slightly apologetic.

So he wasn't all-powerful.

Ani, however, looked pretty proud. "It's better than I thought you'd do." She turned to Ruby. "I know this must be confusing. It's the price of keeping you safe. We're going to help you learn how to be one of us, and eventually Sylva will make up other dangers in her head."

Ruby remembered the hatred she'd seen in Sylva's eyes. She tried not to let her doubt show on her face, or her growing questions about the extent to which she'd traded one prison for another.

It was hard to figure out which questions to ask first. "Access rights to what?"

Fox paused a moment, as if he didn't quite know the answer. "Places and information," he said finally, an answer with no real information in it at all. But his voice and his look were warm enough that Ruby chose not to push him on it yet. "What you're saying is I'm stuck here, doing what I'm told, just like I was stuck there."

"Everybody does what they're told," Fox said.

"You don't. You came and got me."

He laughed. "And you sang 'The Owl's Song' and stood up to Ix."

Dayn simply said, "You're both crazy."

"You wanted to be here, didn't you?" Ani asked.

Ruby nodded. "With all my heart." Except that she'd expected to get here with her friends, at least with Onor and Marcelle. She gave up on understanding anything more until her belly was full. As she finished eating her soup, she watched Ani eat, too, and wondered if she would become a friend. Ani's skin glowed so close to black that she looked almost like metal in certain lights. Her high cheekbones barely showed in a round face with a wide, animated mouth, and she watched people closely. She'd done that all morning, enough for Ruby to notice it.

Besides Onor and Marcelle, Ruby didn't really have anyone she considered a true friend. But she'd apparently be spending time with all of these people, and maybe Ani and Dayn would be like Onor and Marcelle. The thought startled her. She closed her eyes for a moment and swore to herself that she'd get Onor and Marcelle here. She just had to learn her way around first.

"Are you okay?" Ani asked.

Ruby opened her eyes and looked up. "I'm sorry. I was just thinking about my friends." She cleared her throat. "It's all right. The food was great. Thank you." She told them about Kyle and how his food always tasted a bit better, and that got Dayn and Ani talking about food and let Ruby breathe.

For now, Ruby really wanted Dayn and Ani both gone so she could spend time with Fox. In her daydreams, when he came for her he wasn't distant like this at all; he held her and kissed her and whispered that he was glad to see her. Surely those weren't schoolgirl dreams, and it wasn't coincidence that he came for her only after she became an adult.

Ani stood with her plate and gave Ruby a pointed look. Ruby picked hers up and the two of them went into the small kitchen, the close quarters emphasizing that Ani was even taller than Ruby. "It'll be safer for you to stay away from public places for a little while. Don't go to the common kitchens where we were this morning."

Great. A few weeks ago she'd been warned to avoid private places so the reds wouldn't get her. Now she was supposed to hide. "I'm looking forward to a tour."

Ani looked down at her, her dark hair haloed by overhead light so it looked like a circle around her face. "This is a big change for you. Are you okay?"

"Sure."

Ani looked dubious. "Look, I want to make sure you know how the kitchen works here. Someone will be here all the time for a while, but eventually you might be on your own."

Surely Fox could show her. But maybe Ani was really making time for Fox and Dayn to talk. "I didn't mean to become a problem," Ruby said.

"You're not."

"Seems like you have to be my keeper."

Ani smiled, looking almost shy. "I get to learn that way."

"About what?"

"You. What it's like to live in the gray pods."

Ruby pointed at the small oven and the dish box and the storage. "It looks like home. Except cleaner. What's different here isn't the stuff. It's the people."

Ani started clearing food waste into the recycler and stacking the dishes in the small sink. Her movements were spare and graceful. "How so?"

"I don't see many reds stalking the halls, telling you what to do."

"Peacers," Ani said reflexively.

Ruby couldn't keep her voice as calm as she wanted. "They hurt us, just to keep us doing what they say. Just to show us they can." Ruby ran warm water into the wash side, stopping when she had an inch or two. "They're our enemies. They beat us up, and sometimes we die."

Ani stopped and stared at her. "They just have to keep order. That's their job."

"My friend died after two reds raped her and stabbed her. Another friend almost died because he was . . . well, he was where he wasn't supposed to be." She didn't really want to talk about this since she wasn't sure of Ani at all, but she couldn't help herself. "Owl Paulie's grandson. Reds are awful. Sometimes it's their job to kill some of us."

Ani chewed on her lip, looking uncertain. "You can't mean that."

"I do."

Ani's eyes narrowed and she gave Ruby a long look. "It can't be that bad. People would see. Ix at least would see."

"Ix doesn't care."

"Of course Ix cares. It helped us get you here."

Ruby filed the bit about Ix away for later contemplation. It was a good question. "People don't care. The reds we see—they don't care." She thought about Ben. "I mean most of them. They mostly live there, so maybe the ones on gray aren't people you know. But they're evil."

Ani shook her head. "Not any of us here. We'd know."

"How? How would you know?"

"A lot of my friends are peacers, and they would never hurt anyone. Not unless they deserved it."

Anger made Ruby's words stiff. "What would a gray have to do to deserve it?"

Ani pursed her lips and moved around to Ruby's side, taking the dishes from her to stack in the sanitizer.

"You said you want to learn," Ruby reminded Ani.

An awkward silence ensued. Long enough that the dishes all disappeared into safe places.

When there was absolutely nothing left to do, Ani stood in the doorway and faced Ruby. "I guess . . . I guess I know you're right. But it's no one I know. I'm sure of that."

"I don't see how you can be," Ruby whispered, "but I'm willing to believe it's not you. Or Fox. That's as far as I can get, though."

"You'll understand."

Ruby took a deep breath and let it out slowly. "I can see how living here where everything is clean and everyone is friends with everyone else might make it hard to see cruel things, but that's no excuse not to."

"Maybe so." Ani let out a breath. "But don't think we're all friends here. Maybe you had it better down there where all your enemies wore the same color." With that, she turned around.

Ruby took two deep breaths and shook her arms out. Not the time to be so angry. As much as she loved her anger, that wasn't what she wanted right now. It took a long time before she felt ready to follow Ani into the living room, where Fox and Dayn sat on the couch talking in low tones.

Fox looked up when they came in, his smile broad and his strange blue eyes lighting in welcome. He gestured her over to sit beside him on the couch, and when she did, he held her close with one arm. She tried to relax against him even though unfamiliar twinges of pleasure and anticipation kept her spine rigid and her breath from settling.

Dayn didn't miss a beat in the conversation, although he widened his eyes and produced a wry smile that she wasn't sure how to interpret. Ruby caught the last part of whatever Dayn had been saying: ". . . scheduled to play at the right time. It'll need to be a surprise."

The conversation didn't seem to have anything to do with her directly, so Ruby snuggled down a little closer to Fox. His arm tightened around her waist and he spoke to Dayn. "I want some time alone."

Dayn reproduced the wry grin, directing it at Fox. "Self control."

Fox didn't respond to the jab, but simply said, "Three hours." Ruby didn't doubt for a moment that it was a command. She glanced over at Ani and noted that her face had gone blank, her green eyes shifted toward the wall. So she didn't approve either. Oh, well. Ruby was used to doing things other people didn't approve of.

When the door shut behind Ani and Dayn, Ruby heard the lock click into place. Even though her mouth was almost too dry to speak, she managed to get a few words out. "What's bothering them? Why didn't they want to leave us alone?"

Fox smiled and touched her cheek, the gesture intimate but short. He stood up and stretched. "They're protecting my reputation. There are rumors I brought you here to be my lover."

Didn't he? I mean, not just for that, but she had dreamed of him for so many nights. She'd used the idea of him to keep her studying and beading and worrying. She watched him closely, waiting.

Almost nothing frightened her, but she was scared now.

He touched her cheek again, softly, running his finger like fire from the bottom of her ear to the bottom of her chin and then taking it back again. "Do you like the place?"

That wasn't the question she wanted. "Your place? It's a lot like ours down below. I guess it's a little big for just one person."

He smiled and then laughed good-naturedly. "I don't live here. You do. This is why Ani wasn't at breakfast. She was registering this space for you."

Ruby felt her mouth open. "*My* place?"

"Sure. You're a working logistics crew person. You have a job."

She stood still, absorbing.

"Yes, you work for me. For all of logistics, actually, for the people here. You get a place to live. Just like everybody else. Do you like it?"

Of course. She'd have been assigned a hab on gray. Not so big as this, though, not for one. Daria and Kyle were the only people she'd ever met with more than two rooms of their own. She and her mom and two brothers had less room than this.

Except she didn't want it right now.

She couldn't possibly say she wanted to live with him. But she did. Maybe. What did she want? Did she like this place, if it was hers? "Y . . . yes."

She looked around, observing the furniture and the walls and the vid-screens all over again. She'd thought this was Fox's. Or maybe Fox's and Dayn's. She'd thought she'd been sleeping on Fox's bed.

It had seemed too small a place for Fox. For her, huge. Bold.

She swallowed. "Yes. I like it. I do." As she said it she realized it was true. She walked around the room, looking more closely at the soft, unstained couch, the clever metal table in front of it, simple but with lockable drawers for storage, the blank walls she'd be able to decorate or fill with bins like the ones in Daria's beading room.

Even while she circled and looked, Fox was heat in the middle of the room, a constant presence she felt even when her back was turned to him. She made a last smaller circle, ending up standing and facing Fox, close enough to hear him breathing. Not touching. She looked up at him. "Thank you. I haven't said that yet. Thank you for coming to get me, for defending me, for this place."

He leaned down and he kissed her, and she lifted her arms up above her head and put them around him, crossing them behind his back and twining her fingers in his hair.

His hands slid down her back, stopping at the small of it and pulling her in so that she felt his hips against hers.

She kissed him and that was all she did. Her world became the kiss, everything, the rough wet of his tongue, the feel of his body, the way he lightened her and heated her just by being there and so close.

Better than her dreams.

She had never slept with a man, never actually seen lovemaking, but there was no hesitation at all as she led Fox to her bed.

TWENTY-SIX
CALISTHENICS

Onor and Penny worked their way through a closed transport station, degreasing and checking seams in the walls. Empty, the station felt huge and full of echo and extra air. The ghosts of activity seemed to be ready to spring to action at any moment. A small, round floor bot circled itself into Onor's right ankle. He grunted. Even though the bot's sides were designed to be soft, he was going to end up with bruises.

"Step over it," Penny chided him, demonstrating as the poor speechless thing scraped along the wall where Penny stood on tiptoe, running her hand along a seam to check the join. The bot went on, just like it would have whether it hit her or not. If he could figure out how to have the single-minded simplicity of bots, this work would be easy.

This was the third day after his beating. It still hurt when he stretched his arms over his head, but walking no longer sent shooting pains along his spine.

His new quarters had turned out to be a shared bunk situation. It looked and smelled like the orphanage he'd lived in for the five years between his parents' death and early last year. The rows of thin, fabric-walled rooms smelled of old sweat and the feet of previous occupants. Penny lived down the hall. Near her, there was another of the banished students—one who had become an apprentice crèche nurse even though she threw up at the sight of blood, even so little as a scrape on a child's knee. Her name was Nia, and she glanced away every time he entered a room she inhabited.

While he was thinking about Nia's sad face, the bot came back toward him, and he imitated Penny badly, almost losing his balance. At least he missed stepping on the earnest little machine.

Penny laughed. "You'll get it."

The floor bot's scrubbers swooshed, and his own hand slid noisily along the wall.

Penny had turned out to be a reasonable, if taciturn, guide to the small things about his new job. He'd known how to command robots for a long time, but he'd never learned the detailed language of clean-and-repair bots.

Already, there were three models she let him manage, even if the one did keep thrashing him about the ankles.

The first night after the beating, Penny had brought him clean rags to soak his hurts. She'd showed him how to find more rags in the communal kitchen and how to hang them over the stim pot to warm them.

He wouldn't call her a friend, but they had a truce. It kept him from feeling entirely alone.

There were two more sections of wall to go. Behind them, the station did look cleaner. He'd not go so far as to call it clean. At least it smelled better.

He focused down. One thing he'd learned for sure. Penny took pride in what they did. She snarked at him for any sign of slacking or slowing or when he missed a tell that a repair bot should be called. As he slid his cloth up and down the seams, feeling for cracks and testing weld points, he tried to focus completely on the moment.

It was less painful than thinking about anything else.

When they finished, they led the bots back to the facilities lounge and checked them in for the next crew. Jimmy had a soft laugh for Onor. "Ankles still bothering you?"

"Not so much today."

Jimmy laughed again, more genuinely. "Penny says you might feel up to joining us after work today. Bruises and scrapes better?"

Onor drew in a sharp breath. He hadn't told Jimmy anything about being beaten. His face hadn't been marked and he'd done a good job of walking normally the first few days even though his side felt like fire with every step.

Jimmy shook his head. "You didn't think there are secrets here, did you?"

Jimmy hadn't been one of the people who beat him up. "No, sir."

"Don't *sir* me."

Onor nodded.

"Wash up. Ten minutes. By the back door."

Ten minutes felt like twenty. Penny passed him by. The rest of the shift passed him, too.

Finally Jimmy walked out and said, "Follow me," low, almost a whisper. He didn't slow down to see if Onor was following, but Onor kept close.

They walked past the lower entrances to the water reclamation plant toward the trash dump. Horror stories told after lights out suggested to the very young that the trash might grow enough to fill the inside of the ship so that whenever the *Fire* reached its next destination, there would be no people left. Only trash. If Ruby was right, and they were really almost home, the garbage would finally get dumped when the *Fire* slowed.

He wrinkled his nose at the stink of the chemicals that fixed the trash in place and held the dangers in the pile tight inside. Toxins and mistakes and anything that carried illness that had killed anyone on the ship ended up here; everything else was composted or taken back to the most elemental substance possible and reused.

Rumor had it that the trash here was occasionally taken to the empty A-pod and that when they got home and the skin of the *Fire* was pulled away, there would be a whole pod to cut loose and toss into an orbit that would dete-riorate into a sun somewhere. Of course, rumors also placed the bodies of Lila Red and her armies there.

Past the dump, Jimmy turned left, and they stepped through a dogged hatch into a dimly lit space. The empty floor continued as far as Onor's eyes could see before it faded into darkness. Above them, pipes of a hundred widths and colors and markings tangled neatly across the ceiling.

They'd come in under the park. He had been here a few times, in his old pod. Conroy had taken him to show him the lines that carried the grey water from the orchards and the food gardens back to the reclamation plant. This was the outer skin of the inhabited pods; below his feet there was only cargo.

Columns and poles held the pipes up here and there. Figures leaned against them, watching him come in beside Jimmy.

He swallowed, his mouth dry and his heart fast. If they were here to beat him, he would die.

He had always thought that only the reds killed grays, maybe at the direc-tion of the blues or whatever cursed group held power. But here, he felt the danger of his own fellows deep in his gut.

Jimmy did whisper this time. "Relax."

"Why am I here?" Onor whispered back.

"To see if you are one of us."

The man with the split lip stepped out of a shadow and stood in front of Onor.

Onor stopped.

Beside him, Jimmy stopped.

At first, the split-lip man said nothing. He watched Onor's face closely.

When he did speak, his voice was flat and unemotional. "You did not report us."

"No."

"Why?"

This was the trap. Part of the truth had been so they wouldn't beat him again, but that wasn't the answer to this question. "Because there must be some secrets."

"Do you wonder why we beat you?"

Onor licked his lip. "I don't know why you're here. Why I'm here."

"You don't need to know that yet. But you can begin to learn. Will you promise to keep all that we say and do close to your heart? To keep it so close that you do not speak to Marcelle or Ruby or anyone else you know about it?"

"Ruby? Is she okay?"

"You don't care about Ruby right now."

Onor swallowed. They knew more about him than he did about them. He didn't even know the split-lip man's name. Something hot gurgled and hissed through one of the pipes above him and steam escaped from a vent. "I promise."

"Then we will show you a little bit. Follow me."

"What would have happened if I didn't promise?" he asked, feeling immediately foolish for asking.

"We might have let you go back home and sleep."

He didn't think so.

A whistle stopped the conversation, and Jimmy led him to a gathering of about twenty people that centered around a tall man who stood with his back to them as they came up.

Conroy.

Onor didn't need to see his face to know him.

Other bodies pressed in from behind, and finally nearly fifty people had gathered, the whole group centered on Conroy. He nodded at the group, a quick glance. His eyes never fell on Onor. "Ten laps. Go."

There were thirty or so men and fifteen or so women, old and young, but all dirty and wearing gray. As one, they stepped out, settling on a pace that would push the slowest and warm up the fastest. Onor went with them, swept into a tide of running bodies. He had not tried to run since the day he came here, and one of his ribs suggested the idea wasn't good. He held his side but kept up, the pace relentless.

So many feet produced a soft thunder. There would be no one to hear it here.

Part way through the second lap, Conroy came up beside him.

Onor's breath had already grown too labored for him to talk and keep the pace, but Conroy was in no such trouble. "Recovered from your welcoming?"

"Yes." He wanted to know how Conroy knew about the beating, but a full sentence was too much to say.

"I transferred here."

"Rec" . . . pant . . . "cla" . . . pant . . . "mation?" Onor managed to grunt out.

"Yes." Conroy said. "But don't get your hopes up. I'm only junior."

"Why?" They rounded a corner and started on the third lap. The space under the park felt bigger than the available walking space in the park. Of course, that wasn't true, but he'd never gone so fast and been so tired all at once.

"You're here." Conroy's strides came easy to him. "Don't ask about more now. Just do this. Run and work out every day. If you need me, find me in the plant. But there is no help for your sentence. Not now. So just do it well. When it's time for you to know more, we'll tell you."

And then he was gone, and Onor was alone to finish the last half of the last lap, the pain in his side sharp. But he knew this was no place to cry out. He held his side and focused on his steps and kept his world small and tight.

Conroy hadn't sounded upset about the beating. But he had come here for Onor. He had been very clear about that.

TWENTY-SEVEN

THE MORNING AFTER

Ruby woke with the memory of Fox's body imprinted in hers, the feel of his shoulder, the curve of his hip. His weight on top of her, light, part of it held by his hands and knees on the bed. The heat of him. She recalled the way his eyelashes looked in the pale light he'd set for them.

His smell permeated her skin even though he had left her. She glanced at her chrono. It had been longer than she'd thought. She'd slept forever, as if taking Fox had drained all of the fear and anxiety from her and filled her entirely.

She stretched, momentarily languid. Everything was different now. It would always be different. Possibilities beat through her blood, driving her out of bed.

There would be someone waiting for her. Fox had told her that Ani or Dayn or both would be with her all the time, even here.

She dressed and cleaned up, washing little enough that she still smelled of him, and of sex. She would see him at the studio in just a few hours, and maybe she would be able to hold him again.

Ruby found Ani sitting and sipping stim on the living room couch with the lights still down.

A pot of stim sat warming in the kitchen—her kitchen—and she screwed the lid free and poured some into her cup. She sat on the opposite end of the couch, crossing her legs, both more vulnerable and older than she had ever felt before. She wanted to blurt out about Fox, to tell Ani that she'd slept with him, that she was a woman and that a man loved her. Because that seemed like something a girl would do, she didn't do it. "Good morning, Ani."

Ani looked worried. "I was about to wake you. We have to be at the studio in an hour, and you'll want to eat."

"Did anything else happen? With Ellis or Sylva?"

"No." Ani sipped at her stim, the cup now half empty. "No, not at all. I think Fox has them cowed for now. You're the talk everywhere. A curiosity. The rough and dirty girl from the far reaches come to make good. Most of them are rooting for you."

"Them?"

"The people who live here. Peacers, entertainers, project managers, technology people, doctors. Like you have, only mostly knowing a little more."

"We don't have tech people," Ruby mused.

Ani shrugged. "Maybe you do but you don't recognize them. You fixed robots, right?"

"That's mechanics. Putting broken parts back on, cleaning them, making them do tests to prove they can obey."

"What do you do when they don't obey?"

"We dock 'em in storage bays until somebody fixes them."

"Anyway, the techs and everybody else are talking about you. I can't decide whether to take you out all dressed up to show you off, or to grub you down so you stay interesting."

"Don't I get to choose?" Ruby asked.

"What would you choose?"

Ruby closed her eyes and pictured herself walking out with her hair a mess and looking like a robot girl.

She didn't like it.

"Let's dress me up."

"I brought some things that will help. Follow me." Ani grabbed a bag Ruby hadn't noticed from the floor and led Ruby into the small second bedroom. Ani pulled out earrings and a necklace. Blue and gray strands of something flexible and shiny that occasionally met and twined through large red beads. She laid them across Ruby's palm.

The jewelry had better materials than she had ever worked with, each bead uniform in size, the colors bright. "They're beautiful."

"Put them on."

She did, running to the privy to see how they looked. "I love them. How can I thank you?"

"You being here thanks me. Now, come on back."

Next, Ani produced three blue shirts with cleverly cut and stitched necklines. The first was simple, the second had little cuffs at the sleeves, and the third had beadwork that must have taken hours. Not the blue and gray and red pattern of the jewelry, but white and yellow that showed prettily against the deep blue shirt. Ruby stared at the three shirts, then clutched up the simplest one. "This'll go the best with the necklace."

"Take them all. You'll have use for them all."

"Really?"

"They're for you. They wouldn't fit me."

Ruby could count the number of times she'd had a new shirt—brand-new and never worn by anybody—on one hand. Now she had three of them. "Thank you."

Ani took out a small box. "There's one more thing."

"This is too much."

Ani grinned widely, looking impish. "It was easy to talk people into helping."

Ruby took the box but looked at Ani before she opened it. "Are you afraid? Of going home? To Adiamo?"

"Terrified."

Her eyes weren't terrified at all. "And excited?"

"Yes."

"Tell me what you know?" Ruby pressed.

"Open the box."

She did. Inside, she found a pair of wooden hair clips with silver suns and moons in them. Wood for this kind of project was unimaginable. Biomass was recycled. Daria had tried to make her hair clips once, only of metal and beads. They had fallen out of her hair no matter how she secured them. These lay light on her palm and the clasps looked sturdy. "I've never had a pair so nice."

Ani looked pleased. "Neither have I. Lanie gave them to me for you. Now let's change and clean you up."

"I had a shower."

"Okay—but you still need some help." When Ruby frowned, Ani said, "Trust me."

"Okay. You have to tell me what you know about Adiamo."

Ani laughed, leading Ruby into the privy and picking up the brush. "I played the game. We all did. You have it too, right?"

"It's not a game. It's home. It's where we're going right now."

"Shhh . . . I know." Ani was so tall she didn't have to stand on tiptoe to reach the top of Ruby's head for a tangle. "Hold still! Look, what did they tell you? What do you know?"

"We had the game. That's all."

Ani frowned. "Wow. That seems . . . I don't know. Maybe people thought you didn't want to know."

How could Ani be so naïve? "Look, they—you—don't teach us anything you don't think we need to know."

Ani swallowed and looked angry, but her voice toward Ruby was softer. "We have histories. Classes about where we came from. Of course, it's been a long time here, but longer there. Who knows what Adiamo is like now?"

"Wait, what?"

Ani carefully placed one of the clips in Ruby's hair and stood back, her head cocked. "I don't understand the math. Time is different for the people standing still—living on Adiamo—than it is for us. More time has passed for them than for us. So we've had over four hundred years in flight, but they've been going on for a lot longer." She took the clasp back out, brushed at Ruby's hair again, and replaced the clip. "Fox thinks they'll be dead by the time we get home, and Dayn thinks they'll have really fast ships. Now, turn around."

Ruby turned, slower than her spinning thoughts. "What do you think?"

"We need them to be alive. The *Fire*'s falling apart. So that's what I think. That it'll be okay."

"Why does Fox think they'll be dead?"

"Maybe he's just teasing. No, don't look yet. Let me get this one right."

"Okay." Ruby kept her head down. Ani was wearing better shoes than Ruby had on, lace-up shoes that looked like they fit her, and they even had a tiny heel. They made Ruby's boots look old and clumsy. She shouldn't be worrying about boots. Not when they might all die, or their home people might all be dead. Or whatever. Shoes were easier to think about. She sighed.

"What's the matter?"

"Nothing."

"Well, think about how pretty you are. Here, look."

Now she did look older, and pretty. Her clothes looked sophisticated, all except her boots. "Thank you." She also looked clean. The smooth fabric still felt strange against her skin, and the woman in the mirror had her features and her red hair, but couldn't really be her. "I feel . . . different." She stared a moment longer, recognizing the source of her unease. She looked like her mother. She didn't want to become Suri, using sex to gain favors and safety.

But that wasn't why she slept with Fox. That was a thank-you, not a please.

Ani's words made it sound almost like she'd heard Ruby's thoughts. "Being knock-out beautiful will help you get what you need. That's just how people work." Ani picked up the empty boxes and recycled them.

"What about you?"

Ani glanced down at her shirt, which was clean and plain. "I look fine. We'll be late."

"Can you do my hair with one clip? In the back?"

"It might not look as good."

"Can we try it?"

It did look fine, and so Ruby brushed back Ani's hair and fastened the other clip into it.

Ani looked pleased. "Now can we go?"

"Of course."

Ruby grabbed up her journal even though it hadn't proven to work for anything except her own notes here. As she followed Ani through the corridors, she again noticed the woman's grace. She moved even more sinuously that Suri did, and she seemed to do it without thinking about it.

Ruby paid careful attention to the turns they took as they went from corridors of habs through corridors of small rooms where people worked and came back to Fox's studio. Her feet lightened as they neared the door, and she felt a smile on her face even though she hadn't asked it to grow there.

Maybe this was what Carolyne felt for Jay or Lya for Hugh. Just coming into physical proximity excited her nerves and made her feel like dancing or singing. Good thing, since she was likely to be singing soon. Hopefully the headsets wouldn't mess up her hair.

Ani opened the door for her and said, "Good luck. I've got to go to work myself, but I'll be back for you at the end of the day."

Ruby pursed her lips. She'd been hoping Fox would come home with her. Well, she'd have all day to make sure he wanted to, and she would use what she had. She touched her fingers to the smooth hard surface of the hair clip. "Thank you."

Ani leaned in and gave her a quick hug.

As she walked into the studio, Ruby forgot Ani and the hug. She had expected to see Fox and maybe Dayn and the long empty room.

Instead, every chair was full of blue-clad people wearing headphones, a few speaking softly to one another. It took her a while to spot Fox standing near the far end, leaning over a woman with glistening, dark braids that hung below her waist.

Fox stood really close to the woman, his hand resting lightly on her shoulder. Whoever she was, she made Ruby feel drab even in her new clothes.

Fox noticed Ruby when she was only a few meters from him, his smile wide and welcoming. "You look beautiful. I've been talking about you." He turned to the braided woman. "This is Jaliet. Jali, meet Ruby."

Jaliet's cheekbones were high and wide, her mouth generous, her eyes dark, with long, light lashes. Blue ribbons had been twisted carefully into her braids and then used to tie them off at the bottom.

Jaliet's eyes traveled up and down Ruby's body twice before stopping on her face and gazing at her, pleased. "You are stunning. I can work with that."

Ruby didn't know quite what to say, or if she should like any woman Fox had been standing so close to.

Fox placed a warm arm around Ruby's waist, pulling her close enough to him that she felt his body heat. "Jali will work with you on how to stand and move, how to dress, and how to speak."

She knew how to do those things, but she kept her mouth shut, willing to wait him out.

Fox glanced up the row of busy people. "I have work to do for a few hours. Jali will keep you in her studio and Dayn will stay with you in case you need anything. Then, when this place clears out for lunch, we'll start our first real recording session." He leaned down and kissed her on her cheek—cool and fast—and then he was talking to someone else and she might as well have become invisible.

As if summoned from a secret door in the air, Dayn appeared at Jali's side, a sly grin on his face. He nodded at Jali. "We'll meet you there."

The braided woman nodded. "It will only be a few moments."

Dayn gave Ruby a little bow and held out a hand. "Shall we?"

Ruby still couldn't decide if she liked Dayn; he always seemed to be making just a bit of fun of her. She didn't take his hand, but she followed him out of the recording room and down the hallway, feeling like a child being herded back to the crèche by keepers. But she paid attention, determined to learn this new level.

She might as well have been walking through a weird dream, full of strangers, while her old friends stood beyond a curtain, unreachable.

It was easy to understand how the people here forgot the grays existed.

She would remember. She would always be a gray deep inside.

TWENTY-EIGHT

HOW ANI GOT HER STRIDE

R uby threw her pajamas into the hamper, wishing for a metal tool to clang into a metal bin. She stared at the barely-mussed bed and shook her head, anger threatening to flip to sadness. She pulled the covers up and frowned, then swore under her breath, cursing Fox and herself at the same time. Why did she expect Fox to slide into her bed every night, and why did it feel so damned cold and empty when he wasn't here?

She hated it. Having Fox was worse than not having him, except she could no longer imagine not having him. Five weeks ago she'd never had a man at all. Damn.

She slid into underwear and a long shirt and stalked into the kitchen to pour a cup of stim. She didn't bother to look into the living room. She already knew Dayn's long, thin form would be there, bundled under her spare couch blanket, head on her spare pillow, arms up over his face to shield his eyes. He always slept like that when he was here, and he was always here when she slept alone.

He came in without her knowing, fell asleep without actually checking on her. Nonetheless, she felt sure that if an army appeared at her door, he would wake up and take them out.

She leaned against the counter and sipped the stim too fast, then cursed. She couldn't burn her mouth, not now. Her first recording came out today, and there was a chance she'd be asked to sing "Gray Matters" live.

Dayn wandered into the kitchen, rumple-shirted, raising an eyebrow at her naked legs. "Don't you ever wake up in a good mood?"

"Only when you're not here."

Dayn reached around to pour his own cup and stood a little too close. "What does Fox have that women love so much? That's what I want to know."

Ruby ignored him, staring at the day's news vid. The story flipped from a video showing a sludgy breakdown in one of the recycling plants to a picture of her. She smiled out of the screen, tilting her head.

She nearly dropped her cup.

Two days ago, Jali told her to pose as if there was a camera in the room. Jali had driven her to exaggerate until Ruby's cheeks had turned bright red

172

with embarrassment. She'd been glad there was no camera, but apparently there had been, and she was hot in the face again as she watched herself preen. She looked better than she'd ever seen herself, and sexy, and she liked it and didn't like it all at once.

Dayn gave a low whistle. She frowned, keeping her eyes glued to the picture of herself on the screen.

Fox's voice spoke over the image of Ruby as it kept changing perspective. "This is Fox Winter, reminding you that tonight is the release you've all been waiting for. Ruby Martin with her new breakout song, "Gray Matters." Yes, that's right, the gray woman who came up to sing for us. Her voice is as beautiful as her figure. I promise. Listen in to the entertainment hour right after dinner tonight."

The vid slipped to a picture of a sun and planets, and someone else started talking up a class in the orbital mechanics of the Adiamo system, but Ruby still saw her face burned onto the screen.

Dayn watched her with an amused look on his face. "That's probably where he was. Doing something special for you."

She frowned at him and didn't respond, still shocked at the idea of being on the screen.

Dayn shook his head and left her, settling on the couch and staring intently at his journal.

She swallowed and took another sip. Fox could have told her instead of just not showing up, but she wasn't going to complain to Dayn. Instead, she paced and ate fruit and paced some more. What would happen if people didn't like her? They'd recorded the song over and over, and Fox had made her work with two different voice teachers. Mala had taught her how to make her voice sound big, so people could hear it from farther away than she was used to, and Henri had worked with her to coax out long, low notes she hadn't known she could sing.

She refilled her stim cup even though she usually only drank one. She'd written "Gray Matters," and Fox had gone over the words twice. She wrote it to tell a little of her story to the people here.

She wished it would play on the gray levels. She wanted Onor and Marcelle to hear it on their journals. Music that passed between had to be approved, though, and Fox had shook his head and said, "No way," when she'd asked.

She paced, nervous. What if no one liked her song? What if it made Sylva chase her down? Her stomach was weaker than it had ever been before a performance, her hands clammy.

The door opened and Fox stuck his head in. "Did you see it?"

She set her cup down and went over to him, no longer angry. "Thank you."

"You looked good. Even Jali said so."

"Jali never says anything nice."

Fox gave Ruby a faint glare. "Of course she does."

"She's jealous, you know."

He grinned. "Nah. Not at all. She gets dates when she wants them. She almost had a kid with her last one, Eric something or other."

Ruby kissed him. "But she left him for you."

He frowned at her. "Don't you be jealous." She blocked his access to the kitchen.

He waved her sideways.

She gave him a kiss before relenting and making room for him to come in. "Stim?"

"Sure."

She gave him the sexiest glance she could manage. "I missed you last night."

"You needed to sleep. We have a busy day."

"The release isn't until dinner."

Dayn came in and deposited his cup in the sink. "I'm heading out before the flirting around here chokes me."

After he left, Ruby and Fox both burst out laughing. Ruby pressed her body close to Fox's, but he pushed her gently away. "I'm taking you to a class."

"What? Today?" She grinned at him. "I heard there's one on orbital mechanics." She lowered her eyes and looked at him through her lashes, daring him to come near. Sometimes he toyed with her, knowing how much she wanted his touch and withholding it even though he wanted hers as much. Eventually he laughed and stepped over and held her in his arms.

She took in a deep breath, breathing him into her, feeling connected. After three breaths like that, long and slow on the last exhale, she felt more grounded.

"Did Jali teach you that?" Fox asked.

"What? Belly breathing?"

"Yes."

"My very first voice teacher made me learn to breathe. She said it's a way for me to straighten my spine."

He shook his head, amused. "You've got plenty of spine. Today, I want you to be seen. This is a popular class. Part stretching, part martial arts. Jali has been pestering me about getting you started—she swears it will make you more graceful." He picked up her chin so they were looking right at each other. "Besides, I always make my favorite artists try something fresh on scary days. Otherwise, you'll obsess."

She pushed at him playfully. "I won't."

"What were you thinking about before I came in?"

"You."

He pulled her close to him and kissed the back of her neck. "Go change into something comfortable. Something you can move in."

This was a good sign. She hadn't been anywhere since she got here except Jali's and Fox's studios, through the corridors, or to the tiny gym two habs down. Something entirely new made her light and bouncy on her feet.

As soon as she'd changed, she came out and grinned at Fox. "Lead on."

Their destination turned out to be a modified storage hold that she figured hung between pods. Maybe even between levels. Here and whatever was inward of here. The large room was mostly empty, with mirrors all along one side and a few locked waist-high bins on the other side. Handholds on the walls indicated the room didn't always have the same gravity. It smelled clean, and the air was a little chill.

Ani and Dayn were there, along with most of the people she'd met in the corridors that first day. She looked for Jali but didn't see her. There must be fifty people, and a few were still coming in. The mirror wall made it hard to count.

Fox whispered, "I'll come back for you," and turned. Ruby frowned at his retreating back.

She heard her name called and stepped carefully around people sitting and streching until she reached Ani. The floor gave disturbingly under her feet. The quiet talk that wreathed the full room sounded anticipatory. She didn't remember any group exercise sessions at home that didn't feel forced. She'd always tried to find excuses to get out of them so that she could get in her mandatory workouts solo, running or lifting weights.

Ani grinned at her. "Don't look so grumpy. He'll be back. He's always like this the day something he cares about happens."

"Yeah, so what? He abandons his girlfriends?" She hated the words as soon as they were out of her mouth; they were weak words. "So tell me about this?" Ruby asked.

Ani pointed at a door in the far wall, which was opening. "No time. You'll have to learn as we go."

A tall man who appeared to be all muscle and seriousness, with dark hair and dark eyes, came through the door. He wore a loose, flowing outfit with sleeves just past the elbow. His feet were bare. The dark cloth clung to his contours, showing off clear demarcations between muscle groups.

The room quieted instantly, all attention going to the man. "Good morning," he called out, his voice loud, almost a bark. A ritual.

"Good morning, KJ," everyone replied in unison. Another ritual.

Ruby felt awkward for not knowing the cue.

As KJ walked from the door to the front by the mirrored wall, he glanced around the room in a single, graceful sweep. Ruby felt sure he noted her presence even though he didn't slow down as his eyes raked across her.

He stood with his feet squared loosely under his shoulders and his knees ever so slightly bent, arms relaxed at his side. His chin was so straight that she'd have bet he could balance a cup of water on his head.

The rest of the class stood similarly.

Ruby did her best to imitate them.

KJ's arms rose above his head and met, palm to palm, and he stretched high, looking relentlessly forward while he appeared to be gaining height.

She did the same, a full half step behind the class. Maybe more.

He leaned forward, the movement fluid, one leg staying on the ground and the other rising up behind him.

His balance was perfect.

Ani breathed a little harder but held the pose exactly.

Ruby bobbled.

KJ swung the high leg from behind him down and brought it up in front of him, changing his center of gravity.

Ruby followed so slowly that she missed the next change completely.

So it went, Ruby a touch behind in every scripted move, a slide from side to side, a step, swivel, step, hold, and more. At one point, she gasped in surprise, realizing that Jali had been teaching her some of these moves in her private studio.

She missed a whole turn and faced KJ while everyone else faced away from her. Her cheeks flushed hot and she turned back as fast as she could.

Ani whispered to her, "Watch my breath."

Ruby tried, and missed another beat.

"Start where I am," Ani urged.

Stretch, twist, turn, stop, lie down, stretch the right leg over the body and to the floor, do the same with the left, roll onto stomach, push up . . .

Sweat trickled down her back.

She was going to have to redo her hair before the opening of her song. That was the last thought she had that wasn't about following and breathing and staying with the class.

At some point, music seeped into the room, informing the rhythm of movement. It helped her immensely.

She almost caught up, a few of the transitions feeling almost natural.

The music began to rise and speed up. KJ's movements matched it.

The students all leaned forward, balanced on one foot, the other foot out behind them, arms out to either side, head up.

She overbalanced and almost fell on her face.

She stood while the others held a pose, perfectly and irritatingly still, that brought their backs horizontal to the ground.

She glanced at KJ, hoping he was looking the other way.

His eyes met hers, full of suppressed laughter, which was the last thing she'd expected to notice on his face. He mouthed the words, "You're doing well."

Without thinking, she stuck her tongue out at him, a silent response to his silent words.

He grinned, but didn't bobble at all.

She turned away, afraid she'd get lost in belly laughter and break the concentration of the entire class.

Before she could resume the one-footed pose, KJ clapped loudly. Everyone else stood. The music stopped.

He walked out of the room the same way he had come in. If he had broken a sweat, she couldn't tell. This time he didn't look over his shoulder or look across the room at all, and Ruby had the absurd thought that maybe he didn't want to meet her eyes in case he laughed out loud.

As soon as the door closed behind him, people began drifting toward the other doors, conversing quietly.

Ani turned to Ruby. "Wasn't that wonderful?"

Ruby grinned. "Yeah. It was. Tell me about KJ?"

"What about him?"

"I haven't seen him before. Or heard of him. He's interesting."

Ani laughed, her voice brittle. "Don't break your heart on him. He doesn't like women."

"He likes men?"

Ani shook her head. "I don't know. But he doesn't like women. Or at least he doesn't have any. Give it up."

"Hey! I'm with Fox."

A dark look passed momentarily over Ani's face, but she followed it with a broad smile. "I'll tell you what I know. This is what KJ does. Like you sing and Fox records and markets and Dayn takes care of Fox. Like I manage the flow of food from garden to table. KJ teaches movement. And he's very, very good at it."

"I never saw him before."

"We don't much. Not outside of class. I've maybe talked to him two or three times in my whole life."

"But you'd like to, wouldn't you?"

Ani lowered her eyes and looked away, momentarily more vulnerable than Ruby had ever seen her. "Me and half the rest of the women here. He's beautiful."

Ruby felt oddly disappointed. "How often does he teach this?"

"Four times a day." They sidestepped three women who had stopped to talk almost directly in the doorway.

Wow. "How does he have the energy for four times a day?"

"This is what he does."

They were in the corridor now. Someone bumped Ruby from behind, pushing a little, jostling her into Ani. Hot, spicy breath whispered into Ruby's ear. "Whore." The word had spilled out of a slender woman with short brown hair teased up into spikes. Just the one word and she was past them, walking with meaning.

"Bitch!" Ani called after her, the word meant to carry, to label rather than challenge. More like acknowledgment.

"What'd she call me?" Ruby muttered, off balance. Although she was being watched over as if she might break or be stolen any moment, she hadn't seen any fighting on this level. Everything looked like love and respect and a darned good time for all. "Who was that?"

"Don't worry about it."

"Who was that?"

"Chance. One of Fox's old girlfriends."

One of? No wonder she hadn't liked the woman. Ruby clamped her mouth shut, not wanting to destroy the glow of the exercise or say anything bad today, when her first song here was coming out and it mattered whether people liked her. She should think about that now, focus on her debut.

TWENTY-NINE

JOEL

Onor ran. Conroy ran beside him. Onor's breath sounded louder and more desperate than his teacher's, but only by a little. He glanced at Conroy, hoping he was nearly ready for a break. Only small bits of sweat brightened Conroy's face, and his strides fell precisely, just fast enough to keep Onor a little ahead of the pace he liked.

Sometimes the split-lipped man, Aric, led the night's work. On Aric's nights they fought each other barehanded, back and forth across the vast floor until they were almost all bruised. On Conroy's nights, they ran a lot, climbed the walls using the handholds, and lined up and raced each other until Onor's breath made fire in his chest and his thighs burned.

This was Conroy's night; there would be no fighting.

Maybe there would be no rest either. They rounded the whole floor again and again.

Onor's legs turned soft and hot.

Conroy and Onor lapped Penny for a second time, and finally Conroy put up his hands and slowed to a walk. As he did, he leaned over to Onor and said, "Someone important is going visit us tonight. Listen well."

The slower pace snaked through the group unevenly, a few stragglers still running here and there until they realized they could stop.

Conroy led them in a chain through two or three more circles until they were gathered near the middle and their breath had lost its ragged edge. An overhead light threw a pale, yellowish cast across sweaty faces.

"Very good," he said. "Now form lines."

They did, nine lines of about six people each. They sprinted from side to side, catcalling to each other.

The last relay racer started back, and Onor readied himself, one leg bent, his body leaning forward. When his teammate tagged him, he took off, going all out, reaching for longer strides. By the time he touched the far wall and returned, his lungs ached and his labored breathing drowned all but the closest sounds.

After three relays, Conroy drove them through sit-ups and push-ups.

Then he had them all gather in a circle. He said, "You did well, tonight. I'm glad, because you've been watched this practice by someone who matters very much to us."

The others seemed to know what would be happening. Onor felt content to sit, so glad to be able to stop moving he didn't actually care what was coming next. All of the long muscles in his legs burned, and his lungs burned even harder.

Before he felt entirely rested, a man stepped silently out of the shadows. He stood in a spot too dark for Onor to really see his features, but he walked with power. Like Conroy, only more so. He wasn't as big as Conroy, and there was enough light to see that his hair was graying. His uniform might be black or even dark green. It looked cut to fit him and new.

Behind Onor, someone whispered, "Joel," and was shushed.

Conroy confirmed the whisper. "This is Joel. He is part of the power on *The Creative Fire*, a man high in our command. He helps plan the future we'll all share. I only met him myself a few weeks ago, and you should feel trusted and privileged that he has come here."

Joel cleared his throat and spoke slightly louder than Conroy had, his voice meant to be a call for action, a bit of theater. "Thank you for the work you are doing here. I have heard a lot about you, and I'm pleased to meet you."

His diction was perfect and even, a cleaner voice than Onor had ever heard. He seemed to be able to look them all in the eye at once.

"There is a lot that can't be told yet, but I wanted to finally speak in person and see your faces and show you mine. For the next short while we must all work hard together. We must keep our work secret. We will blend the colors of the ship so that some day we can walk wearing red pants and a blue shirt and gray shoes."

He stepped forward into the center of the light and it was clear he wore green. All green. "And a green hat. This is the color of command, and at the moment it is the color I must wear, as you must wear gray. We will all need to work in our places, but we are fighting together to honor each other.

"I believe you are the most important people on the ship. Without you there is no food, no water, no life. Gray is the color of life here, and *The Creative Fire* was designed to honor the work of life rather than to lock it up. I have no interest in apologizing for the choices made by people in the past; my choices are for the future. We can walk together into a good future, a strong future, a fair future."

Joel fell silent. For a moment all that could be heard were the slight sounds of people shifting position and the hums and clicks of the *Fire* herself.

Joel spoke into the quiet he had created. "We will have an exercise soon. It will be real in some ways, and you must be ready, and you must obey Conroy and Aric and your other leaders. I am proud of them, and of you, and happy to see your faces and show you mine. I don't have a date yet, but . . ." a pause, "events are hurrying us up."

Onor wondered if the man meant Ruby and then decided that was silly. All of this had been going on while he and Ruby were still children. Penny had been training most of her life. He settled back to listen.

"We are a mighty army. We are more than you see here. More than one hab and even more than one level. You matter, you give weight to what we do to free you, whether or not we call on you individually. Be vigilant. Be hopeful. Be strong."

A pause. Silence. Breathing.

He continued. "This is a time to be brave. Can you be brave?"

"Yes, yes, yes," chorused voices, and Onor heard his own join in.

"You may hear rumors that people were taken. Those are true. But it is only three people out of hundreds of you—of us—who went to lock up. Stay true. Can you stay true?"

The chorus of yeses came again.

"Can you stay true even if some of you die, if half of you are locked up?"

"Yes, yes, yes."

"Thank you." The man sounded so sincere; Onor believed he meant the thanks.

Then he was gone.

Joel. Onor would remember that name. *Joel.*

THIRTY

THE UNVEILING

There were nearly thirty people in Ruby's hab. Elbows bumped; feet got stepped on; a glass of juice spiked with still spilled on the floor, leaving a sweet, heady scent even after Dayn cleaned it up.

The constant low chatter made Ruby feel like a string had been pulled tight through her temples. The crowd seemed to have weight, to press on her, and she smiled and nodded and shook hands and made small talk, every gesture an attempt to impress. Fox moved beside her, graceful and smooth of speech.

The event had unleashed color throughout the room. The base dress was still always the uniform, but whites and golds and bright yellow lined collars and cuffs, hung around necks, glittered in ears and hair, and decorated belts. Accent colors had shown up at home; she'd made them in the beaded necklaces. But they had never been so bold, and now the whole level felt new again, and strange.

Jali's basic blue uniform had been toned to a soft blue. Bright pink buttons and pink piping along the carefully cut shirt showed off her lithe body. Her black hair hung loose, a dark cloud floating around her face and shoulders, making her look even thinner and more mysterious than usual.

For Ruby, Jali had chosen a dress uniform in the darkest navy permissible, with a white collar, a white belt, and white triangles sewn in the outside of the pant legs. Ruby loved the way the soft material clung to her arms and thighs so that every step felt like walking through a massage. She had chosen only one part of her outfit: the gray, blue, and red beaded necklace she had saved from the trash the day she arrived here.

There was no music. Fox had made that choice, and almost all the choices about food and people.

Her voice teachers, Mala and Henri, were both dressed up in shockingly bright blue matching shirts lined with gold. Mala looked uncomfortable, and Henri so clearly reveled in the attention of various females that Ruby went up to him and whispered in his ear. "You never flirted that much with me."

"Oh, no, how could I?" He glanced slyly at Fox. "But if you want me to?"

"Only if you don't mean it. It's my nerves showing."

She slipped into the kitchen to get a moment's peace. What was she doing? Everything here was so different from home; it made her dizzy. She wanted Marcelle and Onor. She loved it here and she didn't, and nothing was what she'd expected.

She was becoming her mother. Suri would approve of her in this setting. But she'd come here because of Nona, and she needed to remember that.

She downed a glass of water and dodged a serving bot Fox had arranged for. There were only a few minutes left. She could plunge back into the crowd and do this. She could.

She'd started talking stiffly to Jaliet about KJ's class when a soft tone started to rise throughout the room. She stopped. The music stilled her, the moment before her song.

Sweaty shakes descended on her.

She had expected to be excited.

She hated fear.

As Ruby looked around the room, the conversation died away and people started looking back at her. She swallowed.

Jali took her arm and hissed, "Stand up straight. Be brave."

Ruby straightened her back and smiled.

Her own voice spilled into the room, honed by her teachers Mala and Henri, recorded by Fox, who had magicked it into something deeper and more resonant than she would have ever thought possible.

In early memory my mother sings. She tells me
how her mother bent over a broken robot
touching its hard metal joints with her warm hands
twisting a worn bolt so we can fly safe and true.
She must have fixed it. We are here today and
I am singing the women down
to sleep inside the belly of the Fire

In the summer orchard, growth light shines
On the twisted limbs of an orbfruit tree so old
it might have been a seed from home. My father
picked yellow fruit the color of the light

to feed us through all the harvests and
I am singing the strong men down down
to sleep inside the belly of the Fire

At the end of the day, the apprentices
in the crèche dress the children to go home
with tired mothers and fathers and uncles
who have worked all day to keep the Fire
a safe cradle through the dark unknown and
I am singing the parents down
to sleep inside the belly of the Fire

She had crafted two stanzas to describe things the peacers and the logistics crew had never done with their own hands, and the other to end with something they must. The words were hers. Most of the things about the song that had to do with the lilt and timing of them, but Henri had done the score. He had created a long, haunting end that sounded like wind and stars, like the things she imagined lived outside the ship even though she had never seen the universe except in pictures. She had argued with him at first, wanting something angrier, but as she watched people's faces she saw that Henri had been right. The song had become more than she had imagined.

The last note faded.

People came up to her one at a time and congratulated her and asked questions and kissed her on the cheek. They hugged her briefly and commented on her voice. They asked her questions about fixing robots and making the beaded necklaces. One woman engaged her in a long conversation about Owl Paulie and spoke as if she'd known him, which grated right up Ruby's spine and made it hard for her to keep smiling. She did, though.

By the time her hab finally began to empty, her feet had become leaden with pain from standing.

As she watched Dayn usher the last of the guests who weren't part of the song out, she flopped onto the couch and tucked her feet under her. Fox joined her. After the crowded party, the room felt empty even though she and Fox and Dayn and Ani all sat near each other. Henri lounged against a wall; Mala sat on the floor; and Jali perched on the arm of the couch near Fox.

"Play it again?" Henri asked.

Fox complied, and they listened all the way through. Ruby expected the kind of bickering and faultfinding that had accompanied the retakes and the laying down of various sounds across the music. Instead, there was silence, and in the end Henri spoke first, addressing Fox, but looking at Ruby. "You were right. Getting her was a risk worth taking."

Jali reached across Fox's back, leaning into him, placing a hand on Ruby's shoulder. "You did well. Really well."

"No one asked me to sing," Ruby said. She had forgotten about that.

"Yes, they did." Fox said.

"Well? Why didn't I?"

Jali, back in her original position, said, "You did well at the party. You did all that you possibly could."

"I could have sung!" The words blurted out of her. "I can sing for anybody."

Fox kissed her on the temple. "Be patient."

They said that a lot. All of them. *Be patient. We'll let you out into the real world of this level soon. We'll let you out of our sight soon. We'll tell you how things work soon.* Surely she was just tired, and she shouldn't feel this way. Fox loved her, and he was helping make her dreams come true. Some of them anyway.

She set her face into a smile and chose to stay quiet and listen to the rest of the conversation, hoping for any bit of information she could add to the store she was slowly accumulating.

THIRTY-ONE
LESSONS

Onor and Penny and the few others from the barracks who partici-
pated in the late-night training sessions dragged home so late that
he expected to find everyone still asleep the next morning. He
hobbled into the shared galley for a glass of water and found Nia, the other
exiled student, sitting quietly in a corner. Either she hadn't slept or she had
risen very early. Since she usually ignored him he didn't bother to say hello.

To his surprise, she came over and offered him a cup of water. Her voice
sounded soft and hesitant as she asked, "Are you okay?"

"Sure. Tired."

"They make you work this hard to clean?"

He hesitated. "I . . . went for a run."

She took the empty cup from him, refilled it, and handed it to him afresh.
She averted her eyes, and her small hands slid slowly from the cup.

"Thank you."

"You look very tired," she said.

"I am." He looked more closely at her. Circles darkened her cheeks under
her pretty black eyes. "Are you okay here, Nia? How's work?" He was stumbling, sounding awkward. "Can I do anything for you?"

When she looked back at him he saw a little shred of hope in her eyes, like
the tiny pride he'd taken in being able to lap Conroy.

He had been wallowing in himself. Perhaps the reason she had not met
his eyes wasn't about him at all. Even though he still felt depressed, he was
getting better. He didn't wake up at night and stare at the ceiling for hours
anymore. Good enough, at least, to see that someone else might be in pain,
too. He chided himself for being a self-centered bastard and asked her again,
"Can I help you?"

She shook her head.

"Want to just talk? About anything?"

She swallowed and nodded, like the word *yes* was too much to say.

The barracks included a large common room, but it was surely half full of
people. "Would you like to take a walk?" he asked her.

She nodded again. "Can we go to the park? I heard that one of my friends goes there sometimes in the mornings and I'd like to see if she's there."

He felt way too tired and achy to get there easily. "Of course." He set his cup down and grabbed his journal.

Onor led Nia through the corridor outside the barracks. "I haven't seen the park here yet," he mused. "Have you?"

"No, but aren't they all alike?"

"I don't know. I've only seen two."

"Oh."

Nia spoke almost hesitantly. "I almost feel like I shouldn't be going to the park. Like we're not good enough for that now. We're exiles."

"No," he said. "I mean yes, I don't think they'll stop us from going to the park. I haven't seen reds on guard between us and where we used to live. Just between pods."

In the bright light of the corridor Nia looked pale and smeared out. She kept up with him pretty well, trying to stay where she could look at his face. It made him feel like he was taking and constantly retaking a truth test with her, like she was trying like hell to trust him but wasn't quite sure she did, or could.

Eventually he asked her, "What did you leave behind? What were you going to be?"

She laughed bitterly. "Married. In a week. I was going to work in the gardens and harvest and prepare food to store and to eat. I should be chopping tomatoes and washing fruit."

"What's your boyfriend like?"

"Fiancé." She spoke the word like a sigh. "Leff? He's tall and thin. He's handsome in his own way. At least I think so. Some of the girls don't, but that's their loss. He's sweet, too. Kisses me goodnight on the cheek. He asked me to marry him the day before everything broke. He's two years older, so he's already working, back in B. He works in clothes."

"Clothes?"

"Sure. Where do you think your clothes come from? Someone has to make them."

"I just . . . thought it would be robots."

"If robots made them, clothes wouldn't be so scarce." She reached out and touched his uniform shirt, the fingers hesitant and quickly withdrawn. "Besides, they make the red and blue uniforms too. And green ones."

He thought of Joel.

"Anyway, Leff told me to stay away from you and Ruby and everybody. He said you'd cause me trouble."

Onor had a vague memory of Nia studying with them for the last few sessions. "You didn't, did you?"

She shook her head. "I liked how Ruby talked pretty. The way she said it could all be better and we didn't have to let the reds push us around."

He bristled at Nia's tone. "We don't have to."

She was silent for a moment, and then she said, "Look, I know you love Ruby. It's been written on your face from the first time I saw you. But maybe there's never anything more for us than this."

Even though they were close to the park, he stopped her right there in the metal corridor, putting a hand on her slender shoulder. "Meaning you're content never to see Leff again?"

Her eyes widened. "Of course not."

"Or for some red to decide you're cute and he wants to sleep with you?"

She took a step back from him. "They've never done anything like that."

He lowered his voice. "You're lucky. Some of the reds back home beat us, and one of Ruby's friends was raped over and over and she died in Ruby's arms. That's why she's so passionate about all of this. She knows how much it hurts."

Nia stared up at him, keeping her distance. She shook a little.

He was almost whispering now. "Look, I know it feels dangerous." He licked his lips and wished he'd thought to bring water. He couldn't talk about the insurrection army he had just finished running with. "It is dangerous. That's why we're here. But we can't just give up."

"Can we go to the park now?" she asked, her voice small.

"Of course." He should be doing more, convincing her that she had to fight. But before they even made it to the park he had a different thought. Maybe they couldn't all be warriors. Maybe Nia wasn't ready to be anything else. But he wasn't just getting in shape and learning to fight for himself. He was doing it for Nia, too, even if she didn't know how much it mattered. Maybe they were all fighting for Nia, and for the old, and for the babies in the crèche.

Nia was a little ahead of him as they rounded the last corridor into the park. It did look a lot like the one on C, where the sky had literally fallen, except there were a few more trees and they were younger. Stylized symbols of suns and stars and space had been carved into one bench and a simple tree into another.

Nia wanted to walk, so he walked. The exertion warmed his legs up and loosened some of the sore spots. "Tell me about your family?" he asked.

"My mom and dad are both good. Dad works in the common kitchen and Mom's a teacher and they've always done that."

"What do they do when they're not working?"

"Mom likes to dance. She and her sister dance. Dad works out a lot and runs in the park. That's part of why I like coming here." She was craning her head, looking around. Probably looking for her friend. "What about yours?" she asked.

"They're dead. They had an accident, but people say they were killed by the reds."

She looked at him hard, and what he imagined he saw in her eyes was something like, *no wonder you're a revolutionary*. She didn't say that, but she did start walking a little further away from him, as if his wanting them all to be free was a sickness that might rub off on her more than it already had.

He tried to restart the conversation. "Do you have brothers or sisters?"

"No."

"What do you like to do?"

"Do you mean what did I like to do?"

He swallowed. "Sure."

"I liked to grow things. I kept my own garden in the hab. I had basil and oregano and lavender."

She and Kyle would like each other.

She went on. "It's probably all dead."

He wanted to put an arm around her and comfort her, but there was a palpable coolness between them still. He settled for saying, "I hope not."

They went on quietly, Nia still looking for her friend. This was part of the problem. He was prepared to fight for someone like Nia, but she might fight him back. She had listened to Ruby, but only until it cost her. Now she seemed to wish everything were like it had been. "I don't like the work—who wants to just clean all day?" he said. "But now the reds've shown how cruel they are."

"They wouldn't have hurt us without you three leading us into trouble."

"They would still control us."

She walked quietly for a while longer and he thought she was done with the conversation, but then she said, "I was happier before."

"Maybe we should sit down for a minute? Watch for your friend to run by?"

She led him to a bench. "You remind me of my dad. Working out and running until you're too tired."

"It helps me clear my head."

"Dad used to say the same thing."

"What do you do to feel better?" he asked her.

"Nothing. I don't feel better. Some days I don't think I'll ever feel better." She was looking away from him, the light breeze of the park's air circulation system blowing strands of dark hair across her face. After a while she said, "I'll just get used to it. But it feels like I've been thrown away for nothing."

He didn't know what to say. She'd never be strong like the people he ran with under the very same place they were sitting now. Not unless something big changed her, like she got hurt or someone she loved got hurt.

He wanted Ruby, her spitfire and courage and the beauty of her determination.

The roof of the park here was a steady blue with a few fake clouds wandering across it from time to time, as if a wind he couldn't feel blew through the *Fire*. Being with Nia—so much the opposite of Marcelle and Ruby—had taught him more about who he was becoming than he had learned in all the year before.

He jerked as Nia leapt up next to him, waving wildly at a young blond woman jogging toward them in the middle of a wide area of the park path. "Shell, Shell!"

As Nia called her friend, the sheer joy in her voice was so unlike anything Onor had heard from her that it underscored how lonely she must be in their day-to-day barracks existence.

Her friend broke into a crazed grin as she recognized Nia. Onor recognized her from class, a year-mate. She hadn't studied with them in common, but she had been there the day they took the test, watching from near the back of the room. Because he remembered the look on her face that day, he wasn't surprised when the wide grin that had emerged when she saw Nia turned to a grimace when she saw him.

She stopped in front of them.

Nia threw herself into her friend's arms, the two moaning as if their separation had lasted months or years instead of weeks. They eventually detangled one from the other and held each other at arm's length, saying, "How are you?" at exactly the same moment.

Then they both started talking at once, and finally Nia said, "You first."

Shell glanced at Onor then back at Nia, a question clearly written on her face.

Nia glanced at him, and Onor half expected her to ask him to leave. But she managed to give him a pale smile before answering Shell's look. "Onor and I live in the same place. A lot of people live there; one of the lower barracks. I asked him to bring me up to see you, and well, it worked. You're here."

"How come you don't talk to me on your journal?"

"I haven't been able to. Or to get any news. It's like being in lockup, even though I'm at the crèche during the day. But my ID doesn't let me get anything in or out there either, like I was a kid." She sped up, words following words as if they'd been stuck in her throat forever. "They let me go out with Onor today. Not that anyone directly stops you; they just make it clear you shouldn't wander around. I've taken a few short walks, but never this far. There's a lot of robots down there, and I never know if they're watching me. And I'm so tired when I get home."

Onor broke in, asking Shell, "What happened to you? In the reassignment?"

Shell narrowed her eyes. "Nothing except I ended up here. I was studying to work in the water plant and I do. Just a different one." Shell turned back to Nia. "They made it hardest on the fools who followed Ruby."

Nia winced and said, "Have you seen Leff?"

"How? He's not here." Then her voice softened. "Surely they'll let you go back soon. You've gotten permission to get married."

"Before they banned it."

Shell's face hardened. She gave Onor an accusing look, but said nothing.

Onor turned away to let them talk without him.

"Wait," she said. "I have news for you."

Onor turned around, apprehensive.

"Ruby abandoned you. She left you all."

He stiffened. "No." Surely she hadn't.

Shell stopped and looked at him. "I overhead two reds talking. There's more around now, so they must come from the other level. I mean they don't just grow them."

He hadn't seen more reds, but then he spent all his time in the lowest levels of gray.

Shell looked like she was enjoying the uncomfortable way he felt. "They said they heard her sing wherever they come from."

Well, good. He wasn't surprised. He'd been worrying, but he'd have known if she was dead. Surely he would have.

"Her lover came out for her and took her inside."

Onor kept his feet planted. "Fox. I know."

"He lives with her. He's making her into something special. The two reds sounded jealous and a little in awe, like she'd somehow gotten lucky. He must be a big thing there."

Shell was enjoying this far too much.

Onor's mouth tasted bitter. "She hasn't forgotten us. You don't know her. Maybe she can't figure out how to get us in there yet, but she will."

"She's not coming back," Shell said. "Ever."

THIRTY-TWO

A MOMENT OF FREEDOM

Bells started so soft Ruby could barely hear them even though she was awake on the soft bed, ear cocked, naked. The bells grew steadily louder until they engulfed her. She let them keep rising, drawing frustration up her spine with each peal.

She'd asked to choose the alarm settings herself, and Fox had laughed and played five or six choices for her. She had almost no access to the controls for her own house. She could tell the kitchen to start the dishwasher or heat water. Fox, Ani, Dayn, and maybe other people had access, and they directed the systems for her.

The bells rang louder in her ears, as if shaking her awake.

She was alone in her warm bed, but Fox had been beside her until an hour or so ago.

She shouldn't hate the bells. At least she had them. Grays had far fewer voice commands, and they couldn't wake to bells, or the high female-voiced song she had liked, or even the default tones that sounded way too happy for her to stand them.

"I'm awake. Ten minutes."

The room responded, breaking a tone just after it started.

She stood up, naked and still a bit sore and warm from the ways Fox had touched her body the night before. She still smelled of him, too, of sweat and sex and heat. She slid into undergarments and pulled a long sleep shirt over her head. No point in letting Dayn see what she gave to Fox. Dayn had been getting flirty lately.

After she dressed she lay back down and waited for the bells to go off again. She stretched one arm and then the other, one leg and the other, pulled her arms one by one up beside her ears, and arched her back. Her schedule included KJ's class today, and she lay stretching until the bells grew loud enough to force her from bed.

Dayn stood in the kitchen, sipping from a nearly empty cup of stim. He smelled good as she walked past him, and she did her best to keep a body thickness of distance between them. The way he attracted her just by standing around and being insolent stiffened her back. There were women, like her mother, who went from man to man easily. She wasn't going to be one of them.

"What do I do next?" she asked him. "Studio?"

He laughed. "Not my day to keep you. Ani's on her way."

"What if I want to do something no one has a plan for?"

"You have no idea how lucky you are."

Sure she did. She was alive. "You make too many choices for me."

Dayn gestured around the hab. "You could decorate."

"I could have permission to set my own wake-up choices."

He laughed. "Probably a couple of other ways you could develop a spine, too."

She stopped and stared at him, her gaze level and her top teeth worrying her bottom lip. He was right. She was taking this gentle captivity lying down. Some would say that with a sneer and double meaning, and she might have said it that way about anyone else. Her cheeks grew hot. She shouldn't be mad at Fox. She should hate herself instead.

She didn't hate Fox. She didn't.

There was no reason to—he was soft and sweet with her. Damn. She crossed her arms and stood straighter. "All right, Dayn. What do you suggest?"

He shook his head at her. "I'm not that disloyal. But changing your alarm clock's not exactly the defiance I expected you to want."

"You sleep in my living room just because he tells you to."

"I didn't tell you to rebel against Fox." He was laughing at her, but there was an edge in his voice. "Your song sounded like you had a cause, but I'm not so sure. I don't think you really care much about your friends slaving away under your feet."

She grabbed her cup of stim and held onto it tight, biting her tongue and blinking back unexpected tears. Angry ones.

He continued, leaning over her close enough that she could smell the stale stim and sleep on his breath and the soft sweat that beaded his forehead. "As far as I can tell, the only person you love is yourself."

"No," she said, evenly and louder than she meant to.

"Oh, yes." He grinned at her again, clearly having a great time baiting her.

She wanted to yell at him so badly; she could taste the bitter words on her tongue. How did he know who she cared about? He didn't know anything about her or about her friends or about her life. Sure, she'd told them all a few things, but Dayn wasn't gray, and he didn't know what it was like to be afraid. "What do you care enough about to pick a fight over?"

He lost the laughter on his face and in his voice. He gave her a long, rather uncharacteristically somber look before answering. "You. We came for you and fought some people with power for you, and Fox comes almost every night for you, but you're not who I thought you were at all." He was still close, his breath warm on her scalp above her ear. "You're not very brave or very smart or very anything at all. Fox is already getting a little bored of you."

She took a step back from him and then realized what she had done. She set her cup down, then stepped back forward, even closer to him. "You don't have to stay, you know."

"Sure I do. Who's going to tell your hab what to do for you?"

If she'd still had the cup in her hand, she'd have thrown it at him. "I've got class today. I'm going to change."

She didn't let herself cry until she was in the shower, and she managed to stop again during the whisper of time before her water allocation shut off. As she dried the tears and water from her face, her eyes were still red. By the time she'd dressed in loose clothes and pulled her hair back in a band she looked collected.

When she got back out to the kitchen, Ani stood there. She gave Ruby a quizzical look. "What'd you do to Dayn? He laughed on the way out the door and told me to watch you extra closely today."

Ruby kept her voice even as she cut out a protein slice and picked a handful of orbfruit from the fridge. "I just asked him for help, that's all."

"You can trust him," Ani said. "Drink some water. You need to be hydrated for class."

Frustration stopped Ruby's hand midway through its work of putting breakfast on a plate. "Who are you people when you're not with me, and what do you do?" She leaned back, the counter a hard stop just at her waist. "What am I to you anyway?"

Ani let out a long sigh. "Can you just accept that I'm your friend? For now? This talk needs Fox."

Ruby put an orbfruit in her mouth, hoping its sweetness would help her stop sounding bitter. She wasn't really mad at Ani. Ani just happened to be here, now, and her family wasn't, and Ani wasn't Onor or Marcelle, and she wished she knew how they were. She finished her fruit, swallowing hard. "I want to run my own house and I want to be alone from time to time and I want to have at least the freedom I had back home."

Ani nodded, only looking a little surprised. "So what do you want?" Ani asked. "I mean from me, now."

Ruby finished her fruit. "Information. I want to understand what makes this ship tick and what people do and how it's going to be when we get to Adiamo and what Fox wants to change and why Dayn is so pissed off at me."

"I'll tell you what I can on the way to class. Some of those questions aren't mine to answer."

"I heard you the first time."

Ani grimaced. "Don't be mad at me."

"I'm not." Ruby took two deep breaths. Had Dayn really upset her that much? "Sorry. I guess I'm making everyone mad this morning."

"Dayn looked amused."

Great. But Ruby shut up and buckled down to her light breakfast, waiting for Ani to offer up information.

Ani didn't look at her, but looked at the door instead, as if wanting to make sure no one came in.

After the silence had gone on a while, Ruby spoke softly. "At home, Ix can't hear inside our habs. Is that true here, too?"

Ani gave a soft smile. "That's a lie on gray levels, too. But there are rules that keep Ix from passing what it hears inside habs to the peacers. I doubt that still applies if Ix thinks it hears anything really dangerous." She waved a hand at the air, as if the AI were all around them. But that wasn't what she meant at all. "This is your home now. You live here. This is the central logistics level, which is why so many of us are blue. That's the work that gets done here. Out a level—that's the physical work. The *Fire* was designed to be purely that way—for all the body labor to be out there and all the head work and planning to be here, and the command is inward again."

"Wait—they don't teach us this. They don't teach us anything. They even act like the design of the *Fire* is a secret."

"You have the same access that any of us in logistics had as kids. Go study."

Ruby sat back. "What do you mean?"

"Ask your journal. Ask Ix. It'll tell you."

"I hate Ix."

"Ix is the glue on this ship."

"Then Ix is in a unique position to make things fairer by giving up a little more information."

"Ship AI's are controlled by a set of rules they aren't allowed to change. Otherwise they might decide they don't need us."

"But Ix is here to protect us!" Suri had told her that from the time she was a baby.

Ani laughed. "So do you hate Ix or do you like Ix?" She didn't look like she expected an answer, which was a good thing, since Ruby wanted to say she hated Ix, but it had felt like a lie when the same words slipped across her tongue earlier. *Something to think about.*

Ix had helped Fox find her, but it had also helped betray her on test day.

Ani poked her gently. "Look, we've got to go soon. What do you want to know?"

"Command. You said there's a command. That's another level?"

"That's the heart of the *Fire.*"

"Can we go there? Is that the only other level—so there're three? Does it have a color?"

Ani laughed. "No, we can't go there, not easily." She must have seen the look on Ruby's face, since she added, "No, no rules between logistics and workers, like you faced. We can go easier than you got here. Fox went once, when he was about your age. Maybe ten years ago?"

Ruby picked up her plate and put it away. "How did he get there?"

"Someone's daughter thought he was cute." Ani drifted toward the door. KJ hates it when we're late."

"All right. Have you been there? To command?"

Ani laughed. "I'm not very influential."

Ani didn't offer anything else on the way to work out.

Ruby had taken to working near the front of the class, close enough to admire the blue and gold in KJ's eyes and to watch the way he folded the whole class into his very being. A look from him could deepen a stretch, raise a jump, or help a student remember to tighten the top of their thigh to keep from falling out of a one-legged stretch.

Ani stayed near her, and by now they were nearly even, the main difference a bit more grace on Ani's part as they transitioned from stretch to stretch. Ani clearly adored KJ, the look on her face as she watched him showed admiration at least, maybe more. She softened more for KJ than for Fox, although both men clearly attracted her.

At the end of class, KJ didn't walk off like he usually did. He stood, watching the room empty, and Ani stood as well. After the other students had gone, KJ came over to them. His hand fell familiarly on Ani's shoulder, and he asked her, "Do you have a few minutes?"

Ruby stood, slightly stunned that he apparently wanted to talk to Ani and not to her.

"I can find my way home," Ruby blurted out.

Ani bit her lip and gave a meaningful glance at Ruby, as if KJ should intuit that she couldn't be left alone.

"I won't tell Fox."

KJ chose to stay silent, watching.

Ani said, "She needs to be protected."

KJ still said nothing, but his look indicated disapproval for Ani's position.

The longer he was silent, the more indecision took over Ani's face. Ruby could feel how much Ani wanted to stay and be alone with KJ.

KJ had the kind of quiet grace that drew women to him. In spite of that, and in spite of the fact that Ani really did find him attractive and had said so over and over, the tall black woman shook her head.

Ruby interrupted. "Really. I'm a big girl. I can find my own house." She didn't wait. It was the first chance she'd had to walk this level by herself, and she was going to take it. She didn't let herself look back until she passed through the door, sure by the silence that the others had not followed her.

Normally, when they got back to the main level, she and whoever Fox had set to "help" her through class turned left.

Ruby turned right.

No one followed her.

At first it looked very much like the same corridor she should have taken: offices filled with people and interface sets, a mess hall like—but not the same as—the one in which Fox had faced down Ellis. She passed a few knee-high service bots that ignored her completely as they whined and whirred down the hall and a more humanoid bot that reminded her of the one that had fallen through the sky the day she met Fox. She almost expected it to be carrying food to someone, like a servant, but it had a bucket of metals that looked destined for the reuse bin in one hand and a broken chair in the other.

She peered into a long, fecund room that turned out to be an herb and vegetable garden. A few yellowed leaves lay on the floor, wasting without being composted. Water pipes hung from the walls and ceiling, visible. More proof that the *Fire* had never been designed for one level to be separated from the other.

She glanced up, sure that the next level inward, command, hung above her head in the same way that logistics hung above the work spaces she had grown up in. It existed. Onor would want to know, and for the second time that day she wanted to see him so much that the separation was pain.

She turned into a corridor just as a bell rang and people poured into the hallway, going both ways, knotting into groups and chatting with each other. She walked with purpose, pretending she knew where she was going, managing not to flinch at the crowd around her. She'd been in this kind of crowd on this level before, but always with Dayn or Fox or Ani or Jaliet.

A hand fell on her shoulder.

She turned.

Ellis.

Okay. She needed to pretend it was just fine to see him. "Hello, Ellis." Jaunty. Or as jaunty as she could make it.

He looked like he was alone. His blue uniform was perfect, his hair neat and short. He closed a hand over her arm. She had to look down into his eyes. Chances were good she could throw him through the crowd if she had to. But Ellis still radiated power, and people started stepping around them as though he were a familiar fear. "Can I help you?" she asked him.

"Come with me." The hand on her arm tightened.

She pulled away, stumbling into a stranger dressed in red. The man put a hand out to steady her. "Ruby! Ruby Martin!" He looked really happy to see her. "Hey, I love your singing."

"Back off," Ellis said, "I'm talking to her."

"Does she want to talk to you?" The stranger's voice rose enough to catch the attention of a couple of women who had been deep in conversation. They stopped, blocking the people right behind them.

Ruby looked gratefully at the stranger. "Thank you. What's your favorite song?"

Ellis grabbed her arm again.

The two women's eyes grew wide, and they sidled around and disappeared into the crowd.

Her original protector stuttered. "I . . . I like 'The Owl's Song.' The way you did it first, before you got here."

"Really? The sound is cleaner on the one Fox helped me with."

Ellis jerked on her.

Ruby jerked back and turned around to stare at Ellis. "I'm talking to someone here. I'd rather talk to him than to you."

Ellis was staring at the stranger. "Give me your name," he demanded.

The man gave Ruby a plaintive look.

She swallowed and stood on tiptoe, still in Ellis's grip, trying to spot someone else she knew. Anyone. When she turned back, her protector had gone.

She snapped at Ellis. "Let go of me."

"No. Fox promised he'd keep you under control. I see he hasn't succeeded."

"I'm on my way home."

Ellis started walking, not letting go of her, clearly trying to get out of the thinning crowd.

Ruby wanted to kick him and get free. But then she *would* be in trouble.

"I'm here."

Fox's voice, behind her.

Ruby turned, grateful. She jerked free and went to Fox's side. She smiled sweetly back at Ellis. "Nice to see you."

Ellis ignored her, giving Fox a withering look. "The next time I find her wandering around, I'm going to take her, and I'm going to get her into the trouble she deserves."

Fox managed to look calm even though Ruby felt his biceps tense under her fingers. "I keep my word."

"And I'll keep mine." Ellis turned and faded into the crowd. He was short enough to get lost quickly, although Ruby could see the wide swath of distance people made around him for a few moments.

Fox started off in the other direction, pulling Ruby along with him.

It didn't feel very different from Ellis's attempt to jerk her down the corridor.

Fox pulled her close to him and kissed her head. "I know you don't like doing what I say. But that was a close call. Do you understand now?"

She remembered this morning. "I want full rights to my house." She felt a little tease slide into her voice. When he was this close, she could barely control her reaction to him, the smell of him and the way he felt turned her soft. "I want to set my own alarms and control my own doors."

"You don't understand the dangers here yet." His hands roamed her back, a gentling rather than a caress. "I know it felt dangerous on gray, but in the game we're playing, the whole ship is at risk."

"So then tell me more," she whispered into his shoulder.

"When I can. It's not time yet."

"How long?"

"I don't know. Until it's safer."

She hadn't been safe a day in her life. "Maybe until you're tired of me?"

He stopped midcorridor and turned her to face him. "I am not tired of you. I will not become tired of you. You, Ruby Martin, are the most beautiful woman in *The Creative Fire* and I will keep you safe."

She heard the lie in his voice. And again she heard Dayn telling her that Fox was already bored of her. The memory burned in her chest, and she kept walking because that was what Fox expected, but she swore to get away from him before he abandoned her.

THIRTY-THREE

THE LAST BABY

Onor was the first one up, as usual. Even though the ship's temperature was always even, this morning he felt cold. Probably tired. He held his hands in front of the stim as it steeped in the warm water. When it was ready, he poured a cup and took it to the big empty table, meant for ten, and sat down with his journal. Since there was so little to do down here, he'd started reading the news the reds posted to journals every morning. He suspected it was partly lies, but there was fact in it. What crops had been harvested. Who had died in the night, or been born.

Today, there was one baby to report, a girl. The last one on gray for a long time. Even though he did not want children, and had no one to marry, it bothered him this morning.

Maybe because right now, in the big empty kitchen, he felt utterly alone.

Nia had been allowed back to her family two weeks ago.

He ached for Ruby. Nia had known her, but not Penny, not anyone he worked with on the cleaning crew.

He stretched, his back muscles sore from yesterday's work, needing to be warmed before they got sore from today's work. They let him work on his own now; they even sometimes let him take a bot. Today was the second half of a long project to remove old supplies from the medikits and replace them. At least he would be upside, where the ceilings weren't so low and the lights were brighter.

The scrape of hinges alerted him to Penny opening the door and sneaking in, still wearing rumpled sleep clothes. He smiled wearily at her. "Saved you a cup."

She filled her cup and walked around him, sliding under the table on the far side, sitting opposite him. Her lined face looked a bit softer than usual this morning. "I'm sore this morning," she said. Code for we worked hard underground with Aric. They didn't talk about that work here, just about cleaning and about simple things. Or in codes.

"Me, too. I want to go back to reclamation."

"They'll never let you."

"Did you dispose of all of the trash from yesterday?" That was code, too, for *did the old supplies all get saved for us?*

"Mostly."

So she had felt like she needed to deliver some to the recycler like her orders said. It was like that down here, instinct and balance.

Penny was as passionate as a wall; the only real emotion he ever saw on her face was the strange determination that fell over her like a cloak when they and the others followed Conroy or Aric through drills at night. Right now, her eyes focused on a dark blemish on the table, and one hand stroked her cup while the other one curled around the edge of the table.

"How long have you been here?" he asked her.

"On this level or in this barrack?"

"Either." He sipped his stim, knowing from the past that it took the old woman time to gather her thoughts up and prepare them to come out into the world.

It took her so long this time he nearly emptied his cup. He was about to get up and make more when she said, "I was born here. Not in this barrack, but in this place. In this hab. I've never been anywhere else like you have."

"It wasn't my choice."

"Still."

"The ship's the same everywhere."

"Really? Even where your Ruby went?"

"I don't know *that*." He didn't want to talk about Ruby. "Do you have family here?"

"I only had a mother, and she died." She looked up from the table and at him, her face serene. That was how she got through the day, by being even. "Long enough ago that I don't think about her much anymore."

"My mom and dad are dead, too," he offered. "They were killed for . . . disobeying."

"Does that make us alike?"

"It makes me do what I do." Code for work out every night to be one of the people who would help take back *The Creative Fire*.

Penny gave him a measured look. "I've been doing exactly this my whole life. Waiting for change. Be sure you develop patience." She stood up and walked slowly all the way around the table. He watched her progress. Pain showed in her lurching walk and the way she carried one shoulder slightly down. When she got to the kitchen, she picked up the empty stim pot and rinsed it, then reached for the herb pack to start the next pot.

Sitting there, he felt struck by the immensity of it all, by how they were an egg flying through stars, tiny beings inside a small shell inside a big galaxy inside a bigger universe. No matter what choices they made, there were forces that could crush them, and only luck and planning had let them live through so many human lifetimes. It made him get up off his seat and go into the kitchen and reach his arms around Penny from the back, hugging her, and whispering, "Thank you," into her ear.

She stiffened, and when he let her go, she whispered, "For what?"

"Existing."

"I'm a bit happy about that, too."

Two hours later, he handed Penny the perishables from the first kit he'd done—water and syringes of medicine and gel tubes full of energy. She nodded placidly at him as she turned and walked down the corridor. He worked his way quickly through the replacements on his cart, checking the totals for everything against a list that had been sent to his journal.

At the next place, he left the medikit cabinet neat and full, twisted the door shut, and pushed his cart, one wheel clicking as it went.

A door opened just as he walked past it and a familiar voice hissed out, "Onor!" He jerked the cart to a stop, rattling the contents.

"Here."

Onor could barely keep the wide grin off his face long enough to make it into the door. He didn't even mind when The Jackman tugged too hard on his arm helping him inside and stepped on his toe getting the door shut.

A light clicked on, illuminating The Jackman's scruffy beard. His cheekbones were visible.

"Damn. There's less of you. What happened?"

The Jackman grinned and patted his half-sized belly, which still poked out above his belt, although it no longer sagged over it. "Been running. You too. You look like a man."

"Been one awhile."

"Nah. Not so long."

"Too bad you didn't lose your attitude with the weight."

"Too bad you got an attitude."

Onor could feel his face expanding, all grins. They did both look good. "What pod are you in, anyway?" he asked.

The Jackman glanced at the door and pulled Onor back further into the office, where he gestured for Onor to sit on a chair bolted in front of the desk. He settled his still-wide bottom on the surface, his legs hanging over. "I've swept this room, but not the corridor," he explained. "So here's the deal. Me and Marcelle, we're in E-pod. We're doing what you're doing. A bunch of us. Practicing for our day. Also Jinn."

"So how'd you get here?"

"Anybody that knows their way around the maintenance catwalks can move between pods if they have a little oxy. I'm a messenger, sometimes."

"Cool. Is there a message?"

The Jackman laughed. "Always have wanted to run without learning to walk. But I'm proud of you. Conroy says you're doing good, and he trusts you. We flipped to see who went with you. But I do have things to tell you as well as him."

Most of the loneliness from this morning had fled with the sight of just this one face. "Go on. Tell me."

The Jackman leaned forward. "First, tell me about you. I been keeping my ear to the ground, but I wanted to see you for myself."

"I hate my job. Well, mostly." He would miss Penny if he got to go back home. "I'm glad for the workout every night. I'm glad there's more people wanting things to be different. But some say it's been like this, all working out and nothing really happening, like getting ready forever and never being ready. I want to know there's a plan."

"Oh, there's a plan." The Jackman sat up a little straighter. "You and your friends either ruined it or helped it, but you moved it along."

"How is Marcelle?"

"She's good. She's liking exercise like you do, now. Looks better, and she's even getting the kind of attention she always wanted from the men. So I guess nothing like bad news and discipline to make a fighter."

"Marcelle's always been a fighter."

"You're all still kids," The Jackman said, his voice sharp. Then he stopped and took a breath. "Sorry. Not really. But there's plans we've been working on for years, and we don't need another whole mutiny full of people who aren't old enough to understand the cost."

"I lost my parents."

The Jackman stopped a minute and went quiet. But he stayed stubborn. "I told you we've been planning a long time."

Onor tried to imagine what Ruby would say. "And you need our help. You must."

"You sound like Marcelle."

And then Onor couldn't help himself anymore. "Have you seen Ruby? Heard from her?"

"No one down here's seen her. Friends on the logistics level say she's split the place in two. Half the world up there loves her and thinks Fox is the luckiest man in the world for being her lover, and half think it's all a plot."

The Jackman had never liked Ruby. Onor had already known she was with Fox, had sometimes imagined them together in the dark of night when sleep failed him.

The only new information was that some people didn't like her. But that had always been true here, too. So he looked his friend in the face and just asked him, "What do you think?"

"Fox isn't lucky. But maybe we are. She's making more of the people up there curious about us. Bringing them to our side. She sings stuff, like she did down here, only everybody listens."

"Can I hear her? Here, I mean?"

The Jackman looked like he'd just swallowed an unripe orbfruit. "That's part of what I wanted to tell you. Her songs are to be coming down here starting tomorrow. You need to help us get people to listen."

"Did I hear that? You want me to say good things about Ruby?"

"Sure." The Jackman looked miffed, overdoing it a little, as if trying to pretend it didn't bother him at all. "I'm not the boss of this operation. There's people thinking she's making a difference."

"Joel?" Onor asked.

The Jackman laughed. "Not that high up." He looked uncomfortable. "Maybe Ruby's singing is a way to get messages out, to tell people what they need to know. I'm not sure she's doing it on purpose, I kinda think she isn't. But she's got the message we need to get out, the one that says people shouldn't be happy just doing what they're told. We're going to be at Adiamo soon, and whatever happens there will take everybody's attention. We need to change how *Fire*'s run before we lose the time to do it in."

"When do we run out of time? Joel was here, telling us something would happen soon. How soon?"

The Jackman slid off the desk and walked around behind it. "When we tell you. Stay ready. That's what I came to see. If you were ready. I think you are. So just stay that way and be patient. And don't get killed."

Onor swallowed. He'd known all the training was for something big, but The Jackman's words made him a little afraid. He sat up straighter. "I'll be careful."

"And you didn't see me, of course. If anyone asks, you came in here to use the privy."

So the visit was almost over. "You'll like seeing Conroy. He looks good."

"I already did. Go on."

Onor stood up. "Thanks. For stopping by. I needed a friendly face."

The Jackman's voice came out a soft whisper. "Go on, now."

Onor went.

THIRTY-FOUR
HOMECOMING

Ruby stood in the studio, ready to start her first take on "Homecoming." The wires down her cheeks felt like old friends now, she'd worn them for so many days. She glanced at Fox, who stood rather stiffly a seat away from her, his face painted in a frown.

She caught a quick, sardonic grin on Dayn's face. He stood up against the video wall opposite them both, his arms crossed over his chest.

Fox counted down. "Three. Two. One."

The music started.

She bobbed her head to the beat, tapping her right foot softly.

On cue, she launched into the first verse:

> *Long and dark is our night flight*
> *No stars shine inside* Fire's *skin, only*
> *Me and you. And love. We're going*
> *Home*

"Stop!" Fox interrupted her.

She let out a long sigh. "What's wrong now?"

"You're too high. And it should be a touch faster."

Heat flushed her cheeks. "And you hate the song because I didn't write what you wanted me to."

He stared at her.

She didn't blink.

"I brought you here to achieve specific goals."

No kidding. "Did you ever think I might have a few of my own?"

"I understand these people!" He stopped, and when he started again the anger had gone out of his voice, although it still lingered in the set of his jaw. "There is nobody else that can help you like I can. Nobody else can make your voice as good, or get the word out about you the way I can. I'm creating you as a lever. And you know it's for the same things you want. For freedom."

"You want your freedom. Not mine. Or at least, not my people's. You want to run things."

"I'll run them well."

He wasn't even denying it. "You're not the only man on this ship. Nor are you the only person who can operate this equipment. I've heard singers you didn't create."

"But who else do you know who's patient enough to deal with you?"

Fuming, she turned away from him, tapping her foot to try and collect herself. She didn't turn around until she had slowed her anger. His blue-blue eyes looked cold to her. She hated that. She needed him to want her—no, to need her, but she wasn't willing to be his slave to get his attention.

She loved him. She'd loved him since the day she saved him, but he could be intolerable. He loved her, too. She could see it on his face right beside the anger. But they felt too damned close. Love and anger, that is.

Neither of them moved, as if the argument had frozen them in place, glaring at each across a meter of space.

Dayn's choked laughter broke her mood. She laughed, suddenly seeing the two of them facing off in this narrow room. Her own laughter drained the last of her tension.

"Look, what's the harm in recording it? If it's completely awful, it can be erased as a bad take."

"We'll lose momentum—"

"—if I have to take time off to write something else. We'll also lose it if we put out crap. We're entertaining, and my audience deserves a song for *them*. So what if it's not dripping with politics? It's got feeling. It will make them uneasy, and they need to be uneasy. They're way too complacent. So are you."

Fox's eyes had narrowed. He smiled, although not like he meant it.

When she glanced over at Dayn, he nodded at her. She didn't want him, not the way she lived with Fox, not in her bed. But it was a good thing to please him. She'd done this song because he told her to get a spine. Not that she'd tell him that. And no one was ever going to remind her she needed to be strong again, either. A song *for* the people here, *about* the people here. Well, about everybody on the ship. That's what she meant it to be. For every single person in every part of *The Creative Fire*, from the mysterious command to the bowels of gray where Nona had died.

First, she had to get Fox to make it popular, like he had with her other work. "Look, I'll go back and start something else if you really hate this."

He stood still and took a moment to answer. "That could take a week."

"I know. But I can do it, and make another revolutionary song. But then I'm a one-trick girl."

"Oh, no, not that." His frown was finally melting. He shook his head, laughing a little, and he looked like the old Fox, the one who adored her.

She'd won.

He whispered, "I guess I won't know if I hate it or not until I hear it done."

Good. She looked away from him and tapped her ear. She refused to look at Dayn, even though she knew he'd be smiling. The music started.

THIRTY-FIVE

AN AUDIENCE

Ruby stood in front of the mirror in her privy. She'd decorated the walls with pictures of the *Fire*. She'd asked for them, and Dayn had found them. She stared in the mirror and saw herself and the *Fire* behind her, a perfect tableau of what she meant to do.

A club. Finally. Fox was taking her to sing in a club. "Homecoming" had been out for a week, and people in KJ's class had begun to try to work out near her, to greet her, to tell her their names. Except a few, led by Fox's old girlfriend, Chance. They stayed as far away from her as they could. But if she had to draw a line down the room to indicate sides, more people liked her than not.

It would do.

The only thing that would make it better would be to get more support from KJ, make it clear he liked her. Except he never took sides. He was a rock that could shatter her ambition if she spent it flailing against him, so she didn't.

But maybe he'd come tonight.

She brushed a clump of red hair back behind her ear and checked her skin by leaning in close to the mirror. She rubbed a few drops of sweet oil from an orbfruit tree on her wrists and dabbed more between her breasts and on her temples.

Fox waited for her in her living room. He wore a soft blue shirt trimmed in gray, something she'd never seen before. He lifted the shirt a bit to show her a red belt. "I borrowed it," he said.

She kissed his cheek in approval, her stomach light and her feet itching to move. She gave him a long, searching look. "You're not mad at me anymore?"

"For?"

"For 'Homecoming'?"

"I seldom argue with success." He leaned in and gave her a kiss so strong and demanding that she stepped back. "This is like a first date," he whispered into her ear.

"Good. Maybe we'll get to know each other better."

He startled a little.

She smiled. "A tease. And you're right. I'm looking forward to it."

"So let's go."

Not only had he apparently stopped being mad, but he felt more like he had when she first came up here, a little in awe of her and a little unsure. It gave her confidence. As they worked through the corridors, her soft boots were nearly silenced by his lightly heeled black ones, something else new. He'd taken extra care with his dress.

"Where is the club?"

"I should blindfold you," he teased.

"You wouldn't dare."

"We're picking up Jali and Ani on the way."

"And Dayn?"

"Dayn will be there already."

Fox led her to a transportation hub and they boarded a train. As if that weren't surprise enough, either she'd failed to figure out the ship's geography entirely, or they were heading outward rather than inward.

When they stopped outside of cargo, Fox leaned down and whispered, "There's no access to this from gray. You've never seen the train used for people, never been on the train, and you've never seen the bars."

She blinked at him. "We like to drink, too."

"You're not that *we* anymore."

Of course she was! But he could believe what he wanted. "Still, how did you get a bar in cargo?"

"It's post-mutiny. Gave us a way to get anything we needed from cargo without having to go through the gray habs."

The gray levels were surrounded, and she'd never known, even though she'd been to the cargo pods before. The audacity of it worried her.

They stepped off the train into a transportation station much like the one they'd boarded in, except that the walls here were bright with posters and signs all written in light and competing for attention, and music spilled from outside. All of the neatness of the logistics level was gone, replaced with a discordant chaos she hadn't expected. She almost flinched.

He started leading her across the wide-open vestibule of the transportation hub. Jali and Ani went ahead of them, lost in their own conversation.

Ruby marveled yet again at how smoothly they moved. But then, she walked differently now, too. Something about KJ's class. "Stay near me tonight," he whispered. "It's not safe here."

"I've never been safer."

"You know better," he said. "You of all people."

And then they were across the floor and through the door. Behind it, a hallway. Colored lights spilled from three doors, and people chatted in small groups in the corridor. She squinted, thinking. "This used to be storage."

He nodded. "Not for generations. It lay empty until the mutiny, and then we took it for a peacer outpost, and they turned it into a few bars and a few gaming havens and a few places for love, and then word got out." He was grinning.

"You've been here a lot, haven't you?"

"Since I was a teenager. Met my first girl here."

She grimaced. "Have you been here since I came in?"

"Only to prepare the way for you."

They threaded through a small crowd in the hall, still following Ani and Jali, mostly passing faces she didn't recognize, a few she'd seen in KJ's class. As they walked, it grew quiet, as if her and Fox passing sent a shiver through the party atmosphere. Ruby looked down to make sure she hadn't spilled anything. "Do I look okay?"

"You look perfect."

She took a deep breath and tried to relax.

Ani and Jali had disappeared in front of her. They were almost at a door, so that was probably where they'd gone. Inside the door.

Deep drum-laden notes shook the walls and floor as she and Fox entered. The room was black except for a strange white light that strobed around the largely open space, illuminating sets of dancers just long enough for Ruby to glimpse sweaty faces before it moved on, changing targets over and over again. The floor had been covered in something scuffed but soft underfoot. Walls and floor were dark with strings of colored lights at odd angles that illuminated the bones of the room: metal beams that supported a high ceiling and tall, squared-off walls.

Ruby thought she recognized Dayn at the edge of the light for a second, and then the light moved on.

Everything about the room made her twitch with the need to move.

Fox took her hands in his and spun her around, rotating in place while she whirled in a wide circle, and then he pulled her to him and they spun together, her face buried in his coat. They separated, and he gestured to make it clear she should hang on to him and reverse the roles. She leaned back, throwing her head back, and let his weight counterbalance and spin her.

Her heart matched the drumbeat.

Just as she began to feel breathless and slightly dizzy, he stopped her short and held her an arms-length away. He began to side step slowly across the floor, expertly keeping her from being jostled. Two different women came up to kiss him, one on the cheek and one on the lips.

Ruby spotted Ani and Dayn (for sure this time) in a spot of light just in front of them, and then it was dark and smelled of sweat and spirits, and then the light landed on her face, making her blink.

She expected it to move on, but it didn't, bathing her in attention.

Jali was at her other side, whispering. "Listen for your notes."

She blinked again, nodded.

Jali's palm stayed on her waist. Fox held one of her hands and reached for something with the other hand, his hand and half of his arm passing out of the light, her vision too far gone in the brightness to see anything outside of the circle she stood in.

She swallowed, sure something was about to happen.

The room silenced.

Fox's hand returned to the light, cupping something small. He fastened half a headset on her and one of the wires he used for recordings, his movements deft. He clipped a small microphone to her shirt.

A note sounded, a single drum beat.

Then another, and then a third.

Everything else was silent.

The fourth beat told her this was "Homecoming." She had never sung it to drums. She sucked in a long wavering breath, as much air as she could take, and then, exactly on cue, she launched into the first verse of the song.

The first line came out a little shivery.

She drew her next breath deeper and sang louder, stronger.

It grew easier with every line until there was nothing but her voice and the music. Although blinded by the bright circle of white light, she felt the crowd around her on every side. She made a slow circle, her feet and hips reflecting the drum automatically, unstoppably. Her voice bounced back from the high ceiling.

She made the words her gift. These were the people she'd written this song for. The logistics people, the reds and the blues, everyone going home and nervous.

Her people now. In this moment, they were all her people.

On the last long note, noise rose all around her.

Hands reached into the circle of light and figures stepped between her and the ones who wanted to touch her. Fox behind her, Dayn at her right, Ani in front, Jali to her left.

Applause rose, filling the room and echoing off the walls and ceilings. Yips. Catcalls. "More!"

She couldn't stop smiling. The crowd made her light, as if she could float to the ceiling.

"More!" "'Gray Matters'!" "Ruby!"

Fox leaned forward and whispered in her ear. "You had to wait until they were ready for this."

"Can I sing another song?"

"Wait for it." His hands drummed on her shoulders.

"More!" "'The Owl's Song'!" Whistles, a catcall.

Fox's hands slid from her shoulders, and she glanced behind her to see his hands raised.

This time, she knew what to do after two notes. "The Owl's Song."

Then "Gray Matters."

Then they wanted "Homecoming" again.

"Last time," Fox called out.

Silence fell and then the drums filled it.

She started again, the song pulling her feelings out of her like energy waves attached to the notes, like the words pulled her very soul from her and offered it out. She loved this. It felt like what she had been born for—the silence of a rapt audience, the beat of the drum, the sound of her voice filling space and echoing back, her words meant to galvanize, to change.

Someone screamed.

Ruby kept singing, standing on tiptoe and trying to see what was happening.

The light slid from her, questing for a landing place.

A hand reached around her shoulder, Fox's hand, pulling the microphone from her shirt. He spoke into it, "Stay calm," his voice drowned by the rising sounds of panic sweeping into the room.

Dayn's voice, loud in her ear, "Let's go! Move to the back."

"Is there a door?" she whispered.

"We'll have to climb for it." The pressure of his hand on her shoulder pulled her back, Fox and Ani and Jali all staying, a knot of them. Others were doing the same, moving back from the noise.

The circle of light stopped moving near the door they'd come in. Ruby tried to see, stood on tiptoe, her view blocked as the crowd crushed back toward them. Dayn was the tallest of them. His eyes narrowed as he squinted at the doorway.

A stranger bumped back against her, pushing her into Fox.

Ani pushed the man to the side, sliding in closer to Ruby, her breath fast.

"Grays," Dayn murmured. "Grays everywhere."

THIRTY-SIX

THE CARGO BAY

A s he stumbled out of the train car behind Conroy, Onor gaped at the crowded transport station full of grays and, here and there, a red. One flash of blue twenty people away from him. There was no time to count or look for people he might recognize; his job was to follow Conroy and to keep Penny and another man, Hal, with him. It had been a hard ride, the train car swaying and smelling of scared and excited people, so crowded most people stood. Penny clung to him and Hal clung to Penny.

Now, across the floor, they threaded behind Conroy in the same way, a line of four clutching each other, Onor and Penny hand in hand and Hal behind her. Conroy led them to the desk where travelers checked in, handled this time by grays. A young woman recognized Conroy, nodded briefly at the other three, as if counting. She made a mark on a slate and stepped aside.

Another group approached from the other side of the bench. The Jackman, Marcelle, Jinn, and an older man Onor didn't know. Marcelle. Marcelle appeared to be a small group leader just like Onor was.

The Jackman hadn't emphasized the changes in her enough. She'd lost every bit of fat she'd ever had, replacing it with defined muscle. Her hair had been cut short, and her cheekbones and chin had grown prominent. She had a hard look about her until she saw him, and then her face collapsed into a broad smile and softened.

He was so happy to see her that he almost let go of Penny. Marcelle's smile looked like he felt, warm and excited and nervous all at once, and seeing her made him a touch less alone in this crazy drill.

If it *was* a drill. He didn't think so anymore.

The Jackman and Conroy moved warily, their eyes excited, edgy. They went together through a door. He and Marcelle joined up, and he dropped Penny's hand for a moment, holding Marcelle tighter than he ever had.

They followed the leaders down a hall, branched to the left, then the right, and went through a door that looked like it should lead to an ordinary office. Instead, a sloping hall ramped up.

They took it at a run, Onor and Marcelle looking behind and then ahead like twins. Enough of a climb that Onor felt it in his chest, although running practice had given him enough breath to take it. By the time they got to the top, the footsteps of another set of people running behind them pushed them harder.

Maybe they were going up into the other levels. They ran through two close-spaced doorways with thick seals that were almost surely an emergency airlock.

He stopped short when he spotted another train, sleeker and blacker than the one he had just been on. It looked so . . . pretty . . . he wanted to gawk at it, but Conroy didn't stop, and Penny bumped into him, pushing him with her hands, so he kept going. Inside the train car, Conroy went one way while The Jackman went another. Onor had no time to even say a word to Marcelle. He found himself in the very front row, facing a blank wall.

Other people poured in until every seat was taken, but no more, unlike the ride through gray. More disciplined, more exact. He didn't doubt they were elsewhere now. The info feeds on the inside of the train along the ceiling described things and places he'd never heard of before. "Nav group meeting at 1600 hours in the diamond lounge," and "storyteller session at the main mess at 0500 tomorrow." His eye caught a third sign, with Ruby's name in script across the top and a picture of her just more than half dressed, looking like she was dancing.

He stared at it for the rest of the time it took for the train to fill up.

They started moving. The windows were small, and all they revealed was a blur, mostly of tunnel and occasionally of lights or corridors.

Conroy stood up in his seat, hanging on to a lip in the roof. He had turned so he faced the entire car of people, maybe forty or so total. "Pay attention," he bellowed.

The few whispered conversations that had been going on silenced.

"We're going into a position as extras only. We'll be watching doors and making sure no one comes out. We are not to hurt anyone, or to allow each other to be hurt."

"Where are we going?" someone called out.

"I couldn't explain if I tried." He looked pleased, like they were going to a party. "What you need to know is to avoid force at all times unless we tell you otherwise."

"So we don't get locked up?" someone asked.

"Ix'll know," another voice spoke up.

"There's too many of us to punish," a woman said.

Conroy raised a hand for silence. "Our goal is to stand where we're told and to block passage. Hurt no one. Be alert and follow orders. You know who your group leaders are, and they will direct you. Take direction only from them, or from me, or from the man in the back with a beard."

The Jackman raised his hand.

Conroy sat back down, apparently having said all he was willing to. Onor's heart pounded. This was real. He wanted to know more, but he was willing to trust Conroy, who must have reasons for what he chose. He wished he knew if this was a small fight or a big one, or if they were taking over the whole ship.

He would do a good job. That mattered. Doing a good job.

The train stopped and they disembarked. Conroy and The Jackman took up the last of the line. Marcelle was close again, but not close enough to talk to. Posters made of light splashed across high walls, bright and pulsing, screaming for his attention.

The hallways on the far side of the station appeared to be clogged. People jammed the room, milling, the foursomes hard to hold together. By the time the empty train pulled away, Onor was shirt to shirt with Conroy, Penny, and a stranger. Yellow light played across one shoulder and Conroy's head, too distorted to read and so bright it forced Onor to squint.

The collective body odors of fear and adrenaline twisted his stomach. He swallowed and closed his eyes, wishing for clear air. He was thirsty. His small water flask was jammed between his hip and the wall, hard to reach. He stayed thirsty.

After way too long, the pressure in the room eased as people began to stream through the door. He had entirely lost sight of Marcelle, and he could barely follow Conroy and keep in step as they went through the door in their turn. They entered a long hallway, so high Marcelle could have stood on his shoulders without reaching the ceiling. It was just wide enough for four across. Every twenty feet or so, a door opened to the right. The left wall was metal, unadorned except for lights that looked hand strung, like an afterthought.

A cargo container. He recognized the look. They had gone outward instead of inward. He wanted to slow down to really see, but he was swept by the tide, pulled by Conroy and pushed by the people behind him, able only to move forward.

A knot of people on the floor outside of one door included three down on the ground, two in gray uniforms and one in blue.

Conroy cursed and bent down over the fallen blue, a young man with blood streaming from his scalp.

Forward progress stopped in front of the door long enough for Onor to look in. A big room, but dark. A white light played over the door, almost blinding him. Jeez, what dark love did these people have for flashing lights? It was worse than the vestibule outside the train had been. He tried to see through it anyway, shading his eyes. Dark silhouettes of people, men and women. Impossible to make out faces. Noise and shouts spilled over the people inside, the meaning drowned in the sheer number of voices.

Conroy stood up, muttering, and they went on.

A drill siren began to screech through the door they had just passed, confusing him for a moment until he remembered that the drills were for the real thing, and whatever this was it was real and the sirens were a real warning for someone.

They left the door and the single white light behind and went on, the press of people unrelenting for what seemed like a long time. Finally Conroy stopped, leaning against the wall. They were in front of a door, and people moved in the back of the room on the other side, too far away for Onor to see anyone clearly. Steady light revealed people in blue and red clothes—not really uniforms, but more casual clothes—gathered against one wall, with grays between them and the door.

"Stop here," Conroy hissed in a loud whisper. "Stay together and stay here."

They stood, all in a row, with their backs to the smooth wall. Conroy had managed to maneuver them so he stood in front of a door, Onor on his right. Then Penny and Hal. Then The Jackman, then Marcelle. Once more Marcelle was close enough he could see her but not talk to her.

All of the doors he could see now were closed. Now that he could stop and look, he was sure they were all cargo doors and that this was a single big cargo bay, converted to something else. He couldn't say what.

He sidled over to Conroy. "What do we do next?"

Conroy's posture suggested he wasn't interested in questions. Onor stepped back to the precise center between Penny and Conroy. The light above his head pooled his shadow around his feet. With no one walking or talking, it had become uncannily still. Onor had never been in the cargo areas before, only really in the two gray pods. He felt like he was standing on a small crack in the world as he had known it.

He hoped he stood in his parents' footsteps.

THIRTY-SEVEN
SECRET PLACES

When Dayn mentioned the grays by the door, Ruby wanted to race toward them. The crowd pressed in on her, making the idea impossible. She managed to scream up at Dayn, "Boost me up!"

He laughed and obliged, bending down and putting one hand on either side of her waist, his thumbs riding beside her spine and his long fingers hooked around her sides. He heaved her up. The light shone full on the door, drawing her gaze right where she wanted to look. Gray uniforms clogged the door, and then there was a space with only a few people moving in it, also grays.

For a moment she saw someone that looked like Onor peering in the door, shading his eyes. The figure moved on before she could be sure. But it couldn't be him. He wasn't the type to do such a thing; he was too meek.

She wanted to scream at not knowing what was going on, at the sheer injustice of it. She'd finally gotten out of her house, and now look. If she still wore gray, maybe she'd be right here anyway, only out in the corridor. If only she understood what was happening!

Just as Dayn let her slide down through his hands, using his elbows to keep space for her in the press of people, a siren sounded. The light from above, the moving cone, snapped off, and Dayn put his hand over her eyes, startling her so that she bit his palm.

He held her tighter, keeping her eyes covered.

She understood as blinding light forced itself through the thin cracks between Dayn's fingers. He slid his hand slowly away from her face and spoke dryly to Fox, "She bit me."

"She can be like that," Fox answered back.

"Hey!" she protested.

"Go up," Fox said, nodding his head to her right.

The bright white wash of light revealed a set of stairs that hugged the wall and went up and up with turns. The stairs were already filled with people.

Her eyes adjusted enough to pull out details. Cargo pulleys on the top and sides, hand holds in rows everywhere except the floor.

The stairs were designed to work without gravity, the walkways caged. In the harsh light, the room looked taller and thinner than her impression of it had been. The small lights that had looked so festive paled to almost nothing. It was a utilitarian place dressed up for dancing, the mundane core hidden from the dancers with darkness and clever light.

Dayn tugged on her arm and she turned to duck under his arm and mount the stairs. They started up, Jali in front, then Ani, then her. Behind Ruby, Fox. Last, Dayn, slowing the progress of the people behind him so that Ruby and her entourage could breathe.

The stairs were full, the going slow. Even so, far more people milled down below than she had thought, maybe a few hundred.

From here, she could see that grays surrounded the rest of the original crowd, pressing them in toward the stairs and up. Maybe seven grays—no eight—nine. None that she recognized.

They pushed the dancers back from the door, effectively corralling them, although she couldn't see how. They must have weapons of some kind, but they didn't seem to be hurting anyone.

Good. They couldn't. It would ruin everything if grays killed people now. They must know that.

They were talking—the grays talking to the fringes of the crowd they pressed upon, the conversation low enough she couldn't hear it above the heavy breathing of her fellow climbers and the staccato conversations between them.

If she hadn't let fear drive her up the stairs, she could have stayed below and found a way to talk to the grays.

During a moment when progress up the stairs stopped entirely, she leaned back and asked Fox, "Do you know what's going on?"

"No." He put a hand on the small of her back. "Move."

She ducked her head and kept going, taking the second turn, the cage arching above her head like a bubble. When she reached the door, she clung to the metal jamb and looked through it.

A corridor, doors to the right and left. Most of the doors were closed. People blocked the narrow space, moving forward only in chaotic bunches. Jali walked into the crowd, leading them through drifting knots of people and worried chatter, around a corner, and into a hall blocked by four big men.

The biggest one smiled at Jali.

She held up a hand with all five fingers spread. The hall guards nodded and opened ranks until Dayn came though, then closed off the hall again.

A wide open corridor on their right led through heavy-duty metal doors, across a short metal bridge between massive cargo containers, and through another door. Inside, soft light illuminated a tall desk in front of a blank white wall. A blond woman in a severe blue uniform with silver buttons stood behind it, watching them come in. She nodded. "Jaliet. And the Fox. Of course." She leaned forward across the desk and reached her hand toward Ruby, her face serene and controlled. "And you look as feisty as your songs." She glanced at Jali. "Is everything else about her as authentic?"

Jali laughed. "Yes, Olna, although we have taught her some poise."

Olna laughed. "You would teach Captain Garth poise."

"If he needed it."

"Oh, he needs more than that." Olna was still looking Ruby up and down, now smiling. "Welcome. Colin has been waiting to meet you."

The rapid energy of their flight seemed to have dissipated, the cadence of the conversation here gone to almost normal, with only a slight bit of edge in Olna's voice. Ruby took Olna's hand. "Good to meet you." The woman's grip was surprisingly strong.

"Go on," Olna said.

Behind the wall that Olna stood in front of, they found a large comfortable room with a bar along one side and a variety of unmatched furniture arranged rather pleasingly. One wall had an herb garden, its containers and lights almost certainly pilfered from one of the gardens on gray. Thyme and mint scented the air.

A group of people stood at one end of the bar, too far away for Ruby to hear what they said as she came in. In the middle of the room, two men sat opposite each other in chairs, staring at a game board. Another man leaned by himself against a wall, watching. A bodyguard after all the others they'd already passed?

Fox and Dayn stepped away from her, clearly not feeling a need to guard her back in this place. Jali walked up to the bar, leaned over it, and talked with the bartender.

Ani, next to her, looked a little shaken.

"Where are we?" Ruby asked her.

"I've never been here. Not to this room. It must be Colin's base."

"What?"

"I better start with Colin." She paused. "Maybe I better start even simpler. There's the power people like Ellis have. That's the power that comes from the front of command. Do you understand?"

"The power the reds wield at home?"

Ani grimaced. "If you will. But even more, the power that the people who command the ship give the peacers. And that they give us. For example, I'm no peacer, but I move goods around, including food. That's power of a sort. Formal power."

"Okay." No matter what Ani wanted to call it, this was the power she hated with all her being, had ever since Nona died.

"And there's the power that gets other things done."

It felt like she was getting a lecture. "Do people live out here?"

"Yes. But they're not all good people."

Another whole new level to the ship. The only cargo bays she'd been in held stuff, and nothing breathed in those. "How do they manage the life support?"

"Same as everywhere else. With the work done on the outer levels and the organization done by us and the priorities set by command." Ani sounded like she was talking to a two-year-old. "Things work together more than you think. The *Fire* isn't defined by the awesome workers and the mean people who make them work. We all work."

Ruby gave Ani a sharp look. "I'm not as simple as my songs. But how does this exist without Ix and the people in command knowing it's here?"

"Oh, they know."

"Why don't they get these people in trouble then?"

"Sometimes they do."

"I don't understand." In spite of what she'd said to Ani, she felt thick, like a little kid unable to understand a basic math concept. It irritated her, but she needed to understand, so she made herself shut up.

Ani sighed. "Sometimes the formal power structure needs the informal one. To get things done they don't want to do with rules and laws. Or can't."

Fox's hand on her arm drew her away even though she had a few hundred more questions for Ani. She expected him to pull her toward the bar, where

Jali still leaned in and chatted, but instead they went to the group of two. Just her and Fox; Dayn now stood beside Jali.

The bodyguard moved away.

The two men with the game board sat opposite each other. The more imposing of the players was probably twice Ruby's age. His short black hair was streaked with white. He looked up as they came forward and offered a welcoming smile. His eyes appraised her much as Olna's had, in a way that made her feel like she stood on a scale. She met his gaze and smiled back but said nothing, since he said nothing. His opponent was even older, thin and wiry. He watched Fox and Ruby warily, and as they got close, he sneered, "Hey, young Fox, I see you've drug your pet gray up here."

Ruby fingered the sleeve of her blue blouse and clamped her mouth shut.

Fox gestured for her to sit between the two men. He stood behind her, leaning in a bit, as if asserting ownership. He gestured at the younger man, who still watched Ruby closely. "This is Colin."

She held out her hand, and he took it, holding it rather than shaking it, his hand warm. She slid her hand free of his before he let go and dropped her eyes. He felt and looked like power and reminded her of Conroy.

"And I'm Par," the other man said, his voice implying distaste. She reached up and put a hand on Fox's arm. It felt stiff. He didn't like Par either.

"So what's the story?" Fox asked.

Par raised an eyebrow. "It's not your doing?"

Fox tensed visibly. "You think I planned this?" His hand on Ruby's shoulder left her no easy way to slide up and away from the animosity she felt between the two men.

Colin looked amused. "There is a beautiful singer in our midst. We should not worry about petty things when we can discover her." He turned to Ruby. "And how have you liked being with us? Is Fox treating you well?"

Ruby took a deep breath. "I want to know what's going on."

No sign of worry marred Colin's face. "I'll have a report soon. And then I'll tell you what I know. In the meantime, let's talk as if the world were normal. What do you like best about being with us?"

She swallowed, her throat dry. "The opportunity to learn."

"And what are you learning?"

That there was this whole section of ship she had not even known existed. And more. "That I know very little."

He laughed again and glanced at Fox. "Perhaps you have bitten off more than I thought you had," he said. "Or perhaps you are right, and she *will* save us."

Ruby kept a steady gaze, chin up. It was hard to stay here, seated, being appraised like a pretty doll. She should be running back down the stairs and pushing through the door of the club into the hallway she'd seen choked with grays. She should be searching for Onor or Marcelle.

Colin watched her, as if noting the slightest move or change in her breath. She didn't let herself blink. A child's game, but something more here.

"She has spine," Colin said.

Fox responded. "Ellis is after her, and Sylva. She's with me until she learns how to get around here."

"You learn fast, don't you?" Colin asked her.

"Yes." He had gone from appraising to flirting. She bent her head slightly, unsure how to react to the heat he drew up in her body.

"I've collected some of the best people to teach her." Fox rubbed her back in sharp nervous circles and she twisted a bit forward to get away from his knuckles. "But she is only part of our strategy."

A young man burst into the room and Colin waved him over. She could feel a sharp sliver of Colin's attention on her even as he greeted the boy. Fox's hand tightened on her shoulder as if he, too, felt Colin's focus.

The boy trembled in front of Colin, looking earnest and eager to please, if a bit frightened. His full lower lip hung out and he worried at it with sharp white teeth. His shoulders hadn't yet grown out past his waist, and he stood on his right foot while his left foot toed the ground.

"What do they want?" Colin asked him.

"I spoke to one of them. A woman. Named Pix." The boy gave Colin a chance to react before continuing. When he didn't, he added, "She said they wanted us to know they're there." He stopped again for a moment, licking his lips. "She said it's a message that they can go anywhere anytime and that there are more of them than of us."

Colin kept his gaze fixed tight on the boy. "And are they all workers?"

The boy shook his head. "They all wore gray, but I saw one of my teachers and she's one of us. Ms. Paulette, with the long hair."

Ruby leaned in. "They just came to frighten us and then went away?"

"I am not frightened," the boy said, although he smelled like fear.

"What is your name?" she asked.

He drew himself up so his spine was straight and his eyes even with hers. "Haric."

Colin had switched his look from Haric to Ruby. "What do you know about this tactic?"

She shook her head. "Can't you see I'm trying to find out?"

"Fox?"

"I'd be more subtle."

Par spoke. "No kidding. But you might be a subtle part of this. You and your lady."

Before Fox could answer, Ruby asked Haric, "Are the grays still outside? Are they okay?"

"Pix said they were leaving. She wanted us to know they could have hurt us or stopped the train and trapped us here. She said they'd be in touch, and she told me to tell *you* that."

Ruby drew her brows together, trying to remember someone named Pix. No memories surfaced. Probably a fake name. "Me specifically?"

"No, Colin." Although Haric kept looking at her. "You're Ruby, who sings."

She smiled. "Yes."

"I think that's why they came."

Ruby glanced up at Fox. "Are they playing the new songs on the gray levels?"

"I don't think so."

She turned back to Haric. "Why do you think that?"

"Because they weren't all gray. And you make me like the grays better. I met a few today, just now."

Ruby smiled. "Thank you, Haric."

The boy looked at Colin, waiting.

Colin nodded. "Good work. Tell Julie to give you a free treat."

Haric headed toward the group at the bar. Ruby asked, "Where did all the grays come from? Which pod? And how did they mix people?"

Colin shook his head. "I don't know. But I think Fox and I will go find out. You can stay. Jaliet has friends here."

It was a dismissal, but she'd learned more from a half hour with Colin than from weeks with Fox. So she nodded and said, "Thank you."

She lifted her face for a kiss from Fox. He smiled, touched her cheek, and said, "Go to the bar." Then he was gone. When Par followed, Ruby let out a sigh of relief.

Jali arranged them all at the bar so that Ruby was between her and Ani; apparently the women still felt a need to guard her here. Ruby leaned over the bar and requested a glass of orb wine. "Anybody know anything?" she asked. "What that was all about?"

Haric appeared from behind the bar, where he had been rummaging, his eyes wide. Ruby winked at him, suggesting she wouldn't give away any secrets he told her.

The bartender handed her wine. "I wasn't there, but I suspect it was the Freers."

The same group Lila Red had belonged to. The people who had almost succeeded in taking the ship once before. "I thought they had disbanded."

A tall, thin woman on the far side of Ani spoke. "There were always too many freers to kill them all. They just made examples."

Ruby took a long, slow sip of the wine, which was a tad sweeter than she liked. "I thought the Freers were murdered and left to rot in A-pod. That they never even got a good burial, so they can bring the bodies out and scare us if they ever need to."

"Children's stories," Ani said. "Nobody would do that."

Maybe. But Ruby had believed it for a long time. She sighed. "Do you know if anyone was hurt tonight?"

Jali answered. "Colin will find out and tell us."

Not Colin *and* Fox. People who deferred to Fox at home gave him less credit here, as if Colin outshone everyone else in this underground part of the ship.

The talk turned to Ruby then, people asking about her songs and what she intended to do. She parried their simple questions easily while she tried to think about Colin and what it meant that there were people with so much more power than Fox. She watched the entrance, waiting for them to return. She missed Fox in spite of the way his moods toward her shifted one way and then another, and at the same time, she wanted to know Colin better.

In the meantime, the wine helped her laugh and listen and not look as much in awe of this place as she felt.

THIRTY-EIGHT

CONSEQUENCES

R uby's feet ached from standing. She held one at a time up behind her, the blood throbbing through her heels. The first glass of wine had taken an hour to drink. The second tasted even sweeter and took half an hour.

Colin and Fox and Par had made no contact at all. Bodyguards paced the room. Their gazes seemed to scrape Ruby's skin raw as they circled.

Dayn paced. He watched everyone, including the guards. He watched Ruby most of all. She wanted to tell him it wasn't her fault they were here, but he didn't stop long enough for her to have a natural opportunity to talk to him.

Maybe the grays hadn't all gone home. Maybe something had happened to Fox. Maybe there was a fight going on somewhere as they stood here, talking awkwardly and sipping bad drinks.

She eyed Haric. He was too young to be seriously deceitful, so he might give her some real information. He also looked a bit lost, like company might cheer him up. She detached herself from the bar and walked over to the boy. "Show me the game they were playing?"

His eyes lit up. He led her back to the chairs the men had been in before they left. In front of him, a set of blue and gold pieces squared off against each other. After making sure she was settled, Haric sat where Colin had been, pointing at the pieces one by one. "This one's in command and has to be protected at all time." He pointed at three others that didn't look like protection to Ruby, but she nodded as if she understood and waved at him to keep going.

Ani and Jali drifted over to flank her. Her ever-watchful bodyguards, there with smiles and support whether she wanted them or not. She ground her teeth and kept watching the boy. She wanted to ask him more about what he'd seen but sensed he wouldn't offer anything he saw as betraying Colin. So she focused on the game.

Waiting sucked.

Apparently, Ani played, since she offered advice from time to time, complete with words like *holding*, *feint*, and *tactic*.

Ruby struggled to understand without asking questions that would reveal how little she knew. She filed the name away to learn later. *Planazate*. She pointed, "Looks like Colin is winning."

Haric gave her an affronted stare. "Were you listening at all? Green is *losing*. Par can probably beat him in three moves."

One of the guards that was in Ruby's line of sight straightened. She looked up, expecting to see Fox and Colin.

The crowd at the door parted to let in one man. Colin. Alone. "Where are the others?" she blurted out.

"They'll be along. There was a message to send."

"To the grays?" she demanded. She stood to add emphasis. Her knee bumped the board and she almost knocked it over. Haric steadied it. "You aren't hurting any of them, are you?"

He laughed. "You are a little bit of heat, aren't you? You didn't even ask if any of my people are hurt. Or about Fox for that matter."

She stiffened.

He came closer to her, but she didn't move.

Haric backed away, and Colin's glance at Ani and Jali got them moving as well. Ani gave her a warning glare.

Colin kept coming until he stood right in front of her, his hips and chest almost touching her, his chin close enough that her eyes couldn't focus on it easily. His breath smelled like stim and his sweat was musky, almost like Fox's when she aroused him. Ruby wanted to take a step back, but she stood her ground.

"I'm not hurting any grays. I'm on your side," he said.

"Good."

Colin reached for her hand, took it in his lightly. "Let's go have a drink."

She didn't really want another one, but she followed him. As they approached the bar everyone else left it. The bartender gave her another wine and poured a dark, smooth drink into a flat-bottomed cup for Colin without waiting for an order. Then the bartender disappeared as well.

Colin wasn't touching her, but he bulked close enough to reach her if she moved. Her head came to his shoulder. She had to look up to see him watching her, his face impassive but curious and measuring.

Clearly he expected her to feel his power—to be afraid or feel trapped or seduced or something else she couldn't define. She didn't like that in him, this assumption of attraction. Even if it was the only thing about him that wasn't attractive. It was a big thing.

She took the tiniest sip of the wine and managed not to choke on the sweetness. "You're fighting the established order? This place," she waved her hand around at the entire room, "isn't okay, right? Not official?"

He laughed. "It's no secret."

"Well, but it's not about the kind of power that hurts the grays."

He nodded, looking slightly amused.

"So why would they attack you?"

"They sent a warning for someone else."

She wished for a chair to sit in, going back to taking her weight off one foot and then the other. "Did they come here from gray? I heard they used the same train Fox brought me here on."

Colin was silent for a long while before his face softened into the seductive mask he'd worn when they sat around the game table earlier. "You pay close attention." He set his drink down on the top of the bar and stretched.

"So why would you get the warning? Why not Ellis or Sylva? Or command?"

He leaned down and clasped his hands around her waist the way Dayn had earlier and deposited her on the bar. "Because your feet hurt. I pay attention, too."

"You could have asked."

"Doesn't that feel better?"

It did. It also meant she was at his eye level. "Why did they come here?"

"What do you think?"

She swung her legs back and forth, her heels hitting the back of the bar softly. "Does it scare you that they came here? Because you're not working?"

"I am working. Just not for anyone else."

That wasn't the part of her comment she'd expected him to react to. "Did I get the rest right?"

"No." He sipped his drink. "What's going to happen to them?"

She felt as lost as she had when Haric tried explaining the subtle nuances of Planazate. "That's what I need to know. These are my family, and whatever they just did, it was brave. But I don't understand what they wanted or why they came here of all places."

"This is the best place on the ship."

"And you're the most infuriating man on the ship?"

"And I want to know if you can think." His voice had actually gone up a little. One of the guards gave him a look, but he shook his head. "Look. Let's keep this simple. Assume they had three choices. Do nothing. Come here. Go to the logistics level."

"And they were tired of doing nothing. I get that. I got that way, too. But they aren't movers down there, most of them. You keep them scared and compliant. So something made them act . . ."

"Like a handful of songs and a few rumors?"

"It would be nice if that was enough," she snapped. "But a few good beatings might have done it." She stared into his eyes. "And it wasn't me. I would love for it to have been me. But it wasn't."

Colin raised an eyebrow. "Not Fox and his entertainment skills?"

She hesitated. "I don't think so." They wouldn't do this without more provocation than a song from me, would they?

"Maybe partly. But I'm glad you don't see yourself as the only catalyst."

"Of course not." She sipped her drink. "The problems on this ship started before I was born. Whatever got my people moving, they could have come here or gone inward to logistics. This is closer. There's fewer weapons here."

Colin didn't respond, although a slight shine in his eyes encouraged her. She didn't know what to say next. "Well, it's not closer. Not if they used the train. I guess they didn't really want a fight."

"Very good." Now his voice had dropped to just above a whisper. "And so it's not quite mutiny."

"I still don't understand that word."

"The *Fire* has a command structure. Mutiny is overthrowing command."

"I thought it was fighting the reds."

He nodded. "It is. But *why* matters. It's one thing to fight to change something and another thing entirely to fight to destroy that thing. The *Fire* needs structure, and destroying that structure completely could cripple the ship. Especially if it's destroyed by people who know nothing of flying or fixing an old ship destined to die in the next generation if we don't get home first."

She hadn't heard the danger framed so bluntly before. "And the sky falling was a warning of that."

"The sky falling?"

"The rift between blue and gray, abandoning C-pod."

"That was less a warning than an underscore."

"So what about before? Before Lila Red, before we couldn't move around. When the *Fire* left home? What did we have then? Do you know?"

"Think of things in a hierarchy. That's how it is now. Command tells logistics and the peacers what to do, and they tell the workers what to do."

"Right."

"It used to be more like lines. Command at the middle, but part of command was a worker. Not the top, but there. Decisions were . . . more shared."

Damn. "Why did it change?"

He leaned in even closer to her. "I don't know. It happened before I was born. Long before. Ask The Jackman."

"He hates me."

"Oh." Colin stood close to her, but he hadn't touched her except to boost her up onto the bar. He still wasn't touching her, but the way he looked at her felt like he was touching her. "What do you want, Ruby?"

"Fairness."

"Is that all?"

The energy between them felt electric, and scary. She leaned back away from him a little, bracing herself with her palms down. Then she held one of them up. "I wouldn't mind having full access to my own house."

She was rewarded with what looked like the barest bit of surprise in his eyes. "I'll see what I can do."

"Or better yet, real freedom of movement for the grays?"

He remained silent, one eyebrow cocked. He really was infuriating. She choked down another sip of wine. "I still don't know what they wanted here."

"Is anything secret on this ship?"

"Of course not. Ix knows everything."

"So I think you should figure out who and what the message was. You have enough information." He reached a hand out and cupped her cheek. His fingers were cool from holding his glass. She almost expected him to kiss her and found she did and didn't want that, as if her head and her insides fought each other. This was a dangerous man. He could hurt her, but he also had power, and he was less secretive than Fox.

She didn't have to decide whether or not to return his kiss, since he didn't offer it. "I have other things to do. But I will see you again. Figure it out by then."

He let go of her and stepped away, leaving her sitting on the bar alone.

THIRTY-NINE

NEW PLANS

O nor's feet pounded alongside many other feet, his breath ragged and his side hurting. Conroy had herded them all off the train, followed them down here below the park, and made them run. Swore at them to work out the kinks from all that standing. Onor could smell the spent adrenaline left from being on high alert as sweat poured down his neck and the middle of his back.

The faces of the others beside him looked like he felt, tired and confused and sucking for air.

To make it worse, Conroy lapped them, laughing. Onor straightened as he heard him approach, wanting to be a good soldier even though he also wanted to strangle Conroy for making him run right now, when all he wanted to do was lie down and think about what he'd just seen.

Conroy matched him, stride for stride, slowing a little while Onor added enough speed he couldn't talk. Not that it mattered. Conroy could. "You did great. Nice work."

"Why?" Onor took three breaths. "Why did," two more breaths burned up his chest, "we do that?"

"Ruby. She gave us an opening, created allies. They might not last long."

"Why not?"

"Politics. They're volatile, and in this case, they depend on Ruby. If she stops doing what she's doing, we lose the advantage."

If she got hurt, he meant. Or killed.

Conroy paused, and Onor hoped he was searching for his own breath, even though he expected he was just looking for the right words. Eventually, Conroy said, "Stay after. I need to talk to you."

Onor nodded, completely unsure whether his tired body would stay awake for anything else after this.

Conroy ran away, slapping the back of a woman in front of Onor and whispering something too softly for Onor to hear. Before he ran on again, Conroy playfully slapped the woman's butt, and she laughed.

People began slowing and peeling off in various directions. Onor slowed but didn't go all the way down to a walk until most of them were gone. At the end, it was only him and Penny and Conroy and Aric.

Aric took over the role of coach. "Circle to cool. Walk it out! Walk it out!"

Next it was, "Push-ups till I say stop!"

Even as exhausted as he felt, Onor noticed he could pass twenty easily and didn't really feel it until thirty.

He had changed.

"Stop!" Aric called.

Onor looked up to see The Jackman walking toward them between two support columns. His face was sweaty and streaked with dirt on one side, and his whole body seemed to slump with exhaustion.

"Everything okay?" Aric asked.

The Jackman nodded. "No surprises."

Onor pushed himself off the ground and stood, slowly stretching his calves and hamstrings, first one side and then the other. Beside him, Penny stretched out her arms, showing surprising reach given her broad build.

The Jackman greeted Penny first, and said, "Thanks for offering."

She gave Onor a sideways look laced with both sadness and pride, and nodded at The Jackman. "My pleasure."

He turned his attention to Onor. "She's going to pack you. Tonight. I'll get your stuff for you and bring it. You have a new job."

He'd actually come to peace with Penny and the cleaning bots. And he wanted to walk back with Penny and sleep. He looked up at The Jackman. "Doing what?"

"Helping me."

The Jackman looked so tired but so proud of himself that Onor grinned in spite of his weariness. "You don't work, old man. You just tell tales."

"Right. So no reason not to join me."

He glanced at Penny. "But I won't stay here, not in this pod?"

The Jackman shrugged. "Sometimes. But what would my apprentice be if not a wanderer, too?"

He brightened a little. "Will I see Marcelle?"

"Sometimes."

Conroy cleared his throat. "The story we'll tell Jimmy and the other people here is that you got in trouble for what we did tonight and were reassigned. We won't lie, since we're reassigning you."

The Jackman grinned. "And I'll see that you cause trouble."

Onor shook his head. "Aren't the reds going to know?"

Aric spoke up. "Not your problem. It's handled."

"Who helps you?" Onor asked, the question blurting out even though he knew he should shut up.

"We'll tell you what you need to know."

"Okay . . . so I do need to know who we're fighting."

Aric shook his head. "No. Not really. You need to know what we ask you to do and you need to do it. Sometimes we're going to need a messenger to say only what we want them to say and not know more in case they get caught."

So he wasn't going to be a spy. He was going to be a sacrificial piece in a game. He looked at The Jackman.

"I'll keep you safe. It's a waste to have you clean floors."

That was true enough. Onor turned to Penny. She must have helped, must have reported on him and told them how he was doing. He stepped over to her and hugged her. He expected her to be soft around the edges, but she wasn't, not even in the waist. "Thank you," he said.

She blinked hard and looked a bit stunned by the hug. "Yeah."

That was all he was going to get. He turned back to The Jackman. "I'm ready."

They walked together, returning the way The Jackman had come. They went up a maintenance ladder and through a hatch, which The Jackman dogged carefully behind them. He glanced at Onor. "Lesson one. Never compromise the *Fire*. Doesn't matter who you're mad at, the *Fire*'s still a ship, even if you and I have never seen the space it flies through. If we want to have our day, we can't break the *Fire*."

"She's breaking by herself. Remember our old pod?"

"That might have been helped along, too. At least by negligence. Maybe even plan."

"Really?" Onor shivered, suddenly as afraid as he had been the day the sky fell. They started down a corridor Onor knew from his cleaning job. "I thought the ship was getting old."

"It is. And we humans are getting lazy. You'll get some education with this job, not to worry. I have plans for you."

FORTY

MIXED MESSAGES

The first low chime of the morning bells dragged Ruby from a ragged sleep. Surely it hadn't been more than a few hours since they came home from the cargo bay and the grays' attack, or whatever it was. She slid her hand across the sheets, releasing a surprised groan when she found Fox's waist.

So he'd stayed.

She scratched at his back lightly, a caress of her fingernails. He leaned into her a bit but either didn't wake or didn't want to wake.

Fine. At least he was here.

She padded into the kitchen and made a cup of stim.

Her journal lit with an incoming message. She frowned at the idea of a note arriving. Nothing from her old life got here. Fox, Ani, Jali, and Dayn had her address, but they didn't use it.

The note's signature showed that it came from Colin West.

She clicked it open.

No subject line. Just a sentence. "Check your front door."

She stared at it for a minute. Then she took the journal to the kitchen controls and held her palm up to the reader.

It logged her on.

She tried a few things. She could make stim (but she had been able to). She could order food, which she hadn't been able to do. She tried her alarm clock settings. Bingo. She had always been able to get in and out; a child's access allowed that. But now she could lock her own door. She closed her eyes and thanked Colin, and then she sent him back the same two words in a reply. "Thank you."

The secret felt good and bright inside her.

She was still humming when Fox found her in the kitchen. "You're in a good mood."

She laughed, hoping to hide the way she felt thrilled and guilty all at once. After all, she *should* have full access to her own hab. She had had access to all of her mother's habs and to Daria's. Now she felt more at home than she had in all her days here so far. "You took me out."

He put a hand on her shoulder. "This isn't the same ship you woke up on yesterday."

"So?" She tried to weave a tease into her voice, to throw him off the scent of her secret. "So tell me what changed?"

He just stared at her.

"You don't tell me enough to know this. I still don't understand what happens here."

"I know."

She waited, but he didn't say anything. He stood over the sink, looking lost in thought.

"So it's a threat. I got that much. The workers showing the rest of you that they can get to various places on the ship. But no one got hurt, right? And the whole ship needs the workers. Isn't that how it plays out?"

"You're not that stupid."

Ouch. "So educate me."

"I make sure you know what you need to know." He came closer to her, smelling of sleep and a little foul with old sweat. "I understand that you want life to be different. That's the main reason I came to get you. I know how to make you matter to people."

She blinked at him, angry. "I mattered before I got here. You even said that. Just now. I have friends you don't even know."

Dayn came in the front door. He gave her a quirky smile from behind Fox's back, but cleared his throat, announcing his presence.

She kept her focus on Fox. "Don't leave yet. I need to talk to you more."

"I have to go," he said. "Ani will be along in a while and I want you to move in a threesome today. But do the normal things. Go to class." He glanced at Dayn. "Don't let anybody surprise you. If you get confronted or she gets taken, tell me right away."

"Taken by who?" Ruby demanded.

"Anybody." Fox had already turned toward the door, but he stopped. "What your friends *I don't know* did last night was to make powerful people mad. They scared them. That would have been great when we were ready, in about a year." He turned around to Dayn. "She hasn't been communicating with them has she?"

Dayn shrugged.

Fox turned back to Ruby, his eyes uncharacteristically hard. "Have you?"

"I wish."

He sighed. "Don't count Ellis and Sylva powerless, or the people who run them. We need more time to kill their influence. If they take you now, they won't just drop you back in gray and make an accident happen. You'll never see gray—or me—again. So no escaping and running around the ship today, okay?"

She hated his tone, but she nodded in spite of it. If he wouldn't tell her anything, maybe Dayn or Ani would. She wanted a good answer for Colin.

Fox stepped back over to her, leaning down to claim a kiss goodbye, but she stepped away so he almost overbalanced. When he stopped and stared at her she stared back and remembered her access rights.

Someday she could use them to lock him out.

She stared at the place Fox had been for a long time, forcing herself not to cry. Right that moment she never wanted to see him again.

Dayn came over and stood close. He whispered, "Let it go."

As if she would cry on *his* shoulder. She could leave Fox, and maybe she would, soon. Maybe she'd even set the door to keep him out tonight and see how he liked her being on equal footing. But she couldn't leave him for Dayn, or open up enough to talk to Dayn. There was only another trap there.

"Are you okay?" Dayn asked.

She pulled away from him and put her back to him. "Sure. I'm surrounded by friends and family and I have my freedom."

"Sarcasm doesn't sound good from you," he snapped. He lowered his voice. "You've got fans. More than you should by now, more than you would have ever had or known about if it weren't for Fox."

She licked a tear that ran down her right cheek, making sure to keep standing so Dayn wouldn't see. She pulled on her anger, which felt more comfortable by far than feeling lost. It was easy to be mad at Fox for acting like she couldn't know anything, like she'd betray his plans if she did.

"What is Fox planning?" she asked. "He's using me for something. What is it?"

"He's simply addressing an imbalance of power."

"You won't tell me anything either, will you?"

"You're a child, Ruby. You're easy to love, and a lot of us love you. Half the ship loves you. Even Colin. You felt him drawn to you last night. But you can't possibly understand the complex power games around here yet."

She had regained enough emotional control to turn and face him. "Maybe that's what we need. Power that doesn't try to play board games with the people on this ship. Maybe *The Creative Fire* just needs a few simple rules. And one of them is *don't keep secrets*." She was right. She could feel it. She could see how right she was in Dayn's eyes, too, in the way he reacted by withdrawing from her and then licking his lips. "Look. Look at me. I'm doing fine up here. And so would anybody else from home. *We are exactly like you*. And before we get home, before we stop and see the stars for the first time ever, *we need to be together*."

He stared at her for a bit before answering in a very measured voice. "That's what we're trying to do."

"No." She shook her head. "I can feel it. Fox wants to have the power. You too. You'll do better with it, I give you that. You will. But the power has to be in every one of us."

"Ships don't run like that."

Thoughts spun through the back of her head. "Maybe not. Maybe that wouldn't have been the right way to leave home. But it's the right way to go back. We're going to leave the *Fire*. We—who've never seen the outside of the skin of our ship—we're going to see Adiamo. And Fox and Colin and even my songs are petty and small compared to that." She felt like she did when she hit just the right note and kept it, or when she ran in the park at home, her feet skimming the surface and her movement synchronized with her breath. Like she felt in KJ's class when she flowed with him instead of fighting him. "Don't you see? Everything about our world is going to be different. In our lifetimes. And nothing we have been thinking about so far is a big enough response to make us ready for that. We have to get even bigger. We have to use everything we have, every skill, every love, every note of every song."

Dayn stared. He clearly didn't understand her.

But she understood herself for the first time since she'd been among the blues. Maybe for the first time ever. She needed more than anger. She needed driven love. And she needed to write this all down before she forgot it. "Look—we'll talk later, okay?"

Dayn narrowed his eyes at her and shook his head. "I was just trying to make you feel better."

"You did." Her journal still lay on the cabinet where she'd left it when Fox came in. She grabbed it and flopped down onto the couch to write down the things she'd just said.

Just before time to leave, Ani came in. She greeted Ruby with a glare, shouldering past her to the living room.

"Good morning to you, too." Ruby said.

Ani stopped and turned. "Colin seemed like a nice opportunity to you, didn't he?"

"Sure." Ruby looked steadily at Ani, trying to tell how mad she was. It was hard to be sure. "Maybe he is a good opportunity. Maybe it would be nice not to have so many keepers for a while."

Ani looked stung. "Helpers."

"That's like reds are peacers. Use the right words and you no longer believe a thing is itself."

"It's not that way. You're twisting my intentions."

"Am I?" Ruby took a deep breath. "I hope so. I hope your intentions are good. I need a friend."

Ani looked down at Ruby, her height more impressive than usual, since Ruby was sitting down. After awhile her stern look softened some. "You sang well in the club before those scum interrupted us."

"Those scum were my family," Ruby snapped.

"That was your debut. Your first public appearance. We'd been planning it for a week, and now it's ruined."

"Is it? A lot of people heard me sing, and I did good. You just said so."

"Did you know any of them?"

"The people who heard me sing?"

Ani gave her a warning look. "The people who threw us all out of our own club to make a point."

"Did they throw us out or did we run?"

Ani's generous lips thinned and her jaw tightened. But she shook her head and said, "I don't know."

"I don't either," Ruby said. "But if they're scum, I'm scum."

"You're infuriating." Ani scowled. "But that's why Fox went down for you. You make the right people mad. But I'm not letting you get under my skin. Come on. We should go."

Dayn and Ani flanked her as they made their way to KJ's class. When they arrived, Dayn leaned down and whispered in Ruby's ear. "I'll stay by the door. You and Ani go up front."

Well, that's where she usually worked out anyway these days. The front of the class. They got there just as KJ was ready to start. She followed him, stretching into an upside-down standing pose, blood pounding in her ears. She balanced through a series of one-legged stretches, her thighs exactly right, her foot right, one arm or the other extended or flowing back by her side. Ani was beside her, distant and a bit cold in spite of her words about not letting Ruby irritate her, and for once clumsier than Ruby.

A flash of red caught Ruby's eye, a woman, passing her. Bright red clothes, swirling against long limbs, a cut of clothing that Ruby had never seen. Dark hair tied up in a knot on top of her head, pale skin, dark eyes.

She went directly for KJ, stopping him in mid-movement, her slender hand on his chest. She whispered in his ear and then turned and took over his position in the flow of movement.

The class didn't react. It just followed her instead of KJ.

Ruby started to lift her right leg, following the woman.

A hand landed on her back, and KJ's voice whispered in her ear. "Follow me. Both of you. Don't look behind you."

FORTY-ONE
COUNTERMOVES

Ruby followed KJ through the door he always used, Ani hard behind her. The door led to a smaller room that held strange equipment: pulleys and ropes and weights. A round handrail lined mirrored walls. Of more interest, six people stood along one of the walls, wearing the same loose, flowing red robes as the woman who was now teaching KJ's class. They stood almost as still as statues. Their eyes fastened on Ruby.

They looked interested, almost fascinated. They also had something like KJ's calm.

She felt sure she'd never seen any of them before.

KJ led Ruby and Ani through another door and into a hallway, leaving the strangely dressed reds behind. Peacers. Whatever. Why wasn't it ever really clear who her enemies were? Hell, maybe KJ was her enemy. She didn't think so, but how could she tell here?

The hallways led through two locks, taking them out of the separate pod into a place Ruby had never seen. KJ's footsteps were almost impossible to hear, and Ani's were barely louder, so it sounded like Ruby walked the corridors by herself. She tried to do it more quietly, but that slowed her down and Ani shooed her forward, loud again.

They weren't quite running, but KJ clearly wanted distance from whatever he'd seen. By the time he stopped in a nondescript galley, Ruby had lost track of the turns they'd made.

"What happened?" Ani asked as soon as the door shut behind them.

"Sylva. And a group of peacers I don't like. Ten. Coming in the doors at the wrong time for class." He looked directly at Ruby, his eyes so calm she wanted to fall into them and be held there. "Triangulating on you."

"Fox warned us," Ruby said.

"Is this because the grays attacked?" Ani asked.

"No one attacked anyone," KJ replied. "But yes, it has to be a countermove to our move last night."

"Our move? Who is *our*?"

"Joel planned the action last night."

His voice was so matter of fact she couldn't tell whether or not he approved of Joel or of the decision or even of her. Maybe he didn't have any emotions.

He switched subjects smoothly. "I'm going to check for a capture order." He wasn't carrying a journal. None of them were. He slid a slender drawer out from under the table and tapped on a surface. A screen flicked on and he held his hand over it, still, waiting for acknowledgment. The screen gave a soft beep.

Ruby stepped close. What she saw looked a little like a journal home menu, only thinner, and the choices were different. Her fingers itched to play with it.

KJ's hands practically caressed the slender interface, the flow of his fingers and palm placing pressure as precise as the drills he ran them through in class.

"What is it?" she asked.

"A communication tool."

"No. I never would have guessed."

He laughed. "I heard you had a smart mouth."

"I'm just tired of being treated like anything I learn will be used against me."

"Funny. We live that way here. Is it kinder down on the level you came from?"

"Of course not."

"Well, then."

"Maybe it is kinder there," Ruby shot back.

He squinted at the device, paying closer attention than he had been.

She bit her lip, watching him. Words flowed across the screen, just barely too fast to read from her angle. She held her silence.

He looked up, frowning. "There is a contact and detain order for you. But they have to find you first."

"And tha . . . your access—it didn't give your location away?"

"No."

She swallowed. That wasn't possible. "Ix."

"Won't know."

Out of the corner of her eye, Ruby spotted a broad grin on Ani's wide dark face. "How do you make something Ix doesn't know about?" Ani asked.

"Magic."

"You lie," Ruby teased him. "Teach me?"

"We better hide you first."

Not fair. She'd just gotten full access to her hab! "Hide me from the reds?"

"Not all of them. Just the worst."

"Where? Can we go out? I want to see my friends. Are you working for Fox? Why are you helping me?"

He ignored her questions. "Follow me."

Five minutes and two turns and two doorways later, he opened a door wedged between shelves in a big storage room. She hadn't recognized it as a door until KJ opened it and a puff of damp, slightly stale air assaulted her nose. The opening was so small she expected a privy or more storage, but instead a very skinny hallway threaded between this room and the next. KJ turned sideways and slid into the narrow opening, gesturing for them to do the same. Ruby fit smoothly, but Ani was just enough bigger and thicker that she had to squeeze through the narrowest spots.

They turned a sharp corner and went up seven metal stairs, still sideways. Although they were barely moving at a regular walk, albeit sideways, it felt like running away. She had her songs, and Fox for whatever he was worth, and her own access. This was the wrong thing to do. "What can they do to me?" she hissed.

"Lock you away. Kill you. Accuse you of treason."

"What have I done wrong?"

"You exist. People like you." After a moment he added, "No. That's not it. They don't like you. They adore you."

"What?"

"Don't play stupid with me," KJ said. "I've watched you and Fox mold your image. You're trying to get people to love you. And that's scared some of the people who don't. Fox has done a nice job making you, but he won't fight for you if they take you. There's too much at risk for him, and he's playing a larger game."

"He loves me!"

"So you're naïve as well as mouthy," KJ said, a soft laughter riding his voice with the words, softening them so she simply felt stupid.

"She's not!" Ani said.

"You, too?" he responded with a question.

Ruby wished she could see his face. "What makes you think Fox won't fight them? He did once."

"He'll fight that hard again. Maybe harder. But he won't risk getting taken out of the game. He wants his own bit of the running of the *Fire*."

"I know that," Ani said.

Ruby grimaced. "So some of the people in power are scared of me? Really? A dirty little slip of gray?"

"Sarcasm doesn't make you sound smarter."

Ruby bit her lip, keeping a smart-assed reply inside. After they went down another flight of seven steps, using a flimsy looking handrail, she said, "Ani thinks everything is sweetness and light," keeping her voice kind, lightly teasing, at least as best as she could.

"I do?" Ani asked. "I'm scared for you right now."

"But you don't think the reds you know would beat up the grays I know."

KJ turned to face them in the passage, still too narrow for them to walk side by side. "Stop."

"What?" Ruby said. "Arguing?"

He held up his hands and whispered. "Talking. People might hear us through the walls."

She nodded and they want back to scooting quietly sideways. A few times she heard voices on the other side, faint and too fuzzy to understand. Dust made her want to sneeze.

Being quiet had some advantages; she could think. They'd gone a long way through hidden places. Whether or not these narrow halls were hidden from Ix, they were hidden from most people. Someone had built them that way. And if KJ really could talk to people and keep it from Ix . . . and who had he been talking to anyway?

Why was she following him, and where was he taking her?

And who had built these passages?

At one point she whispered a question. "Is Dayn okay?"

"Probably," KJ said. "He's a survivor. Doesn't come to class often enough though. He might have pulled a muscle buying us time to get away."

Ruby laughed and they continued, dust tickling her nose so she sneezed a few times.

KJ stopped. He leaned down and whispered, "Now. When the door opens, follow me. We'll be back among people, and in a very short time, we'll catch a train. You'll follow me and sit behind me and say nothing. Look like you have been here before and like you know what you're doing. In fact, if you can, look very, very bored."

"Bored," she whispered.

"Very bored."

Ani placed a reassuring hand on Ruby's shoulder. "I'll look bored, too."

Ruby nodded. "Great. I love being bored."

The door opened in front of them and they came out into the back end of a galley storage room full of racks of carefully stowed dishes and cups. A thin layer of dust suggested it wasn't used much, although KJ held a silencing finger to his lips.

The other door in the room led to a hallway behind a galley and then into a train station.

Ruby forced herself into a casual stroll and then had to pick up a little speed to catch up with KJ. So not *that* bored.

The train car was nearly empty. Two men wearing blue sat in the front with their heads together. Ruby slumped beside Ani in the back, KJ sitting just ahead of them, blocking any direct view from the doorway.

No one followed them.

When the door closed, Ruby let out a long sigh and slumped further, taking a deep, exhausted breath. Every muscle in her back felt tense, and her legs were sore from the sideways walking. Maybe it would be a long train ride.

It wasn't.

She and Ani followed KJ through even more turns and rooms, passing two people dressed all in green, as well as a blue. Ruby did her best to look bored, even though it had dawned on her that between KJ of the smooth moves and Ani the tall, with the almost-black skin, she was the least likely of the group to draw attention.

The last door that KJ opened led into a small hab sized for the elderly, like the one where Owl Paulie had lived on gray. One room, a tiny kitchen unit along the wall, and a bedroom and bathroom.

"Where are we?" Ruby asked. "What level?"

"This is where we will hide you for now," KJ said. "But you must stay ready to move." He stood against the wall, folded his arms, and closed his eyes.

Ruby flopped onto the narrow bed and lay spread-eagled, staring at the ceiling. Ani looked down at her, silent, worry creasing her brow. Ruby closed her eyes, needing a moment to be inside herself. Ever since the day the sky fell, she hadn't been alone in the park, hadn't felt open spaces or sent birds flying across the sky.

There were people trying to hide her and people trying to find her. She'd just gotten control over her hab, and now that had been taken away. Forces she still didn't entirely understand swirled around her, comprehension just out of her reach. If she let things stay this way, let herself be led from place to place, she'd lose her sense of direction entirely. But if she stepped away, she might be captured, or worse. The one time she'd left Ani's side, she'd needed Fox to save her from Ellis.

Ruby opened her eyes and looked closely at Ani. "It's time I stopped letting people tell me what to do."

Ani blinked at her, looking taken aback. "We had to leave."

"No." Ruby stood up and looked Ani in the eyes. Ani took a step back. "That's not what I mean. But I'm tired of waiting until there's no choice." She leaned back against the wall, remembering the way Fox had shown his power through looking unconcerned the day he brought her here from gray. She knew now that he must have been very worried, but he hadn't shown it. She crossed her arms and smiled at Ani. "It's not about you at all. I'm talking about Fox, and the people who tell you what to do. I'm talking about Colin and KJ and the others."

Ani looked confused, so Ruby took her hand and opened the door. KJ turned to look at her, his face blank. She hadn't picked the easiest person to start with. "I'm not going to just do what I'm told anymore."

KJ looked serene.

"I need to know who is chasing me and who is protecting me. I need to understand who hates who and why, and what the various sides want. What is Colin's role? How does he relate to Fox? What does this Garth, who runs Ellis and Sylva, want?"

KJ remained still, watching her. But he stopped teasing her and gave a tiny nod.

FORTY-TWO
ACTS OF A MESSENGER

Onor and The Jackman walked side by side down a maintenance corridor that ran under the galley row in logistics. The underside of logistics looked worse than the underside of gray. Scuffed walls and banged-up pipes, dirty signs on the wall, graffiti here and there. It smelled like a noxious mix of stale water and bleach and oil. Perhaps there was no Penny here to care enough to force an apprentice to do a good job. "Where are we going?"

"It's your turn to take a message. You've seen Joel. He's on green today, and you need to tell him that we're setting up the meeting for three days from now. Tell him it's all good."

"What meeting?"

The Jackman smiled. "Messengers should never have the whole message."

"But you know it," Onor said. "And you won't tell me."

"You're safer if you don't know. We'll be past the time of secrecy soon."

Onor swallowed back the words he wanted to say. The Jackman wasn't running things, and had to do as he was told, just like Onor. At least he wasn't living in a bunk and dodging cleaning robots anymore. He had no job except to do what The Jackman said, and to train, all of which meant he was more exhausted than ever before, but happier.

This would be his fifth time trusted alone with a message, and the first time he'd been told to find anyone important like Joel. "I'll be happy to. When do I leave?"

"Now." The Jackman gave him directions and then a fierce, sharp hug that smelled of sweat and worry and stim and beard, and felt so like a father's hug that Onor gasped.

At the next turn the two of them split off in separate directions.

It didn't take Onor long to get to the door The Jackman had directed him to, and in moments more he had donned the suit he found waiting there and gone through a double hatch to pick up the maintenance cart he'd been instructed to push along the corridor on green.

The detailed planning that supported the simple movement of messages was almost scary. No one he knew seemed to have more than bits of information—like he had—and yet things lined up. Things he needed waited for him; doors that needed to be unlocked were.

The command level was so small it could fit inside one of the pods in the outer ring. Once inside, the level felt empty to him. Hushed, as if the work of commanding the *Fire* required the kind of thinking there was never time for on any other level.

He found Joel walking through a corridor, which was exactly what The Jackman had told him to expect. The timing was uncannily perfect, unless of course Joel had been pacing and watching for him for a while. Not likely; there was no sign of frustration on his face.

Joel recognized Onor as the messenger, since he stopped and asked Onor how his day was going even though his eyes didn't show any recognition of him.

Onor stammered out, "The meeting will be three days from now," and then sounded more confident as he added, "It's good. It's all good."

Joel accepted the message quietly, and Onor waited in case there was a message for him to take back.

Joel merely said, "Thank you."

Very well. Onor continued down the corridor, counting doors, trying to memorize everything he could about command. The Jackman collected every bit of intelligence Onor brought back, taking notes on a special journal that he never let out of his hands.

Footsteps made him look up. A tall, lean man in red approached him quickly and gave him a startled look. He was young and dark: skin, hair, and eyes. His face looked hard.

Onor turned away from him, a reflex to red, and then forced himself to meet the man's eyes and nod, doing his best to look like he belonged and had a place to go. A job. He hoped the stranger didn't see him shaking.

The man looked past Onor.

Onor continued the way he had been going, looking down at the cart and trying to escape further notice. All the planning in the world couldn't scrape the gray from his bones; his disguise was too thin for conversation.

He didn't hear the man walk away, but when Onor turned, he *had* taken a few steps. It dawned on Onor that the man had made no sound. None. To do that, he must be trying very hard. Even here in green, where everything was softer and cleaner than anywhere else, Onor's footsteps made soft thuds that would have been louder if he'd been moving fast.

The man had apparently decided not to worry about Onor. He was hurrying toward where Onor had talked to Joel.

Whatever was happening, he shouldn't act. He didn't know. Except it felt wrong. Joel's back receding, the stranger moving fast and so stealthy. Before he could finish thinking the situation through, the wrongness of the man caused Onor to call out, "Joel!"

Joel, far enough away to look small, turned and in one fluid move flattened himself against the floor.

The man fired a stunner down the hall, the fast and silent release of the beam frightening. Onor kept the cart between him and the man, who had turned to look at him. The assassin was turning his gun hand as well.

Onor shoved his cart, glimpsing Joel standing up behind the red. Onor's attention returned to himself as the cart slammed into his hip. He shoved it back at the man and ducked behind it, a stunner shot missing him. He pushed off from the wall, slamming his shoulder into the cart, giving it as much momentum as possible.

The cart pinned the red against the wall but left his hands free. His arm came up, pointing back at Joel this time, and then Joel was on him, slamming the arm into the wall so the stunner clattered onto the cart.

Joel pulled the assassin free of the cart and threw him to the ground on his stomach. Joel glanced back up at Onor and barked, "Hold him."

Onor practically tripped over the cart, kicking stunner and cart both out of the way, and threw himself onto the man's back below where Joel had his arms pinned, reaching for the man's free arm and twisting it up. Aric's training began to work Onor's body, giving him the balance and strength to keep the man down.

Joel whispered, "Finish it."

The man bucked under Onor and he tightened his grip, glancing up at Joel. "What?"

"Stay on his legs," Joel said, and then straddled the man across the back, standing. He gripped the man's head and the man screamed "No!" before his breath was cut off.

The crack of the man's neck drew a horrid taste to Onor's mouth, and his hands shook. It didn't matter now; the man didn't need to be held down anymore.

He hadn't been more than a few years older than Onor.

Joel stood and calmly picked up the stunner from the cart and looked it over, then pushed a button on the stock. He shoved the gun into his pants and looked at Onor. "Thanks. How did you know he meant to hurt me?"

The only thing Onor could think to say was, "He was walking wrong."

Joel nodded, looking more closely at Onor now. "You've training."

It wasn't a question, so Onor didn't answer it. He asked one instead. "What do we do about him?"

Joel looked down, showing no apparent remorse for ending the man's life, but also no triumph or happiness. More a weariness. "We'll leave him. It will be a message."

Onor swallowed and returned to the cart, not entirely sure what he should do next. Run away? Walk back down the corridor with the cart as if nothing had happened? Look after Joel, who did not appear to need any looking after?

Joel watched him, surely seeing the uncertainty on Onor's face. In fact, he was looking very closely at Onor, examining him, thoughtful. "Haven't I seen you before? On vid?"

"Probably at Owl Paulie's funeral. I met you underground once, too. After a training. But I doubt you remember that."

"You're gray?"

Onor nodded, sure that would earn him a dismissal.

"Would you like to work for me?"

Onor glanced down at the man on the ground, his eyes sightless and staring at the side of the corridor. He swallowed hard, shaking, perhaps only from the adrenaline of the fight. He had The Jackman expecting him. But Joel was in the middle of everything. "Yes."

FORTY-THREE

RUBY'S VOICE

Colin came up from behind Ruby and cupped her right shoulders with one of his large hands. "Are you ready to record?"

She put her hand briefly over his and then let it fall back into her lap. "I suppose I will never be more ready. And I best do this before I get caught."

"I won't let them catch you," he replied.

This time, there was no Fox, just equipment lying torn from his studio or one like it, a headset and a recording box and a toggle. All of it plugged into a journal like the one she'd seen KJ using the day they ran away from capture, the day after the gray show of force. The journal was the kind that didn't connect to Ix, although there would be no way to broadcast her voice without Ix knowing about it and maybe helping. But that was a puzzle she didn't know enough to unravel. She had her journal with her, but she hadn't needed the warning Colin gave her about keeping it off.

She reached for the headset and fit it over her unruly hair, sliding the jaw microphone into place and doing a brief sound check.

At least she'd paid close attention in the days she'd worked with Fox. She hadn't seen him since the second day she'd been on the run, when he'd brought her the best of her clothes, her journal, and the hairclips that Ani had given her the first day she'd been on the logistics level. He had looked at her with blank eyes, angry perhaps, but holding the anger in. "You'll need these," he'd said, his face flat.

Even though they were in a crowd, she leaned in and kissed him on the lips, and then she had said "Take care," meaning the words as a separation.

His response had been "See you soon." And then a glance away, and then more words. "It will be like it was. You need me."

He had turned and left immediately. Since then, she and Ani had been moved three times, and now they sat in what amounted to a conference room in the middle of the logistics level. She wanted to be back with her own people, with Marcelle and Onor and even The Jackman's hard looks, but she had to content herself with sending them love notes. This would be her third recorded message.

She started in. "People of hard work on this ship, people of the robot repairs and the water reclamation and the trash recycling and the gardens that feed us all. I have not been there beside you for a little while, but my heart is there. My hope is with you. *The Creative Fire* needs you at this moment. It needs your heart and your bravery, your hope and your hard work.

"We cannot stop the tasks that have been set before us. We cannot stop keeping the *Fire* running, for it is truth that without us the ship will die. But it is time for *our* contribution to be recognized. It is time to fight for *our* rightful place among the decision makers.

"I sat beside Owl Paulie and I learned of our history. I listened to the words of Lila Red the Releaser and I learned how the people in power are afraid of you, and that it is fear that drives them to lock us up, to beat us, to kill us.

"I have also sat with people who wear red and blue and green uniforms and who are *on our side*. They are also workers. They take the things we grow and make and they measure these things and ensure that they are distributed back. Many of them strive to give us fairness even though what we get is not often fair."

She wished she could see them. Their faces. She continued speaking to the audience in her head. "My message is simple. Those of us who want equality—and I know it is you, it is all of you who hear these words—we must identify ourselves. We must obtain and wear the colors of *The Creative Fire* all together like a painting of unity. For now, these colors must be shared only with those who we know share our dreams and our goals, with those who want freedom from the people who hold us down and take our production with no return or even appreciation. Our day will come soon, and I will come back among you, and I will encourage you. Not because I'm different from you, but because I'm like you."

She stopped there, thumbing off the sound, and leaned back.

Colin reached for the gear to take it from her head, but she waved him away.

"What else is there to say?" he asked.

She shook her head. "I need to go to them. I'm tired of hiding. After the meeting tonight I *am* going back home."

"I don't think that's smart," he said. "You'll be caught."

"And I won't be caught here?" she snapped.

"I want you to stay with me."

She took the headset off and paced. "I will not trade my freedom for another man. I can't." She looked at him. He had been fairer with her than Fox, had taken nothing. They weren't lovers even though rumor said so, and even though she felt him want her, and sometimes she felt the same heat. This was the first time she had seen him in two days. "I wouldn't be free with you. Perhaps we can go to dinner when this is all over, and then we can discuss what we might want to do."

Of course that was a lie. Everything would change once the fight started in earnest, and then she would be dead, or they would be busy until they arrived at Adiamo. It was not a big lie to tell; she might enjoy dinner with him if such impossibility ever happened. Or more. But she didn't need anything from Colin that he wasn't giving her without sex.

Ruby leaned over him and kissed his forehead. He spent his time organizing people like she spent hers organizing messages, but it wouldn't be enough. Colin could never capture the attention of the people on gray.

She wasn't entirely sure that she could.

KJ and Ani came in, and Colin left, trailing a hand across her shoulder yet again, trying to leave her with a promise she couldn't return and wasn't sure she wanted to. "The message will go out now?" she asked.

"Of course," he said.

Hopefully he wasn't lying. Her attention slid to her slender wardrobe as she waited for Ani.

An hour later she was ready, her hair done up on top of her head with Ani's clips and a new shawl Ani had brought for her lying across her shoulders. She drank tea laced with mint to calm her throat and then stood up at the appointed time and let KJ lead her and Ani through the warrens of the ship.

FORTY-FOUR
THE MEETING

Onor swept through the corridors near the meeting place, an exercise room in logistics that had gone unused since the *Fire* had last circled a planet. He looked for anything out of the ordinary, even a robot in the wrong place or any bit of trash that made no sense.

Joel had designed this meeting. He'd chosen the space. It would be a dangerous moment, when so many people who supported Joel would be gathered in one place. Onor didn't yet know who would be there, but curiosity kept him moving through his new duties, and he checked and double-checked everything, trying to be so precise that Penny would approve.

Confident that no hidden threats existed, Onor went back to wait beside Joel along with three of his other bodyguards. They joked, clearly as nervous as he was. Or almost.

Joel had mentioned Ruby in passing, asking a strange, dark-haired man named Colin to be sure that she arrived to begin the meeting. More than a meeting. The call to arms, the beginning.

Joel hadn't said so, but Onor was certain it was the start of a conflict that would spread out across the *Fire* and go on until an outcome was decided. It felt as if the whole ship had become pregnant with tension and needed the violence of birth.

Joel himself did not look nervous. He stood among his three closest advisors, drinking cups of stim, the choice of drink the only sign Onor could see of how seriously Joel took this evening. On a typical night, the men would sip still and strategize. Even now, they laughed together, apparently telling jokes, the picture of calm.

When it was time, Onor and the other guards preceded Joel through the door and down the hall. As they neared the door, the first beats of "Homecoming" sounded. Onor began to sing as Ruby did, opening the door at the beginning of the second line. "No stars shine inside *Fire*'s skin."

As expected, there were close to a hundred people. Ruby stood on stage and looked toward the door. He saw her recognize him, her green eyes flashing welcome and her smile broadening.

She was dressed in a pure blue uniform and a red shawl.

Of course, he was wearing blue, too. But the borrowed shirt smelled of someone else and fit him loosely across the shoulders, even if it did have his own rank insignia on it, bestowed by Joel.

Ruby's clothes had been made to show her off.

She'd grown taller, fitter. Her hair curled suggestively around her ears and hugged her neck. He felt as if he had stood still while she had gone through years of change, as if she were now older than him. The pride he felt at helping Joel had left, and he was only lovelorn and a bit lost. He shook himself, remembering his duty, going to stand by his boss.

Joel watched Ruby with narrowed eyes. "You know her," he said.

Again not a question. Onor nodded and kept watching the crowd, trying to keep his focus on Joel's safety.

"She is good for us. She is giving us the gray levels, and with them, we may win."

"It puts her in danger," Onor said, trying to decide if a tall man dressed in red was looking too closely at Joel.

Joel laughed and slapped Onor on the back. "After she sings, I'll talk. After I talk, will you introduce us?"

Onor swallowed. "Of course." It would get him near Ruby. He looked for Fox, but didn't see him. Colin—a man Onor had delivered two messages to—stood protectively behind her, and almost everyone in the room looked like they wanted a piece of her, lusted after her. A few ignored her or frowned, or talked in low tones in spite of the fact that Ruby was singing. Onor marked all of those for special watching, or to remember later in case he saw them again.

Ruby sang three songs and then bowed. The audience called out the names of songs she had sung already. She stood quietly on stage with her head down until the room grew still, and then she spoke with no microphone. Her voice carried perfectly, filling even the corners of the large room. "Thank you," she called out. "I am pleased that my songs please you. But we aren't gathered to hear me. I'd like to turn the stage over to a man far more important. I, too, came here to hear Joel North. In fact, I came here hoping to meet him." Her cheeks flushed red, and she walked toward Joel, who stood stock still until Onor gave him a small push.

Joel waved her away from him and said, "No. Not yet. Sing 'The Owl's Song' for us one more time and then I'll speak."

She moved into the song so smoothly it felt like a practiced movement, as if the two of them danced for the audience. Joel stood close to Onor the entire time Ruby sang. His face showed no emotion, but his focus felt so intense it frightened Onor.

When Ruby finished, a full beat of time passed, and then Joel took the stage from her and led a standing ovation, his hands clapping as loud and long as anyone's.

Ruby came and gave Onor a hug, taking all of his attention from the room and drowning Joel's opening remarks in the new ways she smelled of fruit and health and a bit of sweet sweat. She stood beside him for a few moments and then squeezed his hand and went to stand next to Colin. Onor was almost glad to have her a little bit away so that he could focus on watching for dangers in the audience.

He realized he'd missed most of the talk just as Joel uttered his last few sentences, "We can win, together. All of us, workers and logistics and peacers, all on one side. That is what we must make so, what we must be sure happens. And then, we will win our freedom. We will."

A woman at the back stood and clapped, then another, and then half the room was clapping. Maybe more. The people who didn't clap for Joel weren't generally the same as the ones who didn't like Ruby's singing, and Onor was losing track. He shook it off as he and three others stood behind Joel in a half ring, watching as Joel shook hands with each one of the men and women in the room, a rhythm that allowed a few sentences with each as the prior person left. This way, they sent a trickle out into the hallways, steady but uneven.

Onor envied the way Joel remembered names and faces, even the names of people's daughters or parents. He had an unlimited well of social trivia that rose in him and spilled out just the right way to bring tears, laughter, and determination into the eyes of those he spoke to.

This was the first time Onor had seen it used with a whole room of people, and he felt awed by the man he'd come to love being beside even after such a short time.

Onor shut the door behind the last stranger. That left only Onor and a handful of other bodyguards, Ruby and Joel, a tall, dark warrior of a woman named Ani, a silent, perfect man named KJ, and Colin.

Ani had taken up a position close to Ruby, protective of her back.

Onor approved.

Colin spoke first. "It's begun."

Joel nodded and glanced at Ruby. "You should go to the cargo bars with Colin."

She nodded, and then she smiled broadly, as if lit by a fresh idea. "Can I take Onor with me? For protection?"

Colin stepped closer to her.

"You will be safe with Colin," Joel said.

Ruby straightened her shoulders. "Colin will have other things to do. I want a protector I know." She glanced at Colin. "Know well. Who won't be running an empire, but only there for me."

Onor struggled to bite his tongue. He had wanted to be with Ruby ever since they were separated, but now he also needed to be beside Joel.

Ani looked like she wanted to say something pretty badly, but she had the discipline to resist the urge. Joel glanced back and forth between Ruby and Onor, as if looking for some sign they had planned this in advance. Onor sat as straight as he could and looked around the room so it would appear he wasn't hanging desperately on the answer.

The Ruby he had seen last would have kept demanding. But this Ruby stood still in the silence until Joel laughed out loud and slapped Colin on the back. "Let her bring her friend. We can always use a go-between."

Colin looked unhappy but didn't argue.

Joel spoke to Onor. "Do you want to stay with her?"

He swallowed. "I'll do what you'd most like me to do."

"Report on this meeting and then go to Colin."

Colin was in the room now. So what did go to him mean? "Excuse me please, where?"

One end of Joel's mouth quirked up. "To the cargo bars, of course."

The Jackman would know where to find him. But The Jackman would want Onor to provide more information than he had learned so far, and he could already see the look on The Jackman's face when he heard that Onor had gone off to be with Ruby instead of Joel.

Ruby gave him a slow wink that nobody but he and maybe Ani could see. "Hurry."

Joel cleared his throat and stopped Onor with a look. "Tell people—our people—all of them that you see. Tell them it's time. Tell them we're taking our rights back."

Onor went, with a last glance at Ruby. A heavy dose of worry hovered behind her smile. He wondered if he was the only person in the room who knew her well enough to see the worry.

FORTY-FIVE

PERMISSION TO TALK

After Onor left, the room fell quiet. To Ruby, it was as if something had been revealed in the previous few moments that changed the texture of the air itself. The message Joel had given Onor had been for all of them. It was time. She glanced at Joel, pleased to meet his eyes before he looked up at nothing, as if thinking.

Even in Joel's silence, Ruby nearly reeled from the confidence he exuded, the way it seemed like all the energy in the room went toward him. What she worked hard to be, he simply was. Here, in the halls of men who made decisions, anyway.

She would never be so much here, but he probably would not do so well writing the stories of a people. She would write about him though. She would.

In the meantime, between KJ and Colin and Joel, Ruby felt small and slightly overwhelmed, not to mention off balance from seeing Onor.

Joel offered his hand to her. His voice held a conflict: pleasure and worry. "I'm glad to see you in person. You are . . . almost what I expected."

She'd hardly said a word. The greeting puzzled her. "Can you explain that?"

He lowered his voice. "You have changed this ship. You're a wildcard. Ellis's advice to me is to help him lock you up, except that then we might have a true mutiny instead of a . . . power shift. I expected you to be interesting. I even expected you to be beautiful. I should have expected you to have charisma, but I failed."

She loved the sound of him. Because of that, he felt like the same trap Colin represented, only more dangerous. She stepped back.

Joel raised an eyebrow. "I'm no longer sure you're Fox's puppet. We'll leave it at that for now." He turned his attention to Colin and KJ. "We can't waste time. Is there somewhere safe for Ruby to wait until after we meet?"

To Ruby's surprise, KJ said, "She's safest with us, and for the moment at least, her safety is as important as this plan."

"Do you trust her so much?" Joel asked.

"I trust her to do what she is doing well. I wouldn't trust her to follow orders."

Ruby winced but said nothing. He had her right.

"But she can learn," KJ added. "And she has gotten this far. She won't tell tales."

Joel still stood close to her. He looked down, took a hand, and tipped up her chin. "You're not going to put what we say here into a song are you?"

She smiled. "Not until whatever you plan is done."

He laughed at that, a genuine laugh. "Very well."

Both Ani and Colin had remained silent, and neither had been consulted. Ani had no power here. Colin had power on the ship, more than she'd ever seen anywhere, and he had spent far more time with Ruby than KJ. Yet KJ was the one Joel asked about her. She revised her opinion of KJ, recalling the oddly dressed people in ponytails they had passed when they fled the class and the woman who had come in to warn him.

"Can we win?" Colin asked. A question, but not a question. Acquiescence. Obedience.

Joel glanced at Ruby. "Depends on what surprises I can pull off. I'll send you enough troops to reinforce yours and protect the cargo bars, and I may give you some objectives as we go. It will rattle Garth if he gets the message that he's clearly lost you. Are you ready for that?"

"Yes." Colin said the word with such conviction that Ruby believed him. Good.

"People are going to die," Colin continued. "We can't stop until we win. If we do, it's over for us. We will have one chance."

KJ spoke. "We've been slowing for almost a year. I don't know when we get home, but we should be close enough to talk to Adiamo soon. We are nearly out of time."

Ruby broke in. "Let me go to the grays. I can make sure they support you."

Joel looked surprised and a bit put out. Well, if he didn't expect her to join the conversation, that was just too bad.

Colin growled, the sound low in his throat and unhappy. "It will put you in danger."

Joel gave her a measured gaze but said nothing.

She kept her eyes on him, trying to figure out what would make him see her as capable. She chose silence.

It took a very long time, but Joel eventually nodded at Colin. "Have Fox help you get her songs and stories throughout gray. Take her out if you can keep her safe."

Colin laughed. "Fox is not likely to be happy with that assignment."

"Then manage him," Joel said.

Ruby stayed as still as she could.

While the men talked about the strength of their fighters, she paid enough attention to realize Garth commanded the whole ship—everything on *The Creative Fire*—and that there were almost as many reds and blues and even greens that hated him or wanted him out of power as there were people loyal to him. They just weren't as well organized.

At least they had better odds than she'd thought. Garth had apparently made a lot of people pretty angry.

As the men argued through details, her mind kept going to what she might say and how she might encourage her people to fight, even though the odds were against them.

FORTY-SIX

IN THE CARGO BAR

The Jackman hadn't been at the rally. Or if he had, Onor hadn't noticed. But he stood outside the door, waiting, wearing exactly the expression Onor had expected: worry, unhappiness, and a bit of disgust.

"Did you see her?" Onor blurted out, even though he knew better. "Did you know she'd be here?"

They came to a "T" intersection and The Jackman took the rightward corridor. "No good is about to happen."

"Isn't this the fight you've been working for all along?"

The Jackman laughed, bitter and short. "Maybe I'm too used to trying to skulk around the corridors here."

"Yeah, yeah. What about Ruby?"

"If we hurry up, you can catch the next train to the bars."

"So you were listening?"

"Of course. What if you'd gotten in trouble?"

Onor bristled. "I can take care of myself."

"You'll get the chance to prove that. See that you're right."

"There's going to be a real fight this time?"

"You heard Joel."

"How will Ix respond?"

The Jackman shook his head, his eyes laughing but a little spooked in spite of that. "Ix has a long, narrow view. I don't know what it thinks."

They rounded the corner into the train station. "This isn't where we went before," Onor said.

"Brilliant noticing."

"Right."

"There's more than one stop for that train, you know."

The room and the platform were empty. "Where is everybody?"

The Jackman shook his head. "I don't know. It's always emptier on this level, but this feels too empty."

"If there's people on our side everywhere—on all the levels of the ship—how do we know who they are?"

The Jackman was turning in place, looking around. "Sometimes we don't."

The Jackman's breath, and his own breath for that matter, sounded loud in the empty room. The Jackman put up a hand, and they both stopped. "Train," he said.

When it came, the cars were full of reds, peppered here and there with blues. No grays. Of course, he and The Jackman were dressed as blue as anybody. When the doors opened, they stepped on and flattened themselves against the wall of the train car.

The faces in the car were strained, expressions varying from determined to scared. Voices spoke in high, nervous whispers. The train hummed and the whispers spun up Onor's spine. Although he struggled to hear details, all he really got was that there was a fight somewhere already, that people were hurt, and that people were dead. He heard Ruby's name three times.

The train kept going through the next stop—the one they'd used to board the day they went to the cargo bars and just stood. The Jackman leaned down and whispered in his ear. "Get off fast."

"Okay."

They made it out the doors first and The Jackman took off at a quick walk, not even looking back to see if Onor followed. Once they were in the corridor he broke into a slow jog. They passed a pair of reds, The Jackman nodding to them, and Onor again wondered how to tell who was on what side. Then he spotted a tiny ribbon of gray on one of the red's wrists, and it reminded him of Ruby's beaded necklaces.

The Jackman ducked through a door and gestured for Onor to follow. They crossed a large, empty space and came to a set of stairs. "Go on up," The Jackman said.

Onor started up and then stopped, realizing The Jackman wasn't following. He bit back the instinct to ask him to come. "What's going on?"

"The fight. The people we came with on the train will be bringing it here, so get up there before they get to this door. You don't want to be questioned."

He glanced up at the door above him and then back at The Jackman. "Thanks."

The Jackman was already gone. Hopefully he'd heard.

At the top of the stairs, Onor hesitated at the doorway, took a deep breath, and stepped through. Two men grabbed him, one on each arm.

"Hey!"

"Who are you and what's your business here?"

"Onor. Colin told me to come here. To protect Ruby."

One of the guards laughed. "The redheaded snap he's attached to?"

He filed that for future consideration. "Yes. And you best watch out. I came on the last train, and there's a pile of people coming—they'll be here soon. Not friends."

"You talk like a gray."

"That doesn't change the truth." He stood straighter and tried to pull his arms free. They were held too tight. Then one was freed as the man closest to the door let go of Onor and stepped to where he could see the stairs Onor had come up. The guard's face froze and hardened. He said, "He's right. Get Claire to watch him."

A soft beeping started. An alarm. One of the two men must have set it off. Before he had time to figure out why, Onor had been dragged around a corner and into a bigger room. The guard led him to a barstool and gestured to a woman as broad as Penny and taller. "Keep him for us."

She laughed.

The alarm had called people from many nearby places; the room began to fill up and organize. Here and there, Onor spotted the confluence of gray and red and blue that meant friend.

Claire leaned on the bar beside him, close enough to grab him if he moved. As edgy as he was, sitting still made his stomach and dry throat scream. "Does watching me include providing food and water?"

Streaks in the back of her head suggested Claire had been dark haired when she was younger. Strong bones and bright blue eyes told him she had probably also once been beautiful. Now, her eyes and lips were surrounded with fine lines. In spite of her bulk, she looked edged and tight. She reached down, drew out a glass, and filled it without having to glance down. She plopped it on the bar next to him. "A start." Her eyes narrowed. "Now trade. What's up?"

He took a long drink of water, thinking. This was where he was supposed to be, and he'd been called by Ruby and sent by The Jackman. He could talk. "You know about us surrounding this place a few days ago, right?"

"Seemed pretty stupid to me."

"We just want to be able to come . . . well, here."

"News flash. Most people don't care if you're locked out or not."

"There's a lot of *us* who care." He drank more water, which mostly made him hungry. The room was still filling up, although the attention was all near the front, mostly on one of the two men who had grabbed him. He should gather intelligence for The Jackman. "So what *do* you care about?"

"We want the right people in charge when we get home. Garth and his iron-fist gang aren't it. They don't share well."

"Share what?"

"Information. Power." Claire's voice had gotten higher and anger was drawing her severe face into a near snarl. "That's going to be who's attacking. They're on us faster than I thought. I hope to hell we're ready."

"Me, too." Not that he understood what was going on yet, but he knew the stakes. It was the same war his parents had died in. "If I can have some food I might be a little more ready."

She laughed. "The key to all warriors is their belly."

FORTY-SEVEN

A SPEAKING PART

The four of them—Ruby and Ani, Colin and KJ—came into Colin's lair all together through an entrance she hadn't even known existed. The room was so full it almost looked small, even with the high ceilings and bright lighting. It smelled like fear and testosterone and stale stim. Suits and helmets had been laid out along the floor on one side of the room, and three men stood guard over the suits. She couldn't be sure, but it looked like there were fewer suits than people.

She spotted the back of Onor's head resting on his hands at the bar, an empty bowl beside him.

Four or five people were already converging toward Colin. She took advantage of his split attention and went toward Onor. Not only did Colin not make an attempt to stop her, she wasn't even sure he noticed she'd left. Ani, of course, stayed with her like glue. The ever-present, supportive protector.

A tired-looking old woman leaned on the back side of the bar, close to Onor. "Hello, Claire," Ani said, "How is he?"

Ruby didn't want to wait for an answer. She put a hand on Onor's shoulder to feel the rise and fall of breath.

Claire must have noticed Ruby's worried look. She sneered. "I diagnose simple exhaustion. I gave him some food and a glass of wine. He fell asleep as if he were home safe in bed."

Ruby bristled at the woman's tone of voice. "He's my friend. Take it from me, he's never been safe."

Claire turned away, muttering. "Quit thinking only you grays have it tough."

Ani broke in. "Do you have a few more bowls of whatever he had? Only without the sleeping powder?"

The food gave her immediate strength, and Ruby felt oddly content to sit beside Onor while he snored softly. She watched the chaos in the room form itself around Colin and KJ. "I can trust them, can't I?" she mused.

"You can trust Fox, too," Ani replied between bites.

"Really?"

"He came for you."

Ruby snorted. "I can't love a man who keeps me prisoner."

"Or have a friend who keeps you safe?" Ani countered, a lightly hurt look in her eyes.

"Safe is useless."

"So's dead." Ani's lips had thinned and her eyes narrowed, but her focus had shifted to Onor. "Do you love him?"

"He's been my *friend* forever."

A loud thump came from the front of the room. Then a grunt. A scream, cut off. "They're here," Ruby whispered. "Fighting."

"Get behind the bar." Ani pushed on Ruby's shoulder, trying to move her.

Ruby glanced at Onor and then at the front of the room, where KJ and Colin had both disappeared in the crowd. She reached over and squeezed Onor's shoulder. "Wake up."

He sat bolt upright, surprise registering on his face when he saw her.

"Let's go."

"Wait," Ani said.

Ruby took Onor's hand and pulled him off the barstool, heading toward the front. Ani could follow or not.

Ruby pulled Onor close enough to the door to see what was going on. The only real sign of trouble was a man in red laying motionless across the floor. Looming over the body, but paying it no attention, the two big door bouncers stared outward. Everyone else milled behind them, pushing. Then two men dragged the body toward the side of the room.

Colin stood against the wall, facing inward. She pushed through three fairly big men to stand next to him and look out at the room, seeing what Colin saw. A few hundred people, most of them bunched together, facing forward. Blues and reds, men and women. Most of them men. Faces determined and anticipatory. Hungry, almost.

Hot breath and whispers and shuffling created a sort of white noise.

In the far back, by herself, Claire leaned against the bar.

Ani popped out from behind a knot of people. She met Ruby's eyes for a moment, looking betrayed.

Colin noticed Ruby and pulled her in close to him, sharply and for just a moment. Her head came lower on him than on Fox, near his heart, and his arms caged her lightly. He leaned down and whispered in her ear. "Are you ready to talk to them?"

She nodded, her mouth suddenly dry.

"I'll set it up." He let her go. His voice boomed across the room, almost surely loud enough to be heard by anybody foolish enough to be on the stairs outside. "Here we go. We've been waiting for this forever, for our moment to run *The Creative Fire*. But before we can make choices about the ship, we have to win tonight, and maybe tomorrow, and maybe the day after that."

Faces were all turned to him, eyes glinting in the overhead light.

"The doors are guarded again; the stairs are safe. You will go out, and when you return, we will be in charge."

Someone in the crowd yelled out, "Yes!"

"Ix is on our side," he said. "As long as we bring no weapons and do no damage. As long as we respect the *Fire*. We must do that or we will lose Ix, and if we lose Ix, we lose the battle and the war, and we lose any chance at our freedom. Can you all respect the *Fire*?"

A roar rose up, a cacophony of affirmation that included the words *yes* and *now* and *we will*. People smiled, and, in a few places, bigger people boosted smaller ones up so everyone could see Colin's face.

"We are fighting for the *Fire*'s soul."

Colin's words were perfect. They made Ruby's eyes sting as she watched the fighters cheer.

When the sound had died down a bit, Colin continued. "This is not a fight between powers, but a fight between ideologies. Everyone from the outer levels is with us, but in our home, we will have to tell one from the other. No one—not even me—knows all of our faces. Show your sign."

He paused as people held up necklaces and ribbons, buttons and scraps of material knotted into headscarves. All of it was red and gray and blue together, and a few had even added green. Ruby smiled to see the green, knowing instinctively it was right.

She had not created this, could not have created it. Time and stress and cruelty and abuse had made this insurrection, and it went back at least as far as Lila Red, but she *had* given them the sign. Her throat felt thick. She cleared it and sipped water. This was going to be as hard as singing at Owl Paulie's funeral had been.

As if he knew what she was thinking, Colin went on to say, "Most of you know the woman who started this sign."

A few voices said her name. Then a few more. "Ruby! Ruby! Ruuuuuuubyyy!" The calls started to smear together, "RuRuRuby, Ruby," and then developed into a chant, her name over and over. Colin let it build, encouraged it by joining in.

Her heart beat fast, slamming blood into her fingers and toes and heating her cheeks.

Colin leaned down and whispered, "Ready?"

She nodded. "Are they ready to go? Can I send them off?"

Colin glanced at the man beside the door, who nodded. "Yes."

She took a deep breath and let the act of finally speaking quiet her upset tummy and racing nerves. "I grew up walking beneath your feet. We called you reds and blues because all we knew was the color of your uniforms, and mostly we knew the reds and feared them."

They had settled and were watching, but she didn't have them yet. "As I wore used uniforms and worked as a bot repair girl, I dreamed of you. In the moments between work, in the bits of time after school, in my bed when I woke up in the dead quiet of our shift's sleep time, I imagined knowing you and knowing *The Creative Fire*. Because, you see, we didn't know either." She paused, testing. They had become quieter. "My best friend died in my arms out there. My friend Onor's parents died in the fight you are going to."

She looked for Onor's face to point to but didn't see it. Surely he heard her. "You are fighting for yourselves, for freedom of choice when we get home. You are also fighting for who I was, for all of my family and my friends. We have promise and skills and hope and great hearts . . . as do you."

That was almost enough. It was time.

"Stay safe and fight well and treat the people like me from the outer levels as equals and as friends, *and they will help you.* As you go out that door, I'm going to sing for you." She started into "Homecoming":

> *Long and dark is our night flight*
> *No stars shine inside* Fire's *skin, only*
> *Me and you. And love.*

People shuffled past her, the flow outward constrained by the narrow stairs, so she had time to sing the song through three times.

As the last fighter left, between verses, she stopped and took a deep breath, glancing around. Ani had come up and was nodding her head to the beat. Claire, still back by the bar, mouthed the words. Onor was easy to spot in the nearly empty room. He stared at her as if she were some entirely new person. Maybe she was.

Colin said, "Please. Finish the song."

PART THREE

ACTING

FORTY-EIGHT
RETURNING

The last note of Ruby's song lingered in the air. It had sunk deeper into Onor's heart each time she sang it, so that now, when Ruby was done, he *knew*—for the very first time since Ruby had told him so—that they were heading for a home lost to memory, to a place none of them had seen or could even imagine. He knew awe. He knew Adiamo was as real as the *Fire* and much more than a game contained within it.

The song and her delivery made him part of the ship, the *Fire* and the people all together, like one organism in the vastness of space, an organism on its way home.

Home.

Onor had trouble peeling his gaze away from Ruby. Sweat slicked her brow and damp tendrils of flyaway red hair stuck to her temples and cheeks. She had just sung to him with her very essence, and he felt changed by her.

A shuddered breath that shook his very center drove him to refocus on his surroundings. The first thing he noticed was the look on Colin's face, and knew it mirrored his own.

Ruby turned to Colin, seeking his approval.

Onor took a deep breath, unwilling to trust his voice to say anything at all.

Colin embraced Ruby, whispering something for her ears only, smiling, a man tender for a woman. Then he stood and looked around the room.

About a dozen people remained. A woman near the front desk, Claire by the bar, Ani, Colin, Ruby, and a handful of people who now bent to clean up after the chaos of departing soldiers.

Colin looked directly at Onor for the first time since the meeting. His eyes narrowed, and he glanced from Onor to Ruby and back again. He didn't look happy with what he saw. He looked like a man in a trap.

When he spoke, he seemed to be holding Onor to a promise. "The fighting may come here. You must do what she said you would. You must keep her safe. Take her home."

Ruby gasped.

"To g . . . gray?" Onor hated that he stammered and didn't sound as strong as he felt.

"The fighting will be here, I think. I hope. Take Ani with you. Stay very aware, always, every moment. I've already told The Jackman where to find you. He'll keep you safe, but you must defend Ruby. We just announced her presence here to way too many people, so she must not be here."

Did that mean Colin thought there were traitors among the men and women he and Ruby had just sent out the door?

Colin kept pressing. "Be sure she's surrounded by people who will take care of her. She's . . . she's important."

"I know how to help myself if I have to," Ruby said, the words stopping Colin mid-rant.

He turned to her. "No, I suppose I shouldn't underestimate you, should I?"

She laughed in his face, and he laughed back, the tension and the awe and the fear in the room all shattering against their banter so that even Onor felt his shoulders relax.

"Claire will lead you three out the back. Pay careful attention in case you need to return that way. The tunnels are less convenient than the train, but they won't break down."

As Claire came forward, Colin pulled Ruby to him and kissed her on the lips, hard and proprietary, looking up at Onor as soon as he was finished.

Onor managed not to flinch. "I'll keep her safe."

Colin walked out the front door, following the fighters. He glanced back once, and the look on his face told Onor that the man would change places with him if he could.

Onor felt odd wearing gray again, as if he wore a shadow of the past. The shirt hung big on him, but at least it smelled clean. He, Ruby, and Ani had all traded blues for grays. Claire had pulled an oversized gray shirt over a blue one and still looked decidedly uncomfortable, as if the gray color contaminated her.

She moved quietly and deliberately, familiar with the twisted and battered spaces between cargo bays.

Each opening was marked with numbers, and Onor tried to keep track of them as they went, worried he was losing some of the details he'd need to get them back. From time to time he looked over his shoulder, so he'd recognize the way.

The corridors stank of oil and dirt and stale air, and even of dust. He had to fight not to sneeze.

They walked for at least an hour. They crossed open floor and squeezed through narrow openings. Twice they had to crawl up ramps that appeared to have been cobbled together from scraps to allow human traverse.

They'd turned so many times and gone up and down the outside of cargo containers so much that he'd become completely disoriented by the time Claire finally opened a dogged hatch that led to a tunnel, through another hatch, and then into the gray level. "Where are we?" Ruby asked.

"D."

"There'll be more reds *here* than anyplace else," Ruby hissed. "The lockup!"

"Peacers," Ani said, like a reflex.

"Not here, they're not," Ruby replied, equally a reflex.

Claire ignored the entire conversation and fixed her eyes on Ani. "Can you get back to us if you have to?"

"I can," Onor said. Colin had given him the job.

Claire ignored him. Ani's "yes, thank you" came out quite clipped.

Onor wasn't sure which of them was happiest to have the hatch close with Claire on the other side of it. He imagined her stripping off her gray overshirt and becoming herself before she started back.

Onor finally felt free to talk to Ruby. "You were great back there." He put a hand on her shoulder, looking into her eyes, trying to read what she felt for him right then. "Your voice has grown."

She relaxed a tiny bit under his fingers as she let out a long, slow breath. Her eyes dropped away before he could read anything but worry in them. "Is The Jackman supposed to meet us here?"

"I don't know. We should figure out where we are," Onor said. "Do you know where lockup is? I want to avoid it."

Ruby shook her head. Ani answered. "It's below. Under the reclamation plant."

So near where he had been bunking. He laughed. "Figures." Then he glanced at Ruby. "Marcelle lives in this pod now."

Ruby's eyes lit up. "Let's find her."

Ani interrupted. "We should hide."

Ruby shook her head. "Let's get to common. We need to know what's happening. Surely there's someone there."

"Have you gone mad?" Ani's voice sounded strident.

Ruby must have heard fear in Ani's voice, too, since she turned to her and whispered, "We'll keep you safe."

The words shocked Ani into standing straighter.

Before he got caught looking dumbfounded yet again at how much Ruby had grown and changed, Onor started off, hoping he was going in the right direction. Surely Colin had told The Jackman what pod they were in. He'd find them. Besides, Onor was feeling the lack of sleep again. Whatever benefits he'd gained from the uneasy nap on the hard bar surface were draining away from him. If he stopped, he'd crash, and then it *would* be up to Ruby to keep them safe.

Onor peered carefully around each turn before he took it. No reds stalked the halls. In fact, they were entirely too empty. They finally passed a threesome of older workers straggling between shifts, lifting tired hands in greeting. Just as they passed, the tallest of the three narrowed his eyes at them and stopped his brethren. "I don't know you."

"I've just been transferred from D-pod," Onor replied casually.

"Trains aren't running," one of the men said in a hard voice.

The tall one had set his face in a stubborn look. "How do I know you're one of us?"

Ruby laughed, an easy laugh that didn't show any of the tension Onor felt. "We're on your side. There's a fight happening, a fight between us and the worst reds."

"Worst reds?" the man replied.

"Watch," Ruby said. She pulled a necklace out of her pocket and fastened it around her neck. The same blue and red and gray one Daria had made for her just before the test, just before she disappeared. "You'll see this sign, these colors. Maybe some green, too." She pointed at Ani, who wore the sign in a swatch of thin ropes she'd attached to her belt. "Tell people. The ones with this sign are helping you. Even the reds or blues wearing the sign are helping. Helping us."

The tall man looked confused and still dangerous. Then the one who hadn't spoken yet whispered, "Ruby. That's Ruby."

Ruby smiled, lighting up at the reverence in the man's voice. "Yes."

"Where are you going?"

"Common," Onor said.

"No." The expression on the tall man's face had changed entirely, his voice less suspicious as well. "Our children are there. We don't want fighting in common."

"The park?" Ruby asked.

"Under. Go under."

Onor didn't like that. "By lockup?"

Boot steps echoed behind them. Onor didn't need to turn to see if it was reds because the men's eyes widened.

"Hide," the tall one hissed again. "We'll distract them. Now."

The men started forward, a determined look on their faces.

Ruby whispered after them, "Watch for the sign." They ducked into the first doorway they found. A storage room, the walls lined with closed doors and drawers. As the door closed behind them, the light in the room snapped off and they stood in the dark.

"I can't believe Colin sent us here," Ani whispered. The dark accentuated the slight quiver in her voice.

Ruby grunted. "These are my people. They'll protect me. And anyone with me. You'll be okay."

"Shhhh," Onor cautioned as the sound of boots went by outside.

A few breaths after the last echo of a step had died, Ruby opened the door, the light an assault on Onor's eyes.

"There they are!"

Onor prepared to run, but Ruby stopped him with an outstretched arm in front of his chest. "It's our friends."

Sure enough, the same three men. "Do you know what's under the park?" Onor asked. "What happens there?"

The tall one nodded, his eyes showing a tiny bit of surprise and then acknowledgment.

"Can you take us there?" Onor asked.

A smile crossed the man's face. He nodded. They walked quickly, the three strangers no longer slumped.

A group of twenty people milled at one end of the room under the park, apparently waiting for something. Some of them turned and then jostled their neighbors, and soon they were all looking at the newcomers. A few said her name, "Ruby." One called it loudly, sharply. Not happy.

Onor recognized it.

Lya. She, too, had grown thinner, and dark circles smudged the spaces under her eyes. In the time since they had all been broken apart, Lya had changed as much as Ruby, but not in the same way. She looked older and smaller and frightened.

Onor looked for Hugh, spotted him in the back of the crowd talking to a group of men. He didn't recognize anyone else. The group was clearly waiting for something or someone. He'd thought it might be the men they came with, but they had melted into the group as well, joining the waiting, the small talk, most people still looking at Ruby.

Lya raced to Onor and clutched him in an embrace so tight it hurt a bit. He breathed her in, smelling sweat and fear. She trembled.

He brushed the hair away from her face. Her cheek was wet with tears. "What happened?" he asked her. "Are you okay?"

"No." She stepped away from him and glared at Ruby. "No, I'm not. I don't want to fight. I don't want anyone to die." She took a step toward Ruby, her voice trembling but sharp and loud. "It's your fault. This is all because of you." She took another step, her face so angry. Onor grabbed her arm lightly, keeping her from getting closer to Ruby.

"Let it go," he whispered to her. "It's happening now and nothing will change it. We're going to be free. It's the only way."

Lya pulled away and spat at his feet. "Only if we're not dead."

FORTY-NINE

A CHOICE

The industrial light of the storage level below the park made Lya's face look white and nearly dead. Ruby cringed at the look Lya gave her: fear and anger and maybe even hatred all at once. Strong, and dangerous. Ruby didn't dare smile, but she met Lya's eyes. "This has to be done, Lya. I don't like it, and it's not fair. But neither is the way we've been treated."

"You love it," Lya screeched at her. "It's all you ever wanted—attention from everybody. You started this!" She put hands over her face and let out a wracking sob. "You made us believe."

"I didn't make you do anything," Ruby replied, struggling to sound reasonable. "I'm only a singer. I try to draw attention to the things that need to change, but I don't make the injustice."

"We're going to die because of you."

"No, Lya," Onor said loudly enough to address the whole gathered crowd. "You're afraid. It's okay. This is something to be afraid of. But it's not Ruby's fault."

Hugh had noticed the conversation. He came nearer but didn't intervene. Ruby felt as if he was waiting for a chance to talk to her.

A hand fell on Ruby's shoulder from behind, and Onor's eyes lit. She turned to face Conroy as he said, "Well, who do we have here? A slip of trouble come to send us off?" His voice didn't sound unfriendly, but he also didn't seem overjoyed to see her.

"Send you off? Where?"

"Why, to fight for the Gem of the Fire's freedom, of course."

Gem of the Fire? *Gem of the Fire?* That was all she needed. She straightened her back. "Not to send you off."

Conroy raised an eyebrow at her. "Colin or Fox would let you fight? What are you going to do, sing the reds a song?"

First Lya, and now Conroy. "I might. Or I might know those levels well enough by now to help you get around."

Conroy's lips thinned. "You really do mean to go?"

"Yes."

Sure enough, Onor was at her side, whispering in her ear. "You can't do this. I promised to keep you safe."

Ruby didn't take her eyes off Conroy. The room had gone quiet, everyone's attention on her now. "It's the right thing. I can't sing about blood and not ever see it. I'm going." And she would. She would write songs about whatever happened today. She could hear them inside her already, wanting out even though the words weren't there yet.

"You're not leading," Conroy snapped.

She had to laugh. As if she even could lead a fight! "I'm not that stupid."

Conroy appeared to be trying to turn purple. He glared at her and Onor, a look so harsh that Ruby felt Onor step back from it. She had to force herself not to go back with him. She spoke so softly that only Conroy and maybe Onor could hear. "I'll help you."

Only after he nodded did she step back. Conroy went around the group, as far from Ruby as he could get, and started calling out orders. She ignored Onor and Ani, and was careful to do exactly what Conroy asked her to do.

She felt more like her old self again, dressed in ragged grays, her face a mess, her hair streaked with oils from a few places where she'd bumped pipes or walls climbing or crawling through the tunnels between the cargo bars and here. She even smelled like herself again. It felt right, going into the fight, being in gray, being with her people, even arguing with Conroy. It was all familiar and easy, edged with danger.

Surely Joel was out there fighting somewhere. Wherever he was, he would be focused on what he was doing. What could she do? What did she need to do, or better, what one thing could she alone do?

Conroy had finished giving direction. He stood and watched his commands being executed. People lined up and quieted down, getting ready. She went up to him and stood on tiptoe, whispering in the big man's ear in spite of the annoyed look he gave her. "Can I talk to them all for a moment? Please."

He looked at her with a stone face. She could feel him about to say no. "Please. It'll help."

"Damn you."

"Thanks." She almost darted in to kiss his cheek, but she'd pushed him far enough. She cleared her throat and took deep breaths, the same kind Jali had taught her to use to center before a performance.

Finally, all eyes were on her and Conroy. She started: "How many of you have heard my messages over the last few days? Not the songs, the messages?"

Fewer than half raised a hand. Better than nothing, but not enough. "Do you remember tales of Lila Red the Releaser?"

Heads nodded. Most people said, "Yes."

"Good. Think about her name. She wasn't one of us." Ruby paused for a breath, letting it sink in. She noticed a new face on the outside of the circle. Marcelle had changed enough that Ruby failed to recognize her at first. She looked strong and fierce, smiling over the heads of the crowd at Ruby and Onor. It gave Ruby even more hope, made her more sure she was right and that she needed to join these people. "Lila Red came from the inner levels. Yet she fought for us. For just a moment, think of the reds as people who manage the place, who keep things safe." Before anyone could protest, she lifted a hand. "I know. That is not what they are here and now. Not usually. We've all learned to hate most of them."

Murmurs of assent pulsed through the circle. Ani, near her, drew a deep inward breath.

Ruby kept going. "But it is what they were meant to be, and probably what they once were. Some still are. A red named Ben helped me grow up safely, and two reds whose names I don't know killed my best friend. So it goes both ways. Never forget the reds are our enemies, but never forget they are also our friends. Good and bad is more complex than the color of a uniform."

She let a few moments pass, looking at faces, noting that many people appeared willing to agree with her even if others looked set against her. It would do.

"Think of the blues as organizers and managers, like the people who run the crews you work on, only with different worries. Responsible for the whole garden at once rather than just that day's tending crew."

She glanced at Ani and then recalled the way Ani's voice shook when she first came in. "Just like in Lila Red's time, people are working together from all of the levels. I am proof of that. I'm here now, and I've been there, and I will go back there. We will all be able to do that. We will all be able to do that *without fear*."

A slender blond woman who had introduced herself as Gerri said, "How do we know who we're fighting?"

There. That was the question she'd needed. She pointed to her necklace again. "Watch for blended colors."

Three people pulled out the sign, one in cloth, one in beads, one a set of strings that had been braided together to make a necklace. Only a few in the circle looked surprised.

"So you know," Ruby said. "You already understand. What you also need to know is that we need to win now. The *Fire*'s bringing us home, and we need to win before we get close, so we have a voice in decisions when we get there. We need our fair share of the cargo and the decisions. We need what we've worked for."

Gerri snorted. "Why now? We never had any of those things before."

"Yes, we did. When we left Adiamo, we had them all. We had a voice, an equal one to logistics and the peacekeepers—the reds. That's what we're fighting to get back. To have control over what happens to us when we no longer live inside the *Fire*."

Lya spoke up, her voice knotted and miserable. She addressed the crowd rather than Ruby. "People will die," she said.

The crowd's eyes didn't waver from Ruby. Good. She couldn't afford to let fear intrude. "Lila Red died for the same thing. But we're better prepared and there are more of us." She didn't know that, not really. But it was what people needed to hear. "I've been inside, and we have a lot of support. We have so much support that you need to look for the sign on everyone you see in a red or blue or green uniform. A lot of times it's going to be there. And those people are our friends, no matter what color they're dressed in."

A male voice said, "Lila's dead."

When Ruby turned to look, no one met her eyes to admit they'd been the speaker. "I might die, too. But at least I won't die being raped to death or beaten in a back corner of lockup, and I won't be assigned dangerous work and die in an "accident." If any of us die today, we'll die for each other."

A man who didn't identify himself asked, "What will happen when we go out there and fight?"

Good. He'd said *when* and not *if.* She'd done enough, and she could feel Conroy's agitation beside her. "Ask Conroy. I came back to you today, to be here on the right side of this. To support the fight, to be part of it. Not to lead it. I don't know the details of what your leaders want you to do. I do know Conroy, and he's good."

Conroy glared at her but did his job and stepped back up to address the crowd. He told them, "Capture anyone you can. Ix won't support killing anyone unless it's in self-defense. As far as I can tell, it's on our side, but it won't do anything to help or hurt us unless we threaten the *Fire*." He paused and glanced around, as if making sure of everyone's attention. "But that could happen. You should know that. We can die as well. At Ix's hand or the hand of the people we're trying to overthrow. So be careful of each other. And be careful not to get hot and do anything that damages major ship systems. If the *Fire*'s hurt, we all lose. Do you understand?" He waited until the crowd responded to him with affirmations. Then he added, "We're in the right. We're fighting for our voice, our say, our freedom, our safety. We deserve to win, and if we're clever and good and brave, we can win. But the outcome depends on you, and me, and all of us. On our strength and our bonds."

Ruby approved.

The tall man who had led them here helped Conroy distribute stunners. There were enough stunners for about half the people, and Conroy briefly reviewed how to shoot them. Ruby didn't even try to get Conroy to give her a stunner, but she watched carefully. The people who took them already knew how to use them. Marcelle took her stunner as if it were a journal, handling it comfortably.

The people in gray were always fit because they worked hard, but still, she spotted extra muscle and leaner bodies and set jaws and heard resolve in most of the whispers between warriors. Only a few of the voices were laced with fear, like Lya's.

Onor stood beside her, mute, watching her watch.

During a short break in the conversation, she said, "I had to do it."

"Did you?"

She nodded at Conroy. "I'm proud of Conroy and what he's made here. And you were part of it, I know you were. I could never have trained people like this."

He smiled, but his smile carried anger in it, and more steel than she was used to seeing in him. Onor had changed as well.

FIFTY

RUBY'S FIRST FIGHT

An hour and a half later, the group slid through the same doorway that Fox had first taken Ruby through. She walked in the middle of the single-file column, but nonetheless, when her turn to cross the threshold came, she tensed, expecting a welcoming committee.

Instead, the hall was empty.

They snuck through corridors, Conroy in the lead, Marcelle just behind, Hugh in the back, and Lya just in front of Ruby, so that Ruby had to hiss at Lya to keep up from time to time. Conroy's idea of a joke, maybe. Ani and Onor walked right behind Ruby, crowding her whenever Lya slowed down.

She kept expecting to see or hear people, to find a fight.

Instead, she heard their own footsteps and breathing, and from time to time a whispered command from Conroy. She wanted to go check on her hab, to see if it was even still registered to her. Surely there hadn't been enough time for that to change, but she couldn't abandon the group or risk being alone. If she did anything that stupid, Colin would have a reason never to let her out of his sight again. She dragged her focus back to her breathing and to the corridor and to the immediate moment and place.

A sound came from behind them, a woman, calling Ruby's name.

She turned, calling back, "Lanie!" Next to her, Harold. A tall blond man and a short blond woman, both in blue with multicolored necklaces she could actually see from a distance.

Ani and Onor and Hugh stood between Ruby and her friends, Hugh with his stunner up and pointed at Harold. "Hugh, no!" Ruby called.

Hugh dropped his stunner a few inches. Ruby piled out of line and hugged Lanie. "What's happening?" she asked.

Lanie shook her head. "I don't know. We were told to watch for grays out here and to report anything we saw."

"You won't, will you?"

Harold laughed. "Obey? Lanie? She's so happy, you'd think we'd already landed and she was playing under the sky. But you're lucky it's us you found. They'll kill."

"Kill?" Ruby swallowed. "What do you know? Where can we find people?"

Lanie looked at Conroy, who had shown up just behind Ruby. "They tell us you're going to kill people. But you're not, are you? You wouldn't?"

Ruby swallowed and shook her head. "Not if we can help it."

Conroy answered from over her shoulder. "Not unless we're threatened."

Lanie stiffened. "If you kill people, we won't keep helping. You have to promise to do your best to be nonviolent."

Conroy pointed at Hugh's scarred face. "He got those marks for being late, for putting himself in danger. Maybe someone could have just helped him instead of beating him for it." He pointed at Onor. "His parents were killed for getting reds in trouble when they broke their own rules." He looked down at Lanie. "We've all got stories like that. We've all lost friends or family or had them beaten up or locked up. We'll do our best not to hurt anyone, but you just told us they'd kill. Do you really expect a bloodless change?"

Lanie blinked back tears but stood her ground. "Do your best."

Conroy's voice softened. "We will. And we thank you for your support. Do you know where we can find . . . the people who aren't on our side?"

Lanie shook her head. "I can't give away my own. But I won't report you."

Ruby swallowed. "Even Sylva?"

"I haven't seen her."

"Okay." Ruby gave her another quick hug, Lanie frail and thin in Ruby's arms.

"Okay, go on," Lanie said. "We'll go the other way, say we were scared and outnumbered if Ix pops up and shows that we met here."

Seeing friendly faces should have bled some of the tension out. But it didn't get easier to slide through the eerily empty corridors. They took a shortcut through one of the big rooms that were usually full of people working in small segregated spaces. Ruby's heart danced against her ribs. So many places people could hide. If Lanie was right, there was no one here, but what if she wasn't? What if Sylva or Ellis had lied to Lanie and Harold, or changed plans, or had people tracking their progress through the level?

Conroy didn't like this place either. He'd gone dead quiet, every bit of him clearly alert. He started moving faster, not quite running.

They were all in now, and they'd be through pretty quickly.

A yell.

A man in the back, not one of them. A red. Stunner pointed.

One of the women behind Ruby fell, making a small, vulnerable sound and then a thud as her head hit the floor.

Three people shot back, the stunner beams visible only as subtle changes in the air. The only sure signs of the short, fat guns working were flashes of light from the muzzles.

All the shots missed.

Two other people popped up from different workspaces, a blue and a red, firing their stunners, ducking again before Ruby could register who they were. Two more grays fell. A couple she'd met once but didn't know well. She tripped over an uneven spot on the floor, bruising her shin.

The return shots did no good.

Ruby picked up a stunner from one of the people on the floor, holding it awkwardly.

"Through the door. Out! Out!" Conroy barked.

As she passed Conroy, following his orders, she saw him stand on a desk, hunting for a better view. He shot twice, and she heard someone yell. Brave. At least one of them could shoot. He'd be a target there, though. A glance back showed Hugh on a table, too, and a knot of people between her and him. Enemies. She recognized a few faces, no names.

Lya stumbled in front of her and landed on her hands and knees.

Ruby bent down, the heat of a stun beam passing where she had just been. She kept going, eating the floor, spreading herself flat, half on top of Lya. "Crawl," she whispered.

Lya whimpered.

"Now."

Lya started pulling forward, way too slow. Ruby pushed her under a desk and followed her, the two of them huddling together.

Onor stopped in front of them, Ani across from them, her face a darkness in the shadows. She watched Ruby with eyes bright and full of fear and reproach.

Voices called. Conroy grunted once, then Ruby heard a thud. She glanced up, saw that he was still there after all. She knelt and stood quickly, checking for Hugh.

She couldn't see him. "Hugh!" she called, realizing her mistake just as Lya scrambled out from behind her and started heading the wrong way.

Onor tried to block Lya, but Ruby grabbed him. "We're going. Now. It's just stunners. Nobody's dead. I need to know if Hugh is okay."

Onor shook his head, his eyes wide and worried.

She jerked her head back at the door. "How do you know it's safe that way either?"

His lips thinned. Lya was getting too far in front of her, crawling like a madwoman. Ruby launched herself after the fleeing woman. She heard Onor and Ani right behind her.

They passed Conroy. He was unhurt, still ducking and rising and shooting. "Out!" he screamed at them.

She glanced up and saw how angry he was. He wasn't looking at her, and his anger was for far more than her. She fed off it, liking the anger. It fit a fight, felt good in her belly. "Lya," was all she said to him, and then she put her head down and kept going. She heard a few whispered words between Onor and Conroy but couldn't make out what they said to each other.

It seemed to take a long time and a lot of crawling, and each movement was scary. Then Lya rounded a corner in front of her and screamed.

Lya collapsed, still screaming.

Ruby only hesitated a second before peering around the corner. Hugh was on the ground, face down, and a small man dressed in blue was hitting him with a stunner in repeated bursts. The man's face was scrunched up and full of fear and hatred.

Ruby screamed, "Stop!" Onor leapt in front of her, put his head down, and plowed into the man, sending him crashing into the floor. Onor landed on top of him.

Ruby crossed the five steps between them and took the stunner from the man's twitching hand, then stepped on his hand, hard. He grunted, partly from her ravaging his fingers and partly from the blows Onor rained on his side.

Ruby turned to see Lya cradling Hugh's face in her lap, his eyes sightless and staring. Lya's head hung down, her hair covering her face, the ends of it sweeping across Hugh's forehead.

Ani was already kneeling beside Hugh, a hand on his neck, feeling for a pulse.

Conroy and Marcelle rounded the corner. Others followed.

"Onor! Stop!" Conroy commanded. Onor ignored him, slamming his fist into the man's side with a desperation that looked completely wrong on Onor.

"Stop!" Conroy shouted again, and this time Onor gave a final blow and stood up.

"They're gone," Conroy said as he knelt on Hugh's other side. "But we have to get out of here. This is a trap." He glanced at Ani, recoiling at the stunned look in her eyes, and put a hand beside hers. "We have four down. We've just enough people standing to carry them."

He looked at Lya and shook his head.

"I know," she whispered so soft that Ruby could barely hear her. Lya had become a wraith in that short time, a stunned shell of a human being.

"Stopped his heart," Conroy said.

Ruby choked back a soft, keening sob, earning a glare from Lya.

"We've got to go," Conroy said.

Ruby stood up. "I have someplace closer. Trust me."

"Do you *know* it's safe?"

She hesitated. "I'm as sure it's safe as I am that home is safe anymore."

Conroy gave her a wry smile and closed his eyes for a moment before opening them and saying, "Very well. Don't lead us wrong."

She swallowed. "I won't. We'll all fit where I'm going. I promise."

FIFTY-ONE

FOXED

R uby's handprint still opened her door. She didn't realize how afraid
she'd been until it actually worked. She stood just inside the door and
directed the pairs of people supporting groggy stunner victims to come
in and lay them out on the couch and the bed.

"Hey!" Dayn's voice protested, sleepy and angry all at once.

Ruby glanced up to see him coming out of her bedroom, shirtless, with
his hair mussed from sleep. "It's okay," Ruby called to him. Then she told
Conroy and Onor to put Hugh's body on the floor. She'd have liked someplace
more respectful for him, but the couch already held one person and both beds
were full.

Lya collapsed beside the body, her hands shaking, her face so white she
looked physically ill. Conroy crouched beside Lya, talking in soothing tones.

The hab was so full it felt almost like a twisted echo of the party on her
debut night. The shock of fighting, of even being here, played out as wide-
eyed stiffness in some, exhaustion in others. It set Onor pacing. She hadn't
thought past getting here, but now what?

When she felt Dayn grab her arm, she turned on him, too tired to be
handled. "Get them water," she snapped.

He stepped back, startled, and narrowed his eyes at her.

"You told me to get a backbone. I got one. Get these people water."

To her surprise he went into the kitchen. Ani followed, and they came
back balancing three glasses of water each. Marcelle and Onor helped deliver
the water, both curious and a bit shocked. But then she surely didn't look any
better.

Fighting sucked.

After everyone had a place to sit and a glass of water, Ruby backed Dayn
into the wall near the door and looked carefully at him. No colors, no way
to really tell where he stood. Of course, he'd just woken up. He didn't look
like he'd been fighting, but rather—and incongruously—like he had always
looked. As if nothing was going on at all. "Are you one of us?"

"Yes."

She stared at him. He stared back, solid and sure of himself, smelling cleaner than anyone else in the room, looking more confident than anyone except maybe Conroy. She bit at her lower lip for a moment, then said. "Good. Then go home. You're next door. You can watch out from there. We need rest."

Dayn stiffened.

She should use him. "Can you warn us if the fighting comes this way?"

He gave her a quick nod, unhappy and barely acquiescent, and started for the door.

"Oh, and knock when you want to come back."

He reeled as if her words had slapped him, but he went. She let out a long sigh, feeling a little flash of triumph inside the horror of Hugh's death and the awful fight. Then she reset Dayn's door access so he'd *have* to knock.

Marcelle blinked at her, her mouth open, but no words came out. Finally, she stammered, "Who . . . who was that? Where . . . where are we?"

Marcelle's diction was nearly always perfect. A sign of how much stress the fighting had put on them all? Onor was looking at her with intense curiosity as well. "This is my hab," Ruby said. "I live here." She sighed.

Marcelle looked around with interest and Onor frowned but said nothing. Marcelle asked again. "That man. That wasn't Fox?"

"That was Dayn; he's used to watching over me, but he lost track a few days ago." She felt herself grinning and saw Marcelle grinning back. The slight bit of laughter escaping their lips sounded both manic and stressed, and like heaven.

As soon as she regained some self-control, Ruby assigned a door guard and a few nurses and left Ani in charge of making food. Conroy found tasks for everyone else: checking weapons and clothes, stretching, and preparing to leave if they had to. Then he pulled Onor aside and the two of them whispered in a corner.

Ruby sat down in the middle of the room and put her hand on Lya's back. Lya still cried, soft sobs that made more movement than noise, and she didn't look up at Ruby or acknowledge her presence. Ruby felt the sobs through her hand and arm, and focused down on her breathing to keep from joining Lya. There was no way she could afford to look weak, not now. She hummed a bit and then sang quietly, choosing songs that everyone would have heard since they were children instead of songs she'd written.

A few other voices took up the songs with her, the group slowly coming to be more matched up emotionally, the familiar melodies and words acting to calm and unify. As soon as she felt like most of the fighters were more composed, she asked. "Conroy, what do we do now?"

"Wait." He held up his journal. "We'll get orders soon." The look he gave her was approving.

"Do you know what's happening out there?"

He glanced down at the journal, then said, "Not really. Lots of battles. Nothing conclusive."

Ani brought in plates of toast and two carafes of stim, looking apologetic. "This is what we have. We can each have a piece and a half cup."

"I should have stocked the larder a bit better," Ruby joked.

Ani shook her head.

While they ate, Conroy talked tactics and debriefed them, his voice calm.

Ruby got up to help Ani take the plates back to the kitchen and then they went to the privy together. The mirror showed that she looked as bad as she ever had on this level—maybe worse. When she started running her fingers through her tangled hair, Ani handed her a comb.

"You are forever helping me be beautiful," Ruby commented as she took the comb. "Thanks for sticking with me. What do you think of gray?"

Ani ran water into her cupped, clean hands and splashed it on her face before answering. "It's . . . fierce."

"Fierce?"

"You know. Everything feels more intense. Scary. More . . . emotive."

Ruby handed the comb back to her. She stared at the mirror, noting a bruise on her cheek that she didn't remember receiving. "If I hadn't met Hugh . . . no, there's more. If a pair of reds hadn't beat Hugh the day I met Fox, I wouldn't have ever known Hugh believed in me, and maybe none of this would have started. I wouldn't have sung at Owl Paulie's funeral, and that was the beginning."

"You would have found us. Or we would have found you."

"How do you know?" Ruby found a pair of her favorite earrings and put them in. "Maybe it's me that would have been killed. They kill the people that scare them."

"You scare them," Ani said.

"So now you believe me? About people hurting us?"

Ani looked down and away, her face confused and a bit sad. "Yes." She pocketed the comb and started out the door.

"Good," Ruby whispered to the mirror before turning and following her watcher out of the room.

Ani was already running when Ruby came out of the privy. Fox had come, had found them somehow. Maybe Dayn. She should have programmed *Fox* out. Stupid.

Fox stood over Onor, looking down and talking to him, although Ruby couldn't tell what he wanted. Marcelle sat beside Onor, looking up at Fox, her features frozen in fear.

Before she got close enough to hear what Fox said to Onor, Ruby could see that he held a stunner in his hands. "No!" She screamed, hurtling past Ani and skidding to a stop inches from Fox.

Onor kept his eyes on Fox as he said, "There you are."

"There you are," Fox said to Ruby, an odd little echo of Onor's words. "I've been looking everywhere." Fox glared at Ruby, his hand still pointing the stunner in Onor's general direction. "I was just asking your boyfriend here where to find you."

"Stop it, Fox!" Ani snapped, coming to stand beside Ruby.

Onor took advantage of the moment to stand, pulling Marcelle up beside him.

"He's my *friend*," Ruby snapped, "And I'm right here *in my hab*, and I didn't invite you in."

Fox looked awry, his hair mussed and sweat dotting his forehead. "You still work for me," he said.

Ruby let out a bark of laughter. "Surely you don't think I'm that naïve?"

"That's why I came. To keep you safe."

"Put your stunner away." Ruby kept her voice even. Fox couldn't know what they had seen happen to Hugh, how much they needed him to put the gun away.

Fox blinked at her, unmoving.

She almost felt sorry for him. Not quite. "Look, I appreciate it all. Thank you. But I have things to do. There's a battle."

"That's why I'm here."

"No. It's not."

"Of course it is. I have to keep you safe."

"Onor's keeping me safe."

"I see that."

"And Ani."

Fox shook. She couldn't quite tell what emotion drove him to do that. Some anger, some need to control her. Not all of it. He was scared. She knew him well enough to tell.

She fought an absurd urge to hold him. "Look," she struggled to control her voice, "I have a job to do here. Without you, I would never have started it, I wouldn't have known about anything but gray." Damn it, now her voice was quivering. Surely she was just tired. Exhausted. "I'll thank you forever. But I want you to go now." She was breaking up with him, hurting him, forcing it this time. She'd done it inside of herself a long time ago, but this was looking in his eyes. That's why she couldn't talk smoothly, why she felt she was repudiating a piece of her soul.

Fox's eyes darted from side to side, as if looking for a distraction to help him escape.

Onor sidled away from Fox's stunner. He stood as close to Ruby as possible without touching her. Marcelle stepped between Ruby and Ani, all of her attention on Ani. A guard to guard her from her guard. The irony almost made Ruby laugh despite the tense moment.

Ani didn't notice Marcelle's protective stance or how ready she looked, balanced for action. All of Ani's attention had gone to Fox, and his to her.

Conroy watched, almost amused, and intensely curious. Everyone else seemed to have melted into the walls. They were still there, their presence given away by rustles and slight movement, but they'd all gone quiet.

Ani and Fox stood locked in a staring contest full of deeper meaning than Ruby understood. Ani's chin quivered as she tried not to cry.

Ruby chewed at her lower lip, not liking the thick undercurrents she didn't understand.

"Help me," Fox said.

The look Ani gave him held a tiny bit of pity. She was taller than Fox, more regal.

"I love you," Fox said to Ani.

To Ani.

Ruby blinked, even more confused. She held her tongue, watched.

"I can't," Ani said, the words barely more than a whisper. "She's . . . Ruby . . . Ruby has the power to save us all. I can't leave her."

Fox dropped his arm. "I . . . see." His look dismissed Ani then, as if she had been nothing.

Ani took a step back, tilting her head so that she looked over the top of Fox's head instead of into his eyes.

Fox turned to Ruby, then reached out for her.

Marcelle slid between them, quick and sure, bracing herself so her back nearly touched Ruby's chest.

Ruby blinked at Fox over Marcelle's shoulder and then gently pushed Marcelle aside. "It's okay."

Marcelle moved slowly, resisting. Once the space between them was empty, Ruby stepped into Fox and kissed him on the forehead. Then she stepped back and stood beside Marcelle. It took a few breaths before she could get out the words, "Thank you." A breath. "Goodbye."

He looked stunned, then backed up, stepping around Hugh's body. "Don't stay here. The fight's coming this way. Go to Colin if you won't stay with me."

He meant to hurt her with the words. "What else can you tell me? Are we winning?"

"We might have, except I came for you."

He was lying. He wasn't going to give her any real information, not now, not in this state. She couldn't stand the mix of anger and desire in his eyes anymore. "Go," she told him. "I'm sure we'll see each other again."

He left, slamming the door hard behind him.

Ruby felt as if she were being split in two, as if there was a weaker, younger part of her that should be following Fox.

FIFTY-TWO

THE JACKMAN COMETH

Onor felt light as Fox walked away. Before now, he'd only seen Fox once, for a brief moment the day the sky fell. Even so, he'd known who threatened him as soon as he opened his eyes to find the red-haired man poking his shoulder with a stunner. Cocky, clean, full of himself. But oddly, not brave. Fox's hand had been shaking even as he pointed the stunner at Onor.

Marcelle wrapped her arms around Onor, whispering in his ear. "I kept thinking of Hugh. The whole time the stunner was pointed at you, I felt the absence of Hugh."

Onor laughed, giddy for having just escaped death by the hand of his archrival. Maybe this was what it felt like to survive a battle. And Marcelle had been his support. "You'd have never let him stun me enough times for that."

"No." Her voice was a whisper.

Onor felt thick tongued. Still, he pushed Marcelle's embrace aside when he saw Ruby and Ani stepping into the kitchen, looking for a private place to talk. He followed after them, unwilling to let Ruby out of his sight until he got her back on track, got them all under Colin's or Joel's protection. "We're supposed to be finding The Jackman," he said to Ruby's back when he'd almost caught up. "And we have to do something about Hugh."

"I know, and isn't The Jackman supposed to be finding us?"

"Well, but we're not on gray."

"The Jackman always knows where to find you, and Conroy will know when to call the reclaimers."

"Are you really following Conroy?" Onor asked. "Or are you doing whatever you want?"

"Should we have done something different besides come here?"

"No." He stared at her. She was mussed up from all the fighting, she had a stunner strapped to her middle, and she looked just like he imagined Lila Red would look, except Ruby was dressed in gray. She felt as far away from him as the dead revolutionary, and almost as ruthless.

Ani interrupted. "We need KJ. I don't know or trust this Jackman, and besides, he's gray. We need someone who can lead us all." Ani stopped, hand to mouth, suddenly realizing the words that had run out of her mouth. "Someone we know." She looked at Ruby, apologizing with her look, almost pleading. "You could do it, except you're no warrior. We need someone who knows how to fight. Someone we know."

Onor chose to ignore Ani instead of argue with her. She'd clearly just chosen Ruby over Fox. Even without being able to read the nuances, Onor had been able to see that. Ruby needed Ani. She needed more than just him and Ani. "I promised Colin we'd find The Jackman." It felt important to stay on Colin's good side. Onor might have hated the way he looked at Ruby, but that didn't mean they didn't need him. "Colin told me to keep you safe."

Ruby frowned at him. "You sound like Fox."

"Colin has resources, and Joel let him take care of you, and then he asked me to."

Ruby turned in the small kitchen and stood with one hand on her hip, her eyes deadly serious. He knew the look well; he wasn't at all surprised when she spat, "I'm not doing what anyone tells me, except maybe Conroy for the moment. Because I told him I would. But not Ani. Fox. The Jackman. Not even Colin. Not even Joel, who may someday run this ship. And for sure not Garth, who does run it. I am not doing what anyone tells me anymore. Not. Even. You."

The words were spoken to Onor, but even Ani flinched.

Stung, Onor backed out of the kitchen and stood just outside the door. Ruby wasn't going to let him be her keeper, and she really never had, anyway. She'd grown past him for sure now.

He paced. Stepping around people, not stopping to talk to anyone except Conroy. "Do we have orders yet?"

Conroy eyed the kitchen door. "I wish."

Onor stood, waiting, bouncing a little on his toes, wishing he knew what Ruby and Ani were saying behind the closed door. Ruby was a force, an energy that drove him to be brave because she was brave, to question because she questioned. He had orbited her since the day they met. Maybe he would have to be content with watching her back. But if that was what he was going to do, he best not get tangled up with anyone else.

Even Marcelle.

He searched the room until he found Marcelle covering Hugh's body with a blue blanket she'd taken from Ruby's room. Doing what needed to be done, even the hard part of helping Lya stand up.

Before Lya had made it to her feet, a knock at the door startled Marcelle to attention. She looked at the door, then turned to stare at Onor. When Onor heard The Jackman's familiar voice on the other side, he raced to open the door and usher him in. The Jackman looked gaunt, almost hungry, and full of purpose. "Gather them up," he said to Conroy, not stopping to greet anyone. "We've got to go."

Onor remembered Ruby's last words to him, about how she wasn't going to obey anyone, but he went to get her anyway. "The Jackman's here. We need to go."

He saw her begin to refuse, but then she rushed past him, stopping in front of The Jackman. "What's happening?"

The Jackman looked Ruby up and down, taking in her gray clothes and the way her red hair had gone half-tamed at best. When The Jackman spoke, he didn't even sound like he hated her anymore. "They're killing people. We've got to rethink this."

"I know. Hugh."

The Jackman glanced at the body under the blanket and his face grew even harder. "I see."

Ruby shook her head. "Who else?"

"Salli and Jinn. Together." The Jackman paused, looking stricken, almost—for just a second—weak. Then he growled, "They were women, damn it!"

"Yeah. So am I. What are we *doing*? If we kill each other, who's going to run the *Fire*?"

"Someone forgot to remind Garth about that."

Ruby's eyes lit up with sudden purpose. "I need to find Joel."

The Jackman stood still, a dumbfounded look on his face.

Ruby shifted into relentless mode. "I need to be at the center long enough to see the whole picture." She leaned in and grabbed The Jackman by the front of his shirt. "We're going to win. There's as many of us as there are of them, and half of them are on our side."

The Jackman looked into her face. "How do you plan to get near someone like Joel right now?" The Jackman stepped back from her so he could see Onor and Marcelle. He looked at them, one at a time, stopping with Onor. "You too? Is this what you believe? That she—" he sighed.

Onor had never seen The Jackman so torn.

He stopped and stood right in front of Ruby, looking down at her. "I'll take you back to the cargo bars. The fight has been there and gone. But I won't take you into the middle of it."

Ruby shrugged. "Then we'll find our own way."

The Jackman crossed his arms and looked at Conroy, not needing to ask his question out loud.

Conroy nodded.

FIFTY-THREE

THE TABLE

Ruby's belly screamed hunger and her feet hurt. It seemed like she was always standing or walking lately, and her feet always hurt. She glared at The Jackman's back, bent now, looking as tired as she felt. He'd kept them walking through random corridors and tunnels and maintenance hallways full of dirty robots.

Maybe he meant to keep her from being any use to anybody. After all, he'd never liked her, and he'd never made that a secret.

Given the way her feet hurt and her belly had started screaming for food again, they'd been walking and hiding and walking a long time. They'd heard fighting, or what might be fighting—raised voices and running feet—twice. The Jackman had deftly turned them away from it.

She could feel the fight. It existed in the way the mood within the ship had changed, in the way they walked differently through the corridors, more watchful, maybe even a bit afraid. There was even a change in the way the ship smelled, although when she tried to find words for it, they weren't there.

Whatever else she thought about him, The Jackman knew the back warrens of the *Fire*.

Marcelle had stayed behind to take care of Lya. She'd clung to Ruby for a long while. Both thinner and dirtier and scrappier than ever. Conroy was still waiting for orders, but he'd sent Ruby and Onor and Ani with The Jackman.

It was as if her time of being a well-dressed blue was days or even a week behind her instead of only hours or maybe a day.

To keep her feet moving, she started planning the words to a song about change. The ship was going to need one.

The Jackman opened a door, and she expected it to open on another dusty, empty corridor, just like the other twenty or thirty doors he'd led them through.

Just beyond the door, KJ stood ready, hands at his side, clearly prepared to fight. When he recognized them, he stopped and gaped. Blinked. And then relaxed. He stepped aside.

Ruby looked closely, trying to tell if he was glad to see her.

KJ gave no clue.

The room was big, with red couches and chairs bolted to silver walls and a square table with a vid screen embedded in the middle. There were no chairs around the table. Instead, about ten people stood around it, looking down.

Joel stood across the table from her. He looked up, a momentary lightness crossing his features. He waved and then returned to a conversation he was having with Par.

Thank god. Her doubts about The Jackman melted. She turned and planted a kiss on his right cheek, which felt stubbly and wrinkly and dry under her lips.

The Jackman flinched and took a step away from her.

She frowned but didn't take time to worry. She had already recognized Joel and KJ and Par. She looked closer, half expecting Colin, but he wasn't here. There were four others she didn't recognize: two men and two women. Both women were older than Ruby, but one of them—a gray-haired matron—was much older. Only Joel and the oldest woman wore green.

Everyone else in the room was male, and neat, and looked confident. Clearly none of *them* had been fighting or running through corridors.

The table drew her.

As Ruby stepped toward it, KJ stepped between her and the table. He blocked her, but he spoke to The Jackman. "What's she doing here?"

Ruby tried to step around KJ to glimpse the table, but he blocked her again.

She stepped on his foot.

"She's rather difficult," The Jackman said dryly as KJ lifted his foot and leaned into Ruby, one arm around her waist in an imprisoning caress.

Ruby struggled.

"She's also rather hard to say no to," The Jackman said.

Joel spoke from across the room. "Let her come."

The Jackman said, "See?"

KJ grinned at her. There was no anger. If anything, the crook in his smile suggested tenderness and worry. "If you're caught here, Garth will have you killed."

Ruby smiled. "It's no different for you, right? He'd kill you, too?"

KJ nodded.

As she stepped past him she said, "I hope your foot's okay."

"It's fine."

As she stepped up to the table, a set of blinking colors disappeared. Still, her eyes were drawn to the surface, where golden light still glowed in lines and circles.

She recognized the image as a very precise drawing of the *Fire*. She'd seen pale imitations of the picture back in school, when they were trying to teach her about the universe outside of the world she saw inside *The Creative Fire*. It had always fascinated her—an unseen mystery in her life. "You can't come out of the shell," one of her teachers had said. "There is no way to leave the ship while it flies through space. But there is a whole universe out there. We have stories. We have these drawings passed to us from the *Fire*'s makers."

Ruby had repeatedly asked for more detail, to know what the ship looked like from the outside as well as the inside. No one had ever shown her. It hadn't really helped that none of her teachers seemed to really understand the universe—the one outside the *Fire*, or maybe even the one within the *Fire*. And now, in front of her, the *Fire* was drawn in detail and light. Every corridor. On the screen, the ship was round, the open corners full of words and controls. Movement bloomed in various places. Different levels and views were available at a flick of a hand.

She would never have imagined such a thing as the table, or such a place as this room full of the answers to almost every question she had ever asked, existed. She felt completely awed.

The cargo pods were half the ship, maybe more. The gray pods—if you included the two dead ones—took half the rest. Actually seeing the dimensions told her volumes about the control of the ship, about the reasons the cargo bays had become partly taken over, even about the number of reds.

Joel came to stand beside her. She asked him, "Where are we?"

He pointed to a pulsing yellow light in one of the inner levels—but still not the center—of the ship.

She pointed to the very center, which was dark and thick with shapes she didn't understand. "Is that command?"

"No. This is command."

"Here?" An idea dawned on her. "We won?"

He shook his head. "No. Not yet. There are four places like this." Joel pointed to each of them. "They control three. They think this one is broken, and so we're here."

"Ix?"

His eyes looked approving. "Colin told me you're brilliant."

"So what's in the middle?" she said.

"That's where the *Fire*'s guts and brains are, where Ix lives, where pilots go when they're needed."

Wow. She spread her hands out across the whole table, including all of its lights and colors. "Tell me what this shows you."

She expected him to show her the battle, but he didn't. He started with the ship, making sure she understood how to read the labels and how to control the images on the table.

A few of the other people in the room watched, but mostly they gathered in corners. Ruby sensed they were talking about her, but she didn't care. She didn't want to be ripped away from the table in front of her, ever. It was bigger and more important than her hunger or her thirst or her curiosity about the old woman dressed in green. It was simply the best thing she had ever seen, and each time Joel touched a control and brought a new bit of information up, she felt fuller and more complete.

The pulse of fresh and grey water through the veins of the *Fire* fascinated her. So did Joel's quiet explanation of how water acted as lifeline, as ballast, as shield, and as fuel.

The movement of trains. The stopped trains, one for sabotage in the tunnel and the others to cut off parts of the ship and make it hard for people to get around. The train lines that were broken. "Some have been broken for generations," Joel said, "and maybe they never worked."

She needed to know more. She had to figure out how to help. "What did you turn off? When I came up?"

Joel stepped back for a moment, looking around. She caught a nod from KJ and then another one from the old woman. A trio of deciders? Or had she missed some? At least they all agreed.

The lights blossomed again. They started out as gray, red, blue, and green. Thousands of lights, thousands on thousands of lights, tiny, bigger when a lot were clumped together. "It's the battle, isn't it?" she asked. "Who's on our side?"

In response, the lights changed to three colors. Not points, not individuals like the other ones must be. Instead, it was shading. White—the gray pods all colored white. Brown—most of command and some spots everywhere else, a few long lines of brown, quite controlled. And everywhere, like a contamination, tans shaded to darker brown or lighter.

She understood immediately. She pointed at a knot of tans. "These are the people Ix can't tell us about. It doesn't know what side they're on."

Joel laughed. "Mostly Ix knows if the people themselves know. They wear the sign, which Ix can see as well as we can, or they're directly following Garth's orders. Ix can read all of that pretty well. But humans can't always read themselves."

"Are we winning?"

Joel shook his head. "We're not losing yet. It's close."

The other people in the room had slowly gathered back around the table. She felt out of place. Still, she watched, the colors mesmerizing. She was pretty sure she could see battles and movement, and also the simple rhythms of work. The work would have to go on. They would all die if the orchards perished or the water systems stopped working.

She had a hundred questions, but no one looked like they had time to answer them. She put her hands down on the edge of the table, needing something to lean on. She'd been so fascinated that she'd forgotten how much her feet hurt.

The surface under her hand glowed red in the outline of her fingers.

Joel plucked her hand up and backed her away a step or two. "Don't touch the screen."

"I need to sit down."

To her surprise, he backed up with her. Surely he was the boss and had other things to do. "Wait," she whispered. "I'll be right back."

She went to the privy, splashing water on her face and doing her best to comb her fingers through her hair. Walking forever to get here had undone all the repairs she'd managed in her hab, and worse. She pulled her soiled gray shirt off and scrubbed at her body with damp wet hands and a twist of material she ripped from the shirt. Where was Ani when she needed her? For advice. For a comb. She sighed. The mirror showed a topless wild woman with a stunner wrapped around her middle. She pulled the shirt back on and frowned. At least she smelled better.

Joel stood outside, waiting calmly, looking a tiny bit bemused. He led her to one of the couches. She sat awkwardly, the stunner on her hip an unfamiliar object that unbalanced her. "I'll get you water," he told her.

Ruby took the moment to look around. Onor and Ani and KJ stood in the far corner talking. Two peacers had joined them.

Most of the rest of the people still clustered around the table, and Ruby realized she hadn't even noticed if Onor had been able to see the table close-up like she had. She needed time to talk to him. There was too much to do, too much to remember.

Joel appeared beside her with a flask of water and a plate of flat protein crackers and orbfruit. Her hand reached for the food before her brain even recognized it was there.

She watched Joel as he watched her. She hadn't really noticed details about him before. There hadn't ever been a quiet moment like this.

The effort of leading his side—her side—their side—had taken a toll on him. The spidery age lines that edged his eyes ran long. Exhaustion sat deep in his eyes and face, aging him and making him look a bit vulnerable. In spite of that, he was neat, his gray hair combed back from his prominent cheeks and thin lips. His eyes were a lovely blue-green she could swear she'd never seen in another face anywhere.

She'd nearly emptied the plate before she could concentrate on anything other than eating and watching him. "Thank you," she managed to choke out.

He smiled, his teeth an even white, his lovely eyes looking pleased. "You're welcome. I needed a small success."

"So I'm a success?"

"You look much better now, so feeding you must have been a success."

"Are we going to win?"

He shook his head. "I don't know. They're killing us and we aren't killing them. Do the math."

"Even with Ix?"

"Ix can't disobey direct orders, except orders that hurt people."

"But Ix is helping us?"

"Of course. We're right."

She loved how he was sure of himself. The food had given her energy, and she drew more from the way Joel looked at her, as if she were clean and her hair had been done up for a trip to sing in the cargo bar. "We are. I want to help."

"You can. But not now. Now, we're stopping for a bit, resting, getting ready to start all over. Garth has agreed to talk to us in the morning if we promise to keep working."

"You mean the gray shifts?"

"Everyone. But we've set plans in motion."

"What plans?"

He shook his head.

"He'll keep his word?" she asked. "Garth will talk to us?"

He nodded.

"How much time, then? When is morning?"

He laughed. "A few hours yet." He reached over and touched her cheek lightly. "Time to rest."

"I want to help."

"Will you sing me a song? That will help."

He was flirting. In the middle of a battle, this man was flirting with her.

She'd fallen for Fox's flirting, and look how that had turned out. She couldn't give Joel, or anyone else, power over her. Ever. But she could feel him like a magnet. She wanted to touch him, to know how far her head would come on his shoulder. Which was really, really stupid. She shook herself, and a tiny moan escaped her lips. "I'll sing for you."

"Would you like to go someplace more private?"

She would. She did. "As long as you know I have more to offer you than you think." There. She'd got the words out. "I have a good head for strategy and for talking to people. I'm smart."

He looked amused.

"I can help you with the grays. The workers. I can help us win." She was talking too fast. "They matter to you. There are so many of them."

He laughed out loud. "You are a vision. You are who I'm fighting for, you know." He took her hand, pulling her up. "I'm off now. My people told me to rest. You need to rest, too."

She let go of his hand and gestured for him to lead, confused. "I need to know what you believe. Why are you fighting on our side?"

He didn't answer until they were out of the large room, down a hallway, and into what must be his own hab. A small kitchen, a living room, a bedroom. Tasteful, neat, military. Here and there, a splash of color or a bit of homemade craft that suggested a woman took some interest in him, but no real sign of anyone else living there. Of course, maybe this wasn't even his hab.

He went through the door to the bedroom.

FIFTY-FOUR
SONG OF JOINING

Ruby settled down on an oversized light green chair and crossed her legs, waiting for Joel to notice she hadn't followed him to the bedroom. It didn't take long for him to turn around in the doorway. She watched his expression carefully as he reached for her and found she wasn't there. His face registered a moment of surprise, but no anger. He came back to sit opposite her, his expression open and curious. She liked it that he didn't comment, and that she didn't feel pressured.

"The question you asked. About how things were and are. It's a long story."

"I have time. I want it all, but what matters most is how you want the future to be."

"Of course, you want it all." At least he was smiling. Sort of. "I'll tell you the short version of the story. That's all I've got the energy for."

She leaned forward.

"We left Adiamo roughly four hundred ship years ago. You know that."

She nodded. "We went to explore and to bring back the samples and other goods we have in cargo."

"Close enough. Raw materials that Lym wanted. Knowledge. Frozen plants and animals. Video. Our ancestors all volunteered. They chose this life for us."

He sounded a bit . . . put off. Ruby wouldn't label his voice as bitter, but maybe mystified and sad.

"They'd done it before, five other generation ships. None of the other ships had come back by the time we left. So maybe no one knew how hard it is." He shifted and stood. "I need water. Would you like some?"

"Yes."

He brought back the water. "What do you think is the hard part?" he asked her.

"Keeping it all going? Keeping the orchards alive and the robots working and the ship in one piece. There's a lot of ways we could have died, could still die."

He set his glass down. "That's a good answer. But the most true answer is that it's nearly impossible to stay focused and driven."

She laughed. "We have work to do every day, enough to fall into bed exhausted."

"But we don't. Not in command or logistics. The cruelty? The reds who cause trouble?" He must have seen the look in her eyes because he said, "That's how it is. There's nothing new, and this is a very tiny world."

"It took me half a day to walk here."

"We grew up on worlds where we could walk all of our lives and not see everything. You've played the game."

Adiamo. "Is it real? Adiamo? And birds?"

He gave her a funny look. "I was born here, too. But I think so. I think it is, or it was. Let me see if I can get you to understand another way. Your work hasn't changed. When you worked in the robot shop, you did what your parents and their parents and their parents and their parents did."

"So? I'm proud of it."

"Hey, I'm not insulting you. But you did outgrow it."

"Yes." She held a hand to her necklace. "We dream."

"That's exactly it. We all dream, but there's no place to expand here. It's so controlled that it kills our soul. We think it is the whole world, that the universe is inside this ship."

Ruby was silent. Her whole universe was here, and right now it felt bigger than it ever had.

He pursed his lips and took a drink. His voice was so soft she could barely hear it. "None of us knows about the universe. Not you, not me. Not really. No one on this ship has been outside of it. Not even the oldest people, like Owl Paulie, have been outside of the *Fire*."

He had a point. She finished her water and sat back, waiting.

"It's a very bad thing for humans to have nothing new to learn or do. We have this inner drive to create. That's what makes you sing. You've even made a situation where your songs have changed the little world we live in. Because that's what we need to do. Humans. We need to change our world."

"So?"

"Well, if we changed much on the ship, we'd kill it. And we know it. We know how to run the *Fire* but not how to make it or remake it."

She nodded. "We recycle endlessly. But I couldn't make metal from scratch if I had to."

"You may have it better than we do. Workers. You've got things to do, and a way to dream. You can hope to get better jobs."

"Or to be treated fairly by you or become more like you."

He leaned forward. "I know it sounds wrong. But we have less to dream of becoming."

"You have music and art and dance."

He smiled, looking pleased with her. "That's why we support those."

"And now you dream of going home."

"Now we all dream of going home."

That was a good answer. She felt pleased with him, drawn to him. He'd made her think, and the thinking made her want to move, but she sat still and let him watch her. She felt undressed, as if this man was stripping her to bones, only what he was looking for was her soul instead of her body. In spite of that, she still wasn't ready for his touch.

He started again. "Now, be patient with me. I'm going to talk about things that might make you mad, but they weren't my choices. So don't get mad at *me*."

"Okay." She stretched and fidgeted, almost pacing, thinking. Joel simply sat, letting her do half orbits around him.

"People fought. Someday I can share the details of that. Who and why. The outcome was that the peacers were given more power and more people. When we left home there was one peacer to a hundred people. Now there is one to ten."

"But you just said that was part of the problem, reds with too much power." She saw Nona's face again, gone forever. Hugh's now, as well. She felt raw, anger and loss powering some of her agitation. "It is, you know."

"The solution to one problem often makes new problems."

Unfair ones. "How do you know all this?"

"All of our history is available to everyone in command."

"I want to read it all."

"If we win, I'll have Ix give it to you."

"Really?"

"Do you want me to tell you this story?"

"Of course." She stood on tiptoe and stretched up so her fingertips brushed the ceiling. "Then will you tell me what Ix's job is?"

He raised an eyebrow and then laughed. "I don't have to wait for that. Ix's job is to get us home safe. It's that simple."

She furrowed her brow.

"Simple and easy are not the same."

"All right." She didn't think that was all there was to Ix, but she had no way to prove it. She did some of the stretches KJ had taught her, leaking extra energy out on purpose, trying to ground herself and be in the moment. "So people fought."

"They did. Then we put up walls so we could retreat if we needed to. Not me. Not my father. Before that. Before we even got to the first of the planets we went to, and we went to five, in three star systems. There has been more than one fight since then as people tried to free themselves, each from the other. Almost always it has been the workers in the outer pods because those of us on the inside are the only ones who've had time to be oppressors."

"You make it sound so simple."

"I'm simplifying it for you," Joel said. "Can you please sit down?"

She did. "Sorry. So Lila Red was just one of the people who fought one of the fights? But she wasn't from the outer pods."

"According to Ix, there have always been people inside who want a different solution."

"Like you? What do you want?" She wanted to stand up again, to move, but she made herself stay as still as she could manage, though her hands wrung and twisted like live things.

"It's time," he said. "We're coming home. We're almost there. I'm positive we're going to need all of our strengths, and that includes all of you. That's you and Daria and Onor and Marcelle and Conroy and a hundred others I can name."

She shivered a little that he knew so many names. Good.

"And I intend to bring as many of them home alive as I can, and to help us all listen to each other. That's what I want. Because we're going to see the stars."

His tone of voice told her he was done. Everything about his story seemed true to her, a new idea on top of a new idea on top of a new idea. Her blood hummed with new ideas, new energy.

"See the stars," she repeated. She believed him. She believed him completely. She sat back and closed her eyes and whispered, "Thank you."

He let her stay there in silence for a long time. And then he said, "You're welcome." He waited a few more breaths and then said, "Will you sing for me?"

She *had* promised him a song.

Instead of any of the songs he had almost surely heard before, she chose a lullaby in its original version. Well, he had surely heard that, too. But never from her.

He helped her sing the last verse, his voice untrained but decent.

She pleaded thirst.

He brought her wine and water and a small plate with three tiny, sweet snacks on it.

"You are romancing me," she told him.

"You know that."

"I do."

"But you're resisting. Some."

"I am." She took a sip of the wine. It had been pressed from the leavings of the juicing process for golden orbfruit, its color light and its flavor sweet. She only knew this because Colin had served her something like it once. This quality wine didn't exist at home, where homemade stills produced beverages with more bite and less flavor. She let a second sip rest on her tongue and fall down her throat like silk. "I am worth far more than any simple lover. I can bring you the gray levels. I can help you." Her hands shook in her lap. "I can't just go to your bed." Ruby swallowed, waiting. She was afraid to pick up the glass. More wine might cost her the small bit of resolve she had left, or she might spill it and waste a rare drink for nothing.

"Ever?" he asked. Bold. She liked that.

"Until we're equal."

He sat relaxed against the chair opposite her, his legs crossed casually in front of him. He watched her contemplatively, the way one might appraise a fine tool or a particularly good piece of music.

After what seemed like a very long time, he leaned forward. "You are much braver than me."

"No."

"Oh, yes. You are."

"But you . . . you lead so many people. Our own leaders, like The Jackman, work for you."

"And you make people smile."

"I do." She didn't make it a question. It was true. "It's a small thing. Without Fox, I would probably be dead now." She winced, hearing her words sell her short. "But I fought to get his notice." Her hand went to her chest, to the necklace beaded there. "I designed the sign that tells us apart."

"And you wrote the song that brings us together."

The conversation felt like a dance. "I can help you." Her mouth felt dry and her throat thick. "I know I can. And I can learn. Truly, I learn very fast."

His voice was just barely over a whisper. "I've watched you learn."

She took a sip of wine.

"I can help you, too," he said. "If you've lost Fox . . ." He trailed it off, like a question, as if it would matter to him.

"I have."

"I can help you, give you a way for people to hear you. I can give you a voice." He licked his lips, his next words slightly more bitter. "If we win."

"I need to go now. Home. To use my voice. I need to talk to my people."

"Now?"

"Soon."

"It's not safe."

"If I ever let myself be afraid I might as well stop."

He bowed his head. "I understand."

Fox had been stronger than her when she met him, but she'd outgrown him, found he didn't have passion for the same thing she did.

She would not outgrow this man.

He was going to run the ship when they won, and he would be surrounded with things to learn and do, with choices that mattered. "Will you help me get home? I can help us win. I've thought about it. I can go to them, to all the pods, and I can bring messages from you, and I can sing my songs, and I can give them heart. It will help them fight. I can also bring any weapons or knowledge you want them to have."

"I don't want to put you in that much danger."

"You will be in an equal amount."

"So then we are equal."

"We are."

He stood up and extended his hand, and Ruby took it. His hand felt warm and dry and strong.

The bedroom was bigger than any she'd seen on the ship. An intricately knotted hanging on the wall added texture and softness, and the bedspread looked handmade. When she leaned down to take a closer look, she saw that it had been decorated with colorful fabric renditions of birds.

Joel dimmed the lights and slowly stripped her clothes from her. He took her two hands and kept his arms a little stiff, keeping distance between them, simply looking at her for what felt like a very long time. The heat in his hands and his gaze warmed her, even naked. Eventually, she couldn't stand simply being looked at. She pushed his arms to his sides, with effort, and stripped his shirt from him.

When he pulled her to him for a kiss, she tasted the fine wine.

She pushed him backward onto the bed and gave a little leap so she straddled him, leaning down to continue the kiss.

FIFTY-FIVE
PARTINGS

Ruby woke to the memory of Joel's body, taller and firmer and slightly more awkward than Fox's. She lay still, afraid to move lest she forget where his knee had rested on her thigh, or between her thighs, or where his fingers had tightened against her nipples. If she lay still long enough, perhaps the ghost of him would stay in bed with her.

There was a similarity between waking up after a night with Joel and after a night with Fox. Except for her naked body, and the memories of the man, the bed was empty.

The table.

The battle.

Ruby flung the covers aside and went to the privy.

A handwritten note had been attached to the mirror. "Good luck, little gray. I'll find you. Soon." Attached to the note was a chain fashioned of metal loops, and on each loop, there were four tiny beads. One gray, one blue, one red, and one green. She picked it up in wonderment. Where could he have found such a thing? It could be a man's necklace, so maybe it was something he had. Nevertheless, she slid it over her head and put the note into her pocket.

Ruby expected it might be awhile before she saw Joel again. But she was already looking forward to it.

She stepped into the shower. Water poured over her head. She'd find someone to help her go home. Give her people heart. Maybe Ani would still be around and she'd have something pretty to wear. The cascade of warm water stopped long before she felt ready.

She dressed in a clean blue uniform that had been laid out for her, silently thanking Joel. There was no comb, so she used her fingers again.

She opened the bedroom door to find Onor waiting in the living room.

Her face flushed hot, and she stopped dead, swallowing. He made her think of Dayn. She didn't want a keeper. Ever. Again.

Not even if it was Onor.

Onor handed her a cup of stim.

She took it, angry and sheepish at once, looking down at the steaming liquid instead of meeting his eyes. She knew what she'd see in them. "I'm sorry," she said.

His voice shook. "For what, exactly? I need to know."

"That you're standing here right now."

He put a hand out and touched her cheek. She looked up then and saw the pain she had expected in his eyes.

"You will always be one of my two best friends." The words sounded inadequate even as they left her lips. She took his hand in one of her stim-warmed hands. "Always."

His voice shook a bit as he said, "We need to go. There's a status meeting every half hour now, and the next one will be soon."

He turned for the door.

"How is the battle going? Are they telling you anything?"

He blinked and frowned, as if resetting his thoughts. His demeanor didn't look better for it. "There's a thousand dead. Almost all of us. We hold the same territory that we did, nothing more. All of our own level, except lockup and a bit around that, and a few corridors and offices on the logistics level. We're not winning."

"Yet." She could help. "I need to go home."

Onor glanced back at the bedroom door, as if shaming her with her dalliance.

"We need him," she whispered.

"I don't."

She had seen the way Onor looked at Joel, the respect in his eyes. But Joel would have to regain that. "All right. I need him, and you need me. And right now, we need to get to gray. Where's Ani?"

"Do you need her, too?"

She let out a long sigh. "Onor. I will always love you. I love you now. I loved you when we were seven. But you cannot be everything to me."

She expected him to head for the door, but he held his ground. "I hope you know what you're doing."

"So do I." She leaned toward him, offering a hug or a kiss on the cheek or some other thing, but he stiffened and pulled away.

Damn. She'd meant what she said, that she'd always need him.

But there had been magic between her and Joel. Not just sex, not even just during sex. There was power, and with that, she could help bring her people home safely.

She could keep her promise to Nona.

The door beside her burst open and a red glanced at them and barreled past, heading for the bedroom she'd just left.

Damned good thing Joel was already gone.

Onor grabbed her arm and they threaded through two more reds and out of Joel's quarters.

Onor's stunner filled his hand. He pointed it behind them and shot, the sound a rush of deadly softness.

Someone fell. Someone else screamed.

Footsteps started after them.

Onor jerked her left. Pain shot up her arm. "Run!"

She ran. Their footsteps echoed down the corridor, and they came to a two-way choice. "Which way?" she asked.

He shook his head. "Guess."

She chose the right turn, and then another, and then a left. They slowed to a walk, their raspy breath too loud. Hopefully no one would stop them.

"We need to go out," she said. "Back home."

"The trains aren't working."

"We can walk." Her feet were already sore from the long walk here the day before.

It took three hours of walking to find one of the flexible tunnels that led between levels and pods. She'd learned to read the markings on the walls well enough to tell it led outward, to logistics, but not well enough to tell which pod it led to. She closed her eyes. When she opened them again she realized Onor was standing and waiting for her to make up her mind. She was leading again.

This was why he couldn't be everything to her. He needed someone to follow. She stepped through the opening and motioned Onor in, closing the hatch behind them. The tunnel sensed them, leaving lights on for them, pulsing slowly in the right direction.

"Be careful." She started to whistle softly as a way to fill the space with something happier than her fears. With luck, they could slip through and find a path like the one Fox had led her through when he first rescued her. She had lost all sense of location. The corridor felt longer than she expected. Maybe she was just tired. If only she had a way to call The Jackman to her.

KJ had immediate person-to-person communication. She'd seen it the day she and Ani had followed him through the walls.

She whispered, "Ix?"

No answer.

She hissed louder. "Ix!"

No answer. Did it hear her in this corridor, or was it ignoring her, or was it helping her by pretending not to hear her?

With all she'd learned, she didn't know anything.

As soon as they cracked the hatch on the other end of the tunnel, she wished she hadn't. A couple hurrying down the corridor heard the soft wind of opening and turned to spot them.

She had never seen the people before, and they didn't seem to recognize her either.

She turned the other way, hiding her face from the strangers. It should be okay. She and Onor were wearing blue, and while they had the absurd red stunners on their waists, the *Fire* had been full of mixed uniforms the day the sky fell. Surely a long fight like this would cause the same thing.

They came to a T-shaped choice at the end of the tunnel. Boot steps echoed, the sound hard to locate from where she stood. She peered around the corner, hoping that whoever wore the boots was walking away.

People converged from both sides. Sylva led the closest group.

She turned and bumped into Onor. "Trouble," she whispered. "Walk the other way."

"Can we get back to the tunnel?"

"I'm not leading them back to Joel." Or giving away the room with the table. They needed that advantage. She walked close to the wall, leaning close to Onor and talking, trying to look like she belonged here. Maybe Sylva would keep going straight and wouldn't turn to see her. Maybe she wouldn't recognize her.

"He'd want you to." Onor hissed at her. "He'd want you safe."

"I won't risk him." She listened, heard footsteps turn behind her. *Damn.* Running would get her stunned, and she wanted her wits. She should surrender and then find a way to get free. "At the next opportunity, turn away from me."

"I can't do that."

"You have to tell people I've been caught. Tell everyone."

"You haven't been caught."

The footsteps behind her hadn't sped up. She couldn't speed up and pull away. At least not until Onor was safe. "You have to stay free and tell people who has me."

"Who?"

"Sylva. Remember it. Sylva. And stay safe."

They passed the place where they had come into this level. Good. At least Onor couldn't go back that way now. She took more steps, and more. Finally, a branching corridor. "Go, now. Cross and find a place like we just left."

He touched her side, a swipe that might have been accidental but turned out to be a reach for her stunner, which he pulled free of her holster as he finished turning to face their pursuers.

No! There were too many of them. He'd die. Like Hugh. She pulled her hand back to knock the gun out of his fist, saw that he had both stunners, his and hers, pointed at Sylva and her escort. Sylva had at least three or four others with her, maybe more. Ruby couldn't take her eyes from Onor's to look back and see. He looked so full of purpose and fear it frightened her.

She leapt in front of his face, making sure he had no shot. "Run, you idiot," she screeched.

"Why?" he answered, trying to get around.

"Because I need you safe." Of course, it didn't matter now. Her plan had been to separate from him before Sylva recognized her, give him room to escape. But now that he was pointing guns at her enemies, the only choice for either of them was to run. "Let's go!"

She felt the weight of the stun, like a wrench hitting her in the back, and the softening of her limbs as they refused to obey her.

The floor hit her softly, her arms and legs bouncing. She felt no pain from the fall.

Above her, Onor shot two fisted, the slight recoil pushing him away from her as she fell. Her vision shrank to a point of light and stopped.

FIFTY-SIX

THE WATERWAYS

The boneless thud of Ruby's body at his feet made Onor's eyes sting and made his target waver in his vision. The stunners felt light in his hands, like air. Anger tightened muscles.

He recognized the woman from the test day, the severe redheaded one. He shot her.

She fell, the men behind her leaning down toward her, their mouths open in surprise.

Onor reached down and tugged on Ruby's arm. Nothing in the feel of her body resisted his touch or his pull; nothing except breath and blood moved in her. Her eyes, closed, didn't even flutter.

She'd become dead weight. Impossible for him to carry and run.

He glanced up.

Three reds rushed him, one with a stunner out.

He shot again. The closest man tripped over his own feet but held his weapon up, Onor's shot too wild or too weak to bring him all the way down.

No time.

Onor dodged and raced, bruising his shoulders on the walls. He hated every step away from Ruby, expecting each to end with a graceless face-forward fall as someone stunned him.

She'd told him to get away. Tell someone.

His feet flew. Speed dried the water from his eyes, and his vision cleared as he ran. All those nights running.

Bless Conroy.

His legs moved fast, his body responsive.

Bless The Jackman.

The steps behind him sounded farther away. He didn't dare stop and look back.

He'd abandoned Ruby.

Not that he'd had a choice. She'd known that. Told him to do it. Commanded it. Still, it ate at him, drove his feet to keep moving, to find help.

He hadn't seen anyone yet. That must be pure luck. He needed to slow down before anyone noticed him running like a madman.

Dry breath wheezed through his chest as he jogged and then slowed further to a walk. He began to pass others, which made the level feel even more foreign. No one looked emaciated or overweight. No one looked scarred from accidents or red nosed from stim abuse or blown out from drugs.

He started to sound normal, to walk with the right movement and breath, even though he felt the need to find someone to tell, ten people to tell, like a racing sharpness in his blood.

An older man stopped and watched Onor approach.

Onor smiled while he gave the man the barest glance, trying to look like he belonged.

The man nodded, looked like he was about to say something, then nodded again and kept walking.

But surely he'd get stopped soon just for looking tired and worn out, if not for holding a stunner in each hand. He found a small galley and poured himself a glass of water.

Water.

The water system here must be like at home.

The two water systems didn't connect. He and Ruby had tried to climb from one set of pipes to the other when he was an apprentice. But surely he could travel through this level the way he could travel at home, through the catwalks and ramps that allowed maintenance of the pipes.

He looked. There was no good access in this tiny white galley, with its clean silver sink knobs and simple storage drawers for food and utensils. He needed a bigger source of water—a common area or the kitchen or something.

After a glance in the mirror, he washed the sweat from his face and did his best to rake his disorderly hair into something presentable. He looked as scared and lost and angry as he felt, although the mirror didn't show his shakiness. He slid his last power pack into one stunner and pocketed the other.

He checked another galley, a large bathroom, and a crèche before he found a water system access point big enough for a person. It turned out to be a closet behind a school room, the door so clean he almost missed the water symbol in the upper right.

The maintenance infrastructure here looked just like it did on the gray levels: a thin rail for the small repair bots to run around and a slender and compact walkway with just enough room for a human to walk carefully and do a visual inspection. It wasn't any cleaner than his home systems, either.

He followed the grey-water pipe, sure it was heading outward.

A bot whirred by, shaking a tiny bit on its rail. It ignored him completely.

He saw a few more as he crawled and shimmied and sometimes walked upright through the bowels of the *Fire*. Hopefully the bots would all see him as a worker and part of their familiar landscape.

The pipe Onor had been tracking ended up in a group weld he'd already approached from two different angles. There were no seats in the maintenance catwalk, just awkward ways to stand or crouch. His feet hurt. His borrowed blue uniform had torn in two places where he'd snagged it on protrusions, and he had enough grease stains to lubricate a whole maintenance bot.

He stopped.

The day the sky fell and Fox and Ruby first kissed, Fox had been taken up into the sky on a flying cargo cart. It had come from this level.

He started off again, hunting an entirely new thing. Surely there was a place to dock maintenance carts and carry trash in and out and such.

When he found it, he realized he was still out of luck. There were four cargo carts in two different sizes, but none of them would obey his commands. Still, there was a hatch. No window, no way to tell where it went. It was big enough for the flying carts, but there were also hand controls, which must mean there was someplace for an uncarted human to go.

He grabbed a suit and helmet from a rack by the door. If the *Fire* were willing to give him any luck at all, he would get through the door and find a way between levels. If he could get to any gray pod, surely he could ride the train. It couldn't be harder than moving safely all the way from command to gray.

The suit didn't stink quite as badly as the ones he had used when he helped clean out his old home. Staler, and fainter, but still like trapped human. He took a deep breath and slid the helmet over his head, fastening it down to the collar ring.

"Onor."

He startled, and then recognized the voice. "Ix."

"Open the door now and go down."

He didn't understand what the AI meant until he was inside the lock, had closed the door, and heard the air hissing free. He stood on a hatch. There was just enough room to sidle to one side and reach down to pull it open. A metal stair attached to the opening let him drop through and close the hatch above him. "Why that way?" he asked.

No answer at all from the enigmatic AI.

Just like in the water maintenance byways, he now stood on a thin ladder in a tall and fairly slender opening between the levels. The turn through the hatch had kept him oriented the right way.

The ladder led to a series of beams wide enough to walk on and close enough together to jump from one to the other where there were no ramps. Pipes and wires lined the beams. As he stood still, trying to figure out where to go next, it looked as if the whole space breathed, or swayed, or something. His footing felt steady, so it must be part illusion from being inside the skin of the *Fire* in a place humans seldom went.

There were no nearby doors.

He picked a direction and started walking the beams carefully, conscious of the weight that sat above him (the blue and command levels) and of the gray level and cargo holds below.

He started toward the first hatch he spotted in a wall outside the gray pods.

"Next one."

"Thank you."

Damned AI didn't bother to acknowledge even that. Onor climbed through the next hatch, which ended up being a down and then across turn, reversing what he had just done. He remembered looking up from the park the day the sky fell; the gap between levels hadn't seemed so big then.

Home.

"So why didn't you put me in D?" Onor complained. "I bet Ruby's in lockup."

Ix didn't answer.

He started off down the tunnels, jogging, his helmet tucked under his arm but the suit still on to cover his blue uniform.

FIFTY-SEVEN
WAKING

Ruby opened her eyes. A white ceiling above her, blank, fairly clean. She wasn't in a bed, but on something harder and colder.

A lot colder.

Maybe the cold had woken her.

She swiveled her head to the side and found a white wall. Close, maybe a few inches from her nose.

Her muscles responded, let her move her head, but they made her work for the movement. She had to put way too much conscious thought into shifting her gaze or turning her neck.

Tired.

She wanted to go away and wake up again later. Memories floated like fluff and air, coming back slowly. Almost being caught and running and then really being caught.

That memory made her twitch.

Twitching hurt.

She took in three deep breaths, then turned the other way. Another white wall.

She pushed herself up, needing a door.

No door.

A bed—harder than a bed should be, so hard it hurt. At the foot of it, a sink and a privy.

Then a door opened.

That was a problem. A door with no handle for her.

Ellis. She had enough energy to glare at him, but barely. Spitting would have been even nicer, but she couldn't quite get there.

He blinked in surprise for just a moment then said, "You're awake."

She didn't feel any need to reply. The question closest to her tongue was *why hadn't they just killed her?* She was afraid she might not like the answer to that. The next question was *did Onor get away?* And the third was about Joel, whether or not he was free and whether or not he was looking for her, and surely that wasn't a good question either.

Ellis grabbed her arm, holding her close to him. She smelled sour sweat and stim breath. "Can you walk?"

"Where?"

"Can you?"

Bastard. "Maybe."

"Do it."

She thought about sitting cross-legged on the bed and refusing to move, but instead she let him help her down and then shook his arm off. Standing would be tough. The room spun. "Where am I?"

He just stared at her, clearly unwilling to answer.

A stunner shouldn't have put her out so far they could carry her away and place her somewhere else. "What did you do to me?"

"We haven't done anything to you. You started a war."

"Not me."

"Your endangered the ship. You'll be put on trial soon."

Great. "I don't think I can walk yet."

"I'll carry you."

He was an inch shorter than her. The idea was almost funny. Laughing at Ellis wouldn't be any better than the questions she'd thought of earlier. "Give me a minute." She lifted a foot, set it down, lifted the other, shook her arms. Her mouth tasted like metal and soap and medication. "Do you have some water?"

He pointed at the sink, backed off, and closed the door, leaving her alone in the very small space. This must have been built to keep prisoners in. She couldn't think of any other reason for such a room to exist. So she must be in lockup. That meant she was surrounded by her people.

Ruby managed to drink using her cupped palms, use the privy, run her fingers through her hair, and get her legs used to obeying commands again by the time Ellis reappeared.

As she followed Ellis down the hall, two peacers, a man and a woman, slid in behind her. One of the peacers had white hair that contrasted with her brown skin and deep black eyes. Chitt. She winked at Ruby.

Chitt's multicolored strand of beads wasn't visible, but Ruby was willing to bet it was still there.

FIFTY-EIGHT

GATHERING

O nor was almost back to the living habs on B when he heard his name. The voice was familiar, but he couldn't place it until he turned around and spotted Daria standing behind him.

"Come on!" she called, her voice urgent. "To Kyle's."

He'd been going there anyway. "I'm glad to see you."

"We've been watching for you."

"Ruby's been captured."

"We know that. We don't know where she went."

"How do you know that?" Not that he really needed to ask. Surely Ix had told them.

"The Jackman heard it from somewhere." Daria was breathing so hard the words came out in lumps. "He sent messages every direction, but no one's answered him yet. He's practically torn the *Fire* apart looking all over for you."

Onor was still wearing his suit. The awkward overboots clanked on the metal parts of the floor and made it hard to keep up with Daria. "How did you know where to look for me?"

"We didn't. We hoped."

He focused on moving as fast as he could until they got to Kyle's door. As soon as the door opened his stomach screeched in pleasure at the smells of soup and stim leaking into the hallway.

Inside, the room was half full. The Jackman, Daria, Kyle, Conroy, and a few people Onor had seen but didn't know.

"You've still got your helmet with you," The Jackman pointed out. "Dead giveaway that you've been elsewhere."

"Yeah, well, I'm a little tired."

He threw the helmet onto a spare spot on the couch and decided not to say he hadn't wanted to lose his connection to Ix. "Good to see you, too. You know they've got Ruby?"

"They?"

"The red and the same man—Ellis—from the day we took the test.

Anybody remember them?" He looked around. No one from his school class was in the room.

"We know she's been taken," Daria said. "I told you that."

"I need to get her." He stripped off his suit, exposing his filthy blue uniform. "What's the plan?"

"I'll get you clean clothes," Daria offered.

"I might need these."

"I have blues. And take the sign." She handed him a string of beads and material so bold it screamed rebel even from a distance. But, then again, he needed to show where he stood now more than ever. It wasn't like he was right beside Ruby to make it obvious. He put the sign over his head and let it hang over his torn shirt.

"You need to eat," Kyle said, handing him a bowl of rich, spicy smelling soup. "We'll fill you in."

He lifted his spoon. He'd need strength to go after her. "I suspect she's in lockup."

"Eat."

"Do you know where she is?" Onor asked The Jackman.

"No."

Daria handed him a shirt and he changed. "So what are we going to do?"

"You're going to eat. We'll fill you in."

"All right. I'm done arguing." Besides, his stomach agreed with them. He put the spoon in his mouth. At the first taste, his body took over, and Onor was pretty sure he wouldn't be able to stop eating if he tried. After he cleaned the bowl, he looked at Kyle. "Good soup. Did the fight come here?"

"Not much," Conroy answered. "We're too valuable to wipe out. Ix knows it, and I think Garth does, too."

"What are you doing here anyway?" Onor asked, grinning.

"Came to find you."

The Jackman spoke up before Onor could reply. "It was worse in E-pod. Penny's in the infirmary there, got her head banged up."

Not Penny! If only he could be with everyone at once. *Damn.* "She's going to be okay?"

"I think so. If we keep the doctors."

He hadn't thought about that. There was too much to worry about at once. He held out the empty bowl for more. "We have to get Ruby before they hurt her."

The Jackman nodded, but he looked distracted.

"We do!"

"We will. We leave in a half hour."

That was better. Onor settled into emptying the second bowl while trying to listen to every conversation around him at once. It didn't work very well, but he caught the tone of the room perfectly.

Ruby would have stuck her tongue out, said they were all worrying far too much, and offered up a song and maybe a dance. At least a hug. But all he felt was worried, and so tired he was cold in spite of the warm soup filling his belly.

And sad. He had let Ruby be caught. He could have stopped it. Somehow.

After he handed the bowl to a rather-too-grim Kyle, The Jackman came up behind him, close enough to talk just above a whisper. "She screwed you up, didn't she?"

Onor swallowed, his throat too constricted for words to sneak out. What did The Jackman know? That Ruby was Joel's bedmate now? He hadn't really stopped running since he found that out, and now it stuck him to his chair like dead weight. He knew she didn't love him that way, had always known that. Too bad what his head knew didn't seem to get through to his thick, stupid, loving soul.

When he could speak, Onor kept his voice steady. "Ruby hasn't changed at all. She's like she's always been, looking for a way to change the *Fire* so it bends to her will."

"The *Fire*'s metal, and that girl is only flesh. Don't let her hurt you beyond repair while she beats herself to death against the inside wall of a spaceship."

He swallowed, still thick of throat and tongue. "I just hope she isn't dead yet."

"Ix says no."

"Are you ready?" The Jackman asked. "Can you do this?"

"What are we doing?"

"We're going to get her. There are others meeting us at various places."

"Ruby's in lockup?"

"No. She's in command."

Onor grunted. "I just came from there. How the hell are we going to get back?"

"We have help hiding our movements."

"No. You don't. Not enough. There's a table. There's four tables. They show where everyone is. Magic and scary. They can see us now."

"I dropped you off there, remember? I saw it."

"Did you really see it? Did you watch it for hours? Ever?"

"They wouldn't have let me stay. So I didn't ask."

"I watched it, for a very long time." While Ruby had slept with Joel. "I know a lot about the patterns and the battles. I can help."

The Jackman sounded wounded. "I only got a glimpse."

"You can stare at the table for a week after we win," Onor promised. "Let's go."

FIFTY-NINE

PIECES REVEALED

Ruby followed Ellis slowly down the hall, humming "Homecoming" all the way.

He turned and glared at her, so she smiled and continued.

Walking remained hard at first, but eventually her feet started obeying her mind with no extra effort. Thoughts came a bit closer together. Ellis must need her alive, have a plan for her. It would have been so easy to kill her after they'd stunned her.

They stopped outside of a door and Ellis turned to Ruby, his eyes cold and hard. Even so, she saw fear in them. Or maybe she just needed some hope to cling to. "You're not to speak," he said. "If you speak we will make sure you cannot ever speak again. Do you understand?"

Well, maybe he *was* afraid. She lifted her chin and straightened her spine, trying to look as strong, female, and unafraid as she could. A lesson from Jali. "I heard you."

They led her into the biggest room she had ever seen. Rows of tables, seats close together, every seat filled. Faces turned to watch her, curious, suspicious, angry. They all watched her. She saw uniforms of every color except gray. Clean, neat. Not the fighters. The planners. Here and there, even a splash of green.

Sylva. Standing on the far side of the stage, watching, her eyes narrow and her face hard as robot gears.

So many in one place.

Chitt had stopped by the door and faded into a line of reds who stood watching the room, leaving Ruby and Ellis on a stage with a giant screen behind them and one on each side of the room. On the screen, she and Ellis loomed over the group. Her face was pale and her damned hair had gone flyaway again. Whatever camera they were using made her hair look the wrong color of red.

They'd left her in her grunged-out grays to set her apart from everyone else. She smiled, used her hand to capture the worst bits of flyaway hair. She straightened her back.

Maybe she would finally meet Garth, the man who seemed to be behind all this. Colin had showed her vid and a picture, so she knew what to look for: a tall, pale-skinned man with dark eyes, slightly hunched over shoulders, and hair beginning to gray. With well over a hundred in the one room, there were too many people to see them all individually in the crowd

She kept smiling at the crowd, making eye contact, doing her best to own the stage. It would be a great place for a concert. She drew it in her mind and heard the instruments tuning up.

Next to her, Ellis's face looked purple with anger. He should be saying something if he wanted to shift attention away from her, but he seemed to be waiting. Sylva also stood, tapping her toe lightly.

Garth didn't appear to be here. Mostly she saw strangers or noticed faces she'd seen in passing. A reminder, again, of how big the *Fire* was and how she was only one person, and a small, young one at that.

The vid screens snapped away from Ruby to show a close-up of Garth, his face too big to look natural. It appeared on three walls, behind her and on both sides. Coward. If he wasn't here, how was she supposed to influence him or capture him or do anything useful at all?

She hadn't forgotten Chitt, or the fact that Lila Red the Releaser had been like Chitt, or like her. The faces could all be enemies, or a mix.

The projected image of Garth showed details she hadn't been able to see from the picture Joel had pointed out for her on his wall. Garth's cheeks were high and a bit sunken, his lips nearly colorless. His eyes were a bright dark, almost gray, his lashes long and feminine and deep black. Worry lines carved the skin around his eyes and the corners of his mouth.

She expected Garth to talk, but it was Ellis who spoke first. "Ruby Martin, you are here to be judged. Your trial is being broadcast on all of the ship's channels and witnessed by the ship's captain."

Now Garth spoke. He addressed neither Ellis nor Ruby. "People of *The Creative Fire*. We are almost home."

Ruby bristled. He wouldn't be telling the grays that—if he even told the truth about broadcasting to everyone—unless she had done so first. Bastard. Liar.

"And it is time for all of us all to work together. We must do that in the ways that we know. We must have order and discipline. We will begin to enforce discipline rigidly in all areas of the ship."

Right. He was willing to kill. She imagined people stopping to listen and shaking their heads or making bad jokes.

"We do not know what we'll find at Adiamo, whether we will meet friends or enemies. We must stand united in case we find danger. We must stay where we know how to act. We must do our jobs."

The grays must stay slaves. She wanted to get her hands on this vid and edit it so people would hear what he was really saying. He sounded so fervent, so confident, and so wrong.

She had to stay alive to write songs about him.

"Today, we are putting one of our workers on trial. We are doing so because she has been trying to cause change in a time when we can't afford change. We have been patient. She is young, and a girl."

"Woman," she whispered.

Ellis glared at her.

"But we cannot allow mutinous thoughts or deeds in any form, and we will root them out so that we remain strong together to face the growing threats."

She looked back out at the faces. They were difficult to read. Some set hard against her. Some curious. Not that it mattered; this wouldn't be a fair trial. If she were lucky, she'd go to lockup. She did not expect luck. But you made your own.

She took a deep breath and gathered as much strength as she could. She glanced down, noticing that she still wore the necklace Joel had left for her. Surely Ellis and his supporters knew the power of the mixed-color symbol. Yet they were underestimating it, and her, and the people who followed her. All she had to do was glance at Chitt, who looked angry and betrayed and also ready to act. And who had been on Ruby's side since before Fox came for her.

She felt rifts in this room that could crack wide open.

When Ruby let her breath out, she took another one in, feeling it fill behind her belly button, deep. She gathered as much of her anger in to her as she could.

She spoke.

"My most mutinous thought has been that we go home the same way we left, where everyone aboard *The Creative Fire* has a voice."

Ellis grabbed her and pulled her toward him. He stank.

"Let her talk!" someone yelled from the back of the room.

Ellis's hand covered her mouth.

She slimed his sweaty palm with her tongue. A short scream exited her throat and pushed through his fingers.

His hand opened.

She got out the words, "We are not killing you," before he leaned over and replaced his hand on her mouth, whispering in her ear.

She had to stop struggling to hear what he said. "I will see that Fox dies for this if you don't stop."

He was quite behind the times. But for the moment, she stopped. Fox didn't deserve death for coming to get her.

Garth watched her intently from whatever safe bunker he was in.

Ellis accepted her stillness as acquiescence and let go of her face.

She kept her gaze firmly on Garth and spoke a single word loud enough for the whole room to hear. "Coward."

SIXTY

JOEL AND ONOR

To Onor's surprise, they headed to common, where they joined two other groups of about the same size. "Won't they find us here? Where are the reds anyway?"

The Jackman grinned. "We've distracted them. We had help from Ix. Like your directions here."

Onor hadn't told anyone about the voice in the helmet. "How did you know?"

"Ix told me. Ix can give us whatever information we ask for or that it wants us to have. The problem is that it can't hide information the others ask for." He paused. "Are you sure you want to go?"

"Of course."

The Jackman grunted. "You could stay back and be defense. We'll be meeting Joel."

Onor spat. "We may need him."

"See you keep that pride." The Jackman turned and started them off down the same corridor they'd come up. Onor walked near the middle of the pack, beside Kyle. Both were silent, but Onor had the distinct sense that Kyle was as happy to have him around as The Jackman seemed to be.

It seemed like the wrong number of people. Onor counted twenty plus him. Twenty-one. Too many for a stealth operation, too few for a strength move.

The Jackman had an inner sense of the *Fire*'s layout that made the route back through the blue level seem direct and safe. No one had journals with them, but The Jackman muttered under his breath from time to time, his jaw tensing and relaxing, his focus sometimes inward even though they walked though enemy territory.

Onor stumbled over a low lip where two tunnels joined. Kyle steadied him. "Are you okay?"

"Sure. I'll be fine." He breathed and walked and worried. His brain shed its fog and his knees lifted higher. It seemed they hadn't gone far enough when The Jackman ushered them through the locks on the far side of the blue level and through a connector that led to command.

"Go right," The Jackman whispered.

Around a corner, they met up with four other people. Joel, two men, and a woman. Joel stopped and looked hard at Onor, appraising him all over like the first time they'd met in the corridor on green. Joel had passed Onor on his way out, so he knew Onor had been guarding him and Ruby the night they had slept together. In another circumstance, another moment of his life, Onor would have turned away. He wanted to now, but he couldn't. It mattered too much that he be part of the next battle, part of saving Ruby.

Joel had slept with Ruby too easily. He couldn't possibly appreciate her. He probably slept with women all the time; women liked power.

Ruby's choice, too.

Joel waited for a response from Onor. Maybe he expected a punch.

Onor swallowed hard, shoving away his hurt pride to deal with later. "Good to see you again. We should go."

"Good to see you, too." Joel looked past Onor at the group from gray. "Thank you for coming."

Joel turned and led them in the direction they'd already been going, their pace a fast walk.

The Jackman took up the rear and Onor fell back beside him.

Being in the back let him watch Joel, who moved at the front of the group from the first step after he met them, leadership falling to him as surely as he breathed. Joel knew almost everyone's names already, which seemed impossible, and he learned the others quickly, as well as the names of people they knew, asking about family and jobs and dreams in whispered tones.

Twice they passed men who looked the other way. Onor looked for the multicolored sign, even subtly, on their uniforms or jewelry. He didn't see it, but still he felt sure the men were with them. Or trying to take no side at all.

They came to a "T" intersection. Joel steadied his stunner, pointing just in front of him. He and The Jackman separated, one on each side, and people peeled off to stand by one or the other.

Onor hesitated, then followed Joel.

The Jackman gave him a soft nod of approval.

The group split a second time, and Onor worked to stick with Joel again.

Joel stopped in front of a door and whispered. "This is the briefing room. We've got two minutes to wait, then we go in together, all four groups. There are four doors. There are more people able to help than you know about.

"Use your stunners only to threaten unless you're fired on, and then use them to stay safe and to keep each other safe."

Onor nodded.

"Keep Ruby safe."

Joel and Onor shared a look, respect mixed with determination, and all of it salted with the unspoken. They nodded at each other.

Joel opened the door.

SIXTY-ONE
CONFRONTATION

Ruby had created silence in the room with her one word: *coward*. The word seemed to fall into the rift she felt in the room, and she wasn't entirely sure if she would hear cheers or be hit with a stunner next. Garth started to laugh at her. And while he was laughing, the door to her right opened.

Joel burst in, followed by Onor. Both men held stunners out, Onor with one in each hand. Ellis grabbed her, using her to shield himself from them.

Ruby laughed, giddy with the tension and the sudden action. Ellis was demonstrating the very word she had just called his boss. Then other hands were on her, rougher and surer, the wrists thick under a red uniform. She felt real fear then, more afraid than when she'd first walked into the room and realized how many people had gathered to see her charged and damned.

Ruby kicked down hard, slamming her foot against a boot while she tried to twist away. The room spun as her attacker dragged her backward and sideways.

She glimpsed Garth on the vid screen, no longer laughing, his eyes snapping anger and his mouth shut tightly.

Ellis's face passed close to hers, going from fright to slack as he fell, stunned by someone.

Onor standing, yelling her name.

The man who held her, his arm. In front of her face. She bit, tasting cloth.

The crowd, standing and moving, making no real sense. A blur.

The ceiling, her arms pulled tight behind her, her back bent. She screeched as pain arced up her spine.

The other sounds were confusion, and then she started to fall, dragged down as the man holding her slumped in the boneless fall of the stunned.

A hand reached for her. Green uniform. Joel.

She took his hand, and he pulled her close to him and pushed her down. She refused to lay flat even though Joel barked at her to. She sat up crouched, able to see, able to run, but still as small as she could be and do either. Her breath came in great, gasping bits laced with fear and adrenaline.

"Stay there," Joel hissed. He straddled her with his legs, standing over her.

Chaos. Color and movement and screaming. The reds that had been against the wall fought each other. The crowd in the center stood uncertainly, seeming to sway in all directions. Some people held stunners on uncertain targets, others crawled under tables, heading toward the doors. Impossible to make out who was on what side.

Chitt on top of a man twice her size, beating the side of his head with her stunner while he struggled to throw her off.

The Jackman, in what looked like an even fight with a red, blood streaming down his beard, but the red bloodied too, his nose and arm slashed and bleeding.

Joel tried to scream at the crowd, but the noise and fighting drowned his voice.

The doors were clogged by knots of people trying to get out and grays and blues trying to get in, everyone slowed by everyone else.

To her left, a red uniform launched itself at her. Sylva. With a stunner aimed at Joel. Ruby leapt, felt her right shoulder dig into Sylva's neck, knocking Sylva backward.

Sylva grunted and grabbed a chunk of Ruby's hair, pulling.

Ruby landed on Sylva, her head yanked down to the stage floor as Sylva pulled.

Ruby twisted and kicked, getting nothing better than shin.

Sylva was on her, one hand still holding her hair, the other holding the stunner, using it as a bludgeon, slamming Ruby in the cheek so hard she tasted blood.

Ruby felt only anger now, hot and swift. She raised a hand and blocked Sylva's next blow, twisting her arm around Sylva's so Ruby pulled her down, easing the terrible bright pain of the hair pull. She thrust with her legs, getting leverage, rolling over on top of Sylva and pinning her.

Onor screamed from behind. "Lean, Ruby, give me a shot!"

Ruby leaned to her right, feeling Sylva react to the release of pressure and begin to flip her, gaining the advantage again. Sylva's arms felt tight around Ruby's waist, a force. They let go and Sylva fell, loose limbed and stunned.

A glance revealed Onor's triumphant smile

"Nice!" Ruby called to him as she shoved Sylva's inert form to the side and stood.

"That's twice," Onor grinned, turning to block a man racing toward Joel.

From the screen, Garth's voice, rising, someone adjusting the volume. "Stop!"

A momentary hush fell over the room.

Joel shouted, "Freedom!" into the silence

Ruby stepped to his side.

Most of the struggle in the room slowed or stopped, attention shifting between Garth's image, Joel and Ruby, and Onor and the others on the stage.

"We've won," Joel proclaimed. "We've won freedom."

A stunner fired, the beam wide of its mark, missing Joel and hitting the man behind him.

A surge of movement brought down the man who'd fired the stunner.

"More?" Joel asked the crowd, scanning their faces and ignoring the man on the ground.

A scuffle broke out behind them, and Ruby took her cue from Joel, not looking back until she heard Onor's voice demanding something. A quick glance showed him standing over a man on the ground, kicking him.

Ruby stayed close to Joel, more control now in her breathing.

Joel was right. They'd won. Ellis was on the ground, unconscious, and so was Sylva. It was the first time Ruby had ever seen her looking relaxed. Three or four others lay on the stage, stunned or, in one case, beaten. A woman's body lay across the floor at the foot of the stage. But most people stood, and some even sat. Most of the movement and chaos had slowed or stopped.

A great happiness filled up Ruby's belly, the happiness as deep as her anger during the fight, as her fear before that. Not happiness. Triumph. She thought she'd felt that before, but she never had, not really.

She wanted to float with it, giddy.

Except Garth was still watching, and he was far away.

Joel looked up at the picture of Garth. "There are more of us than of you. In case you don't know it, you've lost. We're taking the rest of the ship as I speak."

Everyone in the room was looking at Joel now, some quietly, some with approval or hatred, some merely curious. A few looked stunned and surprised.

Garth regarded Joel, silent and furious.

Onor had come up on Joel's far side, standing close to him, protecting.

Ruby fought to keep her face neutral, to think in the midst of the continued rush of joy at winning this room. It wasn't done yet; she couldn't afford to get ahead of the end of the fight. Mistakes lurked in laziness.

Joel kept his eyes on Garth's. Didn't move.

Ruby watched him, marveling at the strength in his face, the resolve. He was sure of himself, sure past the events in this room.

The doorways had cleared enough that grays and blues and reds who had come in at the same time as Joel—all wearing the multicolored sign in easily visible ways—streamed into the crowd and sorted. Ruby couldn't tell what they were doing, but it looked like they were finding the sign and putting people into two groups. They attended to the stunned or wounded in a third corner of the room.

Good.

She whispered in Joel's ear. "How do we get them? Garth and his supporters?"

To their right, a red swung a defiant fist at a swarthy, dark man wearing the sign and was immediately hit with three stunners. A last burst of fighting?

Garth spoke. "A ship without discipline will fail. We will yet win, and when we do, you will die with Ruby and her friends."

Ruby glared up at him. "Come meet me where we live. Where the workers work and keep *The Creative Fire* going." Her voice rose. "I dare you."

"We will win," Garth said.

"Not today," Ruby said. "We've done it." Only they couldn't leave yet. There was a step to take still. She pursed her lips, feeling what they should do like a word stuck behind her tongue.

Joel pointed up at the screen, an answer to the question she'd whispered in his ear earlier. Three men in green had come up and surrounded Garth, who stood stock still.

He looked startled at the intrusion.

"Ix let them in," Joel said to Garth.

Garth flinched and betrayal touched his face before he hardened it.

Joel turned and looked out at the room full of people. Everyone had stopped, the silence so complete that Joel could speak just above his normal tone. "Watch," he said. He raised a hand and lowered it.

Ruby looked back at the screen. Garth jerked and fell. One of the greens laid a blanket over him. As the blanket covered Garth's face, noise erupted, sobs and disbelief.

He had been shot dead. Not stunned.

She turned to Joel, shocked. They'd won. They didn't need to kill him. Not like that. Maybe if he was right here and fighting them hand to hand.

Then she thought about Lila Red, who had been killed by a captain. But even that didn't take away the feeling of too much cruelty.

She felt unsure of Joel, maybe a bit frightened. But then surely he'd had to kill Garth. He must know what he was doing.

Joel looked out at the crowd, his jaw tight. He stood strong, legs slightly apart, leaning a tiny bit forward. He lifted an arm above his shoulder. She expected him to claim victory, but he did something far smarter. He spoke to the crowd. "Garth had to die for the fighting to stop. Now we are all free."

His audience gave him puzzled looks, but Ruby felt a small, warm smile creeping up her bruised face.

"We are all free," Joel repeated. "We can stop fighting one another, because a ship's crew does not fight. A ship's crew works together. And we have a ship to take home."

Ruby could see it now, feel it. That thing behind her tongue. She called out, "Ix!"

Ix answered her with no hesitation. "Ruby Martin."

This was the final necessary move. Ix. "We want Joel to be captain. Do you recognize him as our captain, so that you will obey him?"

"Joel," Ix said, "Do you wish this honor?"

Joel did what Ruby knew he would. He looked out over the crowd and placed the decision in the hands of the crew. "Are you ready? If you are ready for a new day, I am ready for a new day. I will not betray you. I will bring you home."

The crowd roared so loud that Ruby barely heard Ix say, "I will follow Joel."

SIXTY-TWO

THE END IS THE BEGINNING

R uby wandered through the victory tables, tasting the fresh vegetable soup, greeting people she'd met, meeting people she hadn't. Ani and Onor trailed behind her, guarding while pretending not to. Colin had opened up a string of three cargo bars that connected one to the other and provided bright lighting and upbeat music, and even a small crowd of servers who were all capable of turning to fighters if anything suspicious happened.

So far, nothing had.

The *Fire* was full of pleasure for this moment. She could feel it here, as if the simple relief and happiness of all being on the same side again had erased the bitter feelings. It wouldn't be that simple in the long run, but it was good now.

Joel stood on the far side of the room, deep in conversation with Colin and Conroy, and, oddly, Dayn. But then, this was a time of mixing and of new relationships. At least Fox wasn't here, although she'd see him again, too. She was sure of it. But not so far today.

From time to time Joel met her gaze, leaving her tender and a tiny bit melted.

She and Joel had started on the gray levels, had visited three parts of the ship-wide feast already. They had just come from command, where the atmosphere was a little less boisterous and the food better, if less plentiful.

The guards were the only real sign that the battle had been over for only twenty-four hours. That, and the fact that her feet hurt and her voice was so tired she couldn't sing, even when people asked her to.

Onor leaned over and took her elbow. "Joel wants you."

"Thanks." She walked close to Onor on the way over. He kept his eyes straight ahead, as if he couldn't bear to look at her. She whispered to him. "Thank you for more than this. Thank you for all the things you've ever been to me."

He let go of her arm and looked around the room, approval and loss both registering on his face. "You will always be my best friend," she told him.

"Always," he answered.

She couldn't stand how cold he sounded. "I couldn't have done this without you."

He nodded. Marcelle came up on his other side, grinning from ear to ear. "We did it!"

Ruby smiled at her other best friend. "I know. Will you two help me with the next part?"

"Which is?" Marcelle asked.

"Not today," Ruby said. "We will need to figure that out. Right now, celebrate."

An old man in red reached a hand out for her. She took his hand absently, thinking of Onor, and then realized it was Ben. "Thank you, Ruby," he said.

She leaned down and brushed her lips across the old man's forehead. "Thank you for protecting us."

When they were past him, she told her friends, "I mean it. Without you and Marcelle this would never have happened. At least not this way. We did it together. Got free, got here."

"I know," Onor said. "I know you mean it and I know you love us both, and maybe everyone else, and maybe none of us. It's hard to tell. That's what makes it so hard to love you. You love me back and you don't."

His words stung. "Of course I love you. You're tired."

"We're all tired."

She didn't like the way he sounded at all. She couldn't think of a magic way to help him, and she didn't have a way to offer him any more of her than he already owned. Maybe they were just still exhausted. Maybe it would be better in the future.

Onor stepped back after he delivered Ruby to Joel's side. Even though they had been back together now, she searched Joel's face, needing to know he loved her, maybe needing the same thing from him that Onor needed from her. He returned her gaze tenderly and held her close to him for a moment. "Are you okay?" he asked.

"When we have time, I want to sleep curled up at your side for a whole week."

"We can probably get away for a few hours soon."

"And then?" she whispered, hoping to hear him use tender words with her.

"Then we have to start getting people ready to go home."

ABOUT THE AUTHOR

BRENDA COOPER lives in the Pacific Northwest, which is peopled by many authors, perhaps because it is the home of perfect writing weather. She writes science fiction and fantasy stories and novels, walks dogs, and, when she's not writing fiction, she works for local government and writes blogs about the future.

For more information, please head to http://www.brenda-cooper.com/rubys-song.

ACKNOWLEDGMENTS

Every book is a group effort.

Writers help each other. In this case, specific thanks go to all of those who read the first draft at the Starry Heaven workshop in Flagstaff, particularly to Rob Ziegler and Jenn Reese, who read the full manuscript and gave me great advice and didn't pull punches. Thanks to Sarah Kelley for organizing the workshop and chasing me down to suggest I attend. I also appreciate Brad Beaulieu, who provided some extra support in marketing. Thanks to John Pitts, who is always one of my fine first readers and who has supported my work since before most of it was published; to Louise Marley and Cat Rambo and Melissa Shawl, who read many bits of it along the way in a writer's group; and to my dad, who reads my manuscripts and comments quite well. Every science fiction writer should have a father who is a real rocket scientist.

There are songs in this book. I am not able to sing (well, when I'm alone I often sing, but other people don't like my voice much). So to prepare for this, I attended two songwriting workshops led by the talented Cris Williamson. Any mistakes in the songs are mine, and I appreciate her patience while trying to teach songwriting to a woman who can't hear the difference between notes.

I can't say how pleased I am to have Lou Anders champion this book. He is a fabulous person and one of our finest editors.

As always, thanks to Eleanor Wood, my agent. These are shifting times in the industry, and Eleanor has been steady.

My family's support is valuable beyond measure. Writers are not the easiest folk to live with. We are often somewhere else—either physically or in our heads.

Books are written to be read. Thanks to everyone who has read any of my work, and thanks in particular to those of you have commented on it to me.